THE SHEWSTONE

D1533891

What Reviewers Say About Jane Fletcher's Work

The Celaeno Series

"...captivating, well-written stories in the fantasy genre that are built around women's struggles against themselves, one another, society, and nature."—*WomanSpace Magazine*

"In *Rangers at Roadsend* Fletcher not only gives us powerful characters, but she surprises us with an unexpected ending to the murder conspiracy plot, pushing the story in one direction only to have that direction reversed more than once. This is one thrill ride the reader will not want to get off."—*Independent Gay Writer*

"*The Walls of Westernfort* is not only a highly engaging and fast-paced adventure novel, it provides the reader with an interesting framework for examining the same questions of loyalty, faith, family and love."—*Midwest Book Review*

"*The Walls of Westernfort* is...a true delight. Bold, well-developed characters hold your interest from the beginning and keep you turning the pages. The main plot twists and turns until the very end. The subplot involves likeable women who seem destined not to be together."—*MegaScene*

The Lyremouth Chronicles

"Jane Fletcher once again has written an exciting fantasy story for everyone. Though she sets her stories in foreign worlds where the traditional role of women are reversed, her characters (are) all too familiar in their inner lives and thoughts. Unlike the Celaeno series (which I highly recommend) where there are no men, this series incorporates male characters that help round out the story nicely... Fletcher has a way of balancing the fantasy with the human drama in a precise way. She never gets caught up in the minor details of the environment and forgets to tell the story, which happens too often in fantasy fiction...With Fletcher writing such strong work, readers of fantasy will continue to grow."—*Lambda Book Report*

"*The Exile and the Sorcerer* is a mesmerizing read, a tour-de-force packed with adventure, ordeals, complex twists and turns, and the internal introspection of appealing characters. The author writes effortlessly, handling the size and scope of the book with ease. Not since the fantasy works of Elizabeth Moon and Lynn Flewelling have I been so thoroughly engrossed in a tale. This is knockout fiction, tantalizingly told, and beautifully packaged."—*Midwest Book Review*

Visit us at www.boldstrokesbooks.com

By the Author

THE SHEWSTONE

WITHDRAWN

by

Jane Fletcher

2016

THE SHEWSTONE
© 2016 BY JANE FLETCHER. ALL RIGHTS RESERVED.

ISBN 13: 978-1-62639-554-1

THIS TRADE PAPERBACK ORIGINAL IS PUBLISHED BY
BOLD STROKES BOOKS, INC.
P.O. BOX 249
VALLEY FALLS, NY 12185

FIRST EDITION: JUNE 2016

THIS IS A WORK OF FICTION. NAMES, CHARACTERS, PLACES, AND INCIDENTS ARE THE PRODUCT OF THE AUTHOR'S IMAGINATION OR ARE USED FICTITIOUSLY. ANY RESEMBLANCE TO ACTUAL PERSONS, LIVING OR DEAD, BUSINESS ESTABLISHMENTS, EVENTS, OR LOCALES IS ENTIRELY COINCIDENTAL.

THIS BOOK, OR PARTS THEREOF, MAY NOT BE REPRODUCED IN ANY FORM WITHOUT PERMISSION.

CREDITS
EDITOR: CINDY CRESAP
PRODUCTION DESIGN: SUSAN RAMUNDO
COVER DESIGN BY SHERI (GRAPHICARTIST2020@HOTMAIL.COM)

Acknowledgments

Thanks go to Joanie Bassler for helpful comments on my first draft and for the countless cups of tea delivered to my desk, to Nell Stark for her help with Cynnreord, to Cindy Cresap for picking up on my mistakes and oversights, to Radclyffe and everyone else at Bold Strokes Books for making it such an awesome publishing company, and to the readers who have contacted me providing the extra impetus to get back to the keyboard and start pounding out the words.

PROLOGUE

The boy laughed in Matt's face. "Give me that."
        "It's mine."
"No, it's not. You stole it."
        So what if this was true? He was not the one Matt had stolen the fish from, and he had no right to take it. She took a step back, clenching the fish to her chest.

The boy was at least four years older than Matt, and a foot taller, with straight black hair, dark brown eyes, and light brown skin. He was scrawny, dressed in rags so tattered you could count three ribs in the gap between his shirt and pants. His face was screwed in a mean, hard sneer. In short, he looked just like all the other street children— just like Matt herself.

Except Matt knew she was that bit hungrier. The last time she had eaten was the morning before, a few mangled cabbage leaves, scavenged from rubbish at the market. Today, she had been watching fishermen unloading their boat when they were distracted by a drunken brawl. It was her chance to snatch a fish and make off. Despite being raw, it was the nearest thing to a decent meal she had seen all month, and Matt was not about to give it up.

The sound of movement stopped Matt before she could take another step, and the boy's sneer got broader. He was not alone. Matt twisted to look back. Two of his friends stood there, posing like grown-up rowdy boys. All three were bigger and stronger than Matt. One-on-one, she would still stand no chance in a fight, but could they outrun her?

The leader was the soft target. Matt could read him easily. He was a blowhard who thought she was going to roll over and give up, a puffed up bully when the numbers were on his side. The friends were too dim to do anything other than follow.

Matt let her shoulders slump, just enough to let him think he had won, then she charged, driving her elbow into his stomach. He curled forward, his mouth a big circle, like he was about to spew. "Ooof."

Matt threw everything she had into a roundhouse kick behind his knees, taking his feet from under him, and then she was off.

At the corner, she stopped to glance back. The friends had helped their leader to his feet and waited until he had enough breath to tell them what to do. Matt had known they would not be able to work it out for themselves. Now the chase was on. The boys wanted the fish, and probably revenge. Matt raced away from the quay.

The road took her up the hill, and then through the alleys and winding stairways of Fortaine. Matt knew every street in the city, but so did the boys, and with their longer legs, they were gaining on her. Matt had to shake them off. She darted aside, heading to the main road up from the docks.

The High Street was its normal hectic rat run of horse-drawn carts. Matt ducked around one, hurdled the tailgate of another, and rolled between the wheels of a third. This was where it went wrong. She got through with no worse than a bruise and a scraped knee, but she dropped the fish and dared not go back for it.

Matt ran on until she was sure the boys had given up the hunt. Maybe they stopped to pick up her fish. Matt hoped not. She would rather it squished under a wheel than the bastards get it, but either way it was lost, and she would go hungry another day. Matt slumped against a wall, getting her breath back and refusing to cry. Never show you are upset, even when nobody is there to see.

She was in a part of town she did not normally visit. The maze of narrow-ways around the docks was her home. The only times she left were to scavenge in the markets or to try her luck with the mansions high on the cliffs, with their ocean views and more food thrown away than honest folk could put on the table. Trouble was, they also had armed guards who saw street folk as no better than rats. Some children who went to the high cliffs never came back. Vermin control, they called it.

The chase had taken her to the middle ground of quiet streets and comfy, well-guarded homes belonging to merchants and master craftsmen. The buildings were tall and brick built, with heavy wooden doors and bars on the ground floor windows. Walking along, Matt caught the sweet scent of flowers and perfume. Then she caught something else, a smell that hit so hard it made her gasp—fresh baked bread, just like Ma would make.

A rutted track cut between two buildings, leading to the rear of the houses. Some way down, a donkey cart was drawn up at a gate while the deliveryman chatted. The other man looked like a rowdy boy, hired muscle working as a guard. Normally, Matt would have backed off, but he carried no more than a staff, and the bread smelled so good. She sidled closer, reeled in like a fish on a line. The cart held a basket full of bread and wheels of wax covered cheese. Lumpy sacks suggested apples or potatoes. The barrels could be flour or beer. She recognised fish crates from the docks.

Matt's stomach squeezed so tight it hurt. Her mouth watered and she had to swallow. Her eyes were glued to the food. She could not tear them away, and all the while she edged nearer.

"What do you want, kid?"

The harsh voice broke in like a slap. Matt was almost in touching distance. The deliveryman also stopped talking to look at her.

More habit than anything else, Matt stuck her thumbs in her ears and waggled her fingers while poking out her tongue. The guard made a half-hearted attempt to cuff her ear, but Matt ducked out of range.

Both men snorted with contemptuous amusement, then deliberately turned their backs. The deliveryman leaned his elbow on the cart, just to make sure Matt knew who owned it and that he had his eye on the food. She stood no chance of reaching in to grab anything. They would spot her and she could not outrun them, but Matt could not let the food go. She dropped to the ground, just out of their line of sight, rolled under the cart, and clung on.

The deliveryman eventually finished talking and urged the donkey through the gates. The cart stopped in a yard between the house and the garden. Matt remained hanging to the underside of the cart, even after the man's legs vanished into the house.

Matt peered between the wheels. The garden was split into sections, a neat kitchen patch on one side, with rows of vegetables and herb borders, and an overgrown flower garden on the other. At the back were wooden sheds and iron railings. Matt guessed they were dog kennels even before she heard the barking. The deliveryman returned, along with another pair of stockinged legs. Matt matched them to a woman's voice, most likely the cook. The cart shook as something heavy was pulled off. Matt hesitated. Sneaking inside had been gut instinct. It could get her into big trouble, but was the risk any worse than starving?

The two pairs of legs returned to the house, going through a different door this time. Matt crawled out silently and followed the food down stone steps to a cellar. By candlelight at the far end, the deliveryman dumped his sack in a corner and adjusted its position to the cook's liking.

A row of barrels were lined up inside the entrance, with just enough space for Matt to squeeze behind. By the time the two adults were on their way back, Matt was crouched in a dark corner, wedged between the barrels and the wall.

After ten minutes, all the food was stored and the deliveryman left for the last time. Matt heard a metallic clunk, like a key turning, then cook and candle came back through the cellar and left through an interior door.

Matt was alone with more food than she had dreamed of. The cellar had no windows, but enough light squeezed under the door for Matt to make things out, once her eyes adjusted. Footsteps creaked on the floorboards overhead. There were also muffled voices, but it did not seem as if anyone was coming. She crept from hiding, guided as much by smell as sight.

The crust of the bread was rough in her hands. It broke open, releasing a stronger wave of the wonderful smell that had first snared her. But it was as nothing next to the taste, the flavour of sunlight on farmland, rich with yeast and wheat. The crust crunched between her teeth. The soft dough melted on her tongue. The act of swallowing was a dream. Matt took another mouthful, then clawed off a chunk from a wheel of cheese. The next few minutes were devoted to the glory of filling her stomach. Even if she got caught, she could die happy.

Next, Matt checked the door to the outside, but as she guessed, it was locked. Her only way out was through the house, and that would have to wait until everyone had gone to sleep. Luckily, security was designed to keep thieves out, not in. Matt was sure she could find an upstairs window to drop from. In the meantime, she claimed two crisp apples from an open sack and returned to hiding. With her stomach full for the first time in months, Matt drifted off to sleep.

She was woken twice by people getting supplies, but nobody came near the barrels. The next time Matt woke, the cellar was pitch-black and the house was silent. Working by touch, she stuffed a small loaf of bread, another chunk of cheese, and four apples inside her shirt, then edged open the door to the rest of the house.

A wooden staircase took Matt to the kitchen. The fire was damped down for the night, but still gave enough light to see. Another narrow set of stairs climbed one wall, most likely going to servants' rooms at the back of the house. Matt ignored them. Any window overlooking the garden would not be a good escape route if the dogs were let out at night. Two doors led from the kitchen. A band of light shone under one, so Matt picked the other.

The next room was a dining hall, dark and deserted. The only other exit from here also had light on the opposite side, and when she pressed her ear to it, she heard voices. Matt thought of going back to the cellar for another hour, but now she was moving, she wanted to be gone.

A musician's gallery hung over the end of the room. Matt scrambled onto a table, and the wood panelling provided just enough fingerhold to climb the rest of the way. Up above was so dark she had to run her hands over the wall to find the way out. Matt inched open the door.

A wide balcony ran around three sides of a large hallway. Light from below wobbled across the plaster ceiling and poked through the railing but did not touch the back wall. The voices were clearer now, although still too low to make out the words. Matt edged over and peered down. Three men stood talking in the tiled entrance below, one of them holding a candlestick.

Matt did not know or care who they were or why they were up so late. The street door was what grabbed her attention. Now she knew exactly where she was. The room at the end of the balcony would overlook the main street, and if it was one of the men's bedrooms, her best chance was to get out now.

Matt crept along, keeping to the dark side of the balcony and making as little noise as possible. Just as she reached the door, the tone of the voices changed. Light and shadow jumped across the ceiling. The men were moving, climbing the open staircase to the upper floor, and bringing the candles with them. With a second to spare, Matt slipped into the room before she was spotted.

Moonbeams fell across a large desk rather than a bed. It stood four-square in the centre of the room, covered with papers. Cabinets and bookcases lined one wall. A large casement window jutted over the street to Matt's right. She ignored it and darted across the room to the smaller window opposite, only to discover it was locked, and the voices were getting louder and louder. They would not want to read books this late at night, would they?

Moonlight glinted on a penknife. Matt snatched it up and dug at the catch. Then the doorknob rattled and candlelight flooded the room. A shout came as the catch popped. Matt shoved open the window, ready to dive out, but too late. A hand grabbed her shoulder, hauled her back, and threw her to the floor. She half scrambled up, until a swinging backhand sent her flying again.

"Stop that." A strong voice.

"It's a thief." The man standing over Matt spat out the words. Was he the homeowner or a guard? He was muscled and hard-faced like a rowdy boy, but his shoes were too lightweight to deliver a real kicking, the rowdy boys' favourite way to pass on their employer's messages.

"Yes, but I don't mind thieves."

"Even when they're stealing from you?"

The blow had set Matt's head spinning. She squinted at the first speaker, still standing in the doorway. He was the smallest of the three, but clearly the boss. Everything about him was neat and trim, from his beard to the square set of his shoulders. His clothes were expensive. The light shimmered over his red silk shirt and glinted off gold rings.

He laughed. "If they're good enough to steal from me then they deserve whatever they can get." He waved his hand. "Let the boy up, and we'll see what he's stolen."

"Not a boy," Matt said. She flexed her legs before standing, to make sure they would hold her, but refused to rub the side of her head. Never show you are hurt.

"Ah. Indeed." The boss's smile broadened.

"Bread, apples…cheese!" The shapeless lump fished from Matt's shirt was what remained after her fall.

"Food. Which I'd say she needs more than I do." He paused, tilting his head in thought. "Go down and tell the boys to wait a minute, while I talk to our young thief here."

Once they were alone, the man placed the candlestick on the desk and sat, studying Matt.

"Would you like to introduce yourself?"

"Matt."

"Which is short for?"

"Matilda."

"Pleased to meet you, Mattie. My name is Edmund Flyming."

Matt's mouth was open, ready to correct him. Only Ma called her Mattie. Nobody else was allowed, but the words stuck in her throat. If she had known whose house it was she would never have dared break in. He must like thieves, a third of them in the city worked for him, along with the fences, grifters, footpads, and smugglers. He also ran brothels and gambling dens. Things did not go well for folk who upset him, though street tattle claimed he was a fair boss and a man of his word. He sparked loyalty in his followers, fear in his enemies, and respect from most others.

"Where are your parents?"

"Ma ain't around no more." Matt chewed her lip, wondering how much to say. "Pa would get drunk and hit her. One night was really bad. I hid, and next morning, Ma was gone. Pa said she'd run away."

"Did your father used to hit you as well?"

Matt nodded.

"So you ran away too?"

"Wasn't that. My big sister, Emmy, got pregnant."

"He couldn't hold you responsible."

Matt shrugged awkwardly. "He was the one that did it. After Ma went, Pa started paying attention to Emmy. When she got big, he started looking the same way at me. I wasn't going to end up like Emmy, so I ran."

Something dark, angry, and dangerous flitted across Edmund's face, but not directed at her. "How old are you, Mattie? Nine? Ten?"

"About that, I guess."

Edmund steepled his fingers. "As I'm sure you know, Mattie, I employ thieves, good ones. And you're clearly a good thief. Would you like to come and work for me?"

Matt drew a deep breath, mostly from surprise. The memory of the food in the cellar was enough to sway her, and if she worked for Edmund Flyming, no jumped up bully would dare push her around. Before she could say yes, Edmund went on, as if she might need persuading.

"I know you know sometimes when men say they're being nice to young girls, they're not really being nice, as with your father and your sister. I assure you I've no such interest in children, and no time for anyone who does." He smiled. "You're a good-looking child. So maybe in another ten years I might feel differently, but only if you've managed to turn into a man."

Matt nodded. Edmund Flyming's taste in lovers was also common knowledge in the city. "Yes. Yes, I'd like to work for you."

"Good."

There was a knock at the door and a head appeared. "Are you nearly ready, boss?"

"Yes. And can you wake Pearl? I want her to look after my newest employee." Edmund stood and held out his hand. "Come with me."

Half a dozen men and a couple of women were assembled in the entry hall, large rowdy boys for the most part. The woman casually cleaning her nails with a knife put Matt in mind of whispered rumours about the handymen—handy at putting a blade between their victim's shoulders. But the one who stood out was a man with his hands tied behind his back and a sack over his head.

"That's Will," Edmund said. "He was supposed to be working for me, but he appears to have been doing some freelance work. I want to ask him about it." He crouched down so his head was level with Matt's. "But don't worry. As long as you play fair by me, I'll play fair by you. You can trust me."

Matt stared into Edmund's eyes. She did trust him. In that instant she knew it. She trusted him in a way she had not trusted anyone since Ma went.

A plump, middle-aged woman in bedclothes appeared. She toddled to Edmund's side, showing not the slightest surprise at the bound man.

"This is Pearl. She's going to get you a bath, a place to sleep, and clothes, more food if you want. And sometime you must tell me about your father, his name and where he lives." Edmund reached out and gently brushed the hair from Matt's forehead. "The world is an unfair place. Bad things happen to good people, while it can seem like bad people have all the luck. But sometimes even bad people have accidents."

❖

None of the adults used the word "money," but they had their code phrases for it. Eawynn had no trouble hearing what was really being said.

"I'd be honoured to show my gratitude to the temple," was her father's code for, *I'll give you a lot of money if you take my daughter off my hands.*

"Your piety does you credit," which was the priestess's code for, *Thank you, and the more the better.*

The priestess who talked the most was called Insightful Sister Oracle, sometimes with Most Reverend tacked on the front, to let everyone know she was extra important. The priestess sitting beside her was Assiduous Sister Treasurer. This priestess was also important, although she said nothing and did not smile. However, her eyes lit up every time Eawynn's father mentioned his gratitude.

Two other priestesses were present. One was Stalwart Sister Door-warden, who was clearly not as important as the oracle or treasurer and so did not get to sit down, even though there were spare chairs. She had escorted Eawynn and her father, Thane Alric Wisa

Achangrena, to the meeting room. The last priestess was not even worth an introduction and stood ignored at the back. Eawynn also did not get a seat and stood beside her father's chair.

The priestesses all wore shapeless sea-green robes, held in place with a white rope belt. The material was a coarse, heavy weave. They all had shaved heads and no makeup or jewellery or anything to make them look nice.

Eawynn did not want to become one of them. She wanted to stay in her father's house, with her own room; her nice clothes; her pony, Smudge; her kitten, Dumpling; her books and toys. She wanted to stay with Hattie in the kitchen to spoil her. She wanted things to stay the way they were. But what she wanted counted for nothing. Eawynn fixed her eyes on the wall and tried not to cry. She was not supposed to cry.

"I've kept the child with me, out of affection for her mother. A reminder of what we shared," her father continued. "But I've always known some day I'd have to make other plans for her future. The position is, you'll understand, delicate."

Delicate. That was another code word, one Eawynn had heard many times. Insightful Sister Oracle nodded, her face blank.

"Her mother and I..." Without looking, Eawynn knew the sad little smile on her father's lips. "We were young and in love. We were sure our families would approve the match. Both were of equal standing, but..." Her father's hand waved in a vague gesture, to convey the cruelness of fate. "My love's family had other plans. They kept the birth a secret. What could I do but go along with their wishes? But I ensured the child had a good upbringing, befitting her bloodline."

Eawynn bit her lip. The story was one she had heard before, and one Hattie claimed was completely untrue. According to Hattie, her mother had been a pretty kitchen maid. In those days, her father's sister had been thane, and her father had been free to live the life of a wealthy rake. A boating accident, two months ago, meant her father, unexpectedly, inherited the title. As Thane Achangrena, he was heir to an ancient and noble lineage, the equal of any on the Island of Pinettale. By comparison, Hattie was a cook, a servant, a nobody. No court of law would take her word against his, but Eawynn knew which one she believed.

From time to time, Eawynn would wonder about her mother, and what she had looked like. Her father had passed his colouring to her. Like him, Eawynn had the burnished red hair and pale white skin of the old Rihtcynn aristocracy. It allowed him to maintain the fiction of the doomed love affair with a noblewoman of good blood. But his heavy, drawn face, with squashed nose and narrow set eyes, was as different from hers as it was possible to get. How much did she take after her mother?

"She has received a suitable education for a girl of gentle birth. I'm assured she is an apt student. Although she turned six not a month ago, she knows her numbers and letters and speaks Cynnreord fluently. She can sing prettily and accompany herself on the lute."

Did they have lutes in the Temple of Anberith?

Again, Insightful Sister Oracle nodded, her face revealing nothing. "Her education will continue in the temple. I'm sure she'll become a most valuable member of our sisterhood."

"Yes…yes, quite." Abruptly, her father ran out of steam. He swivelled to face Eawynn.

She searched his eyes for a trace of the indulgent father she knew. Not that he had played much part in her life. He had always been kind, often generous, showering her with gifts, but mostly he had been absent, abandoning her to the care of servants. He was abandoning her again, but this time it was more serious. It was forever.

Eawynn almost gave in to the urge to plead, to beg him not to leave her in the temple. She was sure, if he gave Hattie a fraction of the money he was giving the sisters, the cook would happily take her in. However, being raised as a servant was not fitting for the daughter of Thane Achangrena, not even an unwanted, bastard daughter like Eawynn.

"You'll stay here and become a priestess of Anberith."

"Yes, Papa."

"It's a noble thing, serving a goddess."

"Yes, Papa."

"If you work hard, you'll do well. The sisters are very pleased you're joining them."

And that you're paying them so much. Eawynn nodded.

Her father stood. "Right. Well. Good day to you, Holy Sisters. My steward will be in contact."

Stalwart Sister Door-warden escorted him out of the room, and out of Eawynn's life.

"He hopes to fly high." Assiduous Sister Treasurer spoke for the first time.

"Indeed. He's clearly anxious to divest himself of anything that might drag him down." Insightful Sister Oracle's eye flicked in Eawynn's direction. "He might be a useful friend to the temple."

"Certainly if he pulls off the marriage to the Earl Blaedgifa's daughter."

"Yes. And I hear his prospects are very promising in that direction." Insightful Sister Oracle turned to Eawynn. "So, child. You're to join our community. Don't worry. It's a good life, as long as you're a good girl. Are you a good girl?"

"Yes, my lady."

"You should address me as Beloved Sister."

"Yes, Beloved Sister."

"She seems quick enough," Assiduous Sister Treasurer said.

Insightful Sister Oracle nodded. "Tells me your father you knowing of Cynnreord. Are you liking the language for speaking this?"

Eawynn struggled to understand what she meant, and not because the priestess had switched to the actual language. Her accent was appalling. Insightful Sister Oracle managed to make the flowing ancient words sound as harsh and vulgar as common Tradetalk.

Eawynn replied, also using Cynnreord. "Yes, Beloved Sister, it feels so much more poetic and cleaner."

"Well, he told the truth about that much." Insightful Sister Oracle reverted to Tradetalk, which she clearly felt more comfortable speaking. With her shaved head, it was impossible to tell the colour of the priestess's hair, but her skin was as dusky as any common labourer, or Hattie for that matter, although Eawynn loved Hattie and never held her base blood against her.

"Nurturing Sister Mentor will look after you and introduce you to the other girls in training."

The last priestess finally had a name. She came forward and took Eawynn's hand. "Come with me, child. I'll show you the dormitory where you'll sleep."

Eawynn looked down at their interlinked fingers. Nurturing Sister Mentor's skin was several shades darker than her own, yet she was still lighter than either of the more senior priestesses. Did blood and breeding count for nothing in the temple? Before she was taken away, Eawynn could not stop blurting out the question uppermost in her mind.

"Are you going to shave my hair now?"

For the first time, a smile crossed Most Reverend Insightful Sister Oracle's face. "Not until you finish your training and take your vows as a priestess. And that won't be for another fifteen years."

CHAPTER ONE

The razor blade was a line of ice, scraping over Eawynn's scalp. A lock of red hair floated down to join the others on the white flagstones. Wisps of sweet incense tickled her nose. The rasp of steel on skin was loud in her ears, blending with the chanting of her sister priestesses who formed a circle inside the ring of marble pillars. The Inner Sanctum of Sea and Moon stood on the small headland jutting out behind the elders' residence. The sound of waves, breaking on rocks below, was a background rumble, carried on the dawn breeze.

The winter solstice had passed just seven days before, and the air was cold enough to sting Eawynn's cheeks, but the long night was over. A final six-inch strand spiralled to the ground, twisting as it fell. The light of the rising sun flickered like fire along its length. In the future, there would be no locks, just a month's growth of stubble to be removed by Comforting Sister Infirmarian's razor.

Eawynn was the last of the three initiates to be shaved that dawn. Even in the dim light, she could tell her hair from the common black of the others. But would she be able to pick out the red when the cutting was a bare half inch? Eawynn hoped so. Her noble ancestry might mean nothing to anyone else, but it still mattered to her.

Eawynn knelt, facing the statue of Anberith that dominated the back of the sanctum. The stone was cold and hard beneath her knees. The new sea-green gown provided no more protection than the old grey novice one had done. Overhead, the last stars were fading in the washed blue sky, but no moon had risen that night. The Oblation of the Avowed Supplicants took place at dawn of the new moon, the hair offered to the lunar goddess as tribute, to ensure her return for another month.

Comforting Sister Infirmarian stepped back and gestured for Eawynn to stand. As she took her place among the circle, the cold air was unfamiliar on her freshly exposed scalp. Soon, she would get used to it, Eawynn guessed.

Most Reverend Insightful Sister Oracle, in her role as high priestess, led the cycle of prayers. This was the first time Eawynn had taken part in the ceremony, which concluded with burning the hair. In the initiates' training, Eawynn had rehearsed the Oblation countless times, yet she had not anticipated how long it would take in practice. The ceremony dragged on and on. Of course, this was the extended version, the first after the solstice, where novices were initiated into the sisterhood, but even so! Were they going through it twice? Or was it just anxiety about what would follow, when she would learn her future role in the temple?

The final prayer was not finished until the sun was high above the horizon. The column of smoke floated away in the crisp air as the priestesses filed out. Nurturing Sister Mentor's responsibility for the initiates was over. She gathered them around her one last time, embraced them affectionately, then also left. Her place was taken by the less affectionate form of Insightful Sister Oracle, who beckoned them to follow.

On the short walk, Eawynn tried to reassure herself she had nothing to worry about. She failed. By the time she reached the audience room, her stomach felt as if she had swallowed a snowball. Several elder priestesses were there before them. Who would she be assigned to? Was one looking at her with more interest than normal? But no, they were all acting as if she were invisible, much as everyone had been doing for the last four months.

The only exception was Enlightening Sister Astrologer, who sat at the front, smiling, and that was bad news. Insightful Sister Oracle posed herself regally on the chair beside her rival, and Enlightening Sister Astrologer was so busy smirking she did not even roll her eyes. The snowball started bouncing up and down.

The last elder, Studious Sister Librarian, slipped into the audience room and closed the door. Eawynn fought to suppress a pained expression at the sight of her. Not that Eawynn held any deep personal dislike for the current librarian, but if only her predecessor, Erudite Sister Librarian, had lived for a couple more years, the outlook would be far more hopeful.

Erudite Sister Librarian had been a brusque, opinionated, and irritable woman. She had also been an exceptional linguist and scholar. Was it any wonder she had lost all patience and respect for her fellow priestesses years ago? Eawynn had been the only one who could spend an hour in her company without provoking an outpouring of acerbic comments. Eawynn had also been the only one who could understand what was said, if the librarian, in her sole concession to tact, voiced the comments in an obscure language, such as Pinettia.

Erudite Sister Librarian had unmistakably been training Eawynn as her successor. There really was no other serious candidate in the temple. If she were being honest, Eawynn would concede she could not quite match Erudite Sister Librarian's ability to decipher ancient texts, but felt she had the edge when it came to ease of acquiring languages.

But then, without warning, Erudite Sister Librarian had been taken by a seizure one morning at breakfast, collapsed at the table, and been dead before nightfall. Her assistant, Studious Sister Cataloger, had been promoted to Studious Sister Librarian, surely something nobody could have predicted—or wanted. Eawynn caught her lip in her teeth. Too late now to regret laughing along with Erudite Sister Librarian's biting remarks. How deep a grudge might Studious Sister Librarian be holding?

Insightful Sister Oracle stood and the murmuring stopped. "Welcome to our newest sisters. Our joy that you're now joined with us knows no bounds." She smiled at the other two initiates and the air above Eawynn's head. "You've lived among us for many years and know our humble ways. Now you'll play a full role in our life of prayer and reflection. You'll continue assisting with the daily chores. We have no servants here so all must take an equal share—"

Though it's a long time since anyone has seen you cleaning the latrines. Even with her guts tying themselves in knots, Eawynn could not resist the thought.

"—but you'll now have your own special allotted role. Your former name will be forgotten as you become a true part of our community. To guide your footsteps, you'll be assigned to an elder, who will be your teacher, your confidant, and your friend."

Please don't let it be Enlightening Sister Astrologer. But even if Eawynn was not directly assigned to her, the astrologer's position, second in the temple hierarchy, gave her considerable sway. Would she indulge her petty spite by steering Eawynn into a demeaning role?

A year ago, when Erudite Sister Librarian was alive, Eawynn would have had no worries. Even a mere four months back, she still could have expected favourable treatment. Her father's money and influence assured that. However, this was before her father joined his in-laws in an ill-fated attempt by Earl Blaedgifa to usurp the throne of Pinettale. Ex-Thane Alric Wisa Achangrena's head was currently adorning a spike over the main gates into Fortaine, along with the earl's and a half dozen other relatives. No more money would flow into temple coffers from that source, and overnight, Eawynn had gone from being a symbol of favour at court to being a decided embarrassment.

"Melodious Sister Chorister. To you we entrust the priestess who was once novice Beatrice. Henceforth she'll be known as Harmonious Sister Chanteuse."

No surprise there. Beatrice had a remarkable singing voice. She also had nimble fingers and soft lips, as she had demonstrated to Eawynn more than once. This came to a sharp end with Thane Alric's trial and execution. Eawynn tried to tell herself she did not care. Beatrice had been more trouble than she was worth. In fact, Eawynn had assumed she would be the one to end it, but now Beatrice was acting as if merely being in the same room as her was an ordeal. The on-off "special friendship" was firmly off.

"Studious Sister Librarian—" Insightful Sister Oracle continued.

The rush of relief almost made Eawynn's knees buckle. She caught herself in time. Her fears had been unfounded. Studious Sister Librarian had been able to overlook the gibes and condescension. After all, Eawynn had only been following Erudite Sister Librarian's lead. The new librarian must know she was out of her depth and in need of help. Thanks to Erudite Sister Librarian's coaching, Eawynn could speak six languages fluently, including archaic Pinettia, and read and write three different scripts. Whereas, despite years of study, Studious Sister Librarian could barely manage to hold a worthwhile conversation in Cynnreord.

"—to you we entrust the priestess who was once novice Agnes. Henceforth she'll be known as Diligent Sister Caretaker."

Agnes! Eawynn was not the only one looking surprised. Agnes was well meaning and tried hard, but she needed three attempts to spell her own name. How was she going to cope now that it was longer than five letters? And what could she do in the library? Except maybe clean the bookcases, once someone explained to her how a dust cloth worked.

The bouncing snowball grew spikes.

"Attentive Sister Chamberlain. To you we entrust the priestess who was once novice Eawynn." Insightful Sister Oracle said her name as if it was being dragged from her mouth by a ham-fisted dentist. "Henceforth she'll be known as Dutiful Sister Custodian."

Custodian of what? Eawynn clenched her jaw. There was nothing she could do. Everything was set and sealed, her father's final gift. She had preferred the pony.

Any hope it might not turn out too badly was squashed by Enlightening Sister Astrologer's smug expression. They should have been allies, the only ones with enough noble blood in their veins to be worth mentioning. Yet, since the day Eawynn arrived, the other priestess had seen her as competition. Why? Was it no more than jealousy over who had the redder hair? Of course, recent events had made things even more combative. Just because the queen was her second cousin, Enlightening Sister Astrologer had taken Earl Blaedgifa's rebellion as a personal slight—as if Eawynn had anything to do with it.

The meeting broke up after a round of congratulations which conspicuously did not include Eawynn.

"Come with me." Attentive Sister Chamberlain said nothing else until they reached the Shrine to the Oracle.

On a personal level, the assignment of the chamberlain as her mentor could have been worse. Attentive Sister Chamberlain's niece had married a housecarl of the Blaedgifa family, and she had even gone so far as to offer condolences for the death of Eawynn's father. The issue was more that the role of chamberlain involved the maintenance of temple buildings, and there was no associated task Eawynn felt any desire to do.

The Shrine to the Oracle was some thirty feet wide and twice as long. The walls were made of the same dark basalt as the rest of the temple, but here it felt even more heavy and ominous, even though the high windows let in shafts of bright daylight. Deep alcoves were built into the corners. The ones facing the entrance were occupied by statues of Anberith on raised plinths. Numerous antique star charts hung around the walls. The only other decorations were two long mahogany friezes and a huge unlit incense burner in the middle of the floor.

"Dutiful Sister Custodian, we have ascribed a special role to you." The smile held a tinge of embarrassment.

Eawynn braced herself.

"You're to be custodian of the Shewstone."

How much looking after could a stone need, especially one never on public view? In all her years as a novice, Eawynn was yet to set eyes on it. Admittedly, the Shewstone was the temple's most valuable possession, generating vastly more income than her late father's donations, but why did it need a custodian?

Attentive Sister Chamberlain held up a key. "You're to have this. Guard it with your life."

"Thank you, Beloved Sister."

At the far end of the shrine, two steps down led to a door, which had been locked whenever the juvenile novices thought to try it. Now the key turned smoothly and the door swung open.

The Shewstone Sacrarium was smaller than expected, a windowless cave. Eawynn peered into the darkness until she spotted a lantern and tinderbox on a cabinet by the door. At Attentive Sister Chamberlain's nod, Eawynn struck the flint.

The soft yellow light did nothing to reduce the impression of an underground hole. What little the room had by way of decoration was clearly intended to look expensive and mysterious. The walls were painted black, allowing only a suggestion of strange, twisted carvings. The table was antique, sagging slightly on one side, but still impressive. It might have been from the dawn of time, hewn from ancestral oak by the ancients. The only thing on it was a small silver oil burner. Two chairs were made of heavy square-cut timbers, looking as if the maker had only just discovered the concept of sitting. At the back of the sacrarium, a black metal repository stood on long legs. The front and sides were cast in open latticework, allowing Eawynn to see inside. The Shewstone was a mottled stone orb, six inches across, on a simple silver plinth. The lantern light shimmered over its surface. Patterns swirled, suggesting something inside was alive and moving. When Eawynn got closer, the hairs on her arms stood up. The air was charged with static, as before a storm.

Despite herself, Eawynn felt a moment of awe. But then the question repeated in her head. How much looking after could a stone need?

The answer came. "Your tasks are to make sure this room is spotless. You must keep the lamps filled with oil, and burn incense before supplicants come for a divination. You'll also attend Most Reverend Insightful Sister Oracle when she consults the Shewstone. You'll have to ask her about other requirements. The Shrine to the Oracle also forms part of your responsibility." The elder priestess patted the cabinet. "The equipment you'll need is in here."

Attentive Sister Chamberlain did not stay to watch Eawynn open the cabinet. The sound of her footsteps, crossing the shrine, faded away. Eawynn closed the sacrarium door. She did not want an audience.

Feeling like an actor in a badly written play, Eawynn opened the cabinet door. The skin on her face prickled hot and cold, anger and shame. As suspected, the equipment comprised of a brush, duster, and wax polish, along with a bucket and soap.

She had been given the role of housemaid.

Dutiful Sister Custodian? More like Menial Sister Janitor. She had been consigned to a humiliating role, just to prove the temple placed no importance on its previous contact with the late Thane Alric Wisa Achangrena. As if anyone at court would give a moment's thought to the thane's discarded bastard daughter. Maybe in a year or two, the elders themselves would not be so concerned.

Her father's timing had always been off.

❖

The young buck was everything Matt looked for in a man, oblivious, overconfident, and rich. Her palms itched with the anticipated weight of his purse. She trailed her mark across a square and down a side road, playing her favourite game of hunter and prey. The streets of Fortaine were hers. Fools, like the one she followed, stepped onto them at their own risk. And this one was a prize fool, swaggering along. He felt so highly of himself. Flaunting your athletic build was one thing. Flaunting the size of your coin purse was something totally different.

His clothes were fancy to the point of stupidity. His purple satin pantaloons were so puffed up they wobbled like jelly when he walked. If he went too far, he would get chafed in a most unpleasant way. The toes of his shoes were a foot long, curled back in the latest idiotic fashion. The gold embroidery on his doublet screamed, "Rob me."

By comparison, Matt was dressed to look respectable and inconspicuous. She had a simple loose shirt and leggings, a lightweight leather jerkin, and supple rolltop boots, all in neutral colours. They were the everyday clothes of a craftsman, neither pauper nor gentlefolk. Nothing to mark her out from the crowd, and nothing to hamper her free movement.

The mark minced into the upper market, where imported luxuries like silk and spice were on sale. Matt was a dozen steps behind him, but she was in no hurry. In truth, she did not need to be lifting purses. Edmund had no shortage of people, sharp with the fingerwork, but she liked to keep her hand in. Besides, it was fun.

The mark was like a puppy, loose in a butcher's shop, trying to take it in all at once—the colours, the smells, the noise. He even did a couple of pirouettes, looking at everything and seeing nothing. Matt was also checking out the market, but not the stuff on sale. It was pricey merchandise, but not worth the handful she could get from a snatch and run. The people were her concern. Before she made her move, Matt wanted to know who was out and about that late winter afternoon.

One of Gilbert's lieutenants was leaning against the plinth of a statue, but the rival gang member was no concern. The upper market was neutral turf. Most stallholders Matt recognised. The best place to take the mark was by one paying protection to Edmund, and hence sure to turn a blind eye. A city watch constable was patrolling, but he was old Harry, who was bought and paid for. He would only try to arrest her if she gave him no choice. An indie homed in on her mark, but he backed off when he spotted Matt. Independent pickpockets knew better than to poach from the Flyming gang.

Matt increased her pace just enough to overtake the mark. For a few more steps, she stayed in front, then she stopped dead and jerked around, like a woman who has suddenly remembered she ought to be somewhere else. The mark bounced into her. She had given him no chance to do anything else.

They both managed to stay on their feet, although it was a close call for the mark. Confused apologies followed, while he dithered between anger at Matt's clumsiness and a desire to be gallant with a pretty young woman. Matt bid him good day before he had settled on one or the other.

She marched back the way they had just come, with his purse inside her jerkin. However, before she had gone twenty yards, the mark started yelling. As luck would have it, he had stopped at the next stall and discovered that he and his purse had parted company.

Buffoon that he was, it was possible he would not link the theft to their collision. People like him must be losing things all the time. But it was all a little too recent and too blatant for even old Harry to ignore. Anyway, chase was another of Matt's favourite games. She set off at full pelt.

The shouting went up a notch, so she had been spotted, but it was no cause for worry. The mark's fancy shoes would be a bugger for running in, and old Harry was not going to knock himself out with the effort. Anyone who knew the street life of Fortaine would think twice about tackling Edmund Flyming's adopted daughter, and those who did not would need a god or two on their side to have any hope of catching her.

Matt raced through a few twists and turns. The game was hardly started and already sounds of the chase were falling back. It was so easy, it was boring. Matt decided to put an end to it. She ducked into a dead end alley, blocked off by an eight-foot-high brick wall. Without breaking stride, Matt used a window ledge as a step up, jumped, caught the top, and hauled herself over. She dropped into the backyard of The Dog and Whistle tavern, where the last of the winter's snow still hid between the stacked barrels.

Running footsteps echoed on the other side of the wall. They faltered and stopped.

"I thought…" gasp, "…she went…" gasp, "…in here." Oh, what a lovely toffee-nosed accent.

"Ah. She must've gone another way."

Gasp, "But where?" gasp.

"We'll try the docks." Good old Harry.

Matt grinned. The footsteps faded.

The gateway from the yard opened onto Pillow Row. All things considered, it would be as well to get off the streets for a few hours, enough time for old Harry to give up the hunt without it appearing fishy, and for the mark to cut his losses and go home. In another few days, he would have forgotten what she looked like, should they meet again. If only he knew it, Matt had done him a favour. Perhaps, in future, he would be more careful with his money.

Meanwhile, Matt knew the perfect place to kill a few hours. At the corner of the road was the Honeysuckle Bower, one of Edmund's brothels.

The madam greeted Matt. "Hey there, stranger."

"Hey there, yourself. How's business going?"

"Horizontal." An old joke.

The air was thick with cheap perfume and cheaper beer. The lighting was low to disguise the fading state of the decoration and the women. Sometimes it did not pay to look too closely. Imagination could be a useful tool. Yet the Honeysuckle Bower was far from the worst brothel in Fortaine. The girls were clean and friendly, the bedsprings still had some bounce, and the beer from the cellar was cold.

"Have you got a message from your Pa?"

"No. I'm here on my own account."

Matt had been a regular visitor from the time she entered Edmund's household. At first, just as a messenger, pampered and played with by the whores who wished to indulge their maternal urges. Once Matt reached mid teens, she discovered other reasons to visit the brothel. Her arrival today had been greeted by a couple of whores smiling at her in a way that said they were not thinking of playing pat-a-cake.

Matt pulled the stolen purse from her pocket, tossed it in the air, and caught it so it jingled. "I need to lie low for an hour or two, until someone stops looking for me."

"With an emphasis on lie?"

"Less risk of falling over that way." Matt's grin broadened.

"Yvette's been missing you."

"She's available?"

"I think she'd throttle me if I said no." The madam patted Matt's arm. "Go on. She's all yours."

Already Yvette had detached herself from the group of lounging whores and was sauntering forward, exaggerating the sway of her hips. Yvette wrapped her body around Matt's, kissed her soundly, and then linked arms to lead Matt to the back rooms.

All in all, it was shaping up to be a very good afternoon.

Eawynn positioned the last lamp and stood back to admire the effect. The sacrarium exuded a suitably arcane otherworldliness, without being too blatantly contrived. Everything was in place except the Shewstone itself, which would have to wait. It went without saying that a mere Dutiful Sister Custodian did not get entrusted with a repository key. There was only one, and Insightful Sister Oracle kept it on a fine chain around her neck. She probably slept with it. Eawynn could only hope she was never in a position to find out for sure.

This would be the nineteenth time she played attendant, and the charade had lost its novelty. Admittedly, some humour could still be found in Insightful Sister Oracle's attempts to speak Cynnreord, but even this was wearing thin.

The supplicant and his servant were waiting in the Shrine to the Oracle, with Redoubtable Sister Door-warden hovering nearby. She had taken over from Stalwart Sister Door-warden a month ago, when the elderly priestess could no longer manage the chaperoning duties. Except for in the public sanctuary, persons of a male persuasion had to be accompanied at all times on temple grounds, presumably to ensure they did not do anything inappropriately masculine to offend Anberith. Redoubtable Sister Door-warden was taking her newly acquired duties very seriously. She watched the men with an intensity normally only seen in cats tracking flies on a window pane.

It was not as if the supplicant appeared the age or type to cause trouble, and if he could afford a divination, he must be a person of standing. He was in his late thirties, dressed like a minor noble, in an elaborately embroidered tunic and coat, with fur trimmings, well-cut, of good material and new. His servant's clothes were more subdued. Both men had pale skin, the barest half shade off white. Their high cheekbones, green eyes, and red hair would have been a match for Eawynn's, if her head were not shaved.

"Is all ready?" The client spoke with a lilting accent.

"Yes, sir. Most Reverend Insightful Sister Oracle will be here soon to perform a divination for you."

The supplicant nodded and murmured to his servant. Eawynn caught a few words, just enough to know they were talking in Cynnreord. Where did they come from? Surely not Fortaine, or anywhere else on Pinettale. Who now retained Cynnreord for daily use?

Before the Rihtcynn conquered them, the islanders had spoken a language known as Pinettia. Some still did, in isolated mountain villages. Everyone else had adopted Tradetalk, the mongrel common tongue of the empire, which seemed to consist of removing everything from Cynnreord that would strain the abilities of an idiot, blending in the most vulgar elements from the assorted vanquished nations, and then shifting the vowels, so it could be spoken without fully opening one's mouth.

After the fall of the empire, the conquered lands had gone their own ways, but Tradetalk was still widely understood and used, especially where folk from different nations met. The Island of Pinettale, with its reliance on trade and seafaring, had kept Tradetalk as its own.

Insightful Sister Oracle swept in. In addition to her normal robe, she also wore a cowl, partially obscuring her eyes. Presumably, it was to enhance her mystical air. "Greetings, seeker after knowledge."

"Holy Sister."

"Please follow me."

They left the servant and Redoubtable Sister Door-warden to watch each other outside, or more accurately, for the priestess to watch the servant while he ignored her.

The sense of being entombed was even stronger with the sacrarium door closed. Insightful Sister Oracle waved the client to his chair and pulled out the repository key with a flourish. Once the Shewstone was in place over the unlit oil burner, she also sat and steepled her fingers. She bowed her head so her eyes were lost in shadow. The dramatic effect was marred only by Insightful Sister Oracle's misguided faith in her own acting ability.

Eawynn adopted her normal pose, standing silent and unmoving against the wall. She was unsure why her presence was required. The part she would play was minimal in the extreme. Perhaps it was hoped a second pair of eyes would deter any thought of that inappropriate male behaviour while the elder priestess was concentrating on the Shewstone.

"I am the voice of the oracle, High Priestess of Anberith. Stranger, you sit in the presence of great wonder and mystery," Insightful Sister Oracle began. "Might I be allowed to know your name?"

"I am Waldo of Bousack, a merchant."

Which was the more unexpected, his home or his profession? Bousack was a small town on the north coast. Rihtcynn ancestry was no more common there than anywhere else on Pinettale. Yet both supplicant and servant were red-haired speakers of Cynnreord. From his looks and the way he carried himself, Eawynn would have pegged him as a foreign nobleman. Maybe he had moved to Bousack from the mainland years ago and now considered it his home. But where was he from originally?

If Insightful Sister Oracle shared her surprise, she gave no sign. "You've come needing answers for a matter of great importance."

"Indeed, I have."

A few seconds of silence.

"Whatever you seek, doubt not the Shewstone will have the answer."

"This is what I've been told."

More silence.

"You are here on an auspicious date. Today is the Spring Equinox. Did you choose it for a reason?"

"I knew it was today, but the timing is coincidental."

Eawynn pressed her lips together to control a smile. Maybe this divination would be a little more interesting than the others. Whatever prophetic ability the Shewstone might have, Insightful Sister Oracle's revelations amounted to prodding the clients to reveal what they were hoping to hear, then feeding it back to them, couched in sufficiently cryptic terms to give some wiggle room, should events not pan out as desired.

This supplicant was giving away no clues. Insightful Sister Oracle let the silence drag on, beyond any hope he might break down and blurt something out, but eventually she accepted defeat and beckoned Eawynn to light the burner. This was Eawynn's only role in the pantomime, and one which she would rather have been excused from. Perhaps that was why she was there. Did Insightful Sister Oracle also feel the deep disquiet, even distress, when the flame was lit?

As it heated, the patterns in the stone swirled and writhed in a frenzy, seeming alive. It made a sound, high and faint, trilling like a bird. If Eawynn listened, she could persuade herself there were words in the sounds, although this was just a trick of her imagination, she was sure. But the Shewstone did not want to be over the flame. Eawynn could not shake this fancy, no matter how much she derided herself.

The high-pitched shrilling began. Insightful Sister Oracle leaned forward, holding her hands on either side of the stone, just far enough away to run no risk of burnt fingers. "Ask your question, Waldo of Bousack."

"Thank you. I have to make a decision. An old friend of my father has asked me to join him, backing a new venture, trading with the Verlesie Isles. I've no experience of these lands and wish to know whether it would be a wise investment."

That was it? This time, even Insightful Sister Oracle could not conceal her surprise. Judging by his tone, Waldo himself placed scant importance on the question and had no interest in the answer. Was it just his accent?

The temple charged a staggering amount for consulting the Shewstone, reckoning the premium enhanced the prestige of the divinations. The high price might result in fewer customers, but the net balance was the same. Most supplicants came with matters of life or death, tricky, awkward, insoluble problems. For a straightforward business deal, surely Waldo could find a better source of information. Bousack must have other traders with relevant experience. Why was he not asking them? And he was a merchant, by the tears of the gods. It was his trade. Builders did not consult an oracle for advice on how to lay bricks.

So how was Insightful Sister Oracle going to play this game?

From her pained expression, the elder priestess was asking herself the same thing. Then she closed her eyes and let her head fall forward. She swayed gently from side to side, the portrayal of a very refined trance. When she spoke, her voice was a full octave lower than normal. Her words were in Cynnreord.

"Old ropes holding us but not to go forward. In rocks with waterside salt grow seeds, but big and fat they come over friendly ground."

Eawynn winced. The priestess's accent had not improved over the years, and her grasp of the language would have shamed a three-year-old. Of course, the prophesy was intended to be cryptic and not understood by the client, but that was no reason to sound like an idiot.

Insightful Sister Oracle let her hands drop and opened her eyes. She provided her Tradetalk translation. "Ties from the past do not guide us into the future. The seed that sprouts on rocky shores, will flourish on home soil."

So that was what she meant. Was Waldo equally amused? If so, he hid it well. He bowed his head graciously. "You mean regardless of how this venture goes for my father's friend, it's not the one for me. Better profit will come from investing my money in projects I'm familiar with."

"Yes. I think that's the conclusion one may draw."

Always agree with the supplicant, and it was not a hard call. Waldo clearly had no enthusiasm for the deal. Why he had invested so much in getting an answer was anyone's guess. Maybe he was beholden to his father's friend and needed a good excuse to duck out.

Whatever lay behind it, Waldo seemed satisfied. He stood and gave another of his formal nods. "I thank you, and your goddess, for your help."

This too was unusual. Most supplicants wanted the maximum return from their outlay and would ask as many follow-on questions as they could get away with.

However, Insightful Sister Oracle was not going to detain him if he wanted to go. She extinguished the burner. "Dutiful Sister Custodian and Redoubtable Sister Door-warden will escort you out. The blessing of Anberith be upon you."

"I pray *Anbeorht* guides my way. Good day."

There it was again. Waldo had stressed the original form of the goddess's name, as if correcting Insightful Sister Oracle.

For the seafaring islanders, Anberith was second in importance only to Toranos, the storm god. As goddess of moon and tides, she had been worshipped on Pinettale for centuries. The tribes had given her a score of names—Berrima, Bathine, Abela, and others. Then the Rihtcynn conquered the island, to add to their burgeoning empire. They equated her with one of their own goddesses and had bestowed yet one more name, Anbeorht. As such, she acquired dominion over fortune telling and childbirth. The Rihtcynn Empire had fallen, but the expanded role for the goddess had stuck, along with the corrupted form of her new name.

Where had Waldo lived before Bousack? However, he rejoined his servant and left without revealing any more information to satisfy Eawynn's curiosity.

On her return to the Shrine to the Oracle, Eawynn caught a glimpse of a green robe, disappearing into the sacrarium. She assumed it belonged to Insightful Sister Oracle, but when she drew close, she heard voices.

"…are willing to pay that much for the Shewstone, maybe we could increase the donation for consulting the stars." Enlightening Sister Astrologer was riding her favourite hobbyhorse.

"I don't think that's the way for us to go."

"Can I ask why?"

"You know why. This way, we can give guidance to all, rich and poor. If we increase the donation for your valuable work, poor folk will…"

Not give us any money at all. Insightful Sister Oracle left the words unsaid, but Eawynn had no trouble providing them.

"We could offer the guidance of both the Shewstone and the stars on a sliding scale, related to the supplicants' resources."

"No."

"Why should the prophesy of the Shewstone be placed so highly above the wisdom of the stars?"

"The Shewstone is a unique mystery. Anyone can see the stars."

"The stars reveal the glory of the gods' creation. The Shewstone is a…" Eawynn could almost hear the sound of a tongue being bitten.

"Yes?"

In the absence of an answer, *cheap charlatan's trick*, would have been Eawynn's guess.

"We'll discuss this again."

"And my answer will not change."

Enlightening Sister Astrologer stomped from the sacrarium. Seeing Eawynn standing outside, her expression achieved the almost impossible feat of becoming even more irate. It was a shame. If only Enlightening Sister Astrologer knew it, Eawynn agreed with her.

Long ago, the position of astrologer had been foremost in the temple. The Shewstone, and the revenue it produced, had shifted the power balance. It was no secret Enlightening Sister Astrologer dreamed of reverting to the earlier scheme, and Most Reverend Insightful Sister Oracle had not the least intention of letting it happen.

The high priestess was locking the repository when Eawynn entered. She slipped the key inside her robe and smiled, clearly relieved Enlightening Sister Astrologer was not returning for a second bout.

"I think the divination went well."

"Yes, Beloved Sister."

"Waldo had a trace of an accent. He might have lived on the mainland at some stage."

You don't say. "Probably, Beloved Sister."

Insightful Sister Oracle flashed a condescending smile. "You're doing well. Keep it up." She bustled out.

Eawynn held her tongue until the elder priestess was out of earshot. "I'm so pleased I can sweep the floor to your satisfaction."

She turned up the wicks, so it was light enough to see while she cleaned. Still, the sacrarium felt heavy and oppressive. She paused before the repository. The Shewstone was back in its cast iron cage. The swirling patterns inside were becoming less frenetic. The whistling had faded. Now it sounded mournful, the lament of a lost and lonely soul, trapped in a stone prison.

Eawynn bit her lip. "You and me both."

❖

A thump on the door woke Matt with a jerk.

"Edmund wants to talk to you."

Matt groaned and hauled herself up in bed. A band of sunlight squeezed through the shutters. Judging by the angle, the morning was well advanced.

"What about?"

"He didn't say. He's in the study."

"Is he alone?"

"Got a couple of visitors."

"Anyone you know?"

"Nope."

Matt swung her feet out of bed, yawning. "Tell him I'll be along in a few minutes."

The sheets beside Matt moved and a head appeared. "What is it?"

"I've got to go…" Matt struggled to recall a name. "…honey."

A hand slid up Matt's thigh, its goal clear. "Can't you stay with me a little longer?"

"My father wants to see me."

"Hmmph." But the hand's owner had better sense than to argue.

Matt reached for her discarded clothes. The woman in bed raised herself on one elbow to watch. Marie. That was her name, maybe.

"What does he want?"

"I don't know."

"Do you want me to wait here for you to get back?"

Matt thought about the offer while tying her shirt. Maybe-Marie was pretty. From memory, Matt could also confirm she was agile, enthusiastic, nicely padded, but not overly bright.

"I don't know what he's going to want, or how long I'll be. Better if you get Pearl to show you out, when you're ready to leave."

Maybe-Marie's mouth puckered in a pout. "You won't forget to mention me to him, will you?"

That was it. Maybe-Marie wanted a job in a gambling den. Which might work. She might not be up to mastering the more complex card games, nor any fancy dealing, but she was pretty enough to make a certain sort of punter show off by betting high.

"Yeah. I'll tell him."

"Will I see you again?"

"Maybe, Marie." Matt escaped.

Edmund wanted her to meet the visitors, else he would have waited until after they went. But if they were the sort of people who should not be left waiting, his message would have had more urgency. Matt reckoned there was time to wash her face and have a stab at breakfast.

Pearl was in the kitchen, gossiping with the cook, while helping prepare vegetables, and at the same time, no doubt reviewing the stores, planning orders, and setting menus for the next week. Pearl had started out working for Edmund's grandfather as a whore, but had proved far too good an organiser to stay as one. Her ability to do four things at once had kept the Flyming household running smoothly for decades.

"Morning, Pearl."

"Morning, Mattie."

Pearl was the only person in the world, other than Edmund, who could get away with calling her that. Matt scooped a mug of milk from a churn.

"There's someone in my room—"

"Is she the one with the loud squeal?"

"Umm…yes, probably. Can you see she leaves soonish?"

Pearl shook her head. "I swear, you and Edmund were cut from the same cloth. He's your Pa, right enough."

Matt smiled and grabbed a cinnamon bun. She could not remember when she first called Edmund "Pa" as a childish slip of the tongue, but it had pleased him. Whatever his experience with women might have been, no children had resulted, and Edmund was safely past the stage of youthful experimentation. Before long, it became accepted that Matt was his adopted daughter. In truth, Edmund was more her father than the man who sired her ever had been.

Matt swallowed the last of the bun as she knocked on the study door.

"Enter."

Two strangers were in the room. From their dress and posture, one was the master, the other a servant or henchman. Clearly, they came to strike a deal rather than ask for a job. On the principle of, "the longer the robe, the less the work," the master did not do much. His clothes were immaculate and expensive, but interestingly, he wore no jewellery, not even a signet ring. Both men had swords on their belts, but from the way they held themselves, neither was a skilled fighter nor a handyman assassin. They certainly did not have the muscle to be rowdy boys.

Both had red hair and white skin, which was rare on Pinettale, except among the bloodsucking nobility. Since lords and ladies would never dirty themselves contacting Edmund directly, they must have come from the mainland. Which posed interesting questions. The clothes were new, bought in Fortaine. Apart from being local in style, they showed no sign of travel, no salt or sweat stains. Either their luggage had been lost overboard, or they did not want to advertise their origin with a distinctive type of dress. But why not?

The once-over took less than a second. "You wanted me?" she asked.

"Yes. Come in." Edmund was half sitting on a corner of his desk. "Allow me to present my daughter, Matilda. She'll be the one who undertakes this assignment." He tilted his head to Matt. "These gentlemen have an interesting proposition. I'll let them explain."

The leader treated Matt to his own examination, then cleared his throat. "My name is Waldo of Bousack. I'm in Fortaine because there's an artefact we desire. Have you heard of the Temple of Anbeorht?"

If he comes from Bousack, I'm a cabbage. Apart from the other clues, he spoke in a staccato rhythm, biting off his words, and his vowels were rounded and stressed. Matt had spent enough time on the docks to place his accent due south on the mainland. But though reading him was easy, it was harder to know how to read his question. Every child in Fortaine would know what he was referring to. Yet he was waiting for her to answer.

"You mean the Shewstone?"

"Yes. They call it the Shewstone. I intend to have it."

"You're hoping to buy it?" Two could play the game of asking silly questions. "I can't see them parting with it. Do you know the priestesses reckon it can foretell the future? They rake in the money. You'd be amazed." To Matt's way of thinking, the scam was so brazen even she would have felt a twinge of guilt carrying it out.

"I am very aware of how much they charge, and I do not think it would be for sale, regardless of price. Which is why I've come to your father to see if he can acquire it for us."

"Won't be easy."

"If it were easy, we wouldn't need your services. Do you think you can do it?"

Matt shrugged. "If the money's right."

The Flyming gang did not generally work as thieves for hire, but business was business, and Edmund would not have wasted her time if he had no intention of accepting the job.

"Your father and I have agreed on a price."

Matt glanced over to meet Edmund's eyes. What was he thinking? The Shewstone was just a ball of rock. Could they get away with passing off a replica?

As if hearing her thought, the visitor said, "I arranged for a divination yesterday, so I could first see it for myself. The artefact was exactly as I'd been told. I must have it."

Which meant he might notice if he did not get the genuine Shewstone.

"How quickly do you want it?"

"Within the month. I cannot wait much longer."

Matt nodded. She trusted Edmund already had a plan in mind, and if they could not steal the Shewstone inside a month, they could not steal it at all.

"Sounds good to me."

"I agree." Edmund pushed himself away from the desk. "How shall we contact you when we have it?"

"My companion will walk along the harbour wall, each day at noon. You may pass a message to him there."

So, the visitors intended to conceal their lodging. A vain hope. Edmund would want to know more about their new clients and did not lack the resources to find out. The information would be forthcoming, of that Matt was sure.

Edmund's face gave nothing away. "Then I think, gentlemen, we've covered all that is needful."

The visitors nodded politely as they were shown out.

"What do you make of them?" Edmund asked once they were alone.

"They've come a long way for a lump of rock."

"The mainland around Sideamuda, I'd say."

Matt took a seat in the casement window. "And with money to burn."

"You don't know the half of it."

"How much are they offering?"

"Four thousand yellowboys."

"What!"

"I know. We'd have jumped at half that."

Matt was puzzled. "They didn't strike me as fools."

"Except for being desperate to own a stone ball."

"There is that."

Matt turned her head to look on the street below. The two strangers were walking away.

Edmund joined her, leaning his shoulder against the window frame. "It feels too good."

"And if something seems too good, it probably is. You think they're pulling something?"

"I don't know." He sighed. "We go carefully. Any hint of a problem and we tell them it's off."

"Right. Any idea how we're going to get the stone?"

"Nope. That's up to you."

"Me?"

"We need someone inside the temple. I don't fancy our chances of bribing a priestess, and men aren't allowed in."

"You think I could become a priestess? I'm not sure the haircut will suit me," Matt joked.

"I suspect the haircut would be the least of your problems. Fortunately, there's a less demanding way in for you."

"You're thinking of the hostel for travelling gentlewomen who're too dainty for common inns?"

"Do you think you can play the part?"

Matt laughed. "You doubt my acting ability?"

"I'm not sure about you staying sufficiently virtuous."

"I don't have to be virtuous, just act it. I'm sure that's all the sisters are doing."

"You can't afford to slip. No matter what the sisters are up to when the public aren't around, you should stay in character with your cover story."

"Which is?"

"You're from a quaint little rural spot. You're in town to tidy up the affairs of your recently departed uncle, because you're the only one your family can spare, but you've never been to a big city before and your husband is possessively jealous and wants to be sure you aren't cavorting with sailors and the like."

"Husband?"

"Wife is hardly an option."

"I don't know. If word gets out, they might be queuing up outside my bedroom door." Matt ran the idea past what she knew of the sisterhood and winced. "You're right. Husband is safer."

"You don't have to lift the stone yourself. Just see how it can be done. We'll plan on you staying in the hostel half a month. You can extend it if necessary. But I don't think you have to worry about being recognised afterward. The priestesses don't leave the temple much, and when they do they're surrounded by guards."

"A wig wouldn't hurt."

"True. We'll send a letter to the temple. You can show up a couple of days later."

"Right."

"And remember. Don't take risks. Maybe this man calling himself Waldo is just a clown who doesn't know the price of a thief, but something about this is making my back itch."

"You know me."

"Precisely. That's why I'm saying it. Be careful."

Matt wandered back to her room, which was now empty. Pearl had done her job. But with hindsight, perhaps she should have had Maybe-Marie stay. Matt was facing the prospect of days on end stuck in the temple with only the Virgin Priestesses of Anberith for company. Unless the priestesses were more fun than their tag suggested, it could be her longest period of celibacy since turning sixteen.

Matt closed her eyes and groaned. "The things we do for money."

CHAPTER TWO

*T*he stout walls of Hyth Diepu could have held out against the *ragtag rebel army until loyal reinforcements arrived, but the base-born rabble inside the port city made common cause with the besiegers and rose up. In two days of fighting, the traitors burned the warships in dock and massacred the sailors.*

With the loss of such a significant part of the Rihtcynn navy, the seas would become the home of pirates, and Earl Swidhelm Wisa Gyrwefenna saw there was no hope of keeping Pinettale secure within the empire. He therefore made the hard decision to take full personal responsibility for the island, and named himself King of Pinettale, so that he might preserve a remnant of the noble Rihtcynn culture there for the generations to come.

Or to put it another way, Swidhelm saw his chance and grabbed it. Eawynn sincerely doubted the first king's motives had been altruistic.

The events, and the slant on Swidhelm's actions, were familiar to her. It had been her father's favourite bedtime story, on the few occasions he had seen fit to tell one to her. At the time, Eawynn had preferred Hattie's funny tales of Jibjob the Bear. However, Alric Husa Achangrena had wanted to impress on Eawynn their noble heritage. He could trace his ancestry back to Swidhelm by multiple routes, most directly through Swidhelm's youngest daughter, who had married the Thane Achangrena of the day—his great-great-great-great-great-grandfather.

The library door opened. Eawynn looked up to see who would come in. She was supposed to be reading Holy Scripture rather than distorted history, but after four hours spent cleaning, she needed entertainment, and Wilfrid's *Rise and Fall of the Rihtcynn Empire* was the best option on offer. Given her low standing, being caught out would mean more trouble than she wanted to think about. But how great was the risk? Nobody else was in the library, and the book was written in Cynnreord, using old clerical hieroglyphs. After Erudite Sister Librarian's demise, only three other priestesses could decode it well enough to even get the first idea that she ought to be looking at something else. A stout figure in sea-green waddled into the library, and Eawynn smiled. Redoubtable Sister Door-warden was not one of the three.

Eawynn was about to return to her book, but another person followed the priestess in. This woman was a stranger, of average height, dressed in secular clothing, a long blue surcoat, reaching well below her knees, with matching red collar and stockings. A white shirt and dainty shoes completed her attire. Her skin was the light brown of a commoner, but her long wavy hair held a tint of auburn, proclaiming a modicum of noble blood in her ancestry. Possibly there was another trace of Rihtcynn forebears in the delicate bone structure of her face. Her hands were also well formed with long fingers. She looked to be in her mid-twenties.

"We have nearly one hundred and fifty books in the library," Redoubtable Sister Door-warden announced proudly.

"Really." The overstressed cadence suggested the woman was not quite as impressed as she was trying to sound. A bland smile was plastered on her face.

"While you're staying with us, you may come here to read. Studious Sister Librarian or one of her assistants will help you find a suitable book."

As long as you don't ask Diligent Sister Caretaker. Eawynn still wanted to scream at the injustice. How could a featherbrain like Agnes be assigned to the library? She understood the politics, but it was not being fair to the books.

"Thank you."

Redoubtable Sister Door-warden started to back out, but the visitor was not ready to leave. She tottered the length of the room. Her hands were folded demurely over her stomach. Judging by her clothes, the woman was either an artisan or married to one. She was attractive, but otherwise unremarkable, yet something was odd about her. It took Eawynn a moment to work out what. The woman's manner was timid, mouse-like, with small, teetering steps. Her walk should have been ungainly, yet, like a mouse, her footsteps made no sound, even on the tiled library floor.

At the rear of the library, the woman stopped by the metal grill protecting the proscribed books from unauthorised eyes. Insightful Sister Oracle's permission was needed to even open the grill, let alone read any of the contents.

"Why are these books locked up? Are they valuable?"

Redoubtable Sister Door-warden had followed, making considerably more noise. "All the books are valuable. These ones contain particularly sacred writings that only the elders may read. They hold deep mysteries of our faith."

"Really."

The woman did not sound convinced, and nor was Eawynn. Probably every inquisitive novice in the temple's history had tried to sneak a peek. If any had succeeded, they were not letting on, though this did not stop rumours about the contents. Juvenile suggestions were that the books held erotic bedtime reading or magical spells. Eawynn would now guess they included tips on how to wheedle clues from supplicants, plus maybe a compendium of pretentious metaphors in Cynnreord.

The visitor continued her circuit, although it seemed her eyes spent as much time on the windows as they did on the books. Was she a glazier, come to give a quote for new stained glass? Whatever her interest, Eawynn wished she would hurry up and go. The next ceremony was due soon, and Eawynn wanted to finish the chapter without distractions. But no such luck. The woman stopped by her table.

Eawynn restrained the pointless urge to conceal Wilfred's history. It would merely make her appear guilty. Anyway, even if the visitor was a scholar and could decode the script, how was she to know what Eawynn was supposed to be reading?

The woman looked pointedly at Redoubtable Sister Door-warden, who finally got the idea she was expected to introduce them.

"This is Madam Hilda of Gimount. She's going to be staying in the hostel while she concludes some business in Fortaine." Redoubtable Sister Door-warden gestured with one hand. "And this is Dutiful Sister Custodian."

"Good afternoon." Madam Hilda's smile revealed even white teeth. "May I ask what you're custodian of?"

"The Shewstone."

"Really." For the first time, the woman's interest was unmistakably genuine. Her eyes widened slightly, and her voice acquired depth. "I've heard so much about it. I was hoping I might even see it while I'm here. Would that be possible, do you think?"

Redoubtable Sister Door-warden got her answer in first. "I'm afraid the Shewstone is never on display. You would have to make a representation to Most Reverend Insightful Sister Oracle."

"That's a shame."

The woman's eyes fixed on Eawynn, and here again was an off note. There was nothing timid in that gaze. An intent glinted in their depths that Eawynn found unsettling. Hilda of Gimount had locked eyes with her—a wolf, not a mouse—brazenly sizing her up, and Eawynn did not know how to react. How she ought to react was easy; there was little doubt what advice any elder would give. But how did she want to react? Eawynn was completely at a loss, and that was the disconcerting part. Whatever else was happening in her life, Eawynn always knew her own mind. Was it just a reaction to being ignored by everyone else for months?

Eawynn felt her cheek burning. It did not matter whether it was annoyance or embarrassment. The effect was always so obvious on her pale skin. She looked down at the open page, taking a few seconds to compose her features, hoping the woman would move on. However, when she looked up, Hilda of Gimount was still watching her, but now with an easy grin on her lips, like a woman enjoying a private joke. What game was she playing?

"I'll show you the rest of the temple." Redoubtable Sister Door-warden came to the rescue, albeit unwittingly. She shepherded the visitor to the door. But before Hilda of Gimount let herself be led out, she stopped to throw one last broad smile at Eawynn.

When the door closed, Eawynn let out a long sigh, either of relief or apprehension. She could not say which emotion was uppermost. There was something intriguing about Hilda of Gimount, maybe even dangerous. She was also very attractive. But the last thing Eawynn needed were more black marks against her name. This woman was trouble. Eawynn could feel it in her core.

After a few deep breaths, she returned to Wilfrid's history.

Such true-born Rihtcynn as resided on Pinettale rallied to King Swidhelm's cause. United, they were able to maintain discipline in the army and put down uprisings by the commoners. The victories were hard won. In Anmet and Monflacin, mobs murdered everyone of Rihtcynn blood. Sorrowfully to relate, many noble bloodlines were extinguished. Yet, though sorely tried, King Swidhelm kept a firm grip on Fortaine and dealt ruthlessly with the rabble. Once his capital was secure, he had a stable base from which to launch his campaign to subdue the rest of the island. Five years after King Swidhelm took the throne, Pinettale was again at peace.

Back in the colonnaded courtyard, Matt rubbed her face discreetly, trying to massage her expression into one suitable for a decorous gentlewoman. A cheesy grin was certainly not right. She should have been more careful with the good-looking priestess, but good-looking women were always Matt's weakness. Besides, as Matt read the signs, the custodian had potential, and not just in terms of access to the Shewstone. It was a shame about the shaved head. The custodian was pretty enough to carry it off, but Matt was sure she would be even more attractive with enough hair to run fingers through. The grin threatened to return.

"That was the library. I think I've already told you this is called the atrium." The door warden, on the other hand, was a lost cause, regardless of hairstyle.

"Yes, Holy Sister."

In the middle of the atrium was a neat garden of low shrubs and box hedges. Spring bulbs were in full bloom. The four sides were lined with pillars supporting a low vaulted roof over a wide walkway, somewhere the sisters could take exercise on rainy days. To the north, east, and west, arched passageways gave access to the other areas of the temple. There was no southern exit. The Temple of Anberith backed directly onto the cliffs overlooking the port. As befitting the goddess of tides, the sounds of waves crashing against the shore could be heard everywhere.

The priestess paused by another door. "You saw the audience room when you arrived?"

"Yes, Holy Sister."

They progressed as far as the eastern arch. "As a resident of the hostel, you may come and go through the atrium at will, but you may not enter here under any circumstances."

"I wouldn't dream of it." *I have far more interesting dreams.*

"It leads to the priestesses' private quarters."

Private quarters—dormitories, washrooms, an extra special place to pray, and maybe an orgy chamber. Or maybe not, but the priestesses had to do something for fun.

The circuit of the atrium continued. There was a schoolroom, where the daughters of the gentry could be taught to read and write, an accounting office, where rich people who felt compelled to give away money could do so, and a chart room where a grumpy priestess was calculating something and did not want to be disturbed. They left that last room rather hurriedly.

Matt was also shown into two enclosed halls of a religious nature. The larger was the Shrine to the Oracle. A door at the rear was pointed out as being the unpronounceable whatsit where the Shewstone was kept. Matt nodded and said nothing. Expressing too much interest would be a mistake. She concentrated on small steps, with her elbows clamped to her sides, pulling her shoulders in, and smiling sweetly all the time. Her face was starting to ache.

They concluded the circuit back at the northern exit. "The Sanctuary of Anberith is through here. It's the only part of the temple open to everyone."

I know. I came through on the way here. "Yes, Holy Sister."

Anyway, Matt already had a longstanding familiarity with the large, open-air Sanctuary of Anberith, with its huge statue of the goddess surrounded by a circular reflecting pool. The crowded ceremonies provided excellent hunting grounds for pickpockets.

"The doors on this passage are my special responsibility."

The solid, iron-studded doors were clearly her pride and joy. She was all but fondling them when Matt arrived. Would the priestess drag her back to admire the woodwork again?

"Is this why you are called door warden? Do you have the keys to all the doors in the temple?"

The priestess pouted. "I am charged with ensuring no unsuitable persons are admitted to the inner temple."

In which case you've failed by letting me in. And, between the lines, it was a *no* for a key to the Shewstone door. Presumably, the custodian had one. Matt would have to find out. Again, she had to work to hide a grin.

"I'll show you your room."

The door warden might not be guardian of all keys, but her duties apparently extended to full guided tours, when she was not otherwise busy snuggling up to the atrium gates. She led Matt through the western arch, into an area given over to general domestic buildings. A chimney puffing smoke and the smell of cooking marked the kitchen. They passed by the open double doors to a workshop. A paved courtyard surrounded by stables and a small blacksmith was wedged in a corner a short way off.

The hostel was, fortunately, closer to the kitchen than the stable. It consisted of six private rooms over storerooms. A small, unoccupied cubbyhole was near the foot of the stairs.

"That's where Welcoming Sister Hosteller normally sits, but she's not around at the moment."

The redoubtable sister had an amazing natural talent for saying the obvious. And where did the priestesses get their names? Did they shorten them for everyday use? Would the door warden answer to "Red"? What was the original name of the priestess in the library? Matt was going to have to find out.

Matt's bags were waiting for her upstairs. Her small room was furnished with a bed, a footlocker, and a wardrobe. Between them, they took up half the floor space. A window looked out over orderly rows of vegetables and herbs.

"That's the kitchen garden."

"Indeed, Holy Sister."

The well-tended area was walled off from the rest of the temple, either to stop overweight sisters from taking unauthorised snacks or to stop the cabbages and carrots from joining in with the ceremonies.

"We grow food there."

Matt pressed her lips together, fighting the urge to laugh. Irony would, most likely, go right over the sister's head, but the risk was not worth taking. Fortunately, a reply was not needed.

The priestess clapped her hands together, "Oh yes, food! You'll want to see the refectory."

"That would be nice."

The refectory turned out to be a large hall, conveniently close to the kitchen and the hostel. Two long tables ran the length of the room. At the far end, a smaller table was raised on a dais.

"This is where we eat our meals. You'll have a place at the high table, or if you prefer, you may request meals in your room, if you ask Nourishing Sister Kitchener in advance."

"I wouldn't want to be a bother." *Unless the sister in the library was the one providing room service.*

"Breakfast is straight after the dawn ceremony. Luncheon is at noon. The evening meal is at the sixth bell, unless this conflicts with the tides. For those whose work keeps them up late, a light supper is available."

"That's good to know."

They went outside again. The door warden was, mercifully, running out of things to say. How long before she quit prattling and went back to her beloved gates? "You're free to join in with all the ceremonies."

"I'm looking forward to it."

"Female guests may visit you in your room, if you make arrangements with me. Men are not allowed beyond the atrium, and even there they must be chaperoned by either me or my assistant."

That's fine. I prefer women in my bedroom. Probably best not to say it aloud, although maybe the orgy chamber was not such a farfetched idea. The sisters were human, and for all their talk of chastity, there were certain basic human needs. Again, thoughts of the priestess in the library threatened to give Matt a most indecorous smile.

A nearby door opened, and an elderly priestess emerged. This time the door warden did not hesitate to introduce them.

"Beloved Sister, this is Hilda of Gimount, who'll be residing in our hostel for several days. And this is Most Reverend Insightful Sister Oracle, the leader of our community."

Matt was not absolutely sure of protocol, but gave a half curtsy that ought to suffice and bowed her head. "Holy Sister."

"I've been showing her around."

Her divine reverence gave a weak smile. "I trust you've found it inspirational."

"Yes. I was particularly inspired in the library." Matt liked to be truthful when she could.

"You read?" her snotty holiness sounded surprised.

"My father made sure of it. He said otherwise you could not hope to succeed in business." *Regardless of which side of the law your business was on.*

The door warden said, "I've told Madam Hilda she may read books in the library."

"She may. But the books contain weighty matters that are not easy for the lay person to comprehend. Our guest may find more suitable reading matter in the schoolroom."

"Thank you." *But I already know A is for apple.* Her up-her-own-arse-edness was not endearing herself to Matt. *Smile, smile, smile.*

"You're in Fortaine on business?" Her not-too-holy-to-chase-money-edness, was also a little slow on the uptake, but had eventually registered Matt's words. The sums were running behind her eyes.

"My uncle died recently. I'm here to tidy up his affairs and see what state they're in. There had been some talk of debt, hopefully unfounded." *So don't expect a donation to temple funds.*

"I trust so. You're a follower of Anberith?" The sums were still running.

"I'm a faithful daughter of all the gods. My husband thought it better for me to stay with you. Fortaine is a port city, and sailors are…" Matt smiled like a woman too demure to know exactly what sailors were, other than it was not good.

A bell sounded, interrupting any further pursuit of a donation, though Matt suspected it was only a temporary diversion.

"It's time for the Laudation of the Irresistible High Tide. Will you join us?"

"I'd be delighted to, Holy Sister."

The Sanctuary of Anberith was comparatively empty, no more than two hundred worshippers. On holy days and festivals, half the population of Fortaine would squeeze in, ten thousand or more. Those were Matt's favourite times to visit. At the moment, lifting purses would be too conspicuous and totally out of character for a demure businesswoman from Gimount.

Deprived of her normal entertainment, Matt had nothing to distract her from the ceremony. She had not realised before how unbelievably tedious and overbearing it was. The only amusement was that the chief priestess had adopted a particularly silly headdress for the ceremony.

Matt looked at the statue of Anberith, thirty feet tall. The prayers beseeched her to maintain the cycle of tides. Matt was sure, if the gods took their roles the least bit seriously, then Anberith would continue looking after the sea, whether or not she was asked by a group of hypocritical parasites in fancy dress. Alternately, if the goddess decided she could not be arsed anymore, asking her was a waste of time.

The temple took a tithe of all the wealth passing through the port and levied fines for various shortcomings in its followers, then coerced whatever donations they could from people with more money than sense and capped it all by extorting eye-watering amounts from the sham of fortune telling.

When her time in this world was up and Matt came to be judged, she could only hope the gods would show mercy to an honest thief. But if there was any justice in the afterlife, the fate awaiting the swindlers who lined their own pockets in the name of the gods would be no softer. Matt never stole from anyone who could not afford it, and she certainly never claimed she was divinely ordained to take whatever she could get away with.

The prayers droned on. "I, your most humble servant, give thanks for the grace you have shown me."

Humble! Matt wondered how the chief priestess could say it with a straight face. Did she know what the word meant? The ring of green-clad priestesses began yet another chant, about the seas, the moon, and how happy they were to be so pious. Did any of them have the slightest sense of irony? Some people simply did not deserve to have a nice Shewstone.

The statue of the goddess smiled down, kind, placid, and with just a hint of humour. Matt was sure Anberith would see things her way. Then she caught sight of the attractive priestess from the library. Matt bowed her head to hide her expression. She would relieve the chief priestess of the Shewstone, and along the way, she might even have a little fun.

❖

The wooden frescos in the Shrine to the Oracle were a nightmare to polish. Wax got caught behind the little knobbly bits, and the effort of getting it out would cause smears elsewhere, resulting in the fresco looking worse than before Eawynn started. Each fresco would take all day, and polishing them once a year would surely be enough. However, Attentive Sister Chamberlain had ordered it done twice a month.

Eawynn reached one of her least favourite bits, a selection of fruit spilling from an overturned seashell—not that there was much to choose between it and the rest.

"Is this what you do as custodian?"

Eawynn jumped. Hilda of Gimount stood an arm's length away, smiling.

"Yes. Mostly." Caught off-balance, Eawynn's answer was a touch more honest than she intended. "I mean sometimes. But there's more to it." And now she was babbling.

Hilda gave a knowing smile, clearly amused by Eawynn's disarray. "Of course. I assume there would be. After all, you're Sister Custodian not Sister Janitor."

Eawynn could only hope her smile was not too sickly. Yet maybe she gave something away. Hilda's expression became more serious, with a hint of confusion. "I mean, it would be silly if you spent all your time cleaning and polishing. I saw the book you were reading in the library."

"You understand clerical hieroglyphs?"

"Me? Oh no. I had no idea what it was. I didn't even recognise the letters. Which means you're a scholar who was reading something really obscure. You don't set scholars to do a housemaid's job. I can't see the chief priestess wasting a mind like yours."

That's because you don't see how things are. Even so, Eawynn could not help smiling at the compliment.

"So what else does a custodian do?"

"I assist Insightful Sister Oracle when she consults the Shewstone."

"That sounds more interesting."

Had she known it, Madam Hilda was no more accurate than with her previous assumptions. Eawynn merely nodded.

"The consultations, they take place through there?" Madam Hilda pointed to the back wall of the shrine.

"Yes. In the Shewstone Sacrarium."

"That's a bit of a tongue twister." She tilted her head to one side. "The book you were reading, was that to do with the Shewstone? I imagine there's a lot of arcane stuff you need to know."

And you'd imagine wrong. "Insightful Sister Oracle conducts all aspect of the divination. My role requires no special knowledge. I just assist."

"But you are in training to be the next oracle?"

"No. I don't expect that role will come to me."

While they talked, Madam Hilda had been edging forward. Eawynn suddenly became aware how close she now was. The woman had slipped right under her guard. Scant inches separated them, and her eyes were locked on Eawynn's face. Madam Hilda was flirting. Of that Eawynn had no doubt, and the knowledge set her pulse hammering. Maybe it was a game that would be fun to play along with. But the visitor was not the one standing in jeopardy, and she was not the one who should be calling the shots.

Eawynn took a half step back. It was time to assert her own script. She was not a fluff-headed adolescent. "Is there anything I can assist you with, Madam Hilda?"

"Oh please, call me Hilda, no need for the madam part. And is there anything particular you'd like to assist me with?" While they had been talking, Hilda's expression flitted between amusement and confusion. Humour was now dominant, but then she raised her hands in a conciliatory gesture and backed off. "It's fine. I'm just here looking."

Hilda set off on a slow circuit while she continued talking. "When she was showing me around yesterday, I got the feeling your Sister Door-warden was rather put out that she doesn't have a key to the Shewstone room. Or did I misunderstand her?"

"No. Only three of us have keys. Myself, Insightful Sister Oracle, and Attentive Sister Chamberlain."

"And there's no chance of you giving me a quick peek at the Shewstone?" Hilda gave a conspiratorial grin, then again held up her hands, before Eawynn had a chance to reply. "No. It's all right. Forget I asked. I was just..." She shrugged and continued her inspection of the shrine décor—the statues, the stonework, the incense burner, the windows.

Eawynn sucked in a breath, surprised at herself and how close she had been to agreeing to the request. *So much for my own script.* She would have to do a lot better. What was it about the woman? Eawynn's eyes remained on Hilda, watching the way she walked. The dainty footsteps were those of an old woman, yet a fluidity and grace underlay them, a dancer miming a role rather than genuine frailty.

What game was Hilda playing? *She's flirting with me.* That one was obvious, but was there more to it? Hilda's stockings did not hide the muscle underneath. Her shoulders stayed perfectly aligned over her hips. Eawynn studied the movement, hoping for a clue, only to realise Hilda had turned her neck, looking back with a smile that outdid anything to date.

Eawynn felt her face burn to have been caught out in such blatant ogling. Focusing on the wretched fresco, she re-attacked the wax smears and tried to ignore Hilda's soft laugher drifting through the shrine. For once, the overblown fussiness of the woodwork was a blessing, a job needing complete concentration while she regained her composure. She embarked on her twice monthly battle to avoid getting a wad of wax stuck in the dent where the stick joined an apple.

"Couldn't you get a housemaid to do that?"

Again, Eawynn jumped at the voice by her shoulder. Did the woman's feet make no sound at all?

"We sisters perform all necessary tasks. We don't employ servants. Housework is part of our general duties." Of course, before Eawynn was given the role, nobody had been specifically assigned to cleaning the shrine.

"You've got armed guards outside the gates."

"Only in the outer temple. It would require an emergency for them to enter the inner temple."

Hilda studied her with intense dark brown eyes. "Do you enjoy it, being a priestess?"

Not an easy question. "Serving the goddess Anberith is an honour."

The amusement returned. Hilda was too astute not to spot a question being ducked. "Don't you miss all the things you had to give up when you came here?"

"I was too young to have anything to give up." The pony did not count.

"How young?"

"I'd just turned six."

"Why?"

I was an encumbrance to my father's ambition. "My family thought it best."

"Now you're old enough to make up your own mind. Couldn't you leave, if you wanted to?"

Where do I have to go? "I've taken my vows as a priestess. My life is here, forever."

"You don't know what you're missing."

Oh yes, I do. Hilda was standing very close, holding eye contact.

The pounding heartbeat returned, along with a tingling in her knees. Eawynn locked her legs and prayed she was not going to blush again.

The subject of "special friendships" was well known in the temple. It was never talked about directly, mainly because the gossip mill had an extensive range of code phrases above and beyond the standard euphemism. Once you worked out how to interpret what they were saying, some priestesses hardly talked about anything else.

Among the novices, Nurturing Sister Mentor had been on guard against juvenile crushes and had kindly but firmly taken steps to squash them before they developed further. Yet she was not infallible, as Beatrice and Eawynn had been able to find out. Their experiences had been awkward and hasty, but they had managed to break a few rules.

Eawynn was aware that many priestesses, freed from Nurturing Sister Mentor's oversight, formed questionable bonds with each other, not to mention a few who formed even more questionable bonds with the guardsmen on the gates. Eawynn reckoned no more than a quarter of the sisters could truthfully claim the name of virgin priestess. Though in her own case, further straying looked unlikely. Nobody wanted to be known as a close friend to the daughter of an executed traitor, even had Eawynn desired to pursue such a relationship.

But what of Hilda? She had a life outside the temple. Gossip over breakfast had spoken of a jealous husband, anxious to keep his wife from the temptations of common inns. Eawynn chased the questions around in her head. Where was this conversation going? Which of them was being naïve? Hilda was playing games; that much was certain. Was she bored and seeking a little excitement to pass the time? Was this how she acted with every woman she met or was she making the most being away from her husband? Either way, Eawynn was tired of people playing games with her life. She was not a toy. She would not surrender what little control she had.

Eawynn fixed her attention on the fresco and the awful, crevice-scarred bunch of grapes. But she could sense Hilda's eyes on her. The woman's body was so close, Eawynn fancied she could feel Hilda's warmth, burning through the sea-green robe, setting her on fire.

"Don't you find the life of a priestess lonely?"

"I have the company of my sisters."

"But how much company do they provide?" The subtle emphasis on the word *company* put her meaning beyond doubt.

Eawynn narrowed her focus to each appalling grape, one at a time, while the butterflies in her stomach threatened to drive the air from her lungs. "I'm quite happy."

Eawynn had polished the same grape three times, but was unable to think of anything else. She offered up a silent prayer, imploring Anberith to prompt Hilda to leave.

"I'm pleased you're happy, but if ever there's anything I can do to make you happier, you only have to ask." Hilda's voice was warm and husky.

The polishing rag was dry, removing wax rather than applying it. Abruptly, the jar appeared between her face and the fresco.

"Do you want this?" Hilda's tone had changed to pure humour.

Eawynn could not stop herself. Her head jerked around. Her sight locked on the face of the woman holding out the jar—the level gaze of rich brown eyes; the finely balanced cheeks and chin, framed by curls of auburn hair; the straight, pert nose; the full red lips. Eawynn felt her face burn. She could not speak.

Hilda gave a soft laugh. "Tell you what, I'll put it down here." She carefully set the jar on a ledge and then trotted from the shrine, making no more noise than on her arrival.

Eawynn stared at the doorway while she got her breath back. As prayed for, Hilda of Gimount had gone, and most annoying of all, Eawynn now felt nothing but disappointment.

❖

The wig was itchy, but Matt did not want to risk being caught without it on. She had hoped she would get used to the thing on her head, but after five days it was getting worse, not better. Maybe she could have done without a wig. It was not much in the way of disguise. However, her normal short crop was not right for a genteel wife and businesswoman. At least the weather that day was grey and cold, so the wig was not making her scalp sweat.

Matt stood at the window of her room, watching rain fall on the rows of vegetables in the kitchen garden, until a knock disturbed her. "Yes?"

"I've brought your luncheon." Somethingy Sister Hosteller poked her head around the door.

"Thank you."

"Are you feeling unwell?"

"Just a headache." *The one I would have got if I sat through one more lunch with Unsightly Sister Orifice spouting her tight-arsed drivel.*

No doubt it was intended as an honour for hostel guests to sit at the high table with the top rank priestesses. It was an honour Matt could happily have gone without. Her limit for self-righteous blabbering had been reached midway into her first mealtime. The chief priestess had turned bullshitting into an art form. The tedium was not helped by someone droning out Holy Scripture in the background throughout the entire meal. Did the sisters never take a break and lighten up?

After the hosteller left, Matt put a thick slice of cold pork and a thinner slice of apple on a slab of bread and stood chewing while she continued looking out the window. From a burglary angle, the kitchen garden was the obvious route in and out of the temple, far easier than scaling the cliffs from the beach and less well defended than the front.

Both inner and outer walls of the garden were fourteen foot or more, but nothing a rope ladder could not get you over. From the upper floor vantage point, Matt could see shards of broken glass cemented along the top, but the work was old and more was missing than remained. A leather saddle was scarcely necessary. Somebody had let the maintenance slip. Possibly the same somebody who decided to spend the temple security funds on pretty new uniforms for the guards. Matt was not complaining.

The public entrance to the Sanctuary of Anberith was from Silver Lady Square. It would be hard to cross the open expanse unseen, even at night. Whereas, a maze of narrow streets lay over the garden wall. Yet, this vulnerable side of the temple grounds merited no more than an occasional patrol. The guards were stationed in the big sanctuary during the day, when honest worshippers were allowed in. Then at night, they all went home, except for a few who stood outside the main gates. The sisters and the guards they employed did not have the first idea about security and certainly could not think like a thief.

The Shrine to the Oracle was locked at night but pickable. The same was probably true of the windowless room the Shewstone was in, although Matt had not yet been able to examine it from the inside.

What obstacles might a thief face? To date, she had been taking things slowly, waiting until her presence was no longer a novelty, while familiarising herself with life in the temple. Now was the time to speed things up.

Matt swallowed the last of the pork and picked up one of the floury things the sisters called cakes. Had they not heard about cinnamon or honey? She took a cautious nibble.

Luckily, getting into the shrine promised to be a lot of fun. The oh-so-pretty custodian (whose real name she was yet to learn) was oh-so-easy to read. She was also easy to manipulate. The more direct the comments, the more stubbornly the priestess fixated on what was in front of her face and ignored everything else. Of course, flirting was always fun for its own sake.

Matt felt the grin split her face. How far could she get with the flirting? The custodian was definitely receptive. You did not blush like that just because someone handed you a jar of polish. Matt played with a fantasy of seducing her on an altar. Additional pleasure came from imagining the outrage of the chief priestess. Although from purely practical considerations, it would be far more comfortable to entice the custodian up to her room one night.

Matt threw the last half of the "cake" out the window for the birds to choke on and poured herself a mug of small beer. Thankfully, the sisters' brewing skills exceeded their baking.

Edmund would tell her to forget any idea of seducing the custodian. But then, Edmund would be basing the advice on his own personal experience. Pearl had told enough stories about the trouble Edmund's exploits in the sack had got him into as a youth. Apart from the humour value, maybe Pearl hoped the cautionary tales would put Matt off copying them. If so, it had not worked. She and Edmund were far too similar, and not just in preferring lovers of their own sex. They understood each other perfectly.

Matt loved him for the way he had changed her life, the security he had given her, and the pleasure they took in each other's company. As a child, she had worshipped him as a saviour, a hero. Now, he was her best friend. She trusted, loved, and admired him, and knew the feeling was returned. Edmund was the only father she wanted. The only father she would name as such.

Maybe, more than anything else, what they gave each other was the one unchanging relationship in their lives, unlike their sexual entanglements, which were never simple or pain free or long lasting. Although, on the plus side, no matter how messy the affairs might get, they were quickly over.

Sex was a simple, animal need, enjoyable for all concerned, and every animal other than humans seemed to know this. How much easier if people could take the same uncomplicated approach. Instead they bound it up with absurd expectations and threw obstacles in the way just for the sake of it. Or, as with the priestesses, denying themselves and claiming it made some divinity happy, without a shred of evidence the divinity gave a rat's arse either way.

Why did people make things so complicated? They turned sexual desire into the whole courtship game, the chase and the conquest, with nobody saying what they meant, or doing what they wanted. They played stupid games like "hard to get." Then Matt thought of the custodian and laughed aloud at herself.

Who was she to talk? How much fun those games could be.

Eawynn shut the sacrarium door and turned the key. Her work as housemaid was over for the day. She closed her eyes and gave a few words of thanks to whatever deity might be listening. The whole half hour before dinner was hers, to do whatever she wanted. If only there were something permitted that she actually wanted to do. Eawynn looped the thin chain through her belt and dropped the Shewstone key into the pocket in her robe.

What should she do? The library was her normal choice, but she had finished Wilfrid's *Rise and Fall of the Rihtcynn Empire* and had read all the other books at least twice. She could go to the small garden behind the washroom and watch the sunset over the sea, but the wind was chill that day. She could go for a stroll through the market stalls in Silver Lady Square, but leaving the temple unchaperoned, although not forbidden, was frowned upon, and people found enough reasons to frown at her, without providing them with more.

Eawynn stood in the atrium considering her options. What did she want to do? Or maybe she should ask herself what did she least not want to do. Then, in an instant, the answer came to her. On the other side of the atrium, Hilda of Gimount was disappearing into the passage leading to the Sanctuary of Anberith.

In the days since their encounter by the fresco, she and Hilda had met several times in passing. Each occasion had been regrettably short and they were never alone. The words exchanged were brief and polite, nothing more.

Was Hilda avoiding her? Admittedly, Eawynn's schedule had little free time, and Hilda was reputedly busy, sorting through her late uncle's affairs. However, Eawynn was starting to wonder if she had misread Hilda's intentions. How much that hurt! She did not want to pursue any variant on a special friendship, but equally, she did not want to think the only interest anyone had shown in her for months was a misunderstanding.

The perverse disappointment annoyed Eawynn beyond bearing, but she could not stop herself reacting to the mere sight of Hilda. Each time, her pulse would race and her stomach would flip. They had shared just one conversation. Nothing more. Why act like this? Yet fighting it was pointless. The urge was stupid and reckless, but she had to talk to Hilda, if for nothing else than in the hope of soothing her damaged ego.

Eawynn sped around the walkway and followed her quarry along the passage. Redoubtable Sister Door-warden was in her alcove by the heavy timber doors. Eawynn would have felt sympathy for her. Surely sitting by the door all day was the one allotted role in the temple less interesting than cleaning the shrine and sacrarium. However, Redoubtable Sister Door-warden merely pouted at her.

Eawynn emerged into the open on the other side. The sun had nearly set, casting long shadows across the Sanctuary of Anberith. The water in the circular pool was still, reflecting the statue of the goddess like a mirror and setting her against the pale blue sky. The next ceremony would not be for another two hours, at moon rise, and the wide expanse of flagstones was deserted, except for the uniformed guards who stood sentry while the sanctuary was open to the public.

Eawynn had expected the hostel guest to be going into town. However, Hilda was heading to one of the enclosed shrines. There were four of them, each set in a corner of the sanctuary, and dedicated to a different aspect of the goddess—Anberith of the Moon, Anberith of the Tides, Anberith of the Birthing, and Anberith of the Prophesy. The last of these was Hilda's destination.

At that time of day, the shrine was most likely empty. One private conversation was all Eawynn wanted, to resolve any misunderstandings. Or so she tried to convince herself. Yet the onset of nerves set her legs quivering.

Midway across the sanctuary, Eawynn hesitated and pressed her hand against her forehead. Who was she trying to fool? She was acting like an idiot. But knowing this did not stop her following Hilda. What possible good outcome could there be? Eawynn sighed and carried on walking. At least it was not boring. She was getting very tired of being bored.

The dim interior of the shrine was a triangle, twenty feet across at the base. Directly opposite the entrance, a candlelit statue of Anberith was holding a fortune-telling orb similar to the Shewstone. The walls were painted with mystic symbols, interwoven in patterns.

At first it looked as if the shrine was deserted, but once Eawynn's eyes adjusted, she spotted two figures in a dark corner, away from both the candles and the entrance. Hilda was not alone. A tall man, dressed in everyday work clothes, stood with her. Their heads were close together as they talked, too quietly to be overheard.

Eawynn stopped in the open doorway. Neither person had noticed her, so she could back away. Maybe finding a book in the library was not such a bad idea. But who was Hilda talking to? And about what? Curiosity made Eawynn hesitate a second too long. Hilda glanced over, saw her, and smiled. She addressed a few last words to the man, then trotted over, her smile getting broader with each step.

"Have you come to pray?"

"Umm. No." Which Eawynn immediately realised was a silly answer, depriving herself of the only legitimate reason for being there.

If Hilda was confused, she did not show it. She slipped her arm through Eawynn's. "Good. Then you won't mind having a walk with me."

"No." Eawynn's reply was half squeak. A wave of tremors threatened to reduce her to a heap on the ground. Somehow she managed to remain upright. Even through the material of her robe, the touch of Hilda's arm flooded all Eawynn's senses.

Hilda led her toward the middle of the sanctuary. The effort of putting one foot in front of the other took all Eawynn's concentration, but she was hazily aware of the man's footsteps as he too left the shrine.

"That was a fortunate coincidence," Hilda said, after they had gone a short distance, and Eawynn was starting to re-master the art of walking.

"Oh?"

"That man, Raff. He's one of my uncle's ex-employees. He was bringing me a message, but stopped to ask Anberith for good luck in the future. We just happened to run into each other."

"Oh."

"Things are going well. We've managed to switch funds around and clear some issues. With any luck, I'll be able to go home in another seven days or so."

"Oh." Eawynn clenched her teeth. She had to think of something more intelligent to say. Bad enough that she had set herself up, acting like an idiot. Now she was sounding like one as well.

"I'm pleased we have this chance to talk. I've not been able to see as much of you as I'd like."

There. That was the sop to her ego Eawynn had wanted. Now she could disengage her arm, bid Hilda good evening, and walk away. Except she could no more walk away than fly. Whatever game Hilda was playing, she was winning, galling as it was to admit.

They reached the pool around the statue. Hilda said, "There's something I've wanted to ask you, but you don't have to answer, if it's forbidden or anything like that."

"Yes. What?" She was squeaking again.

"Your name. What did your parents call you, before you came to the temple?"

"Eawynn."

Hilda drew them to a halt and turned to meet Eawynn's eyes. "Would it be too much of a cliché to say that's a nice name? It suits you."

"Thank you."

Hilda continued their circuit of the pool. "You know, even though we haven't had much contact these last few days, I've been watching you."

Eawynn was silent. She could not say *Oh* again, and could not think of anything else.

"Does that bother you?" Hilda asked.

Did it? Eawynn was too worried about her knees giving out to be able to think of anything else.

The kitchen bell rang out, signalling ten minutes to mealtime, saving Eawynn. But did she want to be saved?

Hilda slipped her arm free. "I've got to go wash my hands before dinner."

Eawynn nodded. She watched Hilda walk back through the archway to the atrium. Only once she was out of sight could Eawynn start to shake some life back into her legs, steady her breathing, and wait for her pulse to slow. The effect Hilda had on her was outrageous. Eawynn closed her eyes. The most absurdly outrageous thing of all was that she loved it.

"What sort of idiot have I let myself become?" She asked the question under her breath.

Simple answer—an infatuated, infantile one. It was not a situation Eawynn was ready to tolerate. More to the point, she could not afford to tolerate it. Her position was bad enough as it was. Anything that might happen between her and Hilda could only make life worse, especially if the rumour mill got to work. She had to impose some self-discipline and be sensible. In another seven days, Hilda would be gone.

CHAPTER THREE

Matt picked up the cutpurse before she was halfway across Silver Lady Square. She stopped by a stall to give the would-be thief a once-over. He was young, not out of his teens, and nobody she recognised, either an indie or one of Gilbert's boys. His tracking was so flagrant he might as well have hung a sign around his neck, yet he clearly had no idea Matt was wise to him. Either he was not very good, or he thought she was an easy mark. Either way, he was making a mistake.

Matt headed down Gold Street, with the would-be thief in tow, then cut left onto Waddle Lane by the Yew Tree Inn. Just before it hit the High Street, she turned again into Carter's Passage, the alleyway running along the backs of shops and taverns. As usual, it was deserted in the mid-afternoon. The cutpurse was still a dozen yards behind Matt when a dogleg took her out of his sight. She ducked into a doorway recess and waited.

The cutpurse's footsteps clipped out a steady rhythm as he rounded the corner, but then slowed and stuttered. He finally stopped a yard past the doorway with his back to Matt and scratched his head, clearly bewildered about his vanishing mark.

"You weren't following me, were you?"

He spun around, mouth hanging open. "No. I was just on my way to—"

"And you don't recognise me?"

This time the cutpurse merely frowned.

"Try to imagine me without this wig."

The frown deepened before realisation hit. "No, ma'am. I'm sorry. I didn't mean…" He fled.

So he was not a complete novice, new in town, but he still had a lot to learn—if he survived long enough.

The story of the late uncle gave Matt an excuse to go out whenever temple life became unbearable. The problem was the up-market clothes which pulled in unwelcome interest, although this was the first thief to target her. Before now, the trouble had come from young studs, trying their luck. So far, Matt had only needed to resort to violence once to change their ideas. There was a reason why genteel women rarely walked the streets alone. If she returned to the temple with a bruise or two, the sisters would have no trouble believing she had been attacked, but it might blow her cover if she had to admit to winning the fight.

Furthermore, the surcoat was so long and close cut she could not easily run or climb. The fashion was favoured by the professional classes to show they were not engaged in physical activity. Its effect on Matt was to make her feel vulnerable, and she did not like the feeling. She had kept her outings to the bare minimum needed to keep her sane, not going far beyond Silver Lady Square. This was her first visit home.

Benny was on duty outside the Flyming house. He grinned when he saw her. "Has anyone ever said you look good with long hair? Have you thought about growing it?"

"Has anyone ever said you'd look good with no teeth? Would you like my help? I'm sure I could find a rock."

Benny snorted a laugh.

The familiar home sounds and scents flowed around Matt, washing away the soul-stifling dross of the temple. She tugged off the wig and took a deep breath. She felt her rib cage expand, taking in more than just air. How did the sisters cope? The rules, the constant surveillance, the tedium, the absence of everything that made life worth living. Benny's was the first genuine laughter she had heard in days.

Matt was there because of Edmund's message but was not going to waste the chance to check by with the people she missed the most. She stuck her head into the housekeeper's office. Nobody would ever replace her Ma, but if Edmund was her adopted father then Pearl was a favourite aunt.

Pearl was slumped, dozing in a chair, but she struggled up for a hug. "Good to see you, Mattie."

"You too."

Matt wrapped her arms around Pearl, while fighting to control her shock. Over the last year, the weight had fallen off. Pearl's once soft body was now a bag of bones in Matt's arms. When had it happened? Yes, somewhere in the back of her mind, Matt had been aware all was not well. But only now, coming back after days away, was the change so awfully obvious.

"You here to see Edmund?"

"You don't think I'd visit just for the pleasure of seeing you?"

"Get on with you." Pearl pushed her away, smiling, but dark bags under her eyes spoke of sleepless nights.

"Do you know where he is?"

"Haven't seen him for a while. Ricon is upstairs. He should know."

Matt hesitated, wanting to say something. But what? No easy words came to mind. Nothing that was not bland or stupid. *Are you all right?* Why ask? Clearly, Pearl was not all right. Matt gave an extra hug, to let her actions speak for her.

She found Ricon lounging on a daybed, looking pretty, which was something he was very good at, and he knew it. Despite his vanity, Matt liked him. He was smart and funny and appeared to be genuinely in love with Edmund. He dressed in a strange mixture of scruffy and elegant, with a wispy beard and ponytail, which even more strangely, suited him. He had come to Edmund's notice as a smuggler. The noticing had been of a sort that resulted in the breakup of Edmund's previous romance. So far, Ricon and Edmund had been lovers for nine months. Matt thought he might even last another three and make it to their anniversary, which would be a record.

Edmund's love affairs were definitely mellowing with age. Matt had a vision of him and Ricon, both bald and toothless, sitting in front of a fire wearing fluffy socks and bed robes, drinking warm milk, and then dismissed it, smiling at the fantasy. There was no way Edmund would go down that route.

Ricon did not get up, but settled for an exaggerated wave. "Hey there, gorgeous. How's things going?"

"Well enough, handsome. How about you?"

"I struggle through. But tell me, who's winning the conversion battle, you or the sisters?"

"The battle?"

"Are you corrupting them, or are they making a virtuous woman of you? And for the record, my money's been on you all along."

"I can't claim any credit. From what I can tell, somebody's already corrupted most of them."

"You mean the stories about the sisters are true?" Ricon held his hand to his mouth in mock horror. "Lights out at the eighth bell, candles out at the ninth."

Matt laughed. "With one or two exceptions, I pray I never get to find out."

"I guess we all have certain standards. Are you here to see Edmund?"

"Yes. Do you know where he is?"

"He went to feed the dogs a while back. Might still be there."

"Thanks."

Edmund was indeed sitting by the cage at the rear of the garden. The three heavy jawed mastiffs wagged their tails like puppies when they saw Matt approach.

"Hi, Mattie." Edmund spoke without looking back.

"How did you know it was me? It might have been the butcher coming."

"He's already been today."

Matt put her arm between the bars and scratched a furry head. Very few people could have done that without losing a hand, but Matt had known the dogs since the day they were born. Edmund also was accepted and loved by them. He reached through, patted the oldest mastiff, then stood.

An ancient gazebo was nearby, its frame sagging under the weight of an overgrown honeysuckle. They sat on the weather-beaten bench inside.

"Raff said you wanted to see me. Anything up?" As chance would have it, the story Matt told Eawynn the previous day was true.

She had spotted the messenger by chance. On previous occasions, Raff had asked for her at the atrium gate, posing as her late uncle's foreman.

"No. I just wanted a report." Edmund smiled. "And I've missed you."

"Nothing like as much as I've missed you, and home."

"Not tempted to renounce your sins and become a priestess?"

Matt gave a snort in answer.

"So how's it going?"

"Slowly."

"Good. As long as you're making progress."

"I think so. I haven't got sight of the stone yet. The sisters really are fussy about who they let near it."

"We knew that. That's why you had to be on the inside. Have you checked out the guardsmen they employ?"

"The only one I've recognised is Shorty Potts."

"Bribable."

"Yes. But not worth the cost. They stay outside and aren't in a position to give us trouble unless someone raises the alarm and they come running."

"At which point it's too late to worry about the stone."

"True. The big issue is the round-the-clock ceremonies. There's high tide, low tide, as well as moonrise and moonset." Matt shrugged. "Those aren't so bad. We can predict them. But at any time they can all just decide to get up and stream through the atrium for a quick chant in the sanctuary, right by a door we need to get through. We don't want to be caught red-handed, picking the lock."

"We need the key."

"Getting it won't be easy. The only people with a key are four, tight-arsed high-up sisters. However, the outer shrine door is unlocked during the day."

Edmund frowned but said nothing, letting Matt continue.

"There's also an inner door to the actual room where the Shewstone is kept, which is locked day and night, but I fancy my chances of getting hands on that key far more."

"You smiled as you said that. Let me guess, the key holder is young and pretty, not at all tight-arsed, and you've been winking at her."

"I'm never so crass as to wink."

"I was being figurative."

"I'm thinking I can get close enough to lift the key, take the stone during the daytime, and pass it to one of the boys."

"You're sure it's not the getting close bit making you think this?"

"No. Because even if we pick both locks, it still has to be me doing it. A yeggman could hop over the garden wall and get to the atrium, but what happens if they're spotted? If it's me, I can say I was pacing around because I was worried over my uncle's will and couldn't sleep."

"So getting this pretty priestess in the sack is purely a bonus?"

"I just ask myself what you'd do in my place."

Edmund shook his head and laughed. "Just be careful."

"Aren't I always?"

"No."

As ever, they were on the same page. Matt said, "I'll send word when I've got the stone."

"Any idea when that's likely to be?"

"Another four or five days."

"That long? You've already been there eight. She putting up a fight?"

"Nope. It's me. I've been playing hard to get, and I think it's worked. But I'll speed up. I can't take much more of the temple."

"How will you pass the stone out?"

"Not sure. I've got a couple of ideas. Send Raff over again in two days, and I'll confirm."

"Right. I'll let our customers know."

"Have you found out anything about them?"

"Bits. Still no idea what their real names are, but I've got three fake ones to choose between. I know what boat they arrived on and where they're staying. Some other scraps. It all adds up to half a picture."

"Do you know what they want with the stone?"

"Not a clue." He sighed. "There's something about this I don't like. I'm putting the info in the back drawer. Maybe we can piece things together, if needed."

"Hopefully, it won't come to that." With no witnesses around, other than the dogs, Matt shuffled along the bench and rested her head on Edmund's shoulder.

He slid his arm around her. "What's up? Is temple life really bad?"

"It's not that. I spoke to Pearl on the way in. She's lost so much weight."

"Ah." He tightened his arm in a reassuring squeeze. "Yep. It's not good. But none of us are getting any younger."

She knew that. Edmund's once black beard was now grey. The lines on his face were etched ever deeper, his voice less strong, warning of a future she did not want to think about. What sort of fool needed a Shewstone? Was today not enough? For herself, Matt just wanted to finish with the temple, come home, and take her life one day at a time.

She felt Edmund's lips brush the top of her head. "Don't worry. We'll look after Pearl."

"Look after yourself, too." Matt turned her head and whispered into the cloth of his shirt, not fully intending him to hear. "Love you, Pa."

But he did. "Love you too, Mattie."

Eawynn rubbed the tabletop, trying to remove the smears. The previous client had been sweating profusely. Admittedly, "Will I get away with murdering my husband?" was one of the more nerve-racking questions, but the woman could have worn gloves. Her fingerprints were all over the table and chair.

The divination had been one of the rare occasions where the client had not been given the desired answer. From the information the aspiring murderess had revealed, she was clearly hoping for a *yes*, but Insightful Sister Oracle had played it safe. If the woman went ahead anyway, and the Shewstone prophesy proved false, she was hardly likely to take the story before a judge to demand a refund.

Eawynn adjusted a lamp and lowered her eyes to table level, checking the state of the sweat marks from a different angle.

"So this is it."

Eawynn dropped the polishing cloth and nearly fell. Hilda stood just inside the doorway. "You—"

Hilda held a hand up. "I know, I shouldn't be here. But who's going to know?" She sauntered forward, until she was scant inches away. "I won't tell if you don't." Her delivery suggested the offer applied to more than just her presence.

Eawynn braced herself against the table, grasping the edge with both hands to hide their shaking. Hilda was standing so close her breath tickled Eawynn's neck.

She shut her eyes, fighting to cling to a semblance of composure. "Would you tell your husband?"

"Ah. Him." Hilda sounded amused but then, thankfully— disappointingly—she moved away.

Eawynn picked up the cloth in her clenched fist with no hope of using it. She bowed her head, her eyes fixed, unseeing, on the grain in the wood. *This isn't love. It isn't anything important. You don't know her. Ten days ago you had never set eyes on her. Five more days and she'll be gone. Don't be insane. This isn't love, just a stupid juvenile crush. You aren't fourteen any more. Grow up. It isn't—*

"Can I touch it?"

The question knocked Eawynn back on her heels, forcing her head up. Hilda was standing by the Shewstone repository. "No."

"Forbidden?"

"I don't have a key."

"Not even as custodian?"

"No one does. Most Rev—"

"Don't tell me. Most Revolting Unsightly Sister Orifice is the only one with a key?" Hilda found everything one big joke.

"Yes."

"And she never lets you use it?"

"No. It's never out of her possession."

"Doesn't she trust you?"

"No." Not with the key. Not with anything. At that moment, Eawynn did not trust herself.

Hilda's grin broadened, and she returned her attention to the repository. While Eawynn watched, she examined the wrought iron cabinet in a teasing, arousing display, like nothing Eawynn had witnessed before.

It was as if Hilda forgot anyone else was in the room. She ran her hands gently over the metal tracery, caressing it like a lover. She stroked the top, the sides, sometimes with the palm of her hands, sometime just the lightest fingertip pressure. With her thumbs, she rubbed small, sensual circles on the protruding copper hinges and lock. She drew a line with her forefinger down the middle of the door, riding the curves in the ironwork patterns, then slid her hand underneath the main casing. Slowly and deliberately, she started to delve between the stout metal legs, more and more of her hand disappearing with each purposeful stroke.

Eawynn was mesmerized, unable to tear her eyes away. She felt herself grow wet. She wanted Hilda's hands on her body, to bestow the same treatment she was giving to the unfeeling iron case. The surge of desire was more than Eawynn could bear. How could Hilda ensnare her so totally with such brazen tricks? Eawynn clawed at the remnants of her dignity, trying to muster a defence.

"Please."

Hilda took her hands from the repository and turned around. "Please what?"

"Go."

"Are you sure that's what you want?"

No, Eawynn was not sure, not of anything. Except that she desperately needed a firm footing to her life, and she was not going to get it from Hilda. "Yes."

Again, Hilda advanced until they stood almost touching. "I don't know if I believe you."

What was it with Hilda? Was she really no more than a visiting businesswoman as she claimed? What about the absent husband she found so easy to forget? She was restrained and demure with the other sisters, and so very different when they two were alone together. Or was she? Was Hilda playing these same games with other priestesses? Was that where she had been those other days, when she seemed to be avoiding contact?

Eawynn clenched her jaw. Did it matter? It was all a game to Hilda anyway, wasn't it? Did it matter how many people she was playing it with? Eawynn focused on the opposite wall and drew a deep breath.

"I want you to go." Her voice was firmer than she had expected.

Still, Hilda made no move to leave. Instead she raised her hand, the same hand that had so seductively explored the repository, and brushed Eawynn's cheek. For a moment, Eawynn surrendered and leaned into the touch, letting Hilda caress her face. The contact of skin on skin rippled though her. Her body felt more alive than Eawynn would have believed possible. Tingling waves spread out, over her scalp, shooting down her spine. Her legs trembled. Her breath was ragged, as if she had been running. Her vision blurred.

And then Hilda's hand was gone. "If that's what you want."

Eawynn gasped at the shock.

Step by step, Hilda backed away, and then she was gone, leaving Eawynn alone again, with nothing more than an old polishing rag, tightly balled in her fist.

❖

The temple lay in darkness. Matt prowled the deserted atrium. She knew she was prowling, and she knew she should stop. It was not the way demure ladies walked, but it was hard to control the energy in her legs. Tomorrow, she was going to get her hands on the Shewstone. The excitement was like wine, dancing in her veins, to the rhythm of her heartbeat. Her body felt fully alive. All things were possible. She could stretch up and pluck a star from the heavens, if the price was right.

Matt forced herself to stop and lean against one of the columns surrounding the atrium. She needed to show self-control, not act like a kid on her first job. Carelessness was fatal, as those on their way to the gibbet would agree. The judges would come down hard on a thief caught stealing from a temple, or from anyone else with deep enough pockets for the bribe. Matt closed her eyes and breathed, slow and deep. She was Hilda of Gimount, gentlewoman, wife of a protective husband, too well-bred to frequent bawdy taverns. And she had to act like her, for just a few more days.

The moon was past full, nearing the last quarter. Its light trickled over the garden of knee-high hedges. The cool night air carried the scent of lavender and herbs. Matt let the calm soak into her and pull her back into character, enough to continue walking.

There was a thrill to pursuing a woman, and there was a thrill to pursuing a theft. They were similar and different, and Matt loved them both. She treasured every warm memory of success. With a woman, the fun was in the chase, the anticipation. With theft, the best bit came afterward. Not least of the reward was new respect in the eyes of others. Yet, for both, the high point was the same—the moment of triumph, when you held your prize in your hands for the first time, when you knew you had won.

Matt sighed. Chasing Eawynn had been so much fun, but complete victory was going to elude her. Up until yesterday, Matt had clung to a hope that she could entice the priestess to her room, and that sometime between coming and going, when Eawynn's guard was down, she could take a wax impression of the key. Ultimately, Matt was sure she could do it, but would need longer than she was able to wait.

She would have to fall back on her alternate plan. The game in the Shewstone room had achieved everything she intended. The repository was a joke, and although Eawynn was fighting hard, she could be played so easily. Eawynn was trying to walk her own line, but she tripped at every bump. One slip was all Matt needed.

The circuit of the atrium reached the forbidden eastern archway. Matt stared into the dark shadows. Forbidden—a word that always caught her attention. It made her palms itch, and now she had a different sort of itch. Eawynn would be through there, sleeping in her lonely bed, praying in a private shrine, or sprawled satiated in the orgy chamber. Matt laughed softly. Having got to know the sisters, she could scratch that one off the list.

She was going to get everything she needed from Eawynn, but not everything she wanted, and that came close enough to failure to sting. Matt shook her head. You win some; you lose some—a philosophical viewpoint that never sat well with her. Surely she could just let it go? The world had no shortage of attractive women, and once she was out of the temple she could be assured of all the easy conquests she wanted.

But where was the fun in easy?

Matt could not remember the last time she had wanted any woman so much. Eawynn had a sharp intelligence and a principled veneer, unlike the normal run of women Matt pursued. The game was racing to the finishing line. When she left the temple she would never see Eawynn again, if she did not count spotting her face among the priestesses while lifting purses in the sanctuary. A galling knot formed in Matt's chest, a knot that got more tangled each day. Was it just that Eawynn was unfinished business, a race half run, a battle half fought? She turned from the passage. Conquering Eawynn had started as one step in the plan, but Matt had let herself get caught. She could deny it no longer. The hunter had dropped into her own trap.

Matt slapped her hand on her thigh. This hunter knew how to dig herself out, and she knew where to find plenty of women who could lend her a shovel. She would chalk Eawynn up to experience, a warning to keep in mind for the future.

The sound of a bell kicked Matt out of her brooding. The priestesses were about to go for another moonlit ceremony. Their idea of nighttime fun. How could she develop a soft spot for anyone who chose such a stupid, joyless life? Matt hurried from the atrium. She could plead sleeplessness as an excuse for wandering around, but would then have no good reason to miss the ceremony. She needed to go to bed and sleep. Tomorrow was going to be a big day.

❖

The Shewstone Sacrarium was immaculate and had been for the last half hour. Eawynn pressed her hands against the sides of her head in despair at herself and her own stupidity. The point was long past where she could pretend she was hanging around for any reason other than the hope Hilda would visit her again. She was an idiot, not just for indulging forlorn hopes and giving up all claim to self-respect. She was inviting more trouble than she could handle.

Everyone knew which priestesses had their "special friendships." The temple rumour mill ground on, night and day, tended by enthusiastic sisters who could add two plus two and get five. Everything was grist for the gossip mill. Who was looking, or not looking, at whom. Who had a quarter hour unaccounted for. Whose nighttime visits to the latrine coincided. Who had suddenly started, or stopped, talking to each other.

Eawynn rested her forehead against the cold wall. They might be talking about her already, and if not, they soon would. The abilities of some sisters to ferret out the goings on verged on supernatural. She glared at the Shewstone in its repository. "Have you been telling tales on me?"

A year ago, it would have mattered for her no more than for any other priestess. She would have been free to decide if she wanted to join in with Hilda's games. As long as she exercised a modicum of discretion, Insightful Sister Oracle and all the other elders would have looked the other way. But now? She was an unwanted embarrassment to the temple, much as she had been an unwanted encumbrance to her father. What chance was there that someone would decide to make an example of her, just as a warning to the others, a reminder of the advisability of being discreet?

Her father. He had sired her, kept her like an exotic pet, and then discarded her when it suited him. He had consigned her to a life in the temple and then messed it up for her, though to be fair, that last part had been unintentional on his part and had worked out worse for him. Eawynn could almost wish her mother had refused his advances, assuming there had been a choice in the matter for her. Had she been an unwilling victim, defenceless due to her low rank? Or had she been as Eawynn was now, knowing she was being foolish and reckless, but too inflamed with desire to say no?

Eawynn caught her lip in her teeth to hold back the groan. Often she had wondered whether she looked like her mother, but she had never before thought to ask whether she might be like her. In a few days, Hilda would leave. No matter what might happen between them, at least there would be no bastard as a result, to blame her in the years ahead. As comforting thoughts went, it was decidedly lacking. This time the groan escaped.

In a short time, the Encomium of the Unfailing Low Tide would begin. Eawynn had wasted her chance to read in the library, or more likely, to stare blankly at a page while her thoughts refused to focus. Either way, moping in the Shewstone Sacrarium was serving no purpose, other than making her feel even worse about herself.

Exasperated, Eawynn shoved the cleaning rag into the cabinet and puffed out the lamp. She yanked the door closed with a force only just short of slamming and rammed the key into the lock.

A soft sound brought her to a dead stop. Eawynn looked over her shoulder. At the other end of Shrine to the Oracle, Hilda stood waiting, leaning against the wall.

The light was fading as evening approached, but Hilda was prepared. A candle burned in its holder on a shelf beside her, casting a pool of yellow light. Even in the dimness, Eawynn could sense Hilda's eyes on her, a wolf targeting its prey. The urge to dive back into the sacrarium and hide was all the more absurd, given the way she had been waiting. After a few deep breaths, Eawynn advanced the length of the shrine.

Hilda pushed away from the wall. "I wondered how long before you'd come out."

"I was busy." Eawynn added lying to her list of sins. "You didn't want to come into the sacrarium again?"

"Wasn't me breaking the rules once enough for you?"

No. The honest answer, but an inappropriate one.

Eawynn looked at the exit, willed her feet to move, but Hilda acted first. She placed hands on Eawynn's shoulders and steered her back into an alcove, trapping her, but not so forcefully Eawynn could not have broken free, had her heart been in it.

"I...I need to talk to you. Is that all right?" For the first time, Hilda sounded less than confident. The effect was unexpectedly captivating.

"About what?"

"Don't you know?"

"What?"

Hilda swallowed visibly. "You know how I've been around you. I can't help myself. From the moment I saw you, you've been driving me crazy. I tried staying away, but that didn't help, especially when I realised you feel something of the same for me. You can't deny it, can you?"

Common sense made a last desperate bid to reclaim Eawynn's thoughts. "What about your husband?"

"Forget he exists."

"You can say that?"

"He's never been faithful to me."

"But—"

"But nothing. You're amazing, Eawynn. Do you know that?"

"Me?"

"Yes. You."

Eawynn's heart pounded so hard her body shook in time with its beat. Her breath stuck in her throat, denying her speech. Hilda filled her vision; she could think of nothing and no one else. The dimness of the shrine blotted out the rest of creation.

Hilda's hands stole around her waist, pulling her in close. Her face burrowed into Eawynn's neck. Their breasts pressed hard against each other's. Eawynn could feel Hilda's heartbeat, matching her own. Shoulders, stomach, thighs, shins—a body length of contact. For a moment, they were frozen in place while Eawynn's dreams and imagination were put to the test and found inadequate. The physical solidity of Hilda's body in her arms blew away the mist of fantasy. Eawynn had never, could never imagine a simple embrace would feel so good. The merest hint of Hilda's lips on her throat, and waves rippled through her, down to her toes.

Hilda pulled her head back and stared into Eawynn's eyes, a question hanging on her face. Whatever she saw must have been the answer she sought. Hilda's lips again brushed Eawynn's cheek and then moved, slowly but inevitably, to claim her mouth. Eawynn moaned. If not for Hilda's arms around her, she would have fallen. The kiss grew ever more ardent, ever more forceful. The tip of Hilda's tongue slid along her lips, requesting entry. Eawynn could deny her nothing. The world reduced to the dance of their mouths. Time no longer existed.

Until the sanctuary bell pealed across the temple complex, the call to the Encomium of the Unfailing Low Tide. The shock kicked Eawynn back into something approaching sanity. She wrenched herself free from the encircling arms. Hilda stared at her with hurt, bewildered surprise, but Eawynn could not stay to answer or explain. She fled the shrine.

The evening air outside was cool on her heated face. Eawynn sucked in deep lungfuls. Her heart still pounded, her lips tingled. Her skin was so sensitised the breeze felt like a lover's caress, like Hilda's hands.

From east and west, sisters began to appear, filing through the atrium. She had to join them, to become one of them, but Eawynn was certain the events of the last few minutes must be written on her face, plain for anyone to see. Was it not obvious? Yet no one was looking at her, pointing or staring. The light was fading, and already stars were poking out. Night would be on them before the Encomium finished. Was it just too dark for anyone to spot the change in her?

Eawynn forced her legs into the stately pace of a priestess, on her way to glorify her goddess. She had to act as if nothing had happened. Emerging into the sanctuary, Eawynn felt something tickle her face. She raised her hand to wipe it. Water. A droplet. Confused for a moment, she looked up at the cloudless evening sky. Not rain, but tears. The blurring of her vision confirmed it. Eawynn lowered her face, praying nobody would notice.

In the middle of the reflecting pool, the statue of Anberith stared down, as aloof and austere as ever. How would the goddess look on her? Would she forgive her? Was there anything to forgive? This was not a life Eawynn had chosen, not a life she had wanted. All her options had slipped through the cracks between her aunt's boating accident and her father's ambition. She had felt despair before, and anger, frustration, and resentment, but never this sort of pain. How much more must she give to the temple?

❖

The instant Eawynn was gone, Matt grabbed the candle and raced to the rear door. Eawynn had looked so shocked to see her, Matt had wondered whether she would remember to lock up, but habit had carried her through the custodial duties.

Not that it made any difference. Matt had the key in her hand, lifted from Eawynn's pocket while they kissed. In fact, Matt's memory had been the one that nearly failed. She had been so engrossed, she had almost forgotten the reason she was there. Luckily, she had made her move before the bell rang. Matt grinned. Her weakness for good-looking women was something she must learn to overcome, but she hoped to put the lesson off for a little while longer.

Once inside the windowless room, Matt placed the candle on the table and stepped up to the repository. No expense had been spared. Her examination had told Matt that. The frame was highest quality wrought iron. Its construction was the work of a master craftsman. The open tracery was the perfect blend of strength and beauty, allowing clear sight of the contents, but no weak spots.

The fine copper lock was delicately engraved with entwined animals and plants and gleamed against the jet-black iron. Matt recognised the type. It was the best, most complex workmanship money could buy, made to order. Still pickable. All locks were, given the right tools and enough time. Right then, Matt had neither. The tools she could have found. The quarter hour it would have taken was an unaffordable luxury. Fortunately, there was another way into the repository.

If she had time to spare, Matt would have taken a few seconds to laugh. The locksmith undoubtedly did though, back when the commission was received. The whole workshop must have pissed themselves. And knowing they were dealing with fools, the master should have doubled the price. Matt ignored the lock and focused on the three hinges. These were also copper, also shiny, the delicate style marking them as the work of the same master craftsman.

Polished copper. Beautiful to look at. Soft as shit.

A six-year-old could have popped the door off. The task scarcely required the small jemmy Matt had hidden inside her knee-high boot. None of the hinges put up any resistance. Within seconds, the door was on the floor and Matt had the Shewstone in her hands.

The moment of triumph flowed through her. It was as good as sex. Or as good as sex was sometimes, when it was not that good. Memory of Eawynn's lips batted at the edges of Matt's enjoyment, spoiling the moment a little, not that she had time to savour it.

A full examination was something else time did not allow, just the quick, first impressions. The surface was cold and sparkled like granite, but though it felt like stone, the Shewstone was lighter than expected. Was it hollow? Who had made it? When and why? Matt would find out—if someone paid her to do it. However, she could understand why the aura of mysticism attached to the Shewstone. There was something odd about it. Matt could not shake off the strange feeling that the stone knew she was stealing it, and even more strangely, was happy. Or was this so strange? Matt smiled. How many times had she heard merchants' purses calling to her, begging her to take them?

Matt left the stolen key behind in the lock and the room door ajar. Light glinted off the dangling chain as she raised the candle to her lips and blew it out.

In the nearest corner of the shrine was yet another statue of Anberith, her arms raised in a gesture that must mean something to those knowledgeable in holy sign language. In the course of her temple exploration, Matt had discovered the statue stood on a wooden frame. The solid timbers were completely hidden from sight beneath an embroidered cover reaching to the ground.

Matt lay on her back and slid her head under the staging. Thick timbers angled up to support the statue's weight from beneath, forming a triangle with the legs and the platform. Matt balanced the Shewstone on one and wedged it in place using jemmy and candle. She scooted out and adjusted the hanging drapes, removing any trace of disturbance.

Even if searchers lifted the skirt, they would not see the Shewstone unless they did as she had done and stuck their heads underneath. Worse case, and some thorough, conscientious searcher found the stone, there was still no way to link it back to her.

Matt took a few more seconds for a quick brush down and straightening of her clothes and wig, then she was ready to leave the shrine, easily less than a minute after Eawynn.

The temple bell was still clanging as Matt slipped through the door. She was just in time to catch sight of Eawynn, turning into the passageway on the other side of the atrium. Dusk was falling and the back of the walkway was in deep shadow. Matt sidled along, unnoticed, while the flow of priestesses slowed to a trickle. These were the latecomers, and their thoughts and eyes were on getting to the ceremony. Matt reached the corner of the western archway, and still nobody had seen her.

The last clump of women emerged from the domestic quarter. Matt let them get a few yards clear, their backs to her, before she slipped under the arch. She then coughed and hurried back to the atrium, making just enough noise so the nearest women turned to see who it was. Another hostel guest, Rita from Orbeck, smiled at her

"I was sound asleep. The bell woke me," Matt confided in a half whisper.

Rita nodded sympathetically.

Matt now had four witnesses that she had come from the direction of the hostel, and she had been nowhere near the Shewstone. Most folks' memories were easy to manipulate. Some might even swear they had seen her leave the hostel. The only person who knew otherwise was Eawynn, and she was unlikely to confess.

Matt had chosen her clothes carefully. Not just the high boots. The rest of her attire was a little closer fitting than normal, making it easy for everyone to see she was not carrying the Shewstone, nor anything else suspicious. She would need to attend the next few ceremonies, so she could prove she was never alone in the atrium. Fortunately, it should not be too long until the theft was discovered.

Strategically positioned sisters held torches aloft to light the centre of the sanctuary. The flames reflected off the water. Matt took a spot close enough to Eawynn so their eyes met briefly. A twinge of regret prickled Matt. The kiss had been nice. She would have liked more, but it was not going to happen. She hoped Eawynn would not get into trouble. On the other hand, she hoped Most Revolting Unsightly Sister Orifice choked on her porridge.

Matt looked at the huge statue towering over all. In the flickering light, it looked as if the goddess was winking. Matt had always known Anberith would see things her way.

CHAPTER FOUR

Hilda's lips were butterflies, drifting across Eawynn's breasts. They brushed the line of her collarbone before nuzzling at the pulse point in her throat. A hint of hard teeth was balanced by the tickling tip of Hilda's tongue. The hand on Eawynn's thigh moved higher in its slow advance. She heard herself moan Hilda's name. Her body was melting from the heat of her desire.

The clang of the summoning bell wrenched Eawynn from her dream, in much the same way as it had ripped her from Hilda's arms the day before, although that time had been for real. She gasped and bolted upright in her narrow, hard bunk. The wet warmth between her legs testified how strongly her physical body had been responding to the fantasy embrace. Eawynn raised her hand to her face. Her skin was hot, flushed. She prayed it was not conspicuous in the candlelight. But had she called out in her dream? Had anyone heard her?

The nine sisters who shared her dormitory were getting out of bed and pulling on their robes, ready for the Laudation of the Irresistible High Tide. None were looking at her, and from what Eawynn could tell, none were exchanging significant glances. She scrambled from beneath her thin blanket.

The pre-dawn air was chill on the gap between her long, loose drawers and her short, tight camisole. Eawynn tugged her robe over her head. When undressing the night before, she had left the white cord belt in place and now required only a moment to tighten it around her waist. Open-toed leather sandals completed her attire. Eawynn took her place in the line of sisters filing from the dormitory.

The sky was light by the time the Laudation finished, although the sun had not yet risen. The ceremony had been well attended by those wishing to worship the goddess before beginning their day's work. Even Hilda was there, which was unusual. She rarely showed up early. Had Hilda suffered from troubled sleep too? Eawynn would like to think so. It would go a little way to soothe her pride if Hilda was also paying for the game she had started.

Breakfast followed immediately, and again Hilda was present, sitting at the elders' table. Eawynn tried not to look at her, but it was impossible to keep her eyes away. Hilda was so different when others were around. Her elbows were glued to her sides. Her head sunk down so her chin was almost on her chest. A bland, vacant smile was plastered on her face. Somehow Hilda appeared smaller, less alive; even her shoulders looked narrower. Was it just Eawynn's imagination? Yet Hilda's eyes were the same, shrewd and alert.

Suddenly, Eawynn realised everyone else at the table had finished their porridge. Too much time gawking and not enough eating. How long before people started to wonder what was going on with her? Or was it already too late?

Eyes were turning pointedly in Eawynn's direction when the deputy door warden bustled into the refectory, creating a minor stir. Steadfast Sister Porter whispered something to Insightful Sister Oracle, presumably about an urgent matter, since she and two other elders left their seats immediately and followed the messenger from the hall. Hurriedly, Eawynn made use of the disruption and emptied the rest of her bowl.

The rye bread and broth followed while Diligent Sister Caretaker continued stuttering and mumbling her way through all forty-six verses of "In Praise of the Moon Ascendant." Eawynn concentrated on her food, though it was hard not to choke over some of the more garbled passages. She dreaded the days when Diligent Sister Caretaker was the mealtime reader. Had anyone thought things through when they assigned someone verging on illiterate to the library?

As usual, the inept reading overran, forcing everyone to remain seated, long after the food was gone. Even then, Eawynn had to stay behind. That day was her turn to sweep the refectory floor. The sweat and stickiness of the night clung to her skin, but she would have to wait a while longer before visiting the washroom.

The Shrine to the Oracle and the Shewstone Sacrarium were the only places not on the cleaning rota. Everywhere else, the junior sisters had to take their turn. Eawynn thumped the head of the broom on the floor to release her frustration. In all the sisterhood, she was the only full-time housemaid, yet she still got a full quota of the general chores. It was not fair. *And since when did fairness come into it?*

Eawynn started sweeping in the corner nearest the door. Some sisters must spend the entire meal picking bits off their bread and dropping it on the floor, as there was no other way to account for the amount of crumbs they generated. Eawynn had reached a particularly messy spot when the door opened and Vigilant Sister Chancellor appeared, with two assistants in support.

In the temple hierarchy, the role of chancellor tied for third place with chamberlain, but rather than the maintenance of physical bricks and stones, Vigilant Sister Chancellor was charged with preserving the moral standards of the temple. Her promotion to the role four years ago had surprised many. She was seen as too soft-hearted. However, she had managed to carry out all her duties in a dedicated, unwavering manner, without ending up generally hated, unlike most of her predecessors.

She was now wearing her sternest expression—the sort of stern reserved for junior priestesses accused of serious wrongdoing. "Dutiful Sister Custodian, you're wanted in the audience room."

No need to ask why. Eawynn's stomach tied itself in a knot. She braced the broom on the ground, a moment of extra support while she steadied herself, then leaned it against the wall and let herself be escorted out.

Who had reported her? Someone in her dormitory? Had she been talking in her sleep? Which might work out for the best. She was being called to account when she could be accused of nothing worse than making a fool of herself over an attractive visitor. The informers did not know about the kiss, did they? Eawynn would not tell an outright lie, but what was the chance she would be asked a direct question she could not dodge?

The doubts and calculations raced back and forth in Eawynn's head. However, the moment she stepped into the audience room, she knew all her reckoning was hopelessly off target. One kiss did not warrant all the assembled elders. Everyone over the role of cellarer was there, lining the walls.

A last firm push from Vigilant Sister Chancellor shunted Eawynn forward, to exactly the same spot as all those years earlier, when her father had given her to the temple. She stood directly in front of the high priestess's throne-like chair, but currently it and the supporting chairs on either side were empty. Insightful Sister Oracle was patently too agitated to sit.

She had been pacing from side to side. Now she stopped, glaring in undisguised fury at Eawynn.

"Where is your key?"

The question was so unexpected Eawynn could only gape.

"The sacrarium key. Where is it? Show it to me." Insightful Sister Oracle barked the words.

Eawynn fumbled at her belt, unable to take her eyes away from the vision of rage incarnate. Only when her fingers did not hook onto the chain did she look down, hunting with increasing confusion and alarm. Both chain and key were missing. The knot in Eawynn's stomach twisted into tighter loops, giving her nausea.

"I...I don't know. I must have dropped it."

"Who did you give it to?"

"Give it? Nobody. I lost it. I'm sorry. I don't know how I could be so careless. But I didn't give it to anyone."

Insightful Sister Oracle stomped forward so she was shouting into Eawynn's face. "Who did you give it to?"

"Nobody. Why would you think I'd give it away?"

"Because your accomplice used it to get into the sacrarium and steal the Shewstone."

"My accomp..." Eawynn shook her head. "No, I didn't give it to anyone. I don't have an accomplice."

"Don't lie."

"I'm not lying."

"Treachery runs in the family." Enlightening Sister Astrologer added her bit.

"I'm not lying."

"What does the word of a traitor's bastard count for?"

Murmurs of agreement rippled around the room. Insightful Sister Oracle held up her hand for silence. "Who has taken the Shewstone?"

"I don't know." Eawynn stared at her feet, frantically trying to muster her thoughts.

"What are you hoping to get from this?"

"Nothing." Eawynn raised her head. Passive denial was not going to help. "What could I get? How could I possibly benefit from someone stealing the Shewstone? Think it through."

"Don't you dare tell me to think."

Once in your life wouldn't hurt. "If I wanted to help someone to steal the Shewstone, I wouldn't incriminate myself by giving away my key. Not when I could just as easily hand over a wax impression." Eawynn felt a flare of anger. "You clearly believe I'm totally without morals. But you can't possibly believe I'd be so stupid."

Insightful Sister Oracle's hand lashed out, slapping Eawynn hard across the face. "Silence. We don't need you to..."

Point out the obvious? Eawynn's cheek was burning, but now Insightful Sister Oracle had given vent to her anger, what passed for her brain was able to move on. The accusation against Eawynn was absurd, and the shift in tension made it clear that most, if not all, appreciated the fact. For all the good it would do. The Shewstone was gone, and Eawynn was the only one they had to blame. Negligence might be a lesser crime than theft, but with her current status in the temple, Eawynn was not holding much hope in the way of clemency.

"Take her and put her somewhere secure. We'll search the temple, and pray to Anberith that the Shewstone will be found."

Hands grasped Eawynn firmly by the upper arm, pulling her away. As she reached the door, Insightful Sister Oracle said, "I'll speak with you again."

Eawynn had no doubt of it.

❖

Watching the priestesses search her room was fascinating. Matt had never realised how many places they would not think to look. This was matched by the number of places they looked where she would never have hidden the Shewstone, even if she were stupid enough to keep it in her room. Most interesting of all, each of the three times her room was turned over, the searchers all looked, or did not look, in exactly the same places.

While making mental notes for future use, Matt worked on acting like someone who was trying not to show how angry she was. After all, the priestesses were implying she might be a thief, which was the sort of thing that made decorous businesswomen angry.

"Has there been a theft from the temple before?"

"No."

"Are you sure the thieves won't return? I've little in the way of money with me, but some of the documents are very sensitive."

"I'm certain your belongings are safe." Welcoming Sister Hosteller was clearly torn between irritation at the divine Shewstone being equated to mundane business papers, and her job description of being nice to guests. The irritation part was also unfair, given that the sisters were withholding the relevant information.

"Do we know what was taken?" Matt asked.

"An inventory of the items has been made."

That won't have taken many sheets of paper. Matt merely pursed her lips and nodded.

After the searchers left, Matt went for a stroll. On the second day after the theft, things were quietening down. Restrictions on leaving the temple were lifted, and the guard outside the Shrine to the Oracle had gone. A quick check confirmed the door was unlocked. Letting a man stand in the atrium showed how upset the sisters were, but Matt had to wonder what purpose he had been intended to serve. Were the sisters frightened the thieves would break in again and attempt to return the stone?

Whatever byways her thoughts had travelled down, it would seem Unsightly Sister Orifice finally accepted her Shewstone was gone and she could not get it back with the resources at her command. Matt moved to the sanctuary. A short while listening in on conversations confirmed no word of the theft had passed beyond the temple walls. Most likely, the priestesses would call in the city watch tomorrow, and the hunt would expand. Tonight was therefore the time to get the stone out.

Matt left the temple and crossed Silver Lady Square. She did not want to be away for long, and, in her current getup, entering most nearby establishments owned by the Flyming gang would attract attention. However, the jeweller on Crown Row was safe. The owner made and sold bespoke jewellery, and if you knew the right word, she would buy back the same, no questions asked.

Another customer was peering at a tray of gemstones when Matt arrived, a middle-aged, overweight man in a courtier's outfit. His hair was bleached and dyed henna red. His face was dusted with white powder. Matt bit back a grin. Why bother? No doubt his bloodline was not as aristocratic as he would like, but he was not fooling anyone with the makeup.

An assistant accosted Matt. "Can I help you, madam?"

She held out a locket with an engraved letter F. "The catch is broken and I wondered if it might be repaired."

At the sound of her voice, the jeweller looked over. Trained eyes were not misled by the wig and clothes. She gave a faint nod of recognition. "Excuse me, sir. While you think about it, I'll just see to this young lady."

The powdered courtier smiled in a preoccupied way.

The jeweller held the locket to the light. The woman was a true professional. Even though the courtier was clearly oblivious, she stood so Matt's lips were close to her ear and blocked from view.

"Pass the message to Edmund. Tonight, one hour after sunset."

The jeweller gave no sign of hearing. "Yes. It'll be no problem. A nice piece. We can sort it out for you. When would you like to collect it?"

"I'll send someone."

The jeweller handed the locket to her assistant and gave a formal half bow. "Good day to you, madam."

Matt returned to the temple just in time for dinner, which had become a far more entertaining affair. Unsightly Sister Orifice was so upset she would go a whole quarter hour without uttering a single insincere platitude, but her face said it all. Somebody had pissed on her birthday cake. Only Eawynn's absence spoiled the fun. There had been no sight of her since the theft was discovered. Matt did not like to think of Eawynn in trouble, but how much could they blame someone for misplacing a key? Though admittedly, the sisters could be odd at times.

Had Eawynn tied the loss of the key to their kiss, and if so, had she told anyone? Matt's guess on the second part tended to a *no*. Otherwise her room would have been searched more thoroughly than those of the other hostel guests. Not that it mattered. But was Eawynn too naive to realise how she had been duped, or was she staying silent to protect Hilda of Gimount?

An uncomfortable niggle of guilt had unsettled Matt several times over the previous two days. Mostly she was able to shunt it aside, but now it strengthened into a decided kick. Matt clamped down on the unwanted thoughts. Thieves could not afford a conscience. It was not just a nuisance. It could be dangerous. The hangman did not let conscience get in his way, nor did the bent judges. She could not compete against them if she carried a handicap.

Matt had never pushed Eawynn to do anything she was not willing to do, other than give up the key, and if Eawynn had followed her own rules, she would not have lost it. Or at least, she would not have lost it so easily. Eawynn was an adult, with responsibility for her own life. How she handled that responsibility was her concern. She was clearly miserable in the temple, but not willing to do anything about it.

Matt smiled. She must have livened up Eawynn's dull existence no end. Probably the most fun the priestess had known in years. And in the final analysis, if everything went to hell, Matt was the one who would end up with her neck in a noose. She was the one running the risks.

Matt stayed in her room after dinner, watching the light fade. The clanging bell announced the start of yet another singsong in the sanctuary. Matt opened the window and waited until she heard the distant chanting. Time to move. All the sisters who were taking part in the caterwauling competition would be there. She pulled a heavy cloak around her shoulders and left the hostel.

Possibly, rules were laid down somewhere, saying who was allowed to skip out of ceremonies and when, or maybe it went on the whim of the chief priestess. Matt had not been able to work out any pattern to the times when a sister or two could be found wandering the atrium while everyone else was in the sanctuary. Now though, the walkway and small garden were deserted. The door to the Shrine to the Oracle was unlocked, and nobody stood on guard.

Again, Matt lay on the floor and felt under the wooden platform. The Shewstone was where she had left it, on the joist. Matt slipped it into the small bag she had with her, then slung the bag over her shoulder so the stone lay in the small of her back under her cloak.

The resulting bulge would be noticeable, although moving would make it far less obvious. If she ran into someone who wanted to talk, Matt had to keep facing them, walk away backward, and hope the sister did not think it odd. With luck, it should work. However, she did need to put it to the test. Matt returned to the hostel without sight or sound of anyone.

Just one more step to go.

The chanting stopped as darkness fell. Soon the sisters would be going to their beds. Already, the workshops and kitchen would be closed for the night. When making her plans, Matt thought about waiting until later for this stage, but no matter how late she left it, the sisters' ridiculous, round-the-clock prayers meant she could never guarantee being left alone. Trying to explain what she was doing, wandering around at midnight would be that bit trickier. The last thing she wanted, with the current state of alarm, was to do anything suspicious.

Matt left her room with the Shewstone nestled against her back. This was the riskiest part, and the buzz of anticipation was the best drug in the world. Matt could feel it flowing through her. More sisters would be up and about than during the ceremony, but moonlight played games with shadows, and the darkness was her friend, as it was a friend to all good thieves.

Welcoming Sister Hosteller was still awake and on duty. "Good evening, Madam Hilda. You're up late. Is there anything you need?"

"No, thank you. I can't get to sleep, so I thought I'd see if a walk helped."

"Comforting Sister Infirmarian has sleeping drafts."

"I know, but I'd rather not take one if I don't have to. I'll try the walk first."

"As you wish." The sister let her go.

Lamplight and voices were coming from the atrium, and two priestesses were deep in conversation by the garden gate, but no one tried to hail or intercept her. Matt strolled past the kitchen and storerooms, bidding good night to one sister who hurried by with no more than a distracted smile. As she hoped, everyone had gone from the stable yard by the outer wall. The delivery gate was shut and barred after dark, and since the theft, two guards were stationed outside at all times. This did not matter, since Matt did not intend to use the gate.

Matt stopped and listened, straining her ears. Nobody was moving. She continued in her slow, deliberate pace to the stable door, and then slipped inside. Slivers of moonlight squeezed between the planks. Matt waited for her eyes to adjust, still listening. That evening, only the palfrey belonging to Rita from Orbeck was occupying a stall. The horse was half-heartedly chewing on hay and ignored Matt completely. It was nearly as boring as its owner.

The awkward, snooty bugger surcoat made climbing the ladder far more difficult than it needed to be. Why did anyone think it was smart to pick such stupid clothes? Matt swore under her breath all the way to the top. At the far end of the hay loft a loading door overlooked the street below. The three-foot-square door was bolted shut but not locked. Matt drew back the bar and edged the door open a few inches.

A bend in the wall hid the guards from view, although she could hear their voices, discussing the likelihood one of their colleagues would manage to knock boots with the new barmaid at the Nine Bells. This was, apparently, a major ambition of his, though the speakers did not fancy his chances. Nothing else was visible apart from the row of houses opposite. Matt slipped the bag from her shoulders and tied a length of cord to the handle. Quickly, she lowered it through the opening.

When the bag was halfway to the ground, a shadow detached itself from a gap between two houses. It reached the point directly under the loading door, just as the bag got within reach. Matt released the cord which fell, making only the softest whisper. Then shadow, bag, and Shewstone vanished into the night. The guards' tone did not change as they agreed Spotty Sam stood his best chance with Madam Palm and her five daughters.

Matt bolted the door and clambered back to the ground. Job done. The Shewstone would be in Edmund's hands within the hour and ready for the strangers to collect.

After wishing a heartfelt good night to Welcoming Sister Hosteller, Matt returned to her room and got ready to sleep. She would stay at the temple two more full days, just enough distance so nobody would connect her departure with that of the Shewstone.

Eawynn no longer had a working shrine to be custodian of. Presumably, she would be given a new role soon. This might not involve looking after a key, but could offer other possibilities. Matt grinned and rolled over in bed. Maybe, just maybe, before she left, she would manage one more kiss.

❖

The key turned in the lock to the sound of metallic scraping. Eawynn sat on her bunk and stared at the door, swamped by incompatible waves of relief and dread. *Please don't let me get hiccups.* Nothing good was about to happen, but she did not know how much longer she could stand the boredom. The cell had a bunk, a pisspot, a door, a tiny barred window, and four walls comprised of 1788 bricks. In the previous three days, she had counted them more times than she wanted to think about. Why could they not let her have a book? Indeed, why had they even bothered locking her up? It was not as if she had anywhere to run.

Vigilant Sister Chancellor entered the cell and blinked. "Have you opened your heart to Anberith?"

Eawynn knew she had been expected to pray throughout her detention. As entertainment it came level with counting bricks, but she had spent enough time to be able to answer honestly, "I have."

"Then it's time to face your judgement. Come with me."

Dread got the upper hand. The brick walls taunted Eawynn as she left the cell. Maybe a little more boredom would not be so bad, after all.

Four more priestesses were waiting for Eawynn in the audience room, her judges—Insightful Sister Oracle, Enlightening Sister Astrologer, Attentive Sister Chamberlain, and Prudent Sister Treasurer.

With the chancellor, they represented the five most senior positions in the temple.

Eawynn pressed her lips together to keep them steady. What chance did she stand? How bad was this going to be?

Most Reverend Insightful Sister Oracle had calmed down sufficiently to sit in her chair, but the glare she directed at Eawynn had not softened an iota.

"Dutiful Sister Custodian, you were given the honoured position of guarding the most precious artefact in the temple. I confess I had doubts about your abilities, but I had not expected to be proved so right. Your shortcomings surpassed anything I feared. The key was your responsibility, and yours alone. Can you deny your manifest failure to perform your duty to Anberith?"

Honoured position? Where did she start to respond? Yet there was no defence that would do her any good. The elders would interpret the facts as suited them. "No, Beloved Sister."

"And you still deny giving the key to anyone?"

"Yes, Beloved Sister."

"So you claim it was stolen from you. Where? Do you remember anything?"

Actually, after three days thinking it over, Eawynn had a pretty good idea of what had happened to both key and Shewstone. Although disclosing the truth would do her no good, she could not tell a direct lie.

"The sanctuary is the most likely place for the key to be stolen."

"Yes, thank you for that, but I asked you what you remembered. We could all make a guess. It's a sad fact that, despite our best efforts, thieves and pickpockets operate in the sanctuary, preying on the faithful. Which is why you should have been on your guard. But were clearly in a daze. You didn't even notice the key was missing. It was left to Steadfast Sister Porter to spot the sacrarium door was ajar when she unlocked the Shrine to the Oracle the next morning."

Vigilant Sister Chancellor was sitting at the seat on the left. She now joined in the questioning. "You can't remember anyone touching you, or brushing against you?"

Only Hilda. She could have taken the key. Their kiss had been so all-consuming a row of purple pigs could have danced in and taken it, and Eawynn would not have noticed. But Hilda had neither the time nor the opportunity to steal the Shewstone. She had followed Eawynn into the sanctuary mere seconds later. Throughout the entire ceremony, Eawynn had been unable to tear her eyes from the woman who had just set her ablaze, standing a few short yards away. Immediately after the ceremony ended, the outer door of the Shrine to the Oracle had been locked for the night. The thief was not Hilda. Eawynn would stake her life on it. She had a far better candidate in mind, and confessing to the kiss would only dig a deeper hole for herself.

"I wasn't aware of anyone touching me in the Sanctuary of Anberith."

Insightful Sister Oracle resumed her attack. "You want us to believe the pickpocket was so skilful he was able to loosen the chain from your belt without you noticing, even though you were surrounded by your sisters celebrating Encomium of the Unfailing Low Tide?"

"Maybe I dropped the key."

"So a thief found a key lying on the ground and instinctively knew which door it opened?"

Any answer Eawynn could give would be ludicrously weak.

"Then what? He turned invisible and walked past the guards on the atrium gate?"

"Of course not."

"So while we were at our devotions, he left the sanctuary, went to a spot on the outer wall where he could put a ladder up unseen, then made his way to the sacrarium. Once there, the thief hacked the door off the repository and absconded with the Shewstone."

The timing was clearly impossible. The Encomium of the Unfailing Low Tide was one of the shorter ceremonies. Just to get in and out, the thief would have needed to run the entire way, and that did not take into account removing the repository door. Eawynn had no details of how it was done, but even with the right tools, it could not have been a quick job.

"Well, come on, say something." Enlightening Sister Astrologer joined in.

"The thief might have returned at night. After we were asleep."

"You think so?" Enlightening Sister Astrologer was enjoying this. Her attempt to hide her smile was not working. "Supposing I was to say I was up all night, in the atrium, watching the conjunction of the planets?"

I'd believe you. Eawynn had guessed as much. It was the only explanation that made sense.

Sitting in her cell, Eawynn had gone over the events countless times. She remembered leaving the sacrarium, shutting the door, and putting the key in the lock. Then she had seen Hilda, and all rational thought had fled her head. No one had stolen the key from her belt, because she had not attached it there. Like an idiot, she had left it in the door. She knew it.

Enlightening Sister Astrologer admitted being up all night, stargazing. The astrologer was one of the sisters with a key to the Shrine to the Oracle, so she could consult the star charts whenever she needed, although she did not have one for the sacrarium. She must have gone into the shrine that night to look at a chart, seen Eawynn's key in the door, and taken her chance to get rid of the Shewstone. Eawynn was sure any harm coming to herself was a pure bonus from the astrologer's point of view. Enlightening Sister Astrologer would have had all the time she wanted to go for tools and remove the repository door. The Shewstone had most likely been tossed from the cliffs and was now smashed to pieces, under the waves.

And there was not a shred of proof. If Eawynn told the elders what she suspected, some might believe her, but none would admit it. Without evidence, no case could be made against Enlightening Sister Astrologer. The change in temple finances caused by the loss of the Shewstone would shift the power balance. On the next winter solstice, when the convention of the temple was held, Most Reverend Enlightening Sister Astrologer would become high priestess, and plain Insightful Sister Oracle would be performing her readings with a deck of fortune cards.

Who was going to back the unsupported word of a traitor's bastard against the future leader of the temple? Judging by Insightful Sister Oracle's expression, she did not need the Shewstone to make the same prediction about changes to temple hierarchy, and there was no question who she blamed. Eawynn let her head sag. Owning up to kissing Hilda was not going to help.

"Do you think we're fools?" Enlightening Sister Astrologer's voice was dripping with contempt.

"No, Beloved Sister."

"Then answer me this, how did this thief know you had the key to the sacrarium? Our sisterhood numbers fifty-nine priestesses. Did the thief just get lucky? How did he know whose pocket to pick?"

"I don't know."

"Just like you don't know how he got to the sacrarium in the amount of time available."

"No...I mean, yes."

"Or how to find his way. Did he have a map?"

"How would I know?"

Insightful Sister Oracle cut in. "Because you gave one to him."

"No. I've already said—"

"That you wouldn't incriminate yourself? It's a blatant double bluff. You thought we wouldn't see through your trickery."

"No."

"Yes. Because there's only one way the Shewstone could have been stolen. You were due to finish your duties in the sacrarium a full half hour before the start of the Encomium. Plenty of time to hand the key over and for the thief to get in place, ready to climb the wall as soon as the ceremony started."

"No."

"You could have removed the door from the repository beforehand, to make his job quicker, or at least left the tools there, ready for him."

"Why would I do that?" Eawynn could hear the panic in her own voice.

Insightful Sister Oracle started to speak, but Enlightening Sister Astrologer shouted over her. "Because of your traitor father. You wanted revenge on the temple for supporting the true queen, my cousin."

Insightful Sister Oracle jumped to her feet, not yet ready to relinquish her position. "Sisters, please. Remember we stand in the sight of our lady Anberith." Once the room was silent, she stared at

Eawynn. "Dutiful Sister Custodian, this is your last chance. Will you name your accomplice? Show your contrition by telling us the truth, and we may be lenient with you."

"I had no part in the theft. I swear by Anberith"

Insightful Sister Oracle looked as if she was about to be sick. "Do not name the goddess in deceit. Tell us the truth or be silent. Have you nothing else to say?"

Did she? Briefly, Eawynn considered admitting to both her infatuation with Hilda, and leaving the key in the sacrarium door. Changing her story late in the day was not going to sound good. Nobody would admit to believing her, and it would not dent Enlightening Sister Astrologer's ambitions. The only result would be incurring a worse punishment for herself.

"No, Beloved Sister."

"Your sister no more."

"But—" Eawynn was stunned.

"You conspired in the theft of our most precious artefact. You have desecrated this temple. You have betrayed those who called you sister."

Ice flowed through Eawynn's veins. "No. No, I haven't."

Insightful Sister Oracle ignored her. "Our judgement is that there is no place for you in the Temple of Anberith. Your vows are set aside. Five days hence, after the Affirmation of the New Moon, and before the Oblation of the Avowed Supplicants, you will be cast from the sisterhood. You will be beaten from the temple, never to set foot on its holy ground again. Between now and then, you will spend your time in prayer, to beg the goddess to forgive the wrong you have done to her."

Eawynn shook her head, battling with disbelief. They could not throw her out, could they? What would happen to her? Where would she go?

The expressions around the room displayed varying degrees of anger, sternness, and pity, except for Enlightening Sister Astrologer. Her face held nothing but a contented smile.

❖

"The cart is rather late, isn't it?"

"Yes." Matt worked on acting politely impatient, rather than worried.

"Would you like me to see if I can arrange another one for you?"

"Yes, please. If you could."

She gave Welcoming Sister Hosteller a tight smile. The cart from Edmund was an hour overdue. Matt did not know what was going on, but if she did not leave soon she would have to hang around for another day.

Raff had come to see Matt the morning after she handed over the Shewstone. He confirmed it had got to Edmund safely, and the strangers would be calling the following afternoon to collect it. The only thing left to settle was a date for the cart to take her home. Matt had needed to weigh her itch to see the Shewstone again against her itch to see Eawynn. Eawynn had won. Women would always beat rocks.

However, in the end, neither itch was scratched. Matt allowed an extra day, but this was still not enough. Neither sight nor word of Eawynn was forthcoming. Matt had to admit to increasing concern about her, although this was currently eclipsed by concern over the non-appearing cart. Edmund would not have forgotten her unless something critical was afoot. Fortunately, the cart procured by Welcoming Sister Hosteller arrived promptly. Whatever was up with the Flyming gang, Matt wanted to be there to help.

After a last round of thanks and good-byes, Matt plus her bags were loaded and on the way. Matt's preferred choice would have been going straight home without messing about, but the disadvantage to a real hired cart was that she had to maintain the fiction of returning to her husband for a while longer.

The quickest and easiest route to Gimount was by water. The nearest port to the town was five hours sailing down the coast, and a dozen or more boats made the journey every day. This was the part that forced her to leave early in the morning, in time to board a suitable ship. A decorous businesswoman would have no trouble buying passage, and would then have only a short cart ride home. Playing the role of Hilda meant Matt ended up heading toward the harbour, the opposite direction to the one she wanted. The streets of Fortaine rolled by painfully slowly, on the way downhill to the docks.

The harbour was familiar territory. Once there, Matt paid off the driver and looked around. The Flyming dock handler was a woman known as Jenny the Trip, but neither Jenny nor her sidekick Alf were in sight. Matt's disquiet grew, especially when she saw a couple of Gilbert's boys swaggering around the quay like they owned it.

Had a gang war kicked off while she was in the temple? Raff had said nothing, but these things could flare up quickly and without warning. Quite possibly, Edmund had more serious issues than sending a cart to collect her from the temple. Matt needed to get home quickly, before she was spotted, alone and a sitting target. The disguise of a wig would not stand up if trouble was actively looking for her.

A brass penny paid a warehouse keeper to look after her bags. Matt walked back up the hill, at a quick pace but not fast enough to turn heads. Ideally, a change of clothes would have been her first call, but she did not want to take the time. She left High Street at the junction with Collier's Row. The houses became taller as the shops were left behind, and the streets got quieter. Another turn and the front of the Flyming house came into sight, fifty yards away.

Three rowdy boys were posted outside, which was all the confirmation Matt needed that trouble was afoot. Normally, a single guard sufficed. Then, between one footfall and the next, every idea Matt had about trouble erupted into a nightmare, taking the air from her lungs and sending a fist of ice pounding through her gut.

The guards were not Benny, or Raff, or anyone she recognised. Instead the one facing her had a green bandanna around his neck, the token worn by Gilbert's gang when a fight was in the offing, so when things got hectic they did not end up knifing one of their own by mistake. Three steps more and Matt recognised the faces, all of them Gilbert's boys.

Somehow, Matt kept her feet going, the same even pace, looking straight ahead, not faltering, not hesitating. The rowdy boys were gabbing among themselves, laughing and posing like drunken bravos. If they dared stand brazenly on the doorstep, it could only mean there was nobody in the house to challenge them.

Still, Matt kept walking. She glanced up at the building as she drew level. The front window of Edmund's study had been broken and boarded up. A heavy dent marked the street door. Apart from that, nothing was changed. She passed the doorstep, close enough to reach out and touch the nearest lout. They must have seen her, but paid no attention, not looking past the clothes and hair.

Matt caught a few words.

"...know what the boss is gonna do?"

"We'll find out in time, you can count on it."

"As long as I get my share. I'm not fucking gonna let..."

Then she was past them, walking away—away from her home. The voices faded.

What had happened?

At the next junction, Matt turned off into a side street, then hitched up the damned surcoat and ran. She could not help herself. It might not be sensible, but she had to put distance between herself and the building that used to be her home.

Common sense reasserted itself a short way around the hillside. The last thing Matt needed was to catch the attention of anyone looking for her, and some of Gilbert's boys would be doing that, she had no doubt. She stopped in a small square set around a bird-splattered statue of King Swidhelm I. A flight of steps branched off in one corner. Matt stood at the top, leaned her elbow on the stone handrail, and caught her breath. She stared, unseeing, at the port below. What had happened?

The sun burned down like always. The sounds of the city were unchanged. Seagulls screeched overhead, and the air smelt of salt and tar. Matt closed her eyes and breathed in deeply, waiting for the shaking in her hands and legs to fade. What had happened?

When Matt opened her eyes, she was calmer and knew what to do. Forcing her legs into a comfortable stroll, matching her garb, she set off across Fortaine to the once genteel, but now unfashionable, northern fringe. Here the city had overflowed the old walls and spread into the surrounding countryside. The buildings were large and well-built, but run-down. The people were entrenched and minded their own business.

The Jolly Wagoner was an old style wooden framed tavern, three stories high, with a sprawling collection of out-buildings. For as long as Matt knew, Edmund had rented a room here, a permanently ready bolt-hole, a place to hide in a crisis. Few had heard of it—Edmund and Matt, and Pearl of course, because she knew everything. Even trusted gang members who had worked for Edmund's father and grandfather were not in on the secret. Edmund's uncle Ted had been the last to make use of the room, three years earlier.

The barman did not look up when Matt entered. "Can I help you?"

"You have a room reserved for Robin of Thule," Matt said.

"Top of the stairs, on the right." The rhythm of clinking bottles did not falter.

"Is there a key?"

"Master Robin collected it yesterday."

"He is upstairs now?"

The barman did not answer. He had been well paid for his silence and had said all that was needed. Matt ought to know better than ask, but the surge of relief had overwhelmed her. Edmund was already here. She should never have doubted him. If not for the wretched surcoat, Matt would have leapt up the stairs three at a time. She burst through the door.

The room was an average size, with a bay window providing a view over Fortaine. The walls had not seen fresh paint for decades. The floorboards were bare, stained, and warped. A round table, two narrow beds with foot lockers, and a huge lopsided wardrobe was all the furniture. A man was sitting, slumped, on the side of one bed. He jerked, half standing, when the door opened, but sunk back on seeing Matt. And he was not Edmund.

Matt stared, slack-jawed, as her head tried to catch up. Ricon was so unexpected it took seconds to recognise him, and he did not look his normal self. His clothes were always stylishly scruffy, but she had never seen him look unkempt or dirty. Now, his hair was uncombed and he had not shaved. The brown stains on his shirt front had to be dried blood, and the sleeve was ripped. His eyes were red rimmed slits.

"Ricon? Where's Edmund?"

The tears that welled up and spilled down Ricon's cheeks answered her, even before he spoke. "Edmund's dead. They killed him. I'm sorry. I'm so sorry."

Matt's knees buckled. She shoved the door closed and collapsed onto the bunk facing Ricon. "Gilbert killed him?"

"He was in on it, but it wasn't him or his men. It was that red-haired bastard."

"How?" That one word took all the breath Matt could summon. A steel fist was crushing her lungs.

Rather than answer, Ricon lurched to his feet and staggered to the table. Five wine bottles stood on it, three were empty, and the fourth uncorked. He took a long swig and then held out the bottle. He was drunk, Matt realised, and she did not blame him. The wine was cheap and sharp. It stung the back of her throat when she swallowed but filled a need.

"What happened? Tell me."

"It was when they came to pick up the stone. There was the two from before, but this time they'd got some local muscle. Hired to guard the merchandise, so they claimed. Edmund insisted the two rowdy boys stayed in the hall while he and the foreigners went to his study. I was in the room next door. They'd barely closed the door when the yelling and banging started. Footsteps rushed past my room. I was out in time to see the redheads run downstairs. They both were holding swords. The leader had blood on his. Raff was on duty outside. He heard the racket and came in, but the rowdy boys were ready and pounced on him. Pearl came running from her room, but this fucker he...he..." Ricon's composure unravelled further. "He ran her through."

"Pearl. But she..." The first tear slid down Matt's face. "Why kill Pearl?"

"Why kill anyone? I didn't get a chance to ask." Ricon looked like he was going to be sick. "People were shouting. I heard our folk coming from the back. I was about to go and help, then the front door got kicked in and Gilbert's thugs were all over the place. We were outnumbered. It was hopeless. That's when I thought of Edmund. I rushed to the study and he was lying there on the floor, blood all over." Ricon was now crying in earnest.

"I held him. He was still breathing...just. I shoved the table in front of the door to give us time. I was hoping..." He shrugged. "I don't know what. Edmund told me about this room. Said you'd come here. Said I was to give you this."

Ricon held out a gold signet ring. Edmund's ring. The ring that had belonged to his father, and grandfather before. Matt looked at it, lying in her palm. Her vision blurred as her eyes filled. She could force no words through her clenched teeth.

"Then he died. In my arms. I kissed him and he died. There was banging on the door. The table wasn't going to hold for long. I had to leave him. I jumped out the window. Gilbert had some bugger with a crossbow waiting. Lucky for me he was a lousy shot. Missed me and smashed the glass. I hit the ground and took off."

Matt dragged herself to her feet, drained the bottle, and stumbled to the window. Why? The strangers had offered an insane amount of money for the Shewstone, money they most likely did not have. Gilbert would not have asked a fraction of the amount for his help. Hell's fire, after the last bust up between the gangs, he would have probably done it for free.

The joyless, sunlit world outside the window was swimming in tears. The first sob shook Matt's shoulders. She heard a creak from the bed and then Ricon's arms went around her. For a long while, they stood, holding each other. Their tears mingled as they fell. The loss was a physical pain, tearing at Matt's heart. Air burned her throat as each wrenching sob was dragged into her lungs.

Eventually, the storm eased and Matt was able to speak. She stood, her head resting on Ricon's shoulder, again staring out the window.

"What are you going to do?" she asked.

"This town's not safe for you and me. Now I've spoken to you, I'm heading over to Port Baile, and having a word with Tobias, tell him what's happened. He'll know what answer to give Gilbert."

Matt nodded slowly. Tobias was Edmund's cousin, who ran the Flyming operation on the northern side of Pinettale. She had met him a few times and got on well enough. The cousins looked much alike, but Tobias lacked Edmund's easy charm and flare. He was slower to laugh and quicker to anger, and something in his eyes spoke of a hard, cruel streak, missing in Edmund. He might not be such a good man to have as a friend, but was a worse one to have as an enemy. Gilbert would not escape payback for the part he had played.

Ricon rubbed Matt's arm. "How about you? Will you come with me to Port Baile?"

"No."

"You can't stay in Fortaine."

"I won't. Not for long anyway."

"Where will you go?"

"I'm going to find the red-haired bastard who killed Edmund."

"How?"

"Not sure yet, but I will. If I have to track him to the ends of the earth, I will." Matt stood up straighter and wiped her eyes with the back of her hand. "Tell Tobias not to worry about the man who stabbed Edmund. He's taken care of. Tell Tobias I give my word. I'm not going to rest, until I've put a blade in the fucking shithead's heart."

CHAPTER FIVE

The last time a priestess had been expelled was forty-three years before. Apparently, she had, "in a state of extreme intoxication, shouted lewd and outrageous accusations" at the Sister Oracle of the day. Even so, she might have got away with a lesser punishment, had she not done it in the Sanctuary of Anberith, during a Laudation of the Irresistible High Tide, in front of over three thousand startled Fortaine citizens.

Eawynn had always been amused by the story. Reading between the lines, it was the inharmonious breakup to another "special friendship." It did not sound so funny now, and nothing was ever said about what happened to the ex-priestess or where she went, after she was thrown out.

An hour before dawn, the cell door opened. Vigilant Sister Chancellor stood there with two assistants. "Are you ready?"

Of course she was not ready. How could she be? Eawynn fought the ridiculous urge to hide under the bed or cling to the bars of the window so they must drag her out.

Vigilant Sister Chancellor's eyes softened in sympathy. "Take heart. The Abrogating Ritual of Expulsion will be over quickly."

The ritual did not worry Eawynn as much as the thought of the days, months, and years to come. She had not wanted to be a priestess, but the temple was her home. Life inside its walls was safe and familiar. Outside, she had nothing, not even the father who had abandoned her.

Her father. By all accounts he had gone bravely to the block, greeting the executioner like an old friend. Eawynn took a deep breath to steady herself. She was her father's child. After all, that was what this was really about.

The roar of crashing waves sounded subdued in the darkness. High tide was yet an hour away. A stiff breeze came off the sea, snapping at the ring of torches in the Inner Sanctum of Sea and Moon. The ghost-white pillars swayed in the churning light. Beyond this ring, the moonless night was utterly dark, except for stars peeking through rips in the cloud.

The first time Eawynn had celebrated the new moon here was just three months ago, when she had made her vows as a priestess. Two times since her head had been shaved as an offering to Anberith. This month, she would keep the half-inch-long stubble. The infirmarian's razor would not be called upon for Oblation of the Avowed Supplicants until after she was gone. Who would have thought her time as a priestess would be so brief?

Vigilant Sister Chancellor guided Eawynn to the middle of the sanctum, prompted her to kneel, then stepped back, leaving her alone on the cold flagstones. The other priestesses were present, all fifty-eight of them, forming a complete circle inside the pillars. Even Meticulous Sister Recorder had left her sickbed for the show. Eawynn knew them all, had seen them every day, had heard everything there was of note about them. Some she had thought of as friends. Even those she disliked formed part of the only family she could claim. And they were gathered, twitching in anticipation, to see her cast out. The Abrogating Ritual of Expulsion was a novelty, and they might never get to witness it again.

Most Reverend Insightful Sister Oracle stood before the statue of Anberith. She raised her arms in a suitably dramatic fashion. "Beloved sisters. This is the saddest of days. One of our number has fallen so far from grace that her presence taints our precious community. Though it tears at our hearts, our duty to Anberith, our beloved goddess, demands we purge ourselves of this pollution. The vows of the woman, once known as Dutiful Sister Custodian are set aside. She no longer has a place among us. We can only pray that with true remorse and penance, our lost sister may earn Anberith's forgiveness."

Eawynn could feel the tingle of excitement running around the circle of watchers.

Insightful Sister Oracle gestured to those standing behind Eawynn. "Remove the robes she no longer has a right to wear."

The two assistants helped Eawynn to her feet and then tugged the sea-green robes over her head. Her drawers and camisole went next. Eawynn kicked off her sandals to stand utterly naked in the torchlight.

Never had she felt so isolated and vulnerable. She restrained the pointless urge to cover her breasts or pubic hair with her hands. There was nothing the others had not seen before in the washrooms or infirmary. Yet on those occasions she had been one of many, going about her duties. Here she was alone and on show.

"Make the sickness of her soul visible to all."

One of the assistants handed Vigilant Sister Chancellor a large, floppy brush. With it, she slapped yellow paint across Eawynn's face and breasts and then over her stomach. The watery paint trickled down Eawynn's legs in rivulets, while more dripped off her jaw. The smear that seeped between her lips tasted of sawdust and flour. At least it would wash off.

"Now beat her from our midst, never to set foot on this hallowed ground again."

Vigilant Sister Chancellor swapped the paintbrush for a yard-long cane. Each assistant grabbed one of Eawynn's wrists, stretching her arms out horizontal. The first stroke surprised Eawynn, a line of fire across her shoulders, hurting far more than she anticipated. She clenched her teeth, refusing to cry out. A drop of blood landed by her foot. Vigilant Sister Chancellor might be kind-hearted, but she would always fulfil the requirements of her role to the letter.

After the required five stripes, the assistants released Eawynn's hands. Now she was free to go. Eawynn turned away, wanting to run, to escape, but she would not give them the satisfaction. Her father had walked calmly to his death. She would walk from the temple.

By the time she passed between the pillars, Eawynn had received another four strokes. Still, she refused to run, but now that Vigilant Sister Chancellor had done all her duty demanded, the cane landed with appreciably less weight. A few other sisters accompanied them through the temple grounds. One was Redoubtable Sister Door-warden, needed to unlock the atrium door. Eawynn did not turn her head to see who else.

The flickering torches sent the statue's huge shadow leaping around the walls in a frenzy as they crossed the Sanctuary of Anberith. Eawynn and her escort passed the statue and pool, approaching the final gateway. The blows from the cane were now infrequent, no more than light brushes, like a farmer guiding a cow to market.

They stopped at the main doors. Outside, the rest of the world lay in wait. Abruptly, the fight left Eawynn. She just wanted to be gone, but Benevolent Sister Almoner stepped forward and pointed to a side doorway. "In here."

Eawynn was too sick at heart to ask why.

The small room contained a row of large wicker baskets. Benevolent Sister Almoner lifted a lid. "You may select clothes from those that have been donated for the poor."

Eawynn stared at the jumble of cloth, unable to make sense of what she was looking at. The ebbing wave of emotion was leaving her dazed.

Benevolent Sister Almoner sighed loudly and pulled out a dark brown item. "Put these on."

The loose pants had clearly been intended for someone shorter and fatter than Eawynn. They barely reached to her mid calf. Vigilant Sister Chancellor helped her into them and tightened a string belt around her waist. Benevolent Sister Almoner found a grey shirt which, judging by the smell, had belonged to a fishmonger. The rough material stung the cuts on Eawynn's back as she pulled it over her head. A pair of woven hemp sandals were handed to her. Eawynn slipped them on her feet, although they were frayed and unlikely to see much more service. In a last act of charity, Benevolent Sister Almoner pressed a loaf of hard, dark bread into Eawynn's hands.

When they left the storeroom, Redoubtable Sister Door-warden was already holding open the small wicket gate, set in the outer door.

Eawynn stood before the exit and stared out at her dark, hopeless future. Her legs would no longer obey her. What was out there for her? A hard shove sent her stumbling. Her foot caught on the lower beam and Eawynn fell through the doorway. She crashed to the cobbles in the square outside.

Eawynn tried to muster the will to stand.

"Has there been trouble, Sister?" a confused male voice asked from the darkness.

Three temple guards stood by the huge door, dressed in long grey cloaks and stylised sea crest helmets. One held up a lantern.

"Nothing you need worry about," Vigilant Sister Chancellor answered. "She was one of our number, but no more. She is cast out. Just see she doesn't try to return, or do anything stupid."

The wicket gate closed. The guards continued to stare at Eawynn and, despite their instructions, looked as if they were still trying to work out whether they ought to do something.

The urge to flee could no longer be resisted. Eawynn crawled the first yard, until she got feet under her, then she ran, stumbled, and staggered across Silver Lady Square. The echo of the hemp sandals came back flat and mushy from the surrounding wall of houses.

She reached the edge of the plaza. A dark passageway opened before her and she plunged in, out of the sight of the guards, out of sight of anyone who might witness her humiliation. At the first intersection, she turned left, and mainly by touch, found a deep recess, the top of a flight of steps leading to a cellar.

Already the darkness of night was giving way. To the east, the sky was paling with the approach of daybreak. The wind carried the scent of rain. Eawynn hunkered down, clasping the loaf to her chest. Then the tears came. It no longer mattered. There was no one to see. The drops rolled down her face, tasting of salt and yellow paint. They were tears of anger and shame and fear. Now, she could give in to them.

The sound of footsteps snared Eawynn's attention, reminding her of where she was. She scrubbed her eyes and listened. Multiple feet, coming in her direction. Eawynn slid further down the steps and peered furtively over the top. Two figures, tall and heavily built, rounded the corner. Their feet were clad in boots. Iron nails clacked on the cobbles. Eawynn ducked down deeper, praying they would not see her.

Unhurried, the two men swaggered along the street, exchanging grunted words of conversation. As they passed, Eawynn saw the cudgel one had, swinging in time with his steps. A few yards farther on, a hard, humourless bark of laughter rang out, and then their footsteps faded away, into the sleeping city.

Eawynn's heart was pounding. Maybe those men were honest citizens, about their lawful business. Maybe, if they had seen her, they would have done her no harm. Maybe she had not needed to hide. But there were others in the city who were not honest, who would harm her, and she could not hide from them all.

Eawynn realised that, until then, she had not really known what fear was.

❖

After four days, Matt had got a feel for the pattern of activity in what used to be the Flyming home. At the same time, she had been keeping an eye on how the pieces were falling in the upturned power battle of the Fortaine underworld. She had kept the wig, hacked into a shorter, less fashionable style that was still surprisingly effective at changing the shape of her face. It was hardly a foolproof disguise, but she had seen no sign of any attempt to hunt her down. Maybe Gilbert assumed she had fled to Port Baile, like Ricon, who had headed off two days earlier. Maybe Gilbert had too much else on his mind.

Already there was trouble in his gang. One of his lieutenants had decided Gilbert's share of the action was bigger than needed or deserved, and so had claimed the Clambrook district for herself. A quarter of the gang were now working for this new boss. Meanwhile, Benny had pulled together a crew of rowdy boys and was talking about revenge. Jenny the Trip had re-emerged on the dock and was not budging. Someone in the city watch wanting to make a name for himself had seized on the upheaval as a chance to shut down a few operations. If Tobias Flyming did not make a move on Gilbert soon, there might be no piece of him left to stake.

Yet, while Gilbert's problems could not be too few for Matt's liking, they were not her main concern. She needed information about the man who had murdered Edmund, and she knew one place to get it.

Gilbert's gang were occupying the house, though not using it as a base of operations. A permanent guard was set outside the main door, and a crew of four were always in the building, but the comings and goings stopped around midnight. After that, those inside might party a while, usually with guests from one of Gilbert's brothels, and take turnabout on the door, but otherwise the house was quiet. The rear of the building was unguarded, or at least, no guard Matt need worry about. The occupants of the neighbouring houses, after years of practice, were ignoring everything.

In the quiet hours before dawn, Matt waited, melding with the shadows where the side street branched off beside the house. A dozen yards farther along was the delivery gate—the same gate she had used for her first break-in. The room at The Jolly Wagoner was stocked with clothes and equipment for all occasions. However, Matt needed to trade warmth against freedom of movement. She clenched her teeth to stop them chattering. Not much longer.

From where she stood, she was out of sight of the front door and the guard, but not out of earshot. The door latch clacked as it opened for the last changeover of the night.

"How's it going out here?" A low male voice.

"Fun and laughs like always."

"Tell me about it."

"Better than that, you can see for yourself. I'm off to bed."

"Yeah. Cheers for that."

Matt waited long enough for the old guard to fall asleep and the new one to grow bored, then she was off. She slipped along the side street, far enough so there was no risk of the guard hearing the clink of her grapple catching the top of the wall.

In seconds, Matt was over and in the garden on the other side. She crouched motionless, listening. A soft rustle in the undergrowth gave a moment's warning that she was not alone before she was pounced on. The Flyming mastiffs were trained not to warn intruders by barking, but they still wagged their tails and licked and slobbered like any other dog. Matt hugged them around their necks and wiped her sudden tears on their coat. She had not expected it would cut so sharply to be welcomed home with love.

Of the Flyming household, only the three mastiffs remained. Trained guard dogs were valuable. Perhaps Gilbert hoped to buy their loyalty, given enough time and beef. Meanwhile, the dogs paid no heed to the changes inside the house and kept the rear secure at night, against all strangers—except Matt was not a stranger to them. If Gilbert and his underlings had thought of this, they still had no reason to expect she would pay the house a visit.

The garden was pitch-black. The sliver of the moon barely poked above the horizon. Matt let go of the furry necks and then, working by scent and memory, glided through the garden, the dogs trotting happily at her heel. She passed the overgrown gazebo where she had sat fourteen days before, talking to Edmund. The ghostly echoes remained.

"Love you, Pa."

"Love you too, Mattie."

The last words they had exchanged. Again, Matt's eyes burned. She pushed the memory aside, but at least she had no regrets on this account. She could wallow in grief later if she wished. For now, she had a job to do.

Matt parted with the dogs after a last round of slobbering and head patting. She would miss them, along with everything else. She pulled herself onto the shed roof outside the scullery, and from there, shuffled along to outside the rear stairwell window. The cornice offered no more than two inches of foothold, and the brick facing had hardly anything to claw on to, but it could be done. Matt had demonstrated it to Edmund when she was twelve years old.

"Look, Pa. When you get here, the gap between the frame is too big. All you need is a thin knife."

She flipped the latch on the inside with her stiletto, pushed open the window, and then sat on the sill, looking down on Edmund in the garden.

He laughed and applauded. "Well done."

"Anyone could break in."

"You're not just anyone, Mattie."

"Aren't you going to fix it? Get a better latch?"

"You should always be able to break into your own house."

Was it foresight or whimsy on his part? Matt swallowed, again pushing away the grief.

The latch put up no more resistance than it had thirteen years earlier. Matt slipped inside and crouched in deep shadow, halfway up the stairs, listening. Nothing stirred. The darkness was complete, but she did not need to see. All the house's secrets were known to her. The third step creaked if you stood on the left side. The floorboard in the hall had lifted at one end and could trip the unwary. The hinges on the landing door were offset and would pop if opened too wide.

Matt navigated the hazards. The only sign of life were snores, rasping from one room she passed. Everywhere was in darkness until she reached the balcony overlooking the entrance where a single candle burned below, on the stand by the door.

The scene was so familiar. Matt rested her hands on the rail, heedless of all else. How could the faces she knew be gone? She shut her eyes tightly, trying to believe she only had to open them and everything would be as it should. This was a nightmare. It could not be true. At any moment, a door would open and Pearl would appear, or Edmund's laughter would ring from a nearby room. The world could not have changed so much.

But it had. Matt opened her eyes, and the nightmare continued. The scene might not look so different now, but the house was not the same. She could feel it in her bones, in her blood, in her heart. The entrance hall filled with phantoms, scenes running before her eyes.

Edmund smiled down at her ten-year-old self and the puppy cradled in her arms. "No. She's not a pet."

"But can't I keep her? Bobo loves me. Pearl said you're going to sell her." The puppy tickled, licking her fingers.

"We don't need so many guard dogs, but..." He crouched down so their eyes were on a level. "I think you're right. Bobo will be a very good guard dog. She can't stay in your room, but we will keep her."

And they did. Bobo was dead and buried, five years or more, but three of her pups now roamed the garden at night.

Fifteen years old, she closed the front door, shutting out the sunrise that tried to follow her in. Last night, Yvette, the young whore at the Honeysuckle Bower, had taught her new games to play, and Matt had liked them. She had liked them a lot.

Even at the early hour, Pearl was awake and stuck her head around the door of her room. "Morning, Mattie."

"Ah. Morning, Pearl."

"Had fun, did we?" Pearl smiled, knowing everything. Pearl always did know everything.

The phantoms streamed on by.

Sitting on the bench and counting the day's takings with Taffy and Hogan, to see who had lifted the most.

Six-foot-tall Raff teaching her how to dodge a punch when she was still so young he had to kneel to be at eye level with her.

Falling down drunk after her twenty-first birthday and crawling up the stairs, while Edmund stood, hands on hips, and laughed.

There was no time to acknowledge them all. Matt closed her eyes briefly, asking the ghosts for patience. If Gilbert was not taken care of by the time she returned to Fortaine, she would make him pay.

Matt reached the door to Edmund's study—the room where he had died. She took a moment to brace herself before turning the handle and slipping inside. Again, she was in darkness, but here she would risk a little light. The lamp and tinderbox stood where they always did, on the cabinet beside the door.

Gentle yellow light flowed over the room. Matt forced herself to look at the dark stains on the floorboards. Edmund's blood. His body would be feeding the fishes in the bay, along with Pearl and all the rest. There would be no grave to lay flowers on. She knew that. The stains were the closest she would get. Tears filled her eyes. Matt forced them away. They were a luxury she could not afford. Later she would cry, if she had to.

Edmund's desk still dominated the room. He had told her the information collected on the strangers was in the back drawer. Matt knew what this meant. She knelt and pulled the top drawer halfway out. Then, using fingertips, she slid the bar on the underside of the desk two inches sideways, exposing the small catch. A faint click sounded when she twisted it, and the panel at the rear popped open.

Four rolls of papers lay inside, all bound with ribbon. Matt transferred them to the bag she had brought. They would cover more issues than just the Shewstone, but it was Flyming business, and she would not let it fall into Gilbert's grubby hands. Matt stuffed the bag inside her jerkin and returned the desk to its original state. She had what she came for. Now it was time to go.

After blowing out the lamp, Matt paused and listened at the door. No sound came from the rest of the house. Based on her observations, no one was likely to rise for a while yet. Retracing her steps to the garden should be safe enough, but there was no need. Matt went to the window overlooking the side street.

The latches at the front of the house were more complex than those guarded by the dogs at the rear. They needed two hands to open, one to squeeze the top and bottom while the other pulled the lever. This was the trick that had thwarted her on her first attempt to escape from the study. A burglar could climb up, even smash the window, but would still need both hands free for the latch.

Matt squeezed, pulled, and opened the window. The side street was deserted. Overhead, the first hint of dawn was greying the sky. It was time to be off, but Matt was not quite ready. She sat on the window ledge and stared into the dark room, inviting the phantoms back for just a little longer.

Actually, it was impressive she had got the window open, way back when. She had not known to press the buttons, but had still managed it, using only a penknife. And she had picked the right window, unlike Ricon who had clearly gone out the front.

Edmund spoke to her, a few days after she came to his house. "You've got a thief's instincts. You bypassed the nearer window and went for the side. If you'd got out, you wouldn't have been seen by the guard on the door, and you'd have landed on packed dirt, which is quieter than the cobbles on the main street."

"But I wasn't thinking like that."

"No, you weren't thinking." Edmund smiled. "It was instinct. You're a born thief."

Supposing her instincts had been working a bit quicker? What if she had got through the window that night, before she was caught? What if she had never met Edmund or joined his gang? How would her life have been?

Lonelier, poorer, duller, and most likely, shorter.

"Love you, Pa. And miss you." Matt mouthed the words.

Edmund's ring was on a cord around her neck. She would not wear it until she had avenged him and earned the right. The hard shape under her shirt was a promise to the dead. Matt bowed her head, then pivoted through the window, hung from the sill for a second, and dropped the twelve feet to the ground. She landed making no more sound than a cat. If the guard on the front door heard, he did not bother to investigate. Matt turned and padded away though the sleeping city.

The hunt had began.

❖

Eawynn huddled in the corner, curled in a ball, arms wrapped around her stomach as tightly as she could. Maybe if she squeezed hard enough she could block the painful rumbling. Maybe she could fool her body that her stomach was not empty. But it was, utterly, and had been for over a day.

She had eaten half the loaf the first morning, intending to save the rest for later, only to have it stolen by a street urchin. Since then she had eaten nothing. Two days, while the gnawing in her gut grew ever more savage. How much longer could she go without food? And how many more nights could she endure, like the one coming to an end? The cold had burrowed into her bones, oozing up from the hard stone. What would winter be like in Fortaine? Would she be around to see it?

Soon, the sun would come up. Eawynn clung to the thought, the one hope she could allow herself. Anything more was a pathetic fantasy. Already the light was strong enough to make out brickwork on the other side of the alley. There would be heat again, but nothing for her stomach. She needed money to buy food and something warmer than the temple castoffs. A roof over her head as well would be nice, but she did not want to be greedy with her wishes. Eawynn bit the heel of her hand to stop herself crying.

She had tried to find work. Somebody in Fortaine must need a scribe, but none of the establishments she tried had even been prepared to put her abilities to the test. The clothes were probably what destroyed her chances of being taken seriously. Her claims to be able to read and write six languages had only provoked derision. One bookkeeper had physically kicked her out. The other two settled for threatening to call the city watch.

Eawynn scrunched her eyes shut, grimacing at memories of the only chance to earn money that had come her way. So far, seven different men had offered her, "Three pennies for a fuck." They had all seemed quite serious about it, except maybe the last one, who had obviously already spent all the pennies he had on drink. Despite this, he had been unwilling to take no as an answer. If he had been able to stand, things might have gone badly. As it was, Eawynn had little trouble escaping, although the stench of his breath had stayed with her. Eawynn fancied she could still smell it on her clothes.

The area around the docks was where the poor and the outcasts gathered, as if wanting to pool their misery. Eawynn had spent the first night after her expulsion there, thinking to find safety in numbers. The reverse was true. The dockside was where she encountered the drunk. She should have known better. It was also where she lost the bread. Why had she not taken that as a warning?

This last night, Eawynn had fled up the hillside, to the more affluent areas of Fortaine. The threat of violence was reduced, but she still did not feel safe. She was not wanted among the honest citizens. Most ignored her. Others did no more than watch with suspicious eyes, but some had threatened what they would do if she did not move on. So Eawynn had moved on and at last found an out of the way corner sheltered from the wind and tried to sleep. She might as well not have bothered. Cold and hunger were poor bedfellows. Safety from attack only meant she could starve to death in peace.

A few hours of broken dozing was all Eawynn managed, finally waking well before dawn. The night had done nothing except for sticking icy needles of cramp into her joints. Time dragged by. She was exhausted, yet could not sleep. Then a wave of nausea made her head swim. Absurdly, she felt as if she was about to throw up. How could she? There was nothing to throw. Eawynn sat, hugging her knees, and waited for it to pass. She needed to eat. How much food could you buy for three pennies? How much longer before she was forced to find out?

A sudden ebb in the light alerted Eawynn. Someone was coming straight for where she sat. The dark figure was almost upon her before she realised. How had she not heard? Wallowing in self pity was one more luxury she could not afford. Eawynn turned her face to the wall and cowered into the corner, as if she could make herself invisible by disappearing into the bricks. *Please let him walk on by.*

The stranger was dressed in monochrome, black leather jerkin and boots, dull grey shirt, and loose leggings. They were the clothes of a common tradesman, off to make an early start on a day's work. Or so Eawynn prayed. He strode along confidently, yet his footsteps were almost silent on the cobbles. Even so, Eawynn knew she should have heard him, should have been more alert, for what good it might do her, lacking the strength to either fight off an attacker or run.

The man's pace did not change. If he saw her, he gave no sign. Still the panic frothed in Eawynn's gut. Only when he drew level, still without slowing or speaking, did she let herself relax and raise her eyes to his face. Then he was past, walking away, out of sight around the corner.

In that brief glimpse, Eawynn realised her mistake. Not a man but a woman, and not a stranger. The clothes and haircut had changed, but the face was one she would never forget. It had taunted her dreams for nights. A wave of joy swept all rational thought from Eawynn's head. She started to scramble to her feet, about to call out, then froze.

Hilda of Gimount was not home with her husband, nor was she in the temple hostel. She was prowling around Fortaine by night, dressed like a workman.

Eawynn sat back on her heels and clamped a hand over her forehead. Had hunger driven her mad? Was she suffering from hallucinations? But no. She was sure of what she had seen, which meant Hilda of Gimount was not the honest businesswoman she claimed to be. No great news there. Eawynn had always known, on some level, Hilda was an actress, playing a part. Yet she had still believed there was a core of truth in her story. Now she doubted everything. How much else about Hilda was a lie? Did she have a dead uncle, or even a husband? What had she been doing in the temple?

The obvious conclusion hit Eawynn like a hammer blow. She had no idea how it was done, but Hilda of Gimount had stolen the

Shewstone. The blows did not end there. Eawynn doubled over in anguish. Hilda had flirted with her and kissed her and made her feel special while taking her for a dupe. She had known Hilda was playing games but had still fallen for the sham, and now she was starving on the streets because Hilda had tricked her into acting like an infatuated fool.

Eawynn lifted her head, gasping as she tried to steady her thoughts. As a secondary point, it also meant Enlightening Sister Astrologer was innocent. Eawynn wished she could say she did not know which conclusion was the more upsetting, but in truth there was no competition. The memory of kissing Hilda raked her heart with acid claws. She thumped her fist on the wall. She had to hit something.

What should she do? More to the point, what could she do? If she went to the temple and told them, would anyone believe her?

Insightful Sister Oracle had spoken of earning Anberith's forgiveness. Of course, she had not meant it; the line was merely what the high priestess was supposed to say during the Abrogating Ritual of Expulsion. But if Eawynn helped return the Shewstone, surely it was possible the elders might let her return. As things stood, it was easily the best chance she had. And if nothing else, there was revenge.

Eawynn shoved herself to her feet. If she followed Hilda to the rogues' den, or wherever it was the thief lived, then she could summon the city watch. Her feet were leaden lumps of ice and did not want to obey her, but she forced them to move. They retaliated by shooting daggers up her legs. Eawynn ignored the pain and broke into a hobbling run.

She made it to the end of the alley in time to see Hilda turn into another side road. For the next half mile she followed her quarry, zigzagging across Fortaine. Twice she got too close and was nearly spotted. Once she thought she had lost Hilda, only to catch sight of her again. The emptiness in her stomach was forgotten as Eawynn crept from corner to doorway, keeping to the shadows.

The old city walls were coming into view when Hilda switched direction again, ducking through a gap between two tall buildings. Eawynn reached the opening as Hilda vanished around yet another corner, twenty yards ahead.

The passage was narrow and dark and had been used as a rubbish dump. Eawynn made what haste she could. A broken post snagged her left sandal and the strap gave way, leaving the sole flapping. Eawynn kicked both shoes off. They had been the next best thing to useless. She carried on barefoot, but avoiding broken glass and pottery shards slowed her down. When she reached the corner, there was nobody in sight.

The buildings here looked semi-derelict, the sort of street Eawynn would have imagined for a secret rogues' den. Doorways punctuated the walls on either side. Had Hilda gone into one or was she carrying on ahead?

Eawynn tiptoed cautiously along, looking up at the windows for sign of anyone watching. She drew level with the first doorway, when a blur of motion caught the corner of her eye. A force slammed into her, knocking her to the ground. A knee rammed into her back, biting on the half-healed cuts, and pressing her face into the ground. Then a sharp point pricked under her chin.

"I don't know why you're following me, but it's a dangerous thing to do." Hilda's voice, rich and soft and deadly.

Eawynn had been caught out, over and again. Could she have made a bigger fool of herself if she had tried? In fury, she shouted, "What have you done with the Shewstone?"

❖

"What have you done with the Shewstone?"

The question caught Matt flat-footed. It was not any of the things she expected the incompetent, would-be footpad to say, and the surprises kept getting bigger. Matt felt her jaw drop. The stubble haired guttersnipe was Eawynn, dressed like a beggar.

Matt took the knife away and shifted back on her heels, allowing Eawynn to roll over and face her. When did the holy sisters start tailing people through the streets?

"What are you doing here?"

"I want the Shewstone."

"What?"

"You're a thief. The Shewstone. You stole it, didn't you?"

Matt had still not mastered her surprise, but the question was easy enough. "Yes."

"You've got to give it back."

"I can't."

"I'll call the city watch. They'll be able to—"

"I can't give it back because I don't have it." Matt sheathed the knife in her boot and stood. She had her own questions. "Why are you here, like this? You're a priestess. Why aren't you in the temple?"

"Not anymore. They threw me out."

"Why?"

"Because they think I helped you steal the Shewstone."

"That's stupid."

"Do you think I don't know that?"

"I didn't need any…" Matt stopped and stared down the street, thinking rapidly.

She had chosen the spot because she was unlikely to be disturbed or overheard, but that did not mean she wanted to hang around. Eawynn was a problem that needed a quick solution. The easiest and surest was to slit her throat. The city watch would not concern themselves over one more dead vagrant. It was not a solution Matt was willing to consider.

The second option was to simply walk away. Losing Eawynn in the city would not be a problem. As it was, she had needed to actively work at keeping Eawynn on her tail. When she realised she was being followed, Matt's first thought was that the footpad might be on Gilbert's payroll. She had wanted the chance to ask a few questions in private.

There was one more option. Matt held out a hand to help Eawynn up. "Come with me."

"Where? Why?"

"Somewhere we can talk in comfort."

"Do you think I'd trust you?"

"No. I don't think you're stupid enough to do that. But I'm not staying here, so if you want to talk, you're going to have to come along."

"I could scream for the watch."

"You think they'd pay any attention to someone dressed like you?" Eawynn truly was a total innocent when it came to life on the streets.

Matt started walking. Before she had gone a dozen yards, she heard Eawynn's footsteps hurrying to catch up. Matt smiled, mainly in self-mockery. Why was it always so easy to persuade herself that inviting an attractive woman up to her room was the most sensible thing to do?

Oh well, if Eawynn tried to cause trouble, tying her up was another option. Matt would leave instructions for the tavern staff to release the prisoner after she left town. If the information she hoped for was in Edmund's papers, she would be on the first boat out.

As ever, the barman at The Jolly Wagoner acted as if she was not there, which was not the same as ignoring her.

"I'd like two large breakfasts." Matt gave the order while heading for the stairs. No need to ask if Eawynn was hungry—street folk always were.

Up in the room, Matt stripped off her wig and jerkin, and dropped the bag of papers on her bunk. They would have to wait. If Eawynn were not there, she would have skipped breakfast and gone through the papers until she could put off sleep no longer. However, Eawynn was going to want to talk. Matt could have guessed as much, even without the expression on her face. The women she kissed always did.

Matt leaned her shoulder on the wall by the window, with half an eye on the sunrise and half on Eawynn, who sat at the table, glaring.

"How did you do it? How did you steal the Shewstone?"

"Quite easily."

"You took the sacrarium key from me?"

"Yes."

"While you were kissing me?"

"Yes."

"Did you have the key to the outer shrine door as well? Did you kiss Insightful Sister Oracle?"

"Oh please, no. I have some standards." Matt winced at the thought. "I honestly find you attractive and enjoyed kissing you very much."

Eawynn's glare deepened. If Matt was honest with herself, she knew that line always was going to be a hard one to sell.

"So how did you do it? When did you take the Shewstone?"

"Immediately after you stopped kissing me and ran away."

"But you followed me into the sanctuary. You didn't have it with you."

"No. I hid it in the outer room to pick up later, after all the fuss died down."

"How did you get the repository open?"

Matt could not help laughing. "That was easy. You wouldn't believe how often people spend a fortune on a lock, then screw it to matchwood that splinters if you look at it too hard. The hinges were soft copper. A kid could've taken the door off."

"They said you used tools."

"Just the jemmy I'd hidden in my boot."

"You had it planned all along? The only reason you were waiting for me was so you could steal the Shewstone?"

"Yes. Although getting to kiss you was a bonus."

"You're revolting."

Matt sighed. Any hopes of seduction had been weak to start with and were not getting any better. "I'm sorry you feel that way."

"Sorry? You don't feel sorry at all. I can see it on your face."

"Not about taking the stone. I'm sorry for what's happened to you. I didn't think you'd get into so much trouble. If I'd known, I'd have worked things differently."

The apology had no effect. "But you think it's all right to steal things." A statement, not a question.

"I'm a thief. It's what I do. Taking the Shewstone?" Matt shrugged. "No guilt at all. Your chief priestess has been fleecing people for years. At least I'm honest about what I am."

"Honest! After all your lying, you think you can claim honesty?"

"In comparison to your Unsightly Sister Orifice, yes, I can. The Shewstone is a con trick. It's a ball of rock, nothing more."

"If you think that, why did you bother stealing it?"

"Some people said they'd pay us."

"Us? You're part of a gang? Are you the leader?"

"No, my father is…was…Edmund Flyming." Matt swallowed. Eawynn showed no reaction to the name. There was no reason to expect one. The sisters in the temple knew nothing about life on the city streets.

"He has the Shewstone?"

"No. He's dead. The shitheads double-crossed us and murdered him. They've got it now."

"Do you know where they are?"

"No. But I'm going to find them. And I'm going to kill them."

That got a reaction. Eawynn sat silent for a moment while a succession of emotions chased across her face, starting with surprise and ending in disgust. "You really are a lowlife." Matt might have been something unsavoury, found stuck to the bottom of her shoe.

"They murdered my father."

"That's what you get for being a criminal."

Matt clenched her jaw, unable to speak. The sun poking over the horizon misted as tears filled her eyes. What Eawynn thought did not matter. She had never met Edmund, did not know the man he had been. He was worth a thousand of the parasites in the temple, or the palace.

After a few seconds, Eawynn asked, "What's your real name?"

"Matt."

"Matt. Hilda. Matilda?"

Matt nodded.

"Mattie."

"No. Don't call me that. I answer to Matt." No one would ever call her Mattie again, not if they wanted to keep all their teeth.

Eawynn's eyebrows raised at her tone, but she offered no challenge. "Why did these people want the Shewstone?"

"They didn't say, and I don't care."

"I want the Shewstone back."

"I'll tell them that when I find them."

"I have to get it." Unmistakable misery broke in Eawynn's voice, shattering the hard veneer she had been presenting until then. "If I can get the Shewstone and return it to the temple, they might let me back. I could be a priestess again."

"You're out of luck. Chances are the bastards won't still have the Shewstone when I catch up with them."

"I can't live on the streets."

"You can stay here a while." Maybe Matt owed her, and anyway, the room was paid for. Somebody might as well benefit. "Anything you want, food, drink. Just ask the staff."

"I don't have any money."

"You don't need it. It's taken care of."

On cue, there was a knock. Nobody was around when Matt opened the door, but on the floor was a tray bearing two plates of eggs, bacon, sliced sausage, and mushrooms, along with half a loaf of bread and two tankards of beer. Matt carried it to the table. The desperate look in Eawynn's eyes was one she knew. Matt broke off part of the loaf, took two rashers from a plate and picked up a tankard. Bread, bacon, and beer would do her for breakfast.

"You can have the rest. I'm not hungry."

Eawynn did not need persuading. She tore into the food like a woman who had not eaten for days.

Matt left her to it. She positioned herself on a bed and pulled open the bag. The strangers had come from the mainland and had most likely gone back there, and that was far too big a net to cast. Matt needed details to have any hope of finding them. Edmund had described the gathered information as half a picture. Which half was it?

The smallest roll was labelled "Shewstone clients" in Edmund's neat handwriting. Matt untied the ribbon. While eating her bread and bacon, she sifted through the contents, eight sheets of various sizes, written in different hands, all annotated by Edmund.

Waldo of Bousack was what the leader called himself when about town, which was something he kept to a minimum, except for twice a day, when he and his servant attended ceremonies at the Temple of Liffrea. If they wanted to stay out of sight, yet still thought it important to pray, they must be unusually devout. Were they priests, hoping to get the Shewstone for their own temple?

One informant had traced the strangers to The Royal Standard, where lodgings were taken in the name of Onesta D'Walnia, which was no more likely as his real name, since Walnia was far to the south, and its inhabitants were very dark skinned. A chambermaid reported the men kept apart from the other guests. Both could speak Tradetalk, but between themselves stuck to Cynnreord. Matt pursed her lips. Using the old empire language would not guarantee eavesdroppers could not understand them. So if it wasn't for secrecy, was it their native tongue? In which case it would narrow down their potential homeland.

Jenny the Trip identified the strangers from their description and reported they arrived on the *Sabina*. In the harbour master's log, they were described as Esteman Haswold and servant. The ship had sailed, so Jenny could not question the crew, but she listed its ports of call on the way to Pinettale. One must be where they boarded the ship.

Four other papers added nothing to what was known. It was all less helpful than Matt had hoped. The final sheet was an intercepted letter. Presumably, it was a report home, but this was guesswork, since it was written in a strange, dense script. Edmund's note read, "No luck with translation from normal sources. Will pursue further if events warrant. Courier had verbal instructions for delivery and wasn't willing to share."

Matt looked up. Eawynn had finished the second breakfast and was wiping the plate with a corner of bread. The script looked similar to the book she had been reading in the library the day they met. Matt waited until the last mouthful was gone, then took the other seat at the table.

"Can you read this?"

Eawynn glanced at the letter. "Yes."

Matt sighed. This was not going to be easy. "Will you read it to me, please?"

"Why?"

"It's from the people who took the Shewstone. It might give a clue about where to find them."

Eawynn pulled the sheet to her. "Theodcwen. Min aerende faerath laetlice. Se feondulf—"

"I don't speak Cynnreord." Matt recognised the language, but no more.

"No. I didn't think you would." Matt waited for Eawynn to get over being smug. She started again. "'Great Queen. My mission is proceeding slowly. The criminal we have conscripted...employed...'"

Eawynn paused, frowning. "There's no exact word for it. Um...'tells us the artefact will be in our hands before the moon is reborn.' That's the new moon. 'We have provisionally secured passage on the...' I guess it's a name. It doesn't translate. Ah...'so with the blessing of Liffrea, we will return to your imperial capital a month before the solstice.'" Eawynn's eyes scanned down the page. "The rest is a lot of flattery about how great the queen is and what an honour it is to serve her. I can translate if you want."

"Later will do. Is there a name?"

"Oswald Husa Eastandune."

"This writing, it's not normal letters."

"It's written in clerical hieroglyphs."

"Who uses it?"

"These days? Mainly historians. They developed from pre-empire pictographs, but got superseded by cursive script five hundred years ago. The only people who kept using them were the Rihtcynn priesthood."

Matt smiled. Everything added up. She knew where to go and who to hunt down when she got there. The man who murdered Edmund looked Rihtcynn, spoke Cynnreord, and wrote in an old empire script. He was a priest who would return to a queen in her capital city. History was not Matt's favourite subject, but she knew enough to work out the clues, as could anyone on the Island of Pinettale, or beyond.

Twelve centuries before, the Rihtcynn had burst out of their homeland on the Rihtcynn plains. Their armies had cut a bloody path across the world, enslaving everyone they met. For five centuries, the empire had expanded. The Island of Pinettale was its last major conquest. The wealth of the known world had flowed back to their capital, Cyningesburg. Then stagnation set in and the empire was smothered by its own weight. Just under 200 years ago had been the great upheaval. The conquered lands had risen up and the bloated empire had fallen apart. The Rihtcynn had been pushed back to Rihtcynnedal, their ancestral homeland, except for places like Pinettale, where a remnant had clung to power.

Talk on the docks said the mainland Rihtcynn were getting pushy again, but did not have much to back it up. How much was left of Cyningesburg? Matt assumed it would be in ruins, but the Temple of Liffrea must still be standing, and someone was styling herself queen in the old imperial capital, so maybe she had a building she could pass off as a palace. Matt would find out when she got there. The first step was passage to Sideamuda, historically the seaport for the inland city. Significantly, it was one of the stops Jenny listed on the *Sabina*'s voyage.

The sun had climbed clear of the horizon and light flooded the room. When first they met, Eawynn's head was newly shaved, her hair no more than a dark outline. Now her hair was a half inch in length, and for the first time, Matt noticed its colour.

"Another damned redhead."

"Pardon?"

"This Oswald and his sidekick. They were both redheads. Pureblood Rihtcynn by the look of them."

Eawynn frowned. "I think they might have come to the temple for a divination."

"He said he went to see the Shewstone before deciding if he really wanted it. He'd have given his name as Waldo of Bousack."

"Yes. That was him. He's the one who's got the Shewstone?"

"Yes."

"He's taken it to Cyningesburg." Eawynn was not slow on the uptake.

"That's my guess."

"You're going to follow him?"

Matt nodded.

"You don't speak Cynnreord."

"I think he'll understand my message when I give it to him."

However, Eawynn had a point. Tradetalk was found wherever the old empire's tendrils had reached. Even where other tongues predominated, it was the language of business. Matt could have counted on getting by, using nothing but Tradetalk everywhere except Rihtcynnedal. Everyone knew the Rihtcynn had their crackjaw, antiquated language and would speak nothing else. They despised all other races—Thraelas they called them, thralls.

With her red hair and white skin, Eawynn clearly had a good dollop of Rihtcynn blood, and she spoke Cynnreord. A translator would be useful, especially one who could read prehistoric writing.

If the arrogant jerks gave her trouble, it might even come in handy to have a translator who could pass as Rihtcynn. But was it worth having a translator who was totally pissed off at her? Matt pursed her lip to hide her smile. Why did she even bother asking the question, when it came to a translator as good-looking as Eawynn?

"You're sure you want the stone?"

"It's my only hope of getting back in the temple."

"How about a deal?"

Eawynn's eyes narrowed in suspicion. "What?"

"We both want to track down Oswald Husa Eastandune. Come with me. Help me find him, and I'll get you the stone."

"Do you seriously think I'd go anywhere with you?"

"Only if you want the Shewstone. I'm betting Oswald has it sitting on his altar in Cyningesburg. I'm the one with experience of stealing stones from temples."

CHAPTER SIX

The docks were a deafening maelstrom. Half the population of Fortaine seemed to be on the quay, all pounding their way in different directions, all bellowing their part of different conversations at the top of their voices. But now Eawynn was no longer dressed as a beggar, the porters detoured around her with only a grunt of irritation. Nobody shouted at her. Nobody swore at her. Nobody tried to run her over.

Did clothes make such a difference? Eawynn looked down at what she was wearing, taken from the wardrobe at The Jolly Wagoner—a green jerkin over a large white shirt, both reaching to mid thigh, loose leggings, leather belt, and ankle boots. Respectable, but hardly aristocratic, especially since all was paid for with the proceeds of crime, as was the food in her stomach. Eawynn's conscience gave a dig. She had not stolen the money personally but had no doubts where it came from. Yet what other option did she have? She would pray for forgiveness the next time she visited a temple.

Clearly, no such qualms affected the woman she was learning to think of as Matt. The thief stood a few feet away, talking to another woman, who had been introduced as Jenny the Trip, an elderly hook-nosed harridan, tall and gaunt, with skin like old leather. The pair stood as if they were dock fixtures—feet planted square, arms crossed, shoulders back, heads held high.

No more of Hilda the hunched mouse, elbows glued to her sides, tiptoeing around. She was not even Hilda the seductress, with eyes that smouldered, and lips so softly possessive. Eawynn closed her eyes, fighting the memory. She did not want to think of how completely she had fallen for the crude trickery, of how her pulse used to race at the sight of the woman, or how her body used to respond, aching to be touched. She should never have let herself get caught up in the game. Because, all the time, Matt had been playing her for a gullible slut.

Eawynn felt her face burning with shame and humiliation. She snapped her eyes open. Desperately, she hunted around the dockside for anything to distract her thoughts.

By a warehouse, two urchins, one barely old enough to walk, ducked and dodged between the heavy carts. Wherever they were hoping to get would not be easy. An older boy sat on a barrel, kicking his heels on the side, his expression withdrawn and hopeless. A woman wrapped in rags was curled, unmoving, in a corner, either sleeping or dead. Who would care? Eawynn bit her lip, guilt-struck. She knew what the docks were like. She should have brought something from her breakfast. She could have given it out and made a difference for just one or two, for just a morning.

Farther along the quay, a stout merchant shifted to avoid being run down by an overladen pushcart. Eawynn focused on him. The man was dressed far better than herself, in a long red embroidered surcoat. Yet he was not immune to the chaos. Her gaze carried on down the dockside, picking out patterns in the flow. Maybe three or four still spots existed, she realised, and she stood in the biggest, stillest of all. Or rather on the edge of the still spot centred around Matt and Jenny.

What was it about them? Surely not just the brash posture? Eawynn listened to their conversation. Apparently, Benny and some badly behaved children were running from a bower. This had to be a secret code, since a garden structure would not be giving chase. They had persuaded both of the hired help to go for a swim in the bay, which made Matt inexplicably happy. Tobias was sending over a couple of handymen. Eawynn was unsure whether this was to assist a man called Gilbert, who was doing something with bricks.

The topic moved to an aspect of Matt. "I wasn't born in the house."

"Edmund claimed you. That's enough for most."

"Is it enough for Tobias?"

"He ain't the only one with a shout. Make the fucker pay a kin's due, and you'll get my nod when you come back."

"That's not why I'm doing it."

"I know. That's why it counts."

None of it made sense. Eawynn forced herself to look at Matt. The auburn hair had been a wig. This had come as a surprise, but should not have, once she knew the sort of woman Matt really was—a lowlife criminal who did not possess a drop of noble blood. Her real, spiky, black hair did not have the flowing curls, so there was nothing to detract from the balance of cheek and jaw. Eawynn refused to let herself consider which look suited Matt better.

Brilliant sunlight accentuated the planes of Matt's face. The breeze chased across her loose white shirt in ripples that hinted at the body beneath. Matt's pose radiated confidence. Even when playing the demure merchant, she had always seemed certain of herself.

The only time Eawynn could remember a faltering in that certainty was in the shrine, when Matt had spoken of being crazy for her, in the moments before they kissed. And it had been the crudest, most contemptible sham of all. Eawynn felt sick. She wished she could persuade herself she had not enjoyed that kiss. She hated herself for the way she had felt and for the way she still could not get it out of her head. But most of all, she hated Matt. Put the blame where it was due.

When they returned with the Shewstone, she could still turn Matt over to the city watch. The thief was guilty of enough crimes. Somebody should see she was brought to account. Maybe it was an oversight, but Eawynn had not been asked to give her word on the matter. Even so, having Matt arrested went against the spirit of their agreement. It did not seem honourable. Eawynn pursed her lips. She would not do it, but that did not mean she could not amuse herself with the idea from time to time.

The conversation was drawing to a close. The women clasped each other's forearm and said farewell. Matt swung her bag over her shoulder and sauntered along the quay. Eawynn fell in alongside. Where to start the questions?

"Why is she called Jenny the Trip?"

"To distinguish her from Jenny the Catch."

"And she is?"

"Was. She took a ride, years back. She used to be an indie, who played hide the lady by Newbridge."

Eawynn gave up. *I'm fluent in six languages, and know something of three others, and she might as well be speaking a tenth.*

A few yards farther on, Matt said. "Jenny's got us passage on a ship to Sideamuda. The *Blue Puffin*. It's not taking the most direct route, but it'll get us there, and the captain owed Edmund a favour."

Obviously, somewhere in the midst of the nonsense, Matt and Jenny had exchanged useful information.

Matt branched out from the quay onto one of the deep water jetties. Docked midway along was a medium sized ship with a bright blue seabird as its figurehead. Matt headed up the gangplank.

A seaman hailed them from the rigging. "D'ya want Captain Joachim?"

"Yes."

"Over there." He pointed to the stern, but there was no need to go hunting.

A tall, heavily built man approached. Captain Joachim had clearly been working and was naked from the waist up, beaded with sweat. "You're Matt? Edmund Flyming's girl?"

Matt answered with a nod.

"Jenny said you'd be over."

"Thanks for the passage."

"Ah, it's nothing. Without Edmund, the bastards would've had me swinging." He pointed to a doorway. "You can have my cabin. Like I said, I owed him, big time. Get yourselves stowed. We sail on the tide."

Eawynn followed Matt as far as the doorway. The image conjured up by "Captain's Cabin" did not match the reality. The lopsided room was five feet wide and seven at its longest point. A narrow bunk took up one wall. A tiny triangular desk was squeezed into a corner beneath the single, unglazed porthole.

"How long did you say this voyage was going to be?"

Matt dropped her bag on the floor and shoved it under the bunk with her foot. "I didn't. But it's going to take twenty-two days if we get a good wind."

"And if we don't?"

"We could get smashed on the rocks and never make it." Matt grinned. "Don't worry."

Easy for her to say. Shipwrecked, Eawynn could deal with. The better part of a month, cooped up with Matt in the tiny cabin was more than she wanted to think about. Briefly, Eawynn considered going back onto the dock and curling up beside the motionless beggar woman she had seen. Realistically, that was her only alternative.

Anberith help me.

❖

Pinettale was a dark smudge on the horizon, purple in the dusk. A pulse of light from the Fortaine lighthouse flickered for a while before being lost. Matt leaned against the railing and watched her hometown vanish into the night.

"Have you ever been off the island before?" the helmsman asked.

"No. Never."

"It'll still be here when you get back."

Matt laughed. "Yeah. I'm sure." Along with Gilbert, Tobias, the family, and a shed-load of other issues, but it could all wait. For now, she had just one matter to deal with. Matt bid the helmsman good night and left the aft deck.

Eawynn was in the cabin when Matt got there, sitting at the desk and staring at the wall as if trying to see whether she could bore holes in wood with her eyes. All right, so maybe there were two matters to deal with.

Not for the first time, Matt questioned her own wisdom in bringing Eawynn along. Other options were available if she did not want to travel alone. The Flyming gang was pulling itself together and could have spared the muscle. Volunteers would not have been hard to find. Yet in order to succeed, she would be relying on stealth, not strength, and stealth needed good reconnaissance. Eawynn was the best resource on offer—just not a very happy, fun-to-be-with resource.

A lantern hung from the ceiling. By its light, Matt considered the bunk. It was narrow, but long. Captain Joachim was a good foot taller than either of them.

"There'll be plenty of room for us to sleep top and tail."

"Do you seriously think I'm getting into a bed with you?" The venom in Eawynn's voice would have put a viper to shame.

"You have to sleep somewhere."

"The floor sounds good to me."

"Don't be an idiot."

The glare she received in response made Matt feel empathy with the wall.

"Look, I know you're upset about being kicked out of the temple. I'm sorry. I've said that. If you think the Shewstone is your way back in, we'll get it. I promise."

"That's all you're sorry about?"

"I've told you I don't feel guilty about upsetting your Unsightly Sister Orifice."

"How about me?"

Why did women always take things so personally? Though to be fair, Edmund had always made exactly the same complaint about men. "I never meant to upset you or hurt you."

"So what did you mean to do?"

"I was having fun. We both were. Yes, I was after the key, but you can't deny you were enjoying the game as well."

"How dare you say that!"

"Because it's true. Be honest. Are you upset I hit on you? Or are you upset because you enjoyed me doing it?" Matt could hear the level of her own voice rising.

"You abused me."

"Oh no. You're an adult. I may have strung you along, but I never forced you to do anything."

"You abused my trust."

"Trust?"

"As in pretending to be something you weren't."

"You've never tried to make someone think you're smarter, or funnier, or more interested than you really were, just to get her into the sack?"

"No."

"Then you picked the right calling as a virgin priestess."

"You think you're so funny." The missed beat in the reply made Matt wonder how close Eawynn came to deserving the title.

"Just pointing out you were breaking your own rules, and you knew it. You can't claim total innocence."

"I didn't know you were a thief."

"So that was it. All along, you were thinking, *That Hilda, she's a merchant. Wow. I really get hot for women who spend all day counting money.* Don't kid yourself. You were going for me. I look like this. I sound like this. I act like this." Matt swept both hands downwards with a theatrical flourish, encompassing her body from head to toes. "And this is what you went for. It wasn't the name. It wasn't the job. You fell for me."

"Now I feel sick just looking at you."

"Then you've saved yourself a lot of time. Usually, I have to be banging a woman for three months before she feels that way about me."

Eawynn lurched to her feet. For a moment, Matt thought she was about to get slapped, which was also not unheard of at the three-month mark, but instead Eawynn pulled her woollen cloak from its peg.

"I'm going to sleep."

"On the floor?"

"Yes."

"Fine. Go for it."

Matt was not about to waste any more time. She watched Eawynn wrap herself in the cloak and lie down, facing away. Matt blew out the lantern, kicked off her boots, and got on the bunk.

For a while, she lay staring up at the darkness. How justified was Eawynn in her anger? Or to flip the question round, how would Matt feel if their positions were reversed? It was not an easy trick of mental gymnastics. Matt could not imagine accepting life in the temple. She needed her freedom and would have jumped at any opportunity for some fun, with no recriminations. Was it her problem if Eawynn could not take things the same way?

Then Matt thought she heard a soft sob. Should she say something? A hug was not going to be well received—more the pity. Eawynn's appeal was all the stronger, now she was not wearing the shapeless robes. Maybe a few nice words tomorrow might ease the friction. Would compliments work?

Matt sighed and rolled over. All things considered, it was just as well she had not been planning on any action between the sheets with Eawynn. Matt would not have turned it down. The long voyage would pass quicker, but Matt had to regretfully accept that ship had most definitely sailed.

❖

The spring sun was warm on the foredeck. The sky was cloudless blue. Eawynn made herself comfy, leaning against a crate, out of the breeze. In truth, she had not slept well, though she was not about to admit it to anyone, and certainly not Matt. She might drift off soon. Meanwhile, it was pleasant, lying in the sunlight, listening to the seagulls and the bow slicing though the waves, with the gentle rocking of the deck beneath her.

To the left, or port as the sailors called it, a line of headlands retreated into the distance, the hook of Pinettale. Above the cliffs, green hillside rose to snow-capped peaks. It would be the last land they saw until the ship reached the mainland. Then they would sail along the coast to Sideamuda. Eawynn could see the map in her head. She had spent enough time poring over one.

Her ancestors had come from Rihtcynnedal. They were the rulers and warriors who had brought civilization to the barbarian lands. Even after the fall of the empire, they formed the aristocracy whose firm guidance had seen the Island of Pinettale prosper. And she was going to the place where it had all begun. She was going to walk the ancient streets of Cyningesburg. It was so unbelievable. Eawynn was frightened she would lose all self-control and start jumping up and down with excitement, like a toddler.

Her father had told her tales of the great city. Yet he had only read about it in books. Certainly, Eawynn had never dreamed she would go there. Was that part of the reason she had agreed to this? Otherwise, even the hope of recovering the Shewstone would not justify working with the lowlife thief. Eawynn did not know how she was going to stand the journey.

The only way was to take comfort in the bits she could enjoy, like lying on the foredeck, with nowhere to sweep or polish, no elder sisters to find fault, and no stifling weight of stone. Just ten days ago, she thought her life would be forever in the temple. Strange how quickly things could change, but change could run both ways. She had to go back. There was no place for her in the frightening world outside. Yet for now, she could enjoy the freedom to do nothing but admire the scenery. Drowsiness clouded the edges of her mind.

The sound of a door roused her. Eawynn peered around the edge of the crate. Matt emerged from the cabin, looking decidedly green. With a hand over her mouth, she staggered to the rail and flopped over, to the unmistakable sound of retching.

Eawynn made no attempt to hide her smile. So Matt had a weak stomach? There was a touch of divine justice to it. She did not look the cocksure queen of the harbour now. The arrogant seductress was completely off her game. Although, to be fair, the pose did show Matt's rear end to good effect. Eawynn squashed that thought immediately. Matt was a deceitful, self-serving crook. Eawynn would never let herself see anything remotely attractive about her again.

"Hey, Jon. You're an arse man, aren't you?" a sailor called out.

"Not when they're puking their guts out." The one who answered stood only a few feet from Eawynn.

"Why? You don't need to look at the mantelpiece while poking the fire."

"The sound of spewing would put me off my stroke."

"Just sing a song and hump in time."

"Nah. I'm waiting to see if this other one wants to tan her nice white tits."

Eawynn glared at the man, stunned by his impertinence. Then she realised he had been speaking Kemruhnic. She raised her voice, using the same language. "I can assure you, I'm not going to risk getting sunburnt there."

The way the sailor jumped was all Eawynn could have wished for. "I'm sorry, ma'am. We didn't mean—"

"You thought I wouldn't understand you."

"Nobody else onboard does. But me and Davi come from Kemruhn, and sometimes we muck about."

"I'm a translator."

"Oh." He swallowed. "You won't tell Mistress Flyming what we said, will you?"

"I'm here to translate whatever she needs to know." The sailor looked so nervous, Eawynn relented. "But she probably doesn't need to know that."

"Thanks. I mean, I respect the Flyming family. We all do."

Flyming, a good name for a family of criminals. Did anyone know what the word meant? There was no trace of irony in the sailor's voice. "Your captain said he owed them a favour."

"We all do. Three years back, we docked at Fortaine with a cargo of Ferridian brandy, which wasn't what it said on the papers, if you know what I mean."

Eawynn thought she did, and nodded.

"One of the crew ratted on us. Took a backhander and told a tonnage man."

"A who?"

"A customs officer."

"Oh."

"Anyway, we'd all have been clying the jerk, or dancing on a rope. But Edmund Flyming said he'd sort it out. The papers got shuffled, and the rat went missing. Flyming had his men take him for a swim in the bay."

"Pardon?" Half of what the sailor said was lost on Eawynn, though she had caught the main thrust.

The sailor shrugged. "You know. Tied him up in sailcloth with a few rocks for company and tipped him overboard."

The casual acceptance of murder took Eawynn's breath away. "And the customs officer, did he get taken for a swim too?"

"No. Edmund Flyming said he was an honest man doing his job. Besides, without the papers and the rat, he didn't have no evidence. Flyming was a good man. The sort you look up to. His word was gold." The sailor looked sad. "He'll be missed. We're all here to give his daughter any help she needs. She'll get her sea legs after two or three days. They always do." He pointed to the stern. "If you don't mind, ma'am, I've got to get on. Thanks for keeping that stupid stuff to yourself."

Eawynn watched him go. On the other side of the boat, Matt was all but crawling back to the cabin. What sort of world was this, where a gangster boss and cold-blooded murderer could be spoken of as "a good man"? What sort of people had she become mixed up with?

A swim in the bay. That was a phrase Matt and Jenny had used back in Fortaine. Some people had been murdered and Matt thought it was amusing. That was why the porters avoided her and Jenny. It was fear, enough to intimidate the entire dockside. No wonder the sailor did not want his bawdy comments repeated. Eawynn took a deep breath. All she wanted was to get the Shewstone, return to the temple, and never set eyes on Matt again.

❖

Banks of black cloud crowded over the horizon, swallowing the late afternoon sun. Already, the wind was picking up. The hull smacked down hard between the crests of choppy waves.

Matt eyed the clouds glumly. *Typical. Three days dying in bed while my stomach tried to turn itself inside out and there was beautiful sunshine. Finally, I feel normal again, and this is what I get.*

A sailor ducked down beside her, nimbly tying off a set of rope ends. "You best get inside, ma'am." He smiled. "Don't worry. It's just a squall. We'll be fine, but it's gonna get a bit damp on deck." He hurried to the next item needing to be secured.

Matt gave the thunderclouds another resentful scowl and returned to the cabin. The minimal fittings were already bolted down. She collected any loose items and stowed them in the locker under the bunk. The task did not take long, especially once Eawynn arrived to help. Soon, everything that could be clamped, stored, or tied down had been.

With nothing left to do, Matt sat on the side of the bunk and pouted at the wall. So far, she had seen more than she liked of the cabin interior. Eawynn swung out the seat contraption from under the desk, looking no happier. But then, as if an afterthought, she opened the locker and pulled out a bucket which she thrust into Matt's hands.

"Just in case."

The mocking smile did nothing to improve Matt's mood. This was going to be fun. Up until now, she and Eawynn had done a good job of avoiding each other. Although, conversation was rarely going to be an issue when one person always had her head over either a bucket or the side of the ship. What hope was there they could find something civil to talk about now?

The pitch and yaw became ever more violent. The timbers creaked and groaned. Hammer-blow waves shook the entire ship. Somewhere, something broke free and thumped through the hold. Shouts from the crew pierced the sound of the rising wind. Matt strained her ears for the voices, trying to gauge if any degree of panic was setting in. Then her stomach started to object. Though she hated to admit it, the bucket in her hands was reassuring.

The shutter over the porthole swung back, smacking against the wall. The second time it did this, Eawynn rose to latch it shut. As she stood, her head was caught by a last stray beam of sunlight, sneaking under the clouds.

With each day, as her hair grew imperceptibly longer, the colour was becoming more vivid. When it was fully grown, Eawynn's hair would be red enough to make half the royal family weep with jealousy. Coupled with her white skin, she must be only a step or two from the aristocracy.

"Are you some lord's by-blow?"

Eawynn dropped back onto the seat. "Yes."

"Did your mother tell you who he was?"

"I've no memory of my mother. My father paid her off. He was Thane Alric Wisa Achangrena." There was no mistaking the stiff-necked pride in Eawynn's voice.

"Figures."

"What do you mean by that?"

"The priesthood and the nobles, hand in hand. Parasites, bolstering each other up." The arrogant aristocracy, with their exalted Rihtcynn blood, was guaranteed to put Matt's back up. Why would anyone boast descent from such bloody tyrants?

"Parasites? What would you count thieves as?"

"Some are poor folk, trying to put food on the table after bloodsuckers have skimmed off the lion's share."

"Is that your excuse?"

"No. People like me and my father, we're evening up the balance. The nobles do bugger all, except grow fat off other people's work. They get the priests to say it's what the gods want, and anyone who objects is evil. Then they pay the judges and the city watch to make sure nobody else gets a look in. When it comes to theft, we're gnats. I might lift a purse here and there. Your King Swidhelm stole the whole fucking island."

"He brought peace and stability when the empire was collapsing."

"He got peace by killing anyone who was making a noise."

"Where would Pinettale have gone without him?"

"I know where he went, into a damned great palace, to eat his dinner off gold plates."

"Somebody has to impose order. Civilization doesn't come about by magic. You might not like it, but we need laws for everyone's benefit."

"Really?"

"Yes. Like we need roads, and markets, and an army to keep us safe. Without somebody strong enough to organise things, we'd all be living in mud huts, eating whatever we could scrape together. That's when it didn't get stolen by raiders. You can't deny that under King Swidhelm's linage, Pinettale has never been richer. And not just the nobles, everyone has been better off."

"So if the poor get a pennyworth, it's all right if the rich take the rest of the barrel? Admit it, apart from those days before I picked you up, had you ever been hungry in your life?"

"The life of a priestess isn't easy."

"You reckon?"

"You saw what it was like. We work, dawn to dusk, and we're up half the night. You ate in the refectory. How many gold plates did you count there?"

"Then more fool you not to stay with your father."

"I didn't get to choose. I'm a bastard. When I got in the way of his ambitions, he dumped me at the temple. No, I was never hungry, but I wasn't living a life of luxury."

"And they didn't give you a soft ride, because you're Lord Whatsisface's daughter?"

"Oh, of course. That's why I was sweeping the floor when you met me. I was bottom of the pile. The temple wanted me even less than my father did."

"I don't believe you couldn't have traded on his name."

"Thane Alric Wisa Achangrena? His name would get me nowhere. The last sighting of his head was on a spike over the city gate. I'm not just a bastard. I'm a traitor's bastard."

The name had been vaguely familiar, although court politics had never been one of Matt's main preoccupations. She gave a sarcastic laugh and waved with her fingers, beckoning. "So your father was executed for treason. All right, run it past me one more time. Tell me again how it's important we follow the rule of law and how naughty criminals are."

"At least my father wasn't a murderer or a thief."

"At least my father kept his word." So much for civil conversation. Eawynn jumped to her feet and reached for the door.

"You can't go outside."

"I'm not staying here. I'll find a space in the hold."

"Don't be stupid."

Maybe that was not the best line to calm things down. Eawynn yanked the door open and stepped into the storm just as the ship rolled violently to starboard. A surge of water broke across the deck and swept into Eawynn, knocking her off her feet. The back of her skull cracked against the doorframe as she fell. The outflow washed her listless body against the gunwale but was not strong enough to sweep her overboard.

Matt sprang off the bunk, grabbed Eawynn under the armpits, and dragged her back inside the cabin. She kicked the door shut before another wave hit. Even as she did this, Eawynn started groaning and struggled to sit up, although clearly dazed.

The risk of setting fire to the ship during the storm meant they had not lit the lantern, but Matt had to check for injury. Contrary to common belief, a blow to the head was not a safe way to send anyone to sleep. Matt flipped open the tinderbox. The wild motion of the boat made striking the flint trickier than normal, but fortunately the tinder was still dry. A flame wobbled into life.

Matt turned up the wick. "Look at the light."

"Why?"

"Just do it."

Eawynn scowled but stopped arguing.

"Now keep your head still and follow my finger with your eyes."

"Are you going to ask me my name now?"

"No." Matt stood. "You'll be all right."

Eawynn needed three attempts to get to her feet. The fact she accepted Matt's help on the last one, without complaint, showed how weak and unsteady she was. Holding Eawynn's arm, Matt could feel her shaking, either from shock or cold. Her clothes were soaked through, and a ring of drips fell around her boots.

"You need to get warm."

Eawynn shrugged by way of answer.

Matt reached for the buttons on the wet shirt. "So take these off and get into bed."

Eawynn batted her hands away. "I can do it myself."

"Fine." At least she had stopped acting like an idiot.

Eawynn turned her back and tugged her shirt over her head. Matt opened her mouth to offer more advice, but the words stuck in her throat. Across Eawynn's back were a dozen or more thin lines of cuts and bruises, unmistakably the result of a week-old flogging. The rush of anger caught Matt by surprise. Shit-ugly Sister Arsehole and the other bitches in the temple—they had done this. Matt's hands balled into fists, a reflex action. There was no target for her to punch, but she so much wanted one.

She lost a key and she kissed me. One little key. A key I stole. Matt forced her hands to open, forced her breath to release. Meanwhile, Eawynn removed the rest of her clothes and slipped into bed. Matt arranged the wet material as best as possible for it to dry, then blew out the lantern and lay down on the floor. Night was a long way off, but there was nothing else to do.

I'm sorry. The words were too weak. How about, *Why don't I go give Shit-ugly Sister Arsehole a good kicking for you?* Matt closed her eyes. Given Eawynn's goody-goody ideas about right and wrong, she would not be any happier with the offer than the apology. *You did not deserve it.* A simple truth, and one Eawynn must know without being told. The priestesses were a bunch of evil bitches. Why did she want to go back to them?

Matt lay, staring up into the gloom while the ship heaved and shuddered beneath her. How did Eawynn total up the balance between them? She had accused Matt of upsetting her feelings, but not of getting her whipped. So which had hurt the most? The call was not Matt's to make, and there was no obvious way to settle the score. She would get the Shewstone, and anything else Eawynn wanted, and maybe it would help. However, Eawynn hated her, and that was not likely to change anytime soon. Matt could not say she blamed her.

❖

The ship was rocking gently when Eawynn woke the next morning. Dawn was long past and warm golden light flooded through the open porthole. The storm had blown itself out. Matt had already left the cabin.

The back of Eawynn's skull was tender, but she had no other problems. Her head felt clear. In fact, she felt better than she had since boarding the *Blue Puffin*. Sleeping in a bed definitely agreed with her more than the floor.

Eawynn saw her clothes from the previous night's insanity, hanging to dry from whatever improvised hangers could be found. She reached over and felt the hem of her shirt—a little damp, but wearable.

Eawynn rolled out of bed and got dressed. What had she been thinking? But no. She had not been thinking at all. It had been a case of get out of the cabin or attempt to throttle Matt. *Bad call.* By comparison, Insightful Sister Oracle ranked as mildly irritating.

With a bowl of porridge from the galley as breakfast, Eawynn started to climb the short run of steps to the foredeck, but stopped. Her favourite spot had been taken. All the while Matt had been suffering from seasickness, Eawynn had been free to treat the area as her own. However, now the thief had her sea legs, she had stolen Eawynn's place.

Eawynn dithered. Should she go and demand first taker's rights? That would be not merely childish but unreasonable. Not least because there was plenty of room for two. However, Eawynn had no intention of sitting any closer to Matt than could be helped. The entire length of the ship was less than she would have liked.

Eawynn took her porridge to the aft deck, close by where the helmsman stood. She spooned down her breakfast while scowling at the opposite end of the ship, an activity all the more galling in that the object of the scowls appeared completely oblivious.

This became the pattern for the following days. Whoever got up first would claim the foredeck, with the loser consigned to the rear. At Matt's insistence, they alternated use of the bunk. Eawynn suspected this was partly because one tended to wake earlier after an uncomfortable night on the floor. The person sleeping on the bed missed out on the foredeck, more often than not.

On the fourteenth day out of Fortaine, the mainland came briefly into view, before a blanket of grey mist swallowed everything. The wind stayed low throughout the night and into the following morning.

Eawynn stood in the cabin doorway, peering out. Rain fell in unbroken sheets. The sails hung slack from the mast, billowing in the most desultory fashion in the occasional damp puff of breeze. She was second to rise that day, but could still have the foredeck to herself. Matt had found a seat under a triangle of awning, the only dry patch on deck. Eawynn bit her lip. Should she stay in the cabin? But why must she be the one cooped up all day? She wanted fresh air, and there was enough space.

Matt looked up as she sat down. "Morning."

"Good morning."

Eawynn stared at the rain. Maybe sitting here had been a bad idea. Sooner or later, she was going to have to say something. Meanwhile, Matt was studiously honing a set of three knives. They were short, no more than six inches long. The stumpy handles had open hoops for pommels. The blades were leaf shaped, sharpened on both edges. Weapons, Eawynn realised, not tools. For the first time, she fully faced the idea she was helping on a mission to kill another human being. She would be an accessory to murder.

"Do you really think it's going to make you feel better, killing this man you're after?"

"Yes."

"You don't have to."

"Yes, I do."

"When you've found him, you can go to the authorities, tell them what he's done. Have him tried before a judge."

Matt looked up from the knife. "I'm going to be in Rihtcynnedal, accusing a Rihtcynn priest of killing a Thraelas gang boss, two thousand miles away. Do you honestly think any judge I find will give me the time of day?" She went back to honing. "Anyway, it doesn't matter. This is something I have to do."

"It's murder."

"We didn't start it."

"That's all the justification you need?"

"Yes."

Trying to reason with Matt was pointless. "I guess breeding tells. You're the daughter of a murderer. Killing is in your blood."

"If you believe that bullshit."

"And you don't."

"I hope not. Otherwise I've inherited the blood of a piece of shit passing itself off as a man." Matt gave a humourless laugh. "And a murderer as well."

"But you're still going to avenge him?" Now Eawynn was confused.

"I wasn't talking about Edmund. He adopted me when I was nine or so." Matt put one knife down and moved to another. "I was living on the streets and stole some food from his house. It amused him, so he took me in. Or maybe he saw something in me."

"Were your parents dead?"

"My Ma was. I can't prove it, but the whoreson who called himself my father murdered her. I know it. He used to knock her around when he'd been drinking. Then one day she was gone. He said she'd run off with another man, but Ma would never have left me and Emmy with that pig."

"Emmy?"

"My big sister, four years older than me. The shit got her pregnant, then started eyeing me up. So I ran away."

"You were nine?"

"Maybe ten. I don't know exactly when my birthday is."

"What happened to your father? Didn't you report him?"

This time Matt's laugh was for real. "You have a wonderful idea of how justice works. He was a sergeant in the city watch. Who was going to arrest him? Anyway, he wasn't my father. He sired me, and that's it. And as for what happened to him, Edmund saw to it he got a swimming lesson in the bay."

Eawynn rested her head in her hands as she struggled with the upside-down morality. Maybe this was one murder that could be excused.

Meanwhile, Matt finished honing and slid the knives into a sheath strapped around her calf. She was barefoot, but when wearing her normal boots, the knives would be completely hidden.

"Edmund Flyming was my true father."

"Do you even know what that word means?"

"What?"

"Flyming. It's a word in Cynnreord. It means an outcast, or fugitive."

"Figures." Matt did not seem put off. "His great-grandfather was one of your lot, son of a noble whatever. The family threw him out. So he started the Flyming gang." She fished inside the neck of her shirt and pulled out a heavy gold ring on a chain. "This was his."

It was clearly an old family signet ring, bearing a crest—an heirloom. Did it matter which family it belonged to? Probably not as far as Matt was concerned. She pressed the ring to her lips. Suddenly, her expression crumpled. Her mouth worked, like a child about to start bawling. Her eyes glistened. Before Eawynn could say any more, Matt let go of the ring. Her hand dropped to her ankle and then shot out. One of her knives thudded into the wooden side of the boat and stayed there.

Heedless of the downpour, Matt walked over and tugged it free. She stayed out on deck, her back to Eawynn, and her face to the sky. Letting the rain mask her tears, Eawynn realised.

Matt continued speaking, without turning round. "You think he was a gangster who deserved to die, but he never hurt anyone who didn't deserve it. He played true with those who played true with him. He answered for his own mistakes. He stood up for himself and his family. He took me in when I had nothing. Edmund was the one who cared for me, and kept me safe, and loved me. And I loved him." Raw grief was in Matt's voice. "And that's why I am going to gut the shithead who murdered him."

❖

After days on the *Blue Puffin*, dry land felt strange beneath Matt's feet. She had become so used to the heave of the deck it now seemed as if the flagstones were also bobbing up and down. Finally, she understood why sailors walked the way they did.

The port of Hyth Diepu was both like and unlike Fortaine. The buildings showed the greatest difference. Their functions were easy to recognise, but instead of the grey stone of home, they were coated in white daub. The roofs were orange tiles, rather than slate. High on the hill, overlooking the port, were the stark ruins of a Rihtcynn castle. It was reminiscent of the one at Fortaine, except the one back home had been well maintained and still commanded the town. No king or queen lived in the castle here, Matt suspected.

The ships, sailors, and stacks of cargo were the same. Activity churned up and down the quay to a roar of voices that was also familiar. Yet the differences snuck in. Mostly, she heard Tradetalk, but the local merchants and longshoremen spoke the native language among themselves. For clothing, loose knee-length tunics were common, with either baggy pants or bare legs underneath.

The town was also noticeably poorer. Many buildings looked at the point of collapse, and the repairs to the dock were slipshod, if they were done at all. The contrast in clothes and health between beggars and workers was less marked. Sailors had told Matt that Pinettale faired better than most in the aftermath of the Rihtcynn Empire. Now she had the chance to see it for herself. Maybe King Swidhelm's dynasty had worked out well for the island, although she was not about to admit it to Eawynn.

However, once she made allowances for wealth, the spectrum of humanity was identical. Apart from the upstanding folk, Matt had no trouble picking out the dock handlers, the rovers, and the sneaks. She soon spotted the sort of people she wanted, three old codgers of the female variety, gossiping on the steps of the harbourmaster's office.

They were the best source of news in the world. A thief could never have too much information about her target.

The rain had tailed off, and although the sky was overcast, the air was warm enough. Matt took a seat beside the elderly women, who eyed her inquisitively. No opportunity for fresh gossip would ever knowingly be turned away.

"Morning," Matt started.

They nodded, agreeing with her assessment of time of day.

"I was hoping for some advice and wondered whether you goodwives could help me."

"Maybe. What do you need advice about?" the youngest asked.

"I'm heading along the coast to Sideamuda. I wondered what the word is from there."

"Not good."

"How so?"

"The Rihtcynn are getting ideas again."

"That was what we were hearing in Fortaine. How bad is it?"

"They've always been prickly. Now they're doing it in style. It's getting uncomfortable, if you ain't got red hair."

"Uncomfortable?" How much of a euphemism was it?

"Lot of new rules."

"That's always a pain."

"They're backing it up with hard knocks."

"Is it safe to walk around?"

"As long as you walk where they tell you."

Matt frowned. They were unlikely to tell her to walk to Cyningesburg. "Supposing I wanted to head inland?"

"Then you'd be heading into a tight spot. I'd stay away if I was you."

"I'm afraid I've got business there. Someone I have to see."

They nodded sympathetically.

"What's your advice? Who should I ask for in Sideamuda, if I need help?"

"What sort of help?"

"Somebody who can handle things on the dock."

Matt was subjected to a long, hard examination before anyone spoke. "Fish Eye Ellis would be a good name to remember. He might help you."

She had passed the test. "Thanks."

"So you're from Fortaine, you said?" The middle crone took over.

"Yes. I've just arrived on the *Blue Puffin*."

"What's the word from there?"

It was only fair, turn and turnabout. "Edmund Flyming is dead. Murdered."

"So we hear." Bad news travels quickly. "We also heard that Gilbert, boss of the Three Rings had a hand in it."

"Just a hand, and not the one holding the knife. That was a redhead from the mainland."

"Ah." Three sets of eyes lit up. "Has this redhead returned home?"

"That's the way it looks."

The eldest spoke for the first time. "Flyming. He had a daughter, didn't he? She'd be about your age."

"Yes. She would." Matt stood and smiled. "Thank you for your time."

The *Blue Puffin* would make two more stops before Sideamuda. Two more chances to cross-check information. Matt had made a good start, and she was not yet finished. Loading and unloading the cargo would take a while. She had plenty of time to wander around the market, listen in on conversations, and see what she could overhear.

The flow of traffic took her to the main town square, laid out with rows of stalls. The air was filled with the shouts of traders. The market was an onslaught of sound and colour, and Matt was not the only one checking it out. The chance to explore a new town had drawn Eawynn off the foredeck. Matt spotted her, standing on the steps of the city hall, leaning against a pillar and studying the activity around the stalls with the expression of a natural philosopher studying an anthill.

Matt stopped at the side of the square and watched her. Having a Cynnreord-speaking redhead along might be even more helpful than Matt had anticipated. Eawynn's hair was now nearly an inch long, at the point of changing from spiky stubble to a softer crop. The dark green shirt emphasised the whiteness of her skin, and though she was too far away to see, Matt knew it matched the colour of her eyes. Her face in profile was delicately chiselled.

Matt felt her pulse start to thud. The rhythm was a hammer blow, driving an aching spike, deep into her core. With each day, the effect Eawynn had on her grew stronger. She had been attractive enough when bald and swamped in a shapeless robe. With a full head of hair, she was utterly stunning. Though it was a pointless exercise in self-torment, Matt could not stop herself lingering over the details—the set of Eawynn's narrow shoulders, her straight back and thighs, hips with just enough flare to count as womanly, the suggestion of small, firm breasts beneath her shirt. Eawynn's whole body was neatly put together.

Matt braced a hand on a wall for support, and it was not just the aftereffects of half a month at sea, troubling her balance. *Forget it. She hates you.*

So easy to say sensible things to yourself, but since when did being sensible have anything to do with it?

The *Blue Puffin* dropped anchor offshore from Sideamuda. They would dock the next morning on the high tide, The gentlest of breezes ruffled the waves. Eawynn sat on the foredeck and watched night claim the port. Light from an array of torches glinted across the water, blossoming as the sky darkened overhead.

Centuries ago, her ancestors had set out from here. Some would have been in the army that conquered Pinettale, overthrowing the feuding chieftains who had previously battled for control of the island. Others would have been the governors, scholars, and judges who followed, imposing order. As part of the Rihtcynn Empire, the island had known peace, security, and the rule of law for the first time ever. It was said a naked woman could walk from one end of the empire to the other, carrying a gold bar, and need fear nothing but the cold. Eawynn pursed her lips, then smiled. All right, that was probably poetic licence.

What would her father have said? She was returning to their ancestral homeland. The childish urge to skip and dance was hard to repress. She was really here. Tomorrow they would land, and then they would go on, across the Rihtcynn plains to Cyningesburg.

Eawynn could feel herself shaking at the thought. How would it look? She tried to imagine the pictures in her father's books, brought to life.

A sudden burst of ironic cheers interrupted her fantasies. A knot of sailors sat, playing dice in the circle of light cast by a lantern hanging off the mast. Matt was among them. Eawynn watched her accept a bottle from a sailor, take a long swig, then pass it on.

When they got to Cyningesburg, Matt would attempt to murder someone, and Eawynn would stand back and let her do it. Because then, if Matt kept her word, they would reclaim the Shewstone, so that maybe, just maybe, she would be allowed to return to the temple—the temple Eawynn was no longer so sure she wished to rejoin. Did she really want to spend the rest of her life sweeping floors?

Now that she was not hungry, or terrified by the risk of imminent assault, now that she had the time and comfort to review things, what did she want to do—other than sightseeing in an ancient city and dreaming about her ancestors? Was that really as important as a man's life?

What were her options? With the right clothes and a small cushion of funds, could she find work as a scribe? Would Matt let her go? If she parted company with Matt, how would she get back to Fortaine? Her options were limited.

Eawynn sighed and rested her head on her knees. She knew what she ought to do. When she got to Cyningesburg, she should warn Oswald Husa Eastandune. Maybe she could claim a reward. Then Matt would be captured and executed. This was not an outcome Eawynn was willing to think about.

With all her twisted ideas, mistaking revenge for justice, Matt had genuinely adored her adopted father. *How would I be reacting to my father's death, if I had actually cared a fig about him?* The gangsters had their own warped sense of honour. At least one murder that Matt's father committed had made the world a better place.

Eawynn groaned. What was happening to her morals? Right and wrong were simple enough concepts, or they used to be. Why could she not see a straight path to follow?

At the root, Matt was responsible for the confusion. The woman was uneducated, stubborn, and utterly insufferable. She was dangerous. Eawynn had known it from the moment Hilda of Gimount was introduced to her—enticingly dangerous. And now nothing was simple.

Eawynn opened her eyes and forced herself to look at Matt, half drunk and hunched over the dice. She was a lowlife thug, drinking and gambling in public. She did not have a trace of noble blood in her veins. So how could there possibly be anything attractive about her? But there was. Not just in her looks. Matt was exciting, and before meeting her, Eawynn would never have guessed how easily she would succumb to the lure.

Matt treated theft as a game. *She treated me as a game too.* Eawynn closed her eyes. Tears could still catch her by surprise. The memory of how Matt used to make her feel was still so powerful. *She cheated me. She used me. She tricked and trapped me. She is utterly untrustworthy. I hate and despise her.* Eawynn had to cling to the memory, summoning her anger and hurt, because whenever she stopped working at it, she could feel things softening at the edges. She clenched her jaw. It would be easy to fall into that trap again, if she let her guard down.

What sort of pathetic fool have I turned into?

CHAPTER SEVEN

Ship's crew and other transients must stay in the docks precinct throughout their stay in Sideamuda. Those hoping to enter the town must first get permission from the portgerefa. Anyone found on the streets during the hours of darkness, or in a state of drunkenness will receive one hundred lashes and be barred from future disembarkation. Any damages or losses incurred in the town will be recouped from the ship's cargo. Please follow these rules. It will make your stay here more pleasant for all. Good day." The harbour official turned on her heel and strode down the gangplank.

"Pleasant!" Captain Joachim spat over the side.

"Watch out. There's probably a rule against that too," Matt said.

"You sure about getting off here?"

"I have to. This is where the trail leads."

"I won't be able to take you home. We'll be steering clear of here, what with the new taxes."

"Don't blame you."

"Take care then."

"Of course." Matt clasped Captain Joachim's hand in farewell. She called to the foredeck, "You ready?"

Eawynn left her vantage point and joined Matt at the top of the gangplank.

This port was different. Matt felt it before her foot hit the quay. The white daub and red tiles were similar to other mainland towns the *Blue Puffin* had called by, but the scale of the harbour dwarfed the rest, though not all was in use. Sideamuda had been the biggest seaport of the Rihtcynn Empire; all trade with Cyningesburg had gone through it. After the empire collapsed, the vast harbour was no longer needed. Currently, less than a tenth of the berths were occupied. Ranks of mansions covered the hills overlooking the sea. Yet many were no more than empty shells. The civic buildings were overblown marble constructions of porticoes and colonnades, but everywhere showed signs of poor maintenance.

Yet the mood rather than the architecture was what struck Matt. The bustle flowed across the docks as furious as anywhere, but the sounds were muted. People were talking, but nobody yelled at the top of their lungs. Porters looked around, rather than over their carts, literally keeping their heads down. Everyone was trying not to be noticed. The upstanding folk, the merchants, traders, and sea captains, kept to the sidelines. The rovers, sneaks, and the rest had to be about as well, but for once Matt had trouble picking them out. Most surprising of all, no beggars were tagged on the edges.

What she did see were soldiers in the black cloaks and silver conical helmets of the Rihtcynn Empire. Their large oval shields carried the old imperial crest. Everywhere Matt looked clumps of them were standing sentry. All the harbour officials strutting across the flagstones had their own personal bodyguard.

A high wall rose above the red tiled roofs, protecting the town. Matt guessed the streets between sea and wall made up the docks precinct. It did not leave a lot of space for the ship's crews. How difficult would getting permission to move on be? At least she had a name to ask for. Maybe Fish Eye Ellis could help. She would look for him once they had accommodation sorted.

Matt headed for a wide street where a couple of promising signboards were hanging.

Eawynn tagged along. "Where do we go for transport to Cyningesburg?"

"We don't."

"What?"

"Frigging stupid rules. We have to stay in the dock area outside the city walls."

"You're saying we're stuck here?"

"For a while. From what sailors in Fortaine told me, Sideamuda was on the edge of the area the Rihtcynn still controlled, and they mostly let the port go its own way. Things must have changed. The Rihtcynn have tightened their grip and made things awkward for everyone else. If we want to go into the town, we have to get a special permit from someone called the portgreffer, or something like that."

"The portgerefa?"

"That was it."

"It means harbour master, in Cynnreord."

"Then why didn't they say so?" Matt was losing patience.

"Because it sounds better."

They reached the first swinging inn sign. However, the door and windows were boarded up. A dozen yards farther on, the second inn was still in business, but a small wooden red hand hung in the window, the universal token for *No Vacancies*.

"Damn." Matt looked up and down the street. No other inn signs hung above the passing heads.

"What?"

"Rooms are in short supply." Which might have been predictable, had Matt given it thought.

"Are there other inns around here?"

"I don't know."

"Can we get a pass from the portgerefa so we can look for a room in town?"

"I don't know."

"Who do we ask to find out?"

"I don't know."

"Is there anything you do know, that you'd like to share with me?"

"We need to find somewhere to stay before nightfall, else if we're caught on the streets we'll be flogged."

"Wonderful." Eawynn's voice oozed sarcasm.

"And don't get drunk."

"I didn't intend to."

"Really? I'd been thinking I could use a drink."

"So what do we do?"

"We stand here and ask each other pointless questions, until someone with a big stick comes to collect us."

"There's no need to take that tone."

"It's the one I reserve for people acting like idiots."

"And where does wasting time, throwing abuse around come in your scale of idiocy?"

"Somewhere below—" A heavy hand landed on Matt's shoulder. Their raised voices had attracted attention.

"Haebbe thu aenigne wea, freo?" The soldier was clearly asking Eawynn a question.

"Eall is wel, thance thu."

"Sy beonde heo sum dracu?"

"Na."

The soldier let go of Matt's shoulder, though he kept a stern eye on her, while continuing his conversation with Eawynn. Whatever she said had an effect. The soldier stood up straighter and adopted a courteous manner. After a few minutes of animated talking, with much gesturing between the quay and the town, he smacked his fist on his chest in a salute and marched away.

"Neat trick. What did you say?" Matt asked once he was gone.

"I apologised for my oafish servant."

"Servant!"

"You."

"I guessed." Matt bit back anything else she might say. With Eawynn's looks it was undeniably the best way to play things. "What else did he say?"

"He told me where the portgerefan office is. Also a couple of recommendations for lodgings in town."

"Do you think you can get an entry permit?"

"He thought there'd be no problem for a visiting priestess and her servant. Come on. Follow me." Eawynn handed over her pack and smiled sweetly. "And it'll look best if you carry all the baggage."

❖

The guard captain at the gate studied the permits Eawynn held out, taking slightly longer over the one for Matt, and then waved them through.

"Welcome to our city, ma'am."

"Thank you."

They strolled up the street, with Matt staying a deferential two steps to the rear, carrying both packs. Eawynn fought to control her grin. A pity walking backward was impractical. She could not see Matt's face and had to settle for imagining how little her current role would be to the brash thief's liking.

The nearest of the recommended lodgings, Se Seofan Steorran, was within sight of the gates. Even in this short distance, Eawynn could tell the pace of life was noticeably different inside the city wall, quieter and more sedate. Cynnreord was all she heard spoken loudly, although she caught mutterings in Tradetalk and other languages.

The social stratification was evident. With few exceptions, those making a display of their wealth were of Rihtcynn descent, and the richer the attire, the redder the hair. Knee-length tunics in red and purple, covered in intricate gold embroidery was the predominant fashion.

The Thraelas, the servants and workers, came from all over the known world, a legacy of empire. Skin colour varied from dark cream to jet black. Most hair was brown, but Eawynn spotted one or two yellow heads from the far north.

Many of the poorest had iron collars around their necks. Eawynn frowned and looked away. Slavery was not unknown, even on Pinettale, although it had fallen into disuse and was no longer officially condoned. Those who owned slaves did not flaunt the fact. But of course, it had been commonplace in the old empire.

The dark-skinned owner of Se Seofan Steorran spoke Cynnreord fluently, but with a strong accent. She bobbed up and down as she talked, as if fearing one curtsy was not enough. "You do us honour by your presence, my lady."

"You have a free room?"

"Yes, my lady, if it please you. Allow me to show you the way."

"My servant will take care of the payment. Settle the bill with her." Matt had assured her money would not be an issue.

"Very good, my lady. Do you know how long you'll be staying?"

"No. Is that likely to be a problem?"

"Oh no, my lady. As long as you wish to stay. We would be honoured, my lady."

The servile grovelling was all decidedly wearing. Eawynn was relieved when they finally shut the door. A feeling apparently shared by Matt, who dropped both packs and collapsed onto the larger of the two beds with a groan.

"I think that's supposed to be mine."

Matt lifted her head. "You're joking."

"No. Supposing someone comes in. Don't we need to maintain the show?"

"They'll knock."

"And you want to scuttle across before I call enter?"

Matt stomped four steps to the narrow bunk and threw herself down in the identical position as before without uttering a word, but her face said it all. Again, Eawynn had to fight to hide her grin. She looked out the window, which commanded a view of a small square with a well in the middle.

After a while, Matt sighed and swivelled into a sitting position on the edge of her bed. "I guess the first thing is to see if Oswald Husa Eastandune is still here. He's a priest of Liffrea. We could go to the temple. I'd say it's a safe bet there's one in town."

Liffrea had been the patron god of the Rihtcynn emperors. Predictably, his worship had declined with the empire's collapse. On Pinettale, his following had held up better than in most other places, partly because King Swidhelm had adopted him, and partly because in all the myths, he had a boat. Despite this, even on Pinettale Liffrea had lost his place as King of the Gods. However, in lands where the Rihtcynn stayed in control, his position would be unchanged.

Eawynn nodded. "I'm sure there is. But I should go on my own."

"What? Why?"

"Because we don't have the clothes to pass you off as rich, and you don't have the looks to pass yourself off as Rihtcynn."

"What does that count for?"

"From what we've seen so far, pretty much everything. The soldier at the docks was ready to arrest you, just for raising your voice to me."

"Yes. And I've learned that lesson, thank you."

"Could you fall over yourself grovelling to me, like the landlady here?"

Matt's expression was her answer.

"You won't be able to understand what anyone we need to talk to is saying. All you can do is attract unwanted attention."

Matt gave in. "What do I do while you're gone?"

Eawynn walked out, smiling. "You could unpack my things."

❖

Matt glared at the back of the door after Eawynn left. "If that's what you want." She spoke aloud.

At the foot of Eawynn's bed was a large chest. Matt lifted the lid, then upended Eawynn's pack into it. For good measure, she tossed the empty bag on top. It was very childish and did not make her feel any better.

Matt wandered to the window and looked out. Summer was approaching, and Sideamuda lay far south of Pinettale. The midday sun was high overhead, and the building's shadows were no more than narrow bands along the edge. She should have gone with Eawynn, Matt thought. Maybe she did not speak the language, but she understood the streets in a way an ex-priestess could not. The games were being played in a different style here, but they would be the same games at heart. Should she go out and explore, or would it be more sensible to wait for Eawynn's return?

A door opened below, and an elderly woman tottered out, dressed in old sacks and carrying a wooden bucket. The hostel employee hooked the bucket on the rope over the well and turned the crank. As she did so, her long, unbraided hair fell forward, revealing the iron collar around her scrawny neck. Not a hostel employee—hostel property. Matt felt her lip curl in distaste. The Rihtcynn had not changed.

A couple of red-haired adolescents strolled into the square, a boy and girl arm in arm, clearly enjoying the warm sunlight as much as they were enjoying each other's company. They passed the well as the elderly slave completed winding up the full bucket, but the rope slipped in her hand as she tried to unhook it, and a splash fell on the girl's shoe.

The reaction was immediate. The boy's backhand sent the old woman flying. She lay, curled on the ground, as a succession of kicks followed. Her only action was to shield her head with her arms. All the while, the boy shouted in Cynnreord. Without knowing the words, Matt had no trouble understanding the meaning.

After a final kick, the boy stepped back, but instead of leaving the old woman alone he drew a short sword. Matt took a half step, about to run down, but what could she do? Even if she got there in time, would the boy pay any attention to her? Matt was not a slave, but neither was she Rihtcynn. It was not as if she could speak any language he would admit to understanding. What was the risk she would simply become a second victim?

Two new figures appeared in the square, soldiers in their black cloaks, presumably attracted by the shouting. They stayed by the entrance and called over. "Hwaet alimpende?"

"Ic alaere hie beon eadmedlic." The boy showed not the slightest concern at being caught attacking an old woman.

Another couple of exchanges followed. The last was clearly a funny joke, since the soldiers laughed loudly and went.

The boy turned back to the slave on the ground. He placed the tip of his sword against her flat chest and shouted some more. Matt could see the hopeless fear in the woman's eyes, but at last the boy stepped back and sheathed his sword. He settled for kicking the bucket across the square, then linked his arm with the girl who had watched impassively throughout. Smiling, the pair continued their midday stroll in the sunshine.

The old woman rolled painfully to her knees. She stared at the alleyway where the adolescents had gone. Her expression was bitter, but resigned. Her hand lifted to the iron band around her neck as she adjusted its set on her collar bone. The gesture was habitual, Matt sensed, possibly the woman was unaware she was doing it.

Matt drew a deep breath and turned from the window. Her permit from the portgerefa lay on a table where Eawynn had dropped it. Maybe she would not go out on the streets, not until Eawynn had translated every last word for her. Matt looked over her shoulder. Down in the square, the slave reclaimed her empty bucket and hobbled back to the well. Matt watched her repeat the drawing of water.

The Rihtcynn had not changed.

❖

Once satisfaction at getting one up on Matt had worn off, Eawynn experienced a twinge of anxiety. The sensation did not begin to compare with the first days after her expulsion from the temple, but she did not feel at ease, out alone on unfamiliar streets. Maybe she should have brought Matt along. Not that she experienced any difficulties. The rich ignored her and everyone else got out of her way.

The temple of Liffrea was unlikely to be anywhere other than the centre of town. Eawynn still thought it best to check. She stopped a young man, pushing a hand cart full of pots.

"Excuse me."

He cowered as if wanting to hide under his cart. "Yes, m-m-ma'am, m-m-my l-lady."

"The Temple of Liffrea, which way is it?"

He pointed up the street. "Th-th-th-"

He dared not meet her eyes. Was he simple-minded, terrified, or both? Then Eawynn noticed the iron collar around his neck.

By the time she reached the temple, her feeling of unease had shifted. She was no longer so anxious for herself, but she was less happy about what she was seeing. Her father had spoken of the centuries under Rihtcynn rule as a time of wonder, enjoyed by all. Eawynn had been doubtful whether life was ever so harmonious. These doubts were hardening. The number of slaves was disconcerting. They acted docile, even content, but it was an act, Eawynn was sure. A couple of times she caught angry, hostile expressions, quickly concealed.

Meanwhile, the Rihtcynn and their rich allies seemed oblivious to the fact they were outnumbered by people who had no reason to feel anything but ill will for them. The soldiers were in control for now. The Thraelas were not challenging the social order, but given the right prod, things could change quickly. Eawynn could sense it in the air. She hurried on her way. Perhaps she should be a little more worried for herself.

The Temple of Liffrea was built along familiar lines. Eawynn entered the main sanctuary, dominated by a statue to the god. The open space was three times that belonging to Anberith, back in Fortaine, but the state of repair was poor. The surrounding wall was crumbling in places, and grass sprouted between cracks in the flagstones.

A ceremony was in progress when she arrived. Eawynn stayed through the cycle of chants, analogous to those she knew, although sung in Cynnreord. This, to her mind, was an improvement, unlike the sacrifice of a bull at the climax. The bellowing of the dying animal and blood spraying into the air was something she was very pleased they had abandoned in Fortaine.

When the ceremony ended, Eawynn hurried to catch up with one of the priests before they left the sanctuary.

"Excuse me, Holy Brother."

He blinked, clearly unsure how to address her in return. "Yes?"

"I wondered if somebody I met recently was here."

"Who?"

"Oswald Husa Eastandune."

Eawynn tried to maintain a calm expression. This might easily turn out badly, yet there was no indirect way to get the information. What could she do, hang around the temple and see if she overheard a mention of him?

The name was evidently familiar to the priest. His blink rate increased. "I'm afraid you've missed him. Our beloved brother is gone. He passed through Sideamuda a half month ago."

Eawynn tried to look disappointed rather than relieved. "That's a shame. I found him..." She had intended to say helpful, but sensed this would not fit the priest's expectations. "Inspirational."

"As he is to us all." The smile said she had picked the right word.

Eawynn inclined her head in farewell and left the temple. What to do next? She could go back to the hostel and talk things over with Matt, but what was there to discuss? The Shewstone and Oswald had gone to Cyningesburg, and they had to follow.

Since people were living in the old capital, they needed goods brought in from the outside world, which meant wagons must go from the port. She knew where the portgerefan office was in relation to the harbour, and could find her way there. If the staff were not able to arrange travel to Cyningesburg, Eawynn was sure they would know who could.

From the plaza outside the Temple of Liffrea, a wide avenue ran, arrow straight, down the hillside to the harbour, passing through the most imposing of the town gates, double the size of the ones they had entered by. It would be a more direct route back to the portgerefan office.

Her permit got Eawynn through these gates as easily as the others. However, here she was greeted by a sight she and Matt had missed before. On either side of the gate stood two gibbets, each with a hanging iron cage. Two cages contained shrivelled corpses, and one was empty. The last held a figure whose age was hard to guess, due to the filthy, emaciated state. Only the beard let Eawynn be certain of the condemned man's gender. Breath whistled through his scab-encrusted lips. His eyes were open and moving, tracking the flight of seagulls above the mastheads. Eawynn assumed the convict was being given water, but not food, and was in the final stages of starving to death. Sickened, she hurried by.

At the first intersection, Eawynn turned aside. The lane was narrow, crowded, and stank, but she was pleased to be out of sight of the gibbets and their contents. Even if it was not the best route, the dock precinct was too small to get lost in. At the next junction, she paused, trying to get her bearings. In her head, the portgerefan office was to the left, but the alley looked even less inviting than the one she was on. Should she go back to the main road and simply follow it down to the quay?

Without warning, Eawynn was struck on the back of her head, but not by a punch. Something had been thrown at her. Something soft enough to startle rather than hurt. A lump of horse dung dropped from her hair to her shoulder and rolled off. Eawynn turned in time to see two children running off. Except the girl did not look where she was going and cannoned into a patrolling soldier. The boy got away.

The captured child stopped struggling after the fourth blow she received, possibly because she had been knocked senseless, but that did not save her from another three. Other soldiers arrived, including one with a captain's emblem on his chest, who took command.

"Are you all right, ma'am?"

"Nothing a wash won't fix."

"Don't fear. Your assailant will be severely dealt with."

"I..." Eawynn paused. Was the beating not sufficient? She thought of the gibbet. "What will happen to the child?"

"That'll be for the judge, ma'am. Most likely she'll be whipped or sold as a slave."

Eawynn was appalled. The girl was young, not into her teens. "It was just a childish prank. I'm not hurt. And look, her hands are clean. She wasn't the one who threw it."

The captain shrugged. "Doesn't matter. She ran. She'll do. The Thraelas need the lesson to keep them in their place."

Six black-cloaked soldiers were now at the scene. They formed a cordon around the prisoner and Eawynn. This was when she became fully aware they now stood in the middle of an empty space. The bustle of the docks had drawn back. People watched from the edges with sullen, guarded expressions. Nobody appeared on the verge of doing or saying anything, but it was not hard to sense the repressed anger.

The captain put his hand on Eawynn's arm. "The docks are not a good place to walk alone, and certainly not until the mood calms down. Please, let me escort you to safety."

"I was intending to visit the portgerefan office."

"You have business there, ma'am?"

"I need to visit Cyningesburg and wanted to sort out travel."

The captain looked surprised. "The portgerefa isn't the person you need to talk to. You'll need authorisation. Come, I'll point you to the Gehrecsele."

In formation, the soldiers marched back past the dying convict in his cage and through the gates. The girl was dragged along, unable to walk, though at some stage she recovered enough to start crying.

Eawynn could not refrain from making one more appeal. "I really am all right. Could you not let the child go?"

The captain treated her to a hard, searching look. "You're not suggesting I neglect my duty? I'm responsible for upholding the law. We cannot let these animals think they can get away with insolence."

"No. I didn't mean that, but..." What argument could she use? "I'm a visiting priestess of Anbeorht. My goddess commands me to show mercy to the young."

"My understanding was the silver lady of the moon is the agent of fate, dealing to all the hand they deserve."

It was the aspect of Anbeorht which had given her dominion over prophesy. "Yes, but she's also the goddess of childbirth."

"Then her care is for Rihtcynn mothers, not the children of Thraelas."

Nothing Eawynn could say was going to help, and she might already have gone too far. The captain was looking at her with outright suspicion. The girl was hauled away, but the captain stayed close to Eawynn. He did not lay a hand on her, but she had the feeling he was on the verge of arresting her also.

"If you please, ma'am, I'll escort you."

They walked up the hill. The Gehrecsele, or government hall, was on the same plaza as the Temple of Liffrea. The captain started to lead Eawynn up the imposing flight of steps.

Eawynn made one last request. "Thank you, Officer. Now I know where it is. Before I make my case, I'd like to return to my lodging, get myself clean, and change my clothes."

"I thought you suffered no harm from the assault. Regardless, I'm sure the attendants will make allowances." From the set of his lips, he was determined to see her handed over to the authorities inside.

Did it matter what she wore? There were no clothes in the hostel that would make her look impressive enough to bluster her way to Cyningesburg. She would have to find another way to swing the argument. Eawynn let herself be led inside the echoing entrance hall.

The captain hailed a woman dressed in a purple tunic, with the emblem of a hawk hanging around her neck. "Madam Examiner, this woman tells me she's a priestess of Anbeorht and that she wishes to go to Cyningesburg." He smiled at Eawynn. "Good fortune in your endeavour, ma'am." His tone implied she would need it.

Over the following hour, Eawynn learned that asking to visit Cyningesburg provoked a definite reaction. She was passed from one official to the next, while the rooms and uniforms became steadily more ornate. Then the decor shifted the other way. The doors got heavier, the windows smaller and soldiers started to outnumber civilians. The Gehrecsele would contain law courts and the associated holding prison. As she passed the top of stone steps, a scream echoed from underground. Of course, there would be dungeons. Eawynn wondered if she was about to be taken down into the darkness, but her escort led her on.

Eventually, she was shown into a cell-like room and the soldiers took up stations outside the door. Bars were anchored over the window, but she was not a prisoner—yet. A man and a woman sat waiting for her. The woman wore priestly robes; the man was in civilian dress. They did not introduce themselves.

These were the important ones, Eawynn was sure. These were the people who could give her permission to travel, or could ensure she never left the building. Luckily, she did not need to worry about appearing nervous. Excessive confidence would be suspicious.

The man indicated for Eawynn to take a seat. "We understand you wish to visit Cyningesburg. May we ask why?"

"Yes. Of course." Eawynn had used her time to decide how to play things. Would it work? She would only get the one chance. "I used to be a priestess of Anbeorht, in Fortaine."

"Used to be?" The woman cut in. "How have you left?"

"I confess, I absconded. But I had my reasons."

"Go on."

"I was responsible for looking after a holy artefact, the Shewstone. I tended the sacrarium where it was kept."

Both officials responded to mention of the Shewstone, exchanging a glance, although they said nothing. Eawynn tried not to look relieved, but her story would be on much surer footing if they already knew about it.

"Our high priestess, Insightful Sister Oracle, used it to foretell the future. I was a mere junior. I assisted her, though I never consulted the Shewstone myself. Then one day, when I was alone in the sacrarium, the stone spoke to me. It told me it would be leaving Fortaine, and I was to follow it, to Cyningesburg."

"The Shewstone spoke to you? You're sure?"

"Yes. I mean, at first I didn't believe it. I thought I was maybe going down with a fever and imagining things, but it happened three times. Then, the day after the last time it spoke, the Shewstone vanished." Eawynn held out her hands, palms up. "I hadn't thought it possible for the Shewstone to go like that. So the speaking can't have been my imagination. The Shewstone must have been foretelling the future, and it wants me to go to Cyningesburg. "

"So you followed it?"

"Yes. I had to. I tried to tell the temple elders, but nobody believed me. It was the hardest decision of my life, but I had to obey. I left the temple and made my way here." Eawynn looked the man in the eye. "The Shewstone is in Cyningesburg, isn't it?"

He sunk back in his chair, rested his elbows on the arms, and interlaced his fingers, studying Eawynn intently. "Yes." He looked at his companion. "Do we need to discuss this further?"

The woman pursed her lips in thought. "No. I don't think we need to." There was the faintest stress on the word *we*.

He nodded and faced Eawynn. "You should definitely go to Cyningesburg. There are people who'll want to talk to you."

The wave of relief made Eawynn lightheaded. She had not been totally successful in persuading herself this was the only possible outcome. It did not matter whether the officials in Sideamuda believed her story or not. Whoever had ordered the theft of the Shewstone would want to know how she had discovered where it had gone.

She now had the time it took to travel to Cyningesburg to work on her story. She had to convince Oswald Husa Eastandune she was telling the truth. Otherwise there was a nasty risk he would have her executed. *One day at a time.*

"A supply caravan is leaving the day after tomorrow. You'll have a place on it," the man said. "Present yourself and your baggage on the docks outside the portgerefan office at dawn."

"Will I need to bring my own supplies?"

"Everything you need for the journey will be provided."

"May I bring a servant to wait on me?"

"No servants."

"Will I have to take care of my own belongings?" Eawynn worked on sounding incredulous.

The man sighed. "The only Thraelas permitted in Cyningesburg are slaves. If you're certain you require personal assistance, there's a market in the Golden Lion Plaza every morning. I'm sure you'll be able to pick up someone suitable for your needs."

"Thank you."

Eawynn was escorted from the Gehrecsele, coughing repeatedly in the struggle not to laugh. Matt was not going to like it at all.

❖

"A slave!"

"That's what they said."

"You're serious?"

"It's the only way."

Matt wrapped one hand around the other, clenched in a fist. Maybe Eawynn was telling the truth, but she was enjoying it far too much. Matt started her next sentence three times before giving up.

Eawynn was smirking. "Come on. Don't you think I did well? I've got us both on a caravan to Cyningesburg."

"Yeah. You're a natural liar."

"You don't need to be like that."

"I mean it. You told the bare minimum of lies you had to, and as much truth as you could get away with. It's an art. Congratulations. I couldn't have done better myself. As I said, you're a natural." Eawynn pouted a little, but Matt could tell her amusement was undented.

"We'll need new clothes. How are we off for money?"

"Some sacking for me shouldn't be too expensive." Matt tried not to sound bothered. She might as well take it like an adult, if only to deny Eawynn the pleasure of winding her up. "But as long as I have hands, money isn't a problem."

"You're planning on stealing it?"

"It's what I do."

"Supposing you get caught?"

"I won't."

Eawynn's smirk had gone into retreat. Then it shifted to within an inch of awkwardness. "I suppose we'll have to get a collar for you."

"I'll take care of it." Matt looked out the window. The afternoon was progressing, but she still had a clear two hours before dusk. "I better go now. We've only got the rest of today and tomorrow to sort it out."

"I'll come with you."

"No."

"You think I'll get in the way of your thievery?"

"I'd prefer not having an audience gasp at the wrong time. But more importantly, we should avoid being seen together, until you present me as your latest acquisition."

"I guess we might run into someone."

"Might? I'd lay money on you being followed back here."

"Oh." Eawynn looked suitably rattled.

"We just have to hope they're not too diligent about questioning the landlady."

Matt had no difficulty spotting the watcher in the street outside, but the young man showed no reaction to her. So either he did not know, or did not care about Eawynn's servant. Even so, Matt took her time, making sure she was not tailed before continuing with her plans, which involved finding someone with a large purse.

The mark she selected was a portly gentleman with thinning red hair. His shirt was of the loose smock style favoured in the region, except he had eaten a few too many big dinners for it to be loose. The material was riding up over his expanded waist, revealing the heavy coin purse tied to his belt. Even better, difficulty reaching over his own stomach meant the knot he had tied was likely to slip apart all by itself. Even had Matt not needed the money, he would still have been far too tempting a target to ignore.

The scene she had witnessed from the window told her that colliding with him, no matter how accidental she made it seem, was not wise. She would need a different opportunity. Fortunately, this did not take long. They soon encountered a street corner gathering, listening to someone ranting from the top of a block. Matt could not tell if the speaker was a preacher, a politician, or a rather bad salesman. Not that it mattered. She sped up to enter the crowd a step behind her mark and emerged the other side with his purse hidden inside her jacket.

In a back alley, she transferred a little of the money to her own purse, hid the rest in her boots and left the empty pouch on the ground. This turned out to be a wise move. Before allowing her through the city gate, the soldiers subjected her to a cursory search. This was most likely a case of following rules, judging by their lack of thoroughness. The soldiers seemed otherwise content with her permit, and the story of a mistress who must have fresh fish off a newly docked boat rather than day old stuff from the market in town.

"Plaice or sole. She likes the flat fish."

"Huh."

"Do you know what the catch is today?"

"Ascest se fiscereas."

A firm shove sent Matt stumbling on her way. The soldiers understood Tradetalk, but took it as an insult if you tried to make them speak it.

Matt reached the waterside and stood on the dock looking around. The *Blue Puffin* had just left, which was mixed news. She would have liked a safe base to work from, but on the positive side, it meant there was nobody to question about Eawynn's arrival in Sideamuda.

Normally, Matt would have chosen a central vantage point to stand while she got a feel for the docks. But as she had already seen, the style of the game in Sideamuda was different from the one she was used to. Standing in the same spot for too long would attract attention. She would have to keep moving and act like someone on their way to do something legitimate somewhere else. Yet it was still the same game. All she had to do was study the ripples in the action, see who was watching and who was being watched.

It took Matt two complete lengths of the harbour before she found the person she was after, also striding purposefully along the quay with no sign of getting any closer to his destination. He was a nondescript man, wearing ordinary clothes, who could walk a line through the chaotic crowd as straight as the soldiers' patrols. People got out of his way and did not look back.

The dock handler gave Matt a thoughtful look when she fell in beside him, but said nothing until they reached an empty spot on the quay, allowing a few moments when they would not be overheard.

"Can I help you?"

"I'm looking for Fish Eye Ellis."

"You've found him. What do you want?"

"Could we go to a tavern somewhere, for a drink and a chat?"

"About what?"

"I'd like to buy something. I'm hoping you can help."

CHAPTER EIGHT

Eawynn fastened the studded belt around her waist. The loose pants felt odd, flapping against her ankles when she walked, but the style allowed easy movement and would be cool. The yellow tunic fell to just below her hips and was decorated around the hem with geometric patterns. The matching cloak was big enough to go around her twice. The weight was heavy on her shoulders but would be a welcome protection against the dawn chill. By all accounts, Cyningesburg would swelter in summer and freeze in winter, and the style of dress was designed to meet both extremes.

Her clothes had none of the ornate embroidery seen on the Sideamuda streets, but were good enough to sit comfortably in the lower end of the Rihtcynn costume range. All were paid for with stolen money. She grimaced at the thought. It meant her current attire was no different from anything else she had worn or eaten since setting foot in The Jolly Wagoner. The knowledge troubled her, but what other option did she have?

Eawynn gave the room one last check for missed belongings but found nothing. Matt had taken everything except the new clothes when she left the previous evening. Nothing remained for Eawynn to do, apart from get herself down to the portgerefan office.

The landlady was bobbing up and down by the front door. "Farewell, my lady. It's been a privilege to have you under our roof."

"It's been a pleasant stay."

"You're very kind, my lady."

"I believe my servant settled the bill."

"Indeed she did, my lady."

"She was fortunate to find quick passage back to Fortaine. I've purchased a maid to attend me hereafter."

"Very wise, my lady."

Eawynn pressed a silver coin into the woman's hand. She would happily have got rid of all the stolen coins, but that would be unwise. The landlady would certainly think it strange. Anyway, Matt would only go and steal more.

"Farewell."

"You're very generous, my lady. Safe travels. May the gods guide your footsteps."

The streets were quiet in the early hours, but not empty. The ratio of slaves to free-folk was higher than Eawynn had seen before. She felt guilty at being relieved there was also a strong presence of black-cloaked soldiers. The sentries on the city gates waved her through. Eawynn hesitated. Who knew when she would next have a chance to bathe? She had no wish to go all the way to Cyningesburg with horse dung in her hair, should another person want to use her as a target.

"I wonder if I could have an escort to the portgerefan office?"

At the sergeant's nod, two soldiers joined her for the short walk to the quay. Nine open wagons were drawn up, each pulled by a team of huge, shaggy horses. Longshoremen were busy loading barrels and crates. Other people, presumably the wagon crews, were tending to the horses and harness.

Three Rihtcynn stood watching, two men and a woman. All were dressed in well-worn travel clothes—long, dusty cloaks with muddy hems, sweat-stained shirts, and tough, leather boots and gloves. Despite their appearance, their keen oversight of the work, along with their self-assured posture, left Eawynn in no doubt they were in charge of the caravan.

"Excuse me. I was told to report here. My name is Eawynn Husa Achangrena."

The older man looked her up and down. "Yes. We were told about you. I am Hunwald Husa Earncynna, caravan master. These are my deputies."

But what were you told? The tight smiles and curious looks implied something.

"I bought a slave at the market. She was supposed to arrive here with my bags."

"She has. Over there." Hunwald pointed. He looked as if he might say more, but the action of a longshoreman claimed his attention. "Hey, you. Be careful with that. You're going to drop it." He marched off.

Eawynn nodded to the deputies and went in search of Matt. The caravan master had shown no surprise or suspicion when she spoke of buying a slave. She had gone to the market the previous morning, with the watcher tailing her, and Matt tailing the watcher. Or so Matt said. For her part, Eawynn had been unable to pick the spy out from the crowd. According to Matt, the watcher had spent more time studying the attributes of naked whores on sale than checking up on what Eawynn was doing. He had not stayed close enough to know she had not actually made a purchase.

Eawynn found Matt sitting cross-legged on the ground at the other side of the wagons, gazing out to sea. She was clad in beige, coarse-weave cloth, garments so baggy the style was hard to judge. Thick soled leather sandals were on her feet, and around her neck was an iron collar.

The sight pulled Eawynn up short. Before now, she had found the concept of slavery distasteful, but that had been in the abstract, even when walking by slaves on the streets. *This is what slavery means.* Eawynn had not anticipated the effect seeing the collar would have on her. The symbol turned someone she knew into a possession. *So what does it feel like to Matt, wearing it?* Eawynn swallowed hard and carried on walking.

Matt scrambled up and ducked her head. "Good morning, my lady."

Did you bid a slave good morning? What was the etiquette of this? Eawynn felt absurdly self-conscious, playing a role she suddenly had no stomach for. "Follow me."

She walked far enough to be out of earshot of those around the wagons. "How are you doing?"

"Fine."

"Your contacts had what you wanted?" Matt had been vague, but the collar must have been part of it.

"Yes."

Eawynn saw the collar was formed from two curved iron strips. On either side of Matt's neck, the ends projected out far enough to be fastened together. The heads of large rivets, a half inch in diameter, were flattened discs on each side. A hammer must have been used to seal the collar. A blacksmith's saw would be needed to open it. And Matt had allowed it to be done. Eawynn had trouble tearing her eyes away.

"They're fakes," Matt said.

"Pardon?"

"The rivets. They're fakes. The ends screw together. It doesn't show, because the sticky-out bit covers the join. I saw you were looking." Matt grinned. "I could be out of this in seconds. Probably best if I don't demonstrate right now."

"How did you get it?"

"I was sure there'd be some way to fake collars. I just asked the right man, a dock handler."

"He's an official?"

"Not one the authorities recognise."

A shout rang out from the caravan master. "All aboard. We're rolling."

Matt said, "The bags are on the second wagon from the front. That's where you sit as well."

"What about you?"

Matt's smile took on a wry twist. "I think I walk."

❖

Walking would not have been so bad, had it not been walking at the back in clouds of dust. On top of this, wheels got stuck in ruts with annoying regularity, so Matt and the other slaves had to help shove the heavy wagons free.

The caravan consisted of the wagons, each with a two-man crew, six mounted soldiers as guards, five passengers in the second wagon, including Eawynn, and eight slaves on foot. The caravan master on a pony trotted in the lead, while his deputies were drivers on the first and last wagons. Two scouts also set out with the caravan. However, since they apparently felt their job consisted of staying out of sight at all times, their inclusion in the reckoning was open to dispute.

For the first half dozen miles, the road was wide and well marked, passing through farmland. The fields were vineyards and olive groves, laid out in neat rows. Herds of goats rambled across the rougher patches of ground. Three small villages lay on route. Children stopped to watch them pass, their attention clearly on the uniformed soldiers, but adults continued their work with barely a glance. The caravan also went by scattered farmhouses, where chickens dared each other to run across the road between the lumbering wagon wheels.

To the south, a high mountain chain threw snowy peaks against the blue sky. Their route was heading for the one obvious break in the wall. Before long, the road began to rise, skirting the foothills. By midday, Sideamuda was laid out behind them, a toy town on the edge of the shimmering sea. The view might have caught the fancy of the caravan master, who called the stop for lunch.

The sun was hot enough to have sweat trickling down Matt's back, and the dust had given her a raw cough. She would have been grateful for the break and a chance to catch her breath. However, a number of jobs needed doing, and nobody else would lift a finger when slaves were available.

The lead wagon contained supplies for the journey, the food, and tents. Matt helped prepare the meal, fetching water from a stream. Others slaves led the unharnessed horses down to drink. The lunch was simple fare—sliced sausage, cheese, and bread, with dates and olives, all washed down with weak wine and followed by small spiced cakes. Magically, the two scouts appeared for the first time since leaving Sideamuda the instant wine was poured.

Only once the free-folk were content did the slaves get their even simpler meal of dried fruit, heavy rye bread, and tough jerky, with water to drink.

Matt joined the circle of slaves and sank to the ground, grateful for the chance to rest. She took a bite of her jerky. It required a lot of chewing for not a lot of gain.

"Someone's lost their dog, I see." The man sitting beside Matt was equally unimpressed.

"Or their boots."

Other suggestions followed.

The slaves were mostly young and fit. Three belonged to the caravan master and had taken the lead in allocating tasks. Two others, a man and a woman, were the property of another passenger. They sat holding each other's hand and saying little. A stocky man was attendant to the soldier captain. The last slave was the oldest, although not past middle age. Her exact state of ownership was unclear. None of the Rihtcynn had shown possessiveness around her, or given her orders, and she had been excused from wagon shoving duties.

She joined in. "The really sad thing is, by the time we reach Cyningesburg, you'll be looking back fondly on this jerky."

"How long will it take to get there? Do you know?" Matt asked. Eawynn had already told her the distance was over three hundred miles.

"Eighteen days. The toughest bit is in two days' time. After that it's an easy run across the plains. Except we'll be on bread and water for the last three days."

"Why?"

She pointed at the caravan master's slaves. "They can tell you."

One pulled a face. "The boss skims the money he's given for our food. He daren't touch the free-folks' rations. But he knows three days on bread and water won't kill us."

"He'd have us on bread and water the whole way," another added. "But we might not be strong enough to pull the wagons out of holes."

"I pity you," the older woman said. "I only do this twice a year, at most. You're at it all the time."

"Huh. Tell me about it. The old bastard."

Matt took another bite of jerky and tried to be appreciative. At least water was not in short supply and cleared the dust from her throat.

Much sooner than she would have liked, the call to harness the horses and get moving rang out. Matt slipped the last of her jerky into a pouch, either to chew on the road or keep for the days of bread and water.

The road was becoming less well travelled, which had dual benefits. The ruts were shallower, and a patchy grass covering survived, cutting down on the dust. The walk was still tiring, but no longer such an ordeal, especially once the terrain flattened out. The uplands soil was stony, unsuited to agriculture. Flocks of sheep and goats were the only farming activity.

Matt fell in beside the older woman, who seemed to be knowledgeable and willing to speak freely. "Good to meet you. My name's Matt."

The woman smiled. "I don't know about good. Certainly not here. Maybe good in a tavern a long way away."

"Well, there's that."

"My name's Bertana, by the way." She spoke with a heavy accent.

"I'm guessing there's not much in the way of taverns in Cyningesburg."

"There's a few, just none you or I would be allowed in." She gave Matt a sharp look. "You've not been a slave long?"

"No. Not long at all."

"I thought as much. I could tell by the way you hold your head."

"Oh." Matt would watch carefully and adapt.

"Do you speak Cynnreord?"

"Only a few words. I guess I'll have to learn."

"You only need a few words, enough to understand orders. Slaves mostly stick to Tradetalk."

"Don't the owners want us to speak Cynnreord?"

"As I said, enough to understand orders. Rihtcynn like to think they're the only ones clever enough to speak Cynnreord properly."

"Being an arrogant arsehole obviously comes with the blood."

"Maybe, but I wouldn't recommend saying it aloud. Some slaves will happily try to earn favour by reporting you."

Matt grimaced. A rat was as low as you could get. "Thanks for the warning. But what about you? Have you been a slave long?"

"All my life. I was born one, in Cyningesburg."

"So you know the city well."

"Not as well as I used to."

"You've been away?"

"The city's changed."

"How?"

"It's all down to Theodcwen Aedilhild Wisa Mearcweada Bregu Rihtcynn."

"Who?"

"The theodcwen, or great queen, which translates as empress in Tradetalk. She became elder of the Mearcweada clan when her father died, six years ago."

"She's changed things?"

"Oh, yes. The Rihtcynn have been in a sulk ever since their empire collapsed. They had their puffed up attitude, but they were going nowhere. Even around here their grip was failing. More folk were moving in, pushing them back. Sideamuda was a free port, and everyone was getting along with each other just fine, so I've been told. Cyningesburg was deserted most of the year."

"But you were born there?"

"In the Temple of Liffrea. The priests kept it going. The tribes would gather for ceremonies a few times a year and listen to the old diehards, who still thought they ruled the world. Or that they ought to, and everything else was a temporary setback. But, like I said, they weren't doing anything about it, just sitting around sulking."

"Then the old emperor died?"

"Aedilhild's father never claimed to be emperor. He was elder of the Mearcweada clan—that's what Wisa means, as opposed to Husa, which means *of the house*. There are twelve main Rihtcynn clans, and dozens of smaller ones. When the empire fell apart, they did too, all blaming each other. They spent more time fighting among themselves than bothering anyone else. The last five Rihtcynn emperors before the fall of the empire had been Mearcweada, but nobody cared about it, until Aedilhild took over the clan and started calling herself Empress of all the Rihtcynn. Then we all peed ourselves laughing." Bertana sighed. "We're not laughing now. I've no idea how far she'll be able to take things. She managed to unite all the clans under her. The Langcnifas were the last to give in. They accepted her claim two years back. The following fall, her army moved into Sideamuda. The port was supposed to be a vassal state, but without a Rihtcynn emperor, that meant bugger all. But you've been in the town now. You've seen what it's like."

"Yes."

"Each time I go back, it's worse. This has been my third visit."

"Why do you keep going there?"

"I'm an artist. When I was a child, the priests discovered I could paint, so they had me tarting up all the old frescos. Now Empress Aedilhild has moved back to the old capital, she's trying to restore its lost glory." Bertana shrugged. "She could have twenty of me and still wouldn't get it finished in her lifetime. Especially since they want to repaint the government hall in Sideamuda. I'm not doing the work myself, but I have to oversee it. Which is what I was doing there."

The road rolled over the crest of the highest hill so far. The view from the top was across a wide valley. A dried up riverbed wound its way across the bottom. Matt could tell many decades had passed since water last flowed. Tall trees sprouted from the eroded bed, but once, it must have been a great waterway.

Bertana nodded at it. "That's what did in the Rihtcynn Empire, you know."

"The river?"

"Its drying up. It used to be the River Sidea. Barges could go up it, all the way to Cyningesburg. But just under two hundred years ago, there was a small earthquake. We get them around here from time to time. Nothing unremarkable, except that overnight, the river changed course. Now it flows way to the east, around the end of the Stanscylfa Mountains. It never gets within eighty miles of Cyningesburg." She shrugged. "I guess, in time, the Rihtcynn could have moved their capital, or dug a canal, or something. But of course, nobody was fool enough to give them time."

Matt had heard many explanations for the end of the empire, including the one about a changing river. Most of the other stories were far more entertaining, and more improbable, especially now she was walking the road to Cyningesburg, with the dried up riverbed in sight.

"Do you have any skills?" Bertana asked.

I'm good at stealing things. "Nothing special. I'm a maid to Eawynn Husa Achangrena."

"Then don't count on getting much rest. When you're not running after her ladyship, you'll be lugging stones across the city."

"The rebuilding work?"

"And then some more. The good thing is you'll get plenty to eat and drink. They need healthy slaves for the work. You'll even get beer to drink rather than water."

"So not too bad, if you're fit." The jerky was giving Matt indigestion.

"And can stay out of trouble. The Rihtcynn are fired up and ready to pick a fight. Any excuse will do. It's like sitting next to the fire. Nice and warm, you just have to make sure you don't get burned."

A shout came from the front of the caravan. The wagon with the passengers had got another wheel stuck. Matt trotted forward with the other slaves. She set her shoulder against the tailboard, ready to heave on the word. Sitting directly above her was Eawynn. She was staring across the valley, paying no attention. Her face in profile was delicately proportioned, her fiery red hair just long enough to fall onto her forehead. Matt could see the pulse beating in her throat. Eawynn was irritatingly stunning and stunningly irritating.

Oh yes, Bertana's adage was equally true for many interpretations. There were all sorts of ways to get burned.

❖

The bygone river had carved a pass through the Stanscylfa Mountains. On either side, steep slopes were littered with boulders and twisted trees. Antelope and wild goats grazed on shrubs. Weathered pillars of rock crowned the hilltops. The difficult terrain forced the road to take to the old riverbed, which would have been an even path, were it not for hollows the river had gouged out of the bedrock and shattered boulders that had rolled downhill. Progress was slow, while the slaves cleared obstructions. They covered three miles in twice as many hours. As delay followed holdup, everyone was getting short-tempered, Eawynn included.

Her fellow passengers were not helping. One elderly woman slept most of the time, snoring loudly. This was preferable to her being awake, when she would talk even more loudly about the pains in her joints. Two were teenage girls, related to somebody extremely important. They whispered and giggled to each other incessantly, except for any time someone else had the nerve to address them, when they would act bored and roll their eyes. The last was a rich, middle-aged landowner whose conversation consisted of boasting about the size of his inheritance. Eawynn suspected he was trying to flirt with her, but was doing it so badly it was hard to be sure—unlike Matt, who did it so very well.

Eawynn leaned back so she could look up the road. Matt was with the slaves, helping to lever a sheep-sized boulder out of the way. The male slaves had stripped to the waist. Matt had a cloth band wrapped around her chest. It kept her breasts out of view, and out of harm's way, but left her shoulders and midriff bare. Dust and sweat drew patterns on the muscles of Matt's arms and stomach, sliding as she moved.

Eawynn realised she had, unconsciously, caught her lower lip in her teeth. She released it and pressed her lips firmly together but did not take her eyes away.

"They're just playing around, if you ask me." Eadbald, the landowner, was an unwelcome interruption.

I didn't ask you. "I think they're doing their best."

"A taste of the whip would have them put some back into it. If I was in charge I'd get them working."

"Really?" *If I were in charge, I'd get the useless lumps of soldiers off their horses and helping, rather than preening for the benefit of the idiotic girls.*

"Yes. I know these barbarians. On my land I own three hundred or more. If any of them were dawdling about like that, I'd have the skin off their backs. My land produces over five thousand bottles of wine each year and as much oil, and you can't do that with slackers."

Eawynn closed her eyes. How to make the oaf shut up?

"It's how Thraelas are. No discipline. No mind to work. It's not surprising the world has fallen apart since the empire left it to go its own way."

"Some parts are doing all right, I think."

Eadbald snorted in contempt. "When the empire reached them, the savages were grubbing in the mud, running around half naked. We gave them everything they have. Without us, they'd still be living like animals. Of course, parts are making some sort of fist of things, using the roads and towns and ports we built for them. But things are changing. The empire will rise again. Then we'll see some real improvement."

"We can but hope." Silence was the improvement Eawynn was mainly hoping for.

"We gave the world everything and got not a shred of gratitude for it. It'll be different this time around."

It sounds rather similar to me.

"Ah. Now I've got you smiling." Eadbald's tone was triumphant.

"Yes. I was just thinking how much you reminded me of my father."

The boulder toppled over with a thump, leaving the road clear, and Eadbald shut up. A double win from Eawynn's point of view.

After another laborious mile, the surrounding hills retreated, taking the fallen rocks with them. The pace increased thereafter. By evening, they reached the edge of the Rihtcynn plains, the land known as Rihtcynnedal. The dead river valley was now broad and shallow. The road climbed its southern rim.

The land was drier this side of the Stanscylfa range. Gently undulating grasslands rolled away to the horizon. Immense herds of antelope, wild cattle, and horses stretched across the plain, the foundation of Rihtcynn wealth. Eawynn looked back. The sun had dropped behind the foothills. Wisps of cloud were tinged pink.

"Hold the horses and set camp." The caravan master called an end to the day's journey.

This was the third night, and the routine of pitching camp was becoming familiar. The soldiers and wagon crews unharnessed their own horses, but everything else was left to the slaves. The older woman got the lightest jobs, tending the fire and cooking. The others would raise tents, feed and brush the horses, and dig latrines.

Eawynn took a seat on a low bank, close by where the fire was being prepared. She was not sorry the day was over. It had been unpleasant all around. She watched as tinder started to smoulder.

The female slave lighting the fire clearly enjoyed a privileged position, something that annoyed Eadbald enormously. He had acted as if it was a personal insult, although he knew no more about her than Eawynn did. The woman had not been forced to clear rocks, and Eawynn did not think it was due only to her age. Even cooking seemed more by choice on her part. What was her story? Did Matt know?

Eawynn looked around, searching. She spotted Matt some way off, digging the latrine. Eawynn frowned. Matt must be exhausted after all day spent clearing paths. Who had ordered her to dig? The slaves were treated as a communal resource, but Matt was supposedly private property, and was not obliged to join in with setting camp, and certainly not if her owner gave different orders.

"Matt."

Matt looked up.

"Come here."

Matt handed her spade to another slave and jogged over. "Yes, my lady?"

Eawynn thought quickly. She could hardly order Matt to sit and chat. "I'm thirsty. Get me a cup of wine."

"Yes, my lady."

By the time she had the wine cup in her hand, Eawynn had thought of another light task. "It's getting cold. I left my cloak in the wagon. See if you can find it."

Matt returned shortly. "Here it is, my lady."

"Good. Put it around my shoulders."

As Matt did so, the tips of her fingers brushed the back of Eawynn's neck. A shiver ran through Eawynn and she closed her eyes. She did not think it had been done on purpose, not least because Matt was not to know the effect her touch had. However, Eawynn knew exactly how she was feeling, and she could not pretend, even to herself, that she was motivated solely by concern for Matt's tiredness. The sensible thing was to send Matt back to digging, but she was not going to.

"Anything else, my lady?"

What could she say? Brush my hair? Remove my boots? Eawynn knew she was playing a dangerous game, all the more dangerous because she was enjoying it. Already her pulse was racing. *Just because you can pretend you're in control, doesn't mean you are.* She looked at Matt, standing before her. Matt's expression was impassive, obedient, but deep in her eyes was a spark of annoyance. In its way, that was just as enjoyable as everything else about the game, and just as much of a trap.

"My bag. Get it from the wagon. I want to look for something."

"My lady." Matt bowed her head and trotted away.

Eawynn let out her breath and took a mouthful of wine. The first flames were running over the firewood. Smoke trailed away on the breeze. Eawynn leaned forward to feel the warmth on her face and took another sip. Matt had bent her heart out of shape once, Eawynn was not going to let it happen again. She had her litany ready, along with all the prepared memories of shame. *While you were kissing her, she was pickpocketing you. I'm sure she laughed about it afterward, maybe even boasted to her friends.* Eawynn would not let herself fall again.

Raised voices broke in upon her thoughts. Eawynn glanced round. One of the soldiers had got angry over something. He swung a punch, presumably at a slave who had annoyed him. Eawynn looked away. The treatment meted out to slaves was the hardest things she found in dealing with her fellow travellers. Eadbald was a brutal bigot, and the rest were no better.

"You thief!" The soldier was shouting now.

Eawynn dropped her wine and leapt to her feet. The soldier swung a second punch, knocking his victim to the ground beside the wagon. He reached into the driver's footwell and pulled out the horsewhip. "I'll teach you."

Eawynn arrived as he raised his arm. As she suspected, the slave was Matt. Eawynn moved between them. "What are you doing?"

"She was trying to steal my bag."

"Don't be ridiculous." *If she was trying to steal from you, you wouldn't know a thing about it.* Eawynn ripped the whip from the soldier's hand and jabbed the end of the handle against his chest.

He protested. "That's my bag she took."

Eawynn looked down. A dropped pack lay by her foot. She yanked the top open and pulled out the first item, her spare camisole. "Does this look like yours?"

"Oh."

A ring of watchers had formed. Another soldier called out. "Hey, Saba. I moved your bag over there."

"Oh." He was starting to look shamefaced. "Well, you know what Thraelas are like. They'll steal anything."

"Like you trying to run off with my camisole?"

"I wouldn't have kept it."

"You should be a bit more certain before you start punching people."

"She's just a slave."

"And you're just a halfwit."

"What?"

Around the circle, a degree of surprise was creeping in. Eawynn realised she was close to slipping out of character. No true Rihtcynn would have any concern for a slave's well-being. She had to hit the right note. "Do you know how much I paid for her?"

"Oh. Sorry."

"If you've permanently injured her, I'll expect you to buy me another."

"I just hit her once."

"Come and see me before you start trying to damage my belongings."

He gave an awkward shrug and turned away. The circle of watchers broke up.

Matt was now sitting. Eawynn switched to Tradetalk but maintained the Rihtcynn facade. "Be more careful in future." She walked back to her seat by the fire, calling over her shoulder, "And get me another cup of wine."

The sky overhead was darkening. Eawynn stared at the flames. The dancing firelight was mesmerising, something to focus on while she tried to calm her thoughts. The flood of anger subsided, leaving her drained. Eawynn's hands were shaking; her whole body was shaking.

"My lady."

Eawynn looked up. Matt was holding out another mug. A red blotch that would turn into a bruise marked the side of her face, but she seemed otherwise unharmed. Eawynn clenched the mug in her hand and a took a gulp. Too quick. The wine burned the back of her throat, making her cough.

"My lady?"

She waved the offered help away. "Go and do whatever."

Eawynn watched Matt walk away. The frantic urge to rush to Matt's defence had been instinctive. The flood of emotions it released was impossible to disentangle. Eawynn's heart was still beating hard in her chest. *She cheated me. She used me. I hate and despise her.* The familiar litany, and it was no longer true. Maybe she enjoyed tormenting Matt, but she could not make herself hate her.

❖

By the time Cyningesburg came into view, the nature of the landscape had changed again. The river valley was now ten miles or more across, the sides carved from red sandstone. The road ran along its flat bottom. Once, the flood plain had been rich farmland. The broken shells of deserted farmhouses dotted the scene, and the outlines of ancient fields were still visible, but without the life-giving river, only yellow grass and thornbushes still grew. The winter rains would bring greenery back to the land, but not enough to support the mightiest city the world had ever seen, or so Bertana told Matt.

Cyningesburg was built atop a spur jutting from the eastern valley wall. As the caravan drew closer, it dominated the skyline. Battlements and towers were black in the shadow, red where the sunlight hit, the colour of Eawynn's hair. The road was paved, but time had not left it untouched. Finger-like sand drifts crept over it, stones were missing, and weeds sprouted in the cracks. On either side, monuments to dead heroes lined the way. The caravan swung east, crossing the riverbed on a massive stone bridge. Twelve arches supported the weight.

After miles of desolation, the flood plain was now filled with activity. Everywhere were horse pens, smithies, and tents. Soldiers drilled on foot and horseback to the shouts of officers. Smoke rose from the forges. It was an army in waiting, but for what? The guards took their leave of the caravan and joined their comrades.

"You said the land won't support a city anymore," Matt said to Bertana, who was walking beside her.

"It won't."

"So why is an army here? How does the empress think she's going to keep this going?"

"Her majesty has not advised me of her plans." Bertana grinned.

"No. But you must have heard something. What's the word among the slaves?"

"Something's up, but when I left here, two months ago, nobody knew what."

Another mile and the route began to ascend the side of the valley. A long, slow climb followed. They reached the top as the sun was passing its zenith. From here, the scale of Cyningesburg became apparent. The buildings on the spur might be the grandest, but they represented a tiny fraction of the abandoned city. Mile upon mile of crumbling walls stretched out—houses, shops, temples, and workplaces. Windblown sand heaped against the walls, while shrubs clawed a foothold between the stones.

The caravan crossed what used to be a grand square, dominated by the statue of an emperor or general. Rows of fluted columns lined the perimeter, all in pitted red sandstone. The road joined a wide avenue leading to the citadel on the spur. Here the state of repair showed a noticeable improvement. The sand and shrubs were cleared, the walls shored up, and statues cleaned.

Black-cloaked soldiers manned the imposing gateway to the citadel. Massive lions, their mouths carved in a frozen roar, supported the arch on either side. The sentries stood motionless, offering no challenge to the caravan as it passed through. The band of shade under the arch was cold after the sunshine, and then they were out again.

To a first glance, all trace of decay had gone from inside the citadel. The buildings lining the main avenue rose as proudly as when they were first built, but down the side streets, Matt saw the crumbling bricks and missing paving. Yet work was in hand. Scores of slaves were hauling, resetting, cleaning, and plastering, under the gaze of whip-bearing overseers. Stone by stone, Cyningesburg was being reborn.

The wagons carrying supplies for the city peeled off at one of the wider cross streets, toward a busy market. A hundred yards farther on, the remaining two wagons rolled into a square, the largest Matt had ever seen, and stopped. They had reached their destination. Monumental buildings opened onto the square. All were adorned with statues and bas-relief. One was clearly a temple and another opulent enough to be a palace. Five domed roofs, shaped like the soldiers' helmets, swept upward in pointed spires. A third building was adorned with friezes of soldiers and battles. The military theme extended to the statues and hanging banners. Was it the army headquarters or the city hall?

The passengers disembarked. The teenage girls and old woman were escorted away by relatives. The overdressed man hung on, bombarding Eawynn with his thoughts about something, despite the blatant lack of encouragement she was giving him.

The atmosphere was changing, becoming hard and brittle, as if something might snap. The caravan master stood at Eawynn's side, guarding her. Was he concerned she might run away? Matt moved closer, although still keeping a respectful distance back. She could hear what was said, not that she understood a word. A small group had emerged from the palace, three officials and a bodyguard of soldiers. They marched across the square, toward the wagons and Eawynn.

The overdressed man was still spouting his monologue, but then he noticed where everyone was looking, and also glanced back. He broke off mid-sentence, threw out a quick, "Beo gesund," and hurried away. Clearly, he recognised at least one of the approaching officials. Matt felt a sudden jolt, realising that she did too. Striding forward in the lead, dressed in priest's robes, was the man who had murdered Edmund.

Would Eawynn recognise him? And would he recognise either of them? Of course, with the story Eawynn had given, it would help rather than harm their chances in her case. But for Matt it would be fatal. She ducked her head in her best servile pose. Fortunately, a slave did not merit the merest glance.

"Wilcuma, freo," Oswald said.

"Wilcuma, leof," Eawynn replied.

"Ic oncnaewe thu baede waere hercyme."

"Gea."

"Folge mec."

More than ever before, Matt wished she could understand Cynnreord. What was going on?

Eawynn turned her head, "I have to talk with some people. Stay here and mind my things." The words were offhand, revealing nothing.

"Yes, my lady."

Matt stood by the bags, watching as Eawynn was escorted across the square and into the palace. Her mouth was dry and her palms were sweating. This was absurd. She never felt like this, not even on the riskiest job. But on those occasions she was the one making things happen, the one whose skill was put to the test. Now it was down to Eawynn, and she was the one running the most risk.

Matt gazed around, trying to act like a curious new arrival. She resisted the urge to wipe her hands on her legs, in case someone was watching. For herself, if things went wrong, she might spend months carting stone around Cyningesburg, until she got the chance to put a knife in Oswald's heart. For Eawynn, things could get far nastier, far quicker.

Maybe Eawynn was enjoying the role of mistress a little too much. It was nothing Matt could not handle. Eawynn was infuriating, stiff-necked, strait-laced, and could get under Matt's skin like no woman she had met before. However, the thought of not seeing her again was a cold knot in Matt's gut. And there was not a thing she could do but wait.

CHAPTER NINE

The palace was even more impressive inside than out. Any trace of neglect had been repaired or hidden. The walls were newly plastered and either embossed with interwoven designs or painted with vivid scenes. Colours burst from the walls. The pillars were draped in banners, all bearing the imperial crest. Light glittered off gold leaf everywhere. The tiled floors were polished to a shine.

They had crossed the plaza in silence. Now Eawynn's escort spoke. "I should introduce myself. My name is Oswald Husa Eastandune."

Eawynn was certain word had been sent ahead and he already knew who she was. Her task was to stay in her role. "I am Eawynn Husa Achangrena. But if I remember correctly, that was not the name you used, last time we met."

"Ah, yes. You were a priestess in Fortaine. I regret the deception, but I was on a secret mission."

"Your mission, was it…"

"Yes?"

"At the time, I didn't connect the disappearance of the Shewstone with your visit, but seeing you here. It can't be a coincidence. Your mission concerned the Shewstone."

"I cannot reveal any details, but yes. Obviously."

"You took it from the temple? How?"

"That may be a story for another time." He smiled. "It has taken me a moment, but now I recognise you. I must say, shaving your hair was a crime. I am pleased you've abandoned the practise. You shouldn't hide your heritage."

He was changing the subject. Eawynn did not mind, although it would be interesting, sometime, to hear his version. "I had no choice in the matter. All priestesses were required to shave their heads."

"And those preposterous names."

"It was traditional for all temples in Fortaine."

"In Cyningesburg, priests use titles for their positions. I am Leader of the Sacred Council. But a noble name is something to be proud of and shouldn't be discarded."

"I don't think most in Fortaine had a noble name to begin with. Maybe the Thraelas started the practice to disguise their origins." Eawynn guessed making derogatory remarks about Thraelas would be well received. Oswald's smile said she was right.

"Indeed."

They reached a pair of double doors, the widest so far. Resplendent soldiers stood guard. In unison, they opened the way for Eawynn and her escort to enter.

Any fears she was on her way to the dungeon vanished. This room put the rest of the palace to shame. It was an audience chamber worthy of an empress who claimed dominion over the known world. A small group gathered at the far end, a dozen or so elegantly dressed courtiers, around a woman seated on a high throne.

Eawynn paced the length of the chamber, remembering Matt's advice. *Don't act the part. Become it. Don't stop to think that a word you say isn't true.* How good an actress was she?

Empress Aedilhild Wisa Mearcweada Bregu Rihtcynn was no more than four or five years older than Eawynn. They looked so similar they might have been sisters. The empress wore a deep red tunic, embroidered with gold. She also wore a golden breastplate, although it looked more ceremonial that military. Gems glinted on her bracelets and the torque around her neck. Her head was crowned with a sunburst.

Beside her stood an elderly man, tall and stiff backed. He had a jewelled band around his brow, over what remained of his thinning hair. His was turning white with age, yet its depths still held the last hint of red.

Oswald moved to the side. Eawynn walked the final few yards alone and dropped to one knee, bowing her head. "Your Imperial Majesty."

"You may stand." Empress Aedilhild gestured to the elderly man, clearly inviting him to conduct the questioning.

He took a half step forward. "I am Ceolwulf Husa Elbacnola, Steward to her Imperial Majesty.

Eawynn bowed her head again. "I am Eawynn Husa Achangrena."

"We understand you were told to come to Cyningesburg."

"The Shewstone told me."

"The Shewstone?"

"Yes."

"It spoke to you?"

"Yes."

"In what language?"

"Cynnreord, I think."

"You don't know?"

"I speak six languages. As long as there's nothing about the words to catch my attention, I often don't stop to think which of them it is." Eawynn knew it might sound odd, but it was true.

"What exactly did the Shewstone say?"

"The first time, I must admit, I paid little attention. I thought I was imagining things."

"You'd not heard it speak before?"

"Only when the high priestess conducted her divinations, and it sounded different then. I think what it said to me was, *Soon I am going to Cyningesburg. You must follow.*"

"Just that?"

"Yes."

"It gave no clue why?"

"No."

"Did it speak to anyone else?"

"I don't know, but I doubt it. The Shewstone was locked away. Apart from me, only the high priestess had access, and if it spoke to her in Cynnreord, she'd struggle to understand." She caught Oswald's eye. "You heard her butcher the noble language."

Oswald smiled. "Indeed I did. I must say, at the time I didn't know you spoke Cynnreord. I compliment you on keeping such a straight face."

"It wasn't easy."

"The two of you met in Fortaine?" Ceolwulf pounced on the words, frowning suspiciously at Oswald.

"Briefly," Oswald answered.

"Did you speak together?"

"Not in private."

Ceolwulf was wondering whether Oswald had told her to come to Cyningesburg, Eawynn realised. Judging by their tones and the way they looked at each other, the two men were not the best of friends. However, the steward's doubts were not shared by the rest of the group, who were mainly looking confused.

"Why would the sylph want her here?" a woman standing at the back asked.

Other voices joined in. "What role could she have?"

"Might Iparikani have something to do with it?"

"It's even harder to see why he might get involved." Ceolwulf's attention returned to Eawynn. "You're sure about the words?"

With the possible exception of the steward, they believed her. That much was obvious. The empress and assembled courtiers were quite happy the Shewstone might speak and have access to hidden knowledge. Only the why of it gave them a problem. Fortunately, there was no pressure on Eawynn to provide an answer. She could act as confused as she liked, but she must not change her story.

"It said it was coming to Cyningesburg, and I should follow. Maybe I misinterpreted it, but that's what I remember." Eawynn looked at the frowning faces. "Whatever the reason, I'm grateful. Where else should someone of Rihtcynn blood be? The empire is rising again." That was the right line. It drew smiles.

"It's possible the sylph spoke for Eawynn's benefit, rather than its own. They're notoriously helpful," Oswald said.

Ceolwulf's frown deepened as his eyes switched between them, ending up on Eawynn. "You're pleased to be here in Cyningesburg?"

"Oh yes. If you'd spent as much time as I, living among the Thraelas, you'd not even think to ask." More of those present were on her side, Eawynn could feel it.

Even the empress smiled and said, "I can imagine. As to what you were told, who can know the mind of a sylph? They do not think as we do. But your lineage. Who was your father?"

"Thane Alric Wisa Achangrena."

"I thought as much. We heard of his fate."

That was less good. Eawynn had no idea why the news had got as far as Cyningesburg, but there was no point hiding what they must already know. "He was executed as a traitor."

"Maybe to the upstart regime on Pinettale. Swidhelm and his accursed lineage are the true traitors. Swidhelm betrayed the empire. It was an evil day when he claimed the island for himself."

Who would have thought it? One matter on which Aedilhild and Matt were in agreement.

Empress Aedilhild continued. "We were in contact with Earl Blaedgifa. Had he succeeded in overthrowing the usurpers, he'd have acknowledged our claim to the empire and would have ruled as our vassal. We gave the earl what help we could. Sadly, it was not enough. In supporting him, your father died loyal to the true sovereign of Pinettale. He didn't deserve a traitor's death."

"I knew nothing of this." Eawynn's face had probably said as much.

"We'd heard his three children were imprisoned."

"His legitimate children." Eawynn had never met her half brothers and sister. "I'm the result of a youthful indiscretion, but my father acknowledged me and gave me the right to his name."

"Ah." Empress Aedilhild leaned back in her throne, a familiar expression on her face. "Your mother. What do you know of her?"

"I've no personal recollection, but my father spoke of her often." Eawynn gathered herself; she might as well go for it. "He said she was a noblewoman, of birth equal to his. They were young, and in love, and certain their families would agree to their marriage, so they were a little hasty. Which was when they learned my mother's family had other plans and wanted her betrothed to a rich, elderly lord. She bore me in secret. Her family disowned me, but my father didn't. He raised me for the first few years of my life, for the sake of my mother's memory. When I was old enough, he sent me to become a priestess of Anbeorht."

"As has happened to many before you in a similar situation," Empress Aedilhild said.

Ceolwulf was still not happy. "Did you enjoy being a priestess?"

"It was an honour to serve the goddess, but…"

"But?"

"I think, had my father known more about the workings of the temple, he might have found another place for me. Blood and breeding count for nothing there. If anything, my ancestry worked against me. They gave me the most menial tasks, and I know, for at least one elder, it was purely due to jealousy of my bloodline. I don't know whether Oswald Husa Eastandune has spoken about the practise of shaving one's head and renouncing one's name. It's just so the Thraelas can hide their base-blood. They wish to drag everyone down to their wretched level." Eawynn had the entire room. It was impossible to say too many bad things about anyone who was not Rihtcynn.

Ceolwulf would clearly have liked to probe further but accepted the mood was behind Eawynn. He sighed and faced the throne. "Empress Aedilhild, if you please, as your steward, permit me to give you my advice."

"Go on."

"I admit some things still puzzle me. Maybe they'll become clear in time, but as you wisely pointed out, a sylph's motives might never make sense to mortals. However, it's evident that, for whatever reason, it directed this woman to us, the natural daughter of a nobleman who died in your service. She's a priestess of Anbeorht and, to date, the cult of Anbeorht has been sadly neglected in Cyningesburg. I propose Eawynn Husa Achangrena resume her devotions here."

Empress Aedilhild nodded. "Anbeorht. Goddess of fate and childbirth. It is our time. A new empire is to be born. Let us take this as a sign."

Everyone smiled; a few even applauded.

❖

Waiting in the square was unbearable, straining Matt's acting to the limit. The urge to pace was making her leg twitch, and she could no longer gauge how long she spent looking in any given direction. In the end, the only way she could disguise her agitation was to push the bags into a sunny spot, lie down using them as a pillow, with her back to the square, and pretend to sleep. Luckily, this was exactly the sort of behaviour expected from a slave. All she then had to do was close her eyes and keep still.

"Stand up."

Matt sprang to her feet. Eawynn had returned with only a junior priest as escort. Somehow Eawynn had done it. She had sold her story. An urge to hug her swept over Matt, but she managed to restrain herself.

Matt ducked her head. "I'm sorry, my lady."

"Get the bags. We're being shown to my lodgings."

"Yes, my lady."

The priest led them across the square and down a road running alongside the temple. He chattered away in Cynnreord the entire time. They passed beneath an archway at the rear and entered a series of small interlinked courtyards. This was clearly domestic accommodation, presumably belonging to priests. The buildings were two stories high, built of red sandstone with tiled roofs. External stairways gave access to the upper floors.

The priest took them up one such set of steps and into an apartment consisting of three moderately sized rooms. All had large unglazed windows overlooking the courtyards below. The furniture consisted of a table and bench in the first room they entered and an unmade bed in another. Matt dropped the bags by the doorway.

"Her bith eower bur," the priest said with an encompassing gesture. "Ic ahope eall beon wel."

"Gea. Thance thu," Eawynn replied.

A lengthy conversation followed, involving a lot of pointing from the priest and a lot of nodding from Eawynn. Eventually, the priest said, "Beo gesund," bowed, and left. Matt watched him go before pushing the door closed. Again, the urge to hug Eawynn presented a challenge.

Matt leaned against the wall behind her, trapping her hands in case they developed a mind of their own. "You did it."

"I think so."

"What happened?"

"It was surprising." Eawynn sat on the bench and leaned her elbow on the table. Her expression hovered somewhere between bemusement and satisfaction. "For the first time in my life, my father's name was a help."

She ran through the entire meeting with Empress Aedilhild and her court.

Matt let her finish before asking, "Did you recognise Oswald?"

"Yes. He's the one who came to the temple in Fortaine."

"He's also the shithead who murdered Edmund."

"So you're going to murder him in revenge?"

"Yes."

"You promised you'd help me reclaim the Shewstone."

"And I will. Don't worry. I'm not about to rush over and stab him the first chance I get, much as I'd like to. I want to make sure I can have my revenge, and take the Shewstone, and get us both safely out of here."

"I'm meeting him tomorrow in the Sanctuary of Liffrea, an hour after dawn. He's going to explain my new duties to me."

"Like I said, I'm not going to rush into things. Tomorrow is safe." Eawynn would not meet Matt's eyes. Killing Oswald was just one more source of conflict between them. A change of subject was in order. "What's a sylph?"

"I'm not sure what they mean by it. It seemed to be their name for the Shewstone, but a sylph is actually a mythical spirit. Maybe they think one talks to us via the Shewstone. They obviously believed something supernatural was going on."

"We know they're gullible. They wouldn't have gone to the trouble of sending Oswald to get the Shewstone if they thought it was just a ball of rock. They'd more likely be surprised if it didn't speak."

In which case, maybe she should finish her business with Oswald sooner, rather than later, before the empress and her lackeys started wondering why the magical Shewstone was not talking to them. However, discussing this with Eawynn was not a good idea.

"Do you think they're hoping the Shewstone will help them reclaim their empire?" Eawynn asked.

"Then they really are desperate."

"The army encampment looks serious."

"Last time around it took them five hundred years to go from grabbing Sideamuda to invading Pinettale. It might get nasty for folk on the mainland, but I don't think you and I need worry too much. Especially if they're relying on the Shewstone for help."

A large wicker basket stood at the end of the table. Eawynn lifted the lid and peered in. "Ah. Good." She pulled out a water pitcher and a wax writing tablet. "There are temple stores, where we can get bedding, spoons, candles, and other domestic stuff. If I put together a list, they should hand it over to you. While I write, you could go to the courtyard and get water."

Matt grabbed the pitcher and headed to the well they had passed on the way in.

Two other slaves were already there, both women. They smiled at her. "Welcome."

Matt smiled in reply.

"You're new in town?"

"Yes. Arrived today."

"There's worse places to be, for people like us."

"So I've been told." Matt took her place in line. "What else can you tell me?"

"About what?"

"Anything. What do you think I ought to know?"

A series of answers followed, the women taking turns. "Don't walk through the army camp at night."

"Don't walk anywhere at night, if you can help it."

"The beer from low-town tastes best."

"Try to avoid being sent to work on the outer wall. They're shifting some big stones. Two slaves were crushed yesterday."

"Stay clear of the steward's men. They carry a little red fly-whisk, made from horsehair. They'll mostly ignore you, but they piss off the other Rihtcynn who'll take it out on you afterward."

"The steward." The slave scowled as she lifted her full pitcher. "He's the one who set the empress off, giving her the ideas. Without him, she'd never have tried rebuilding the empire. She wouldn't have an army. I'd be with my family, and my husband would still be alive." She looked as if she wanted to say more, but turned and left.

Once she had gone, Matt asked the remaining woman. "Is that true? Is the empress just a puppet?"

"It's more complicated than that. Steward Ceolwulf might have started things, but it's running away with him. It's no secret Oswald, the priest, is after his job. There's been scheming over secret missions and more—"

An impatient shout came from a window. "Cleace. Astynte dolspraece."

"Whoops. Better go. Be safe." The second woman also left.

Matt could make a guess at what had been shouted. It probably counted as one of the orders she ought to understand. Maybe Eawynn could give a few lessons.

She lowered the bucket into the well. Where were they getting water? Perhaps underground cisterns stored the winter rain. In which case, it would not keep an army going for long. What were the empress's long term plans?

However, for them, things had gone surprisingly well. Undoubtedly, there would be tricky bits ahead, but Eawynn had access to the top of society and she had access to the bottom. For the meantime, her two biggest issues were learning enough of the crackjaw language to stay out of trouble, and resisting the urge to hug Eawynn.

❖

Eawynn got to the Sanctuary of Liffrea a few minutes early. She spent the time trying to ignore the bloodstains around the main alter. What would be required in her role here? Her training in Fortaine had contained nothing about slitting animal's throats.

"Welcome." Oswald Husa Eastandune arrived.

"Good morning."

"Are your rooms to your liking?"

"Yes, thank you. I wasn't expecting quarters to myself. Junior priestesses shared a dormitory in Fortaine."

"We have no shortage of space, and you're officially High Priestess of Anbeorht in Cyningesburg."

"By default."

"For the moment." He smiled. "Before we go to the shrine of Anbeorht, I thought, you might like to see the Shewstone."

"It's here? In the temple?"

"Yes. I'll show you."

The Temple of Liffrea was part of a large complex of temples, each dedicated to a member of the Rihtcynn pantheon. The buildings formed a maze of courtyards and walkways. Eawynn was lost by the time they reached a narrow doorway. A complement of four sentries stood outside. Steps led to an underground crypt, forty-foot square, with a low, vaulted roof supported by four pillars. Two more black cloaked soldiers stood guard in front of a round altar directly opposite the entrance. Five-foot tall candelabras lit the crypt, one on either side of the dais and one by each of the pillars. The Shewstone was balanced on a plinth in the middle of the altar.

"We're keeping it safe for Iparikani."

The name did not belong to any Rihtcynn god Eawynn recognised. But should she? "You haven't got the Shewstone under lock and key?"

"Thieves generally have more difficulty with soldiers than locks."

"How did you take it from the temple in Fortaine?"

"I hired the services of a notorious criminal."

"How did he manage to steal it?"

Oswald shrugged. "I didn't waste time asking for details before I sent him to the gods to answer for his many crimes. The world's a better place without curs like him."

"But only after he'd got you the Shewstone?"

"Of course."

Eawynn focused on the altar while she tried to resolve her feelings on the matter—an impossible task. Colours, deep within the Shewstone flowed in the candlelight. Without the deliberately reduced lighting of the shrine in Fortaine, or the latticework repository, she could see it better than ever before.

"It's not talking to you now." Oswald stood at her shoulder.

"It never did when anyone else was around."

"Maybe the sylph has said all it needs to."

"The sylph? Why do you call the Shewstone that?"

Oswald studied Eawynn thoughtfully. "You don't actually know what the orb is, do you?"

"I only know what I was told by my elders in Fortaine."

He laughed. "In which case, the little you do know is wrong. It's not a charlatan's toy for telling lovelorn girls the name of their future husband or other quackery. It's a prison."

"A pris…" Eawynn stared at the Shewstone. "There's a sylph in there?"

"Yes."

"How?"

"Somebody got the better of it. The who, when, and how are unimportant."

So what was important? "Why do you want it?"

"Ah. Now you're on the right track."

Oswald walked around the dais until he was directly opposite Eawynn. He rested his hands on the altar and leaned forward, the pose of an orator, ready to give a prepared speech.

"The Rihtcynn Empire was the highpoint of human existence. Order, stability, culture, we gave them to the world. We taught the savages to farm and build and read. Then, one natural calamity, and the Thraelas destroyed it all. They ruined everything that was good and noble. Across the known world, they massacred our people and tore down all we'd built. But, believe me, the lesser races will pay for their crass treachery. Because with this orb, we'll undo the ancient wrong. We'll set the world on the path of greatness again."

"The sylph will do it?"

"No. Sylphs are weak, ethereal beings. But its soul will be a suitable feast for one who can, Iparikani."

"Who is?"

"A mighty demon from the netherworld. In exchange for the sylph's soul, Iparikani will return the Sidea river to its former course. He'll imbue our armies with unbeatable might, and we'll reclaim all that was taken from us. Steward Ceolwulf has made contact with Iparikani, and an agreement has been reached."

"That's amazing." What else could she say?

"Our plans are complete. Ceolwulf has concluded the best time for the ritual of summoning will be dawn on the summer solstice."

Eawynn counted days in her head. "About twenty days from now?"

"Nineteen."

"What about the sylph?"

"Its soul will be consumed by the demon. A small price."

Perhaps not from the sylph's point of view.

Oswald may have read the disquiet on Eawynn's face. He continued. "Its existence has been nothing but torment since it was confined. I think it would welcome the end. And it'll have the satisfaction of seeing its prison destroyed forever."

"The Shewstone will be lost?"

"It's part of the ritual. But come, we've spent enough time here. I must show you the shrine of Anbeorht."

They had nineteen days to save the Shewstone. How were they going to do it? Did Matt have any ideas? Eawynn had other questions, some of which could be put to Oswald while they walked.

"How has Steward Ceolwulf managed to contact a demon?"

"A good question. However, he has not chosen to share this information." Oswald did not sound overly happy.

"How did you find out about the Shewstone and the sylph to start with?"

"That one I can answer. It was pure good fortune. After the Langcnifas joined us, Empress Aedilhild wanted advice on how to proceed with the campaign. We'd heard of the prophetic abilities of the Shewstone, and some wanted to consult it. I must confess, I was foremost in saying it was a waste of time and money. Fortunately, not everyone listened to me." He flashed a smile. "The envoy we sent was an elderly cleric who was knowledgeable in arcane law. As soon as she saw the orb she knew it for what it was. I was sent to confirm her discovery, and if it proved true, to bring the orb back to Cyningesburg."

The shrine of Anbeorht turned out to be an open air terrace, tacked on to the rear of a larger temple dedicated to the primary Rihtcynn lunar deity. It contained a medium sized statue of the goddess, a plain altar, and not much else. Apart from on Pinettale, Anbeorht was never a major immortal in the Rihtcynn pantheon.

Oswald indicated the barren space. "As Steward Ceolwulf said, the worship of Anbeorht has been sadly neglected. I'm pleased you're here to set things right. Up till now, responsibility for this shrine has been shared among the priesthood. You'll now take sole charge of the shrine and all its ceremonies."

"Is there anything in particular you're expecting?"

"You're the one with knowledge of what's appropriate for Anbeorht. Whatever you deem will be most pleasing to the goddess."

Eawynn looked around. "Maybe a little more in the way of decoration."

Oswald smiled. "I'll assign slaves and resources to you. But no need to get too settled. When we've re-established the empire, don't be surprised if you find yourself high priestess in Fortaine."

A harsh voice broke in, startling Eawynn. "That will surely be a decision for the entire council." Steward Ceolwulf had joined them and did not look happy with what he had overheard.

Oswald was not put off. "You know of a better candidate?"

"Don't think I haven't spotted what you're up to, filling posts with your protégées." Ceolwulf shot a disdainful look in Eawynn's direction. "She obviously made a strong impression when you met her in Fortaine. Was it her piety or her prettiness that caught your attention?"

"Neither. In truth, I barely noticed her."

The steward advanced until he was inches from Oswald. "You expect me to believe that! You think I'm an old fool, but once I've summoned Iparikani, and our beloved empress has regained her rightful place, then we'll see who's the fool."

"You're welcome to cling to that hope if it gives you comfort."

After further glaring, Ceolwulf gave a snort of contempt and turned on his heel.

Oswald sighed deeply once the steward had left. "I'm sorry for that. Ceolwulf and I do not always see eye to eye."

Eawynn had gathered as much and thought it wiser to stay out of the conflict.

He continued. "He thinks he can keep all the glory for himself. He wanted to send one of his cronies to Fortaine. I didn't let him get away with that, and I'm not going to let him run away with things now." He smiled at Eawynn. "But you don't need to worry. Work out what you need to show due honour to Anbeorht, and let me know if you have any problems."

Oswald also went, leaving Eawynn with a long list of issues to mull over. Would they be able to rescue the Shewstone? Nineteen days was not a lot of time to play with. Even if they could, did she want to? She could genuinely take her place in the new empire. As long as she managed to keep out of the battle between Oswald and Ceolwulf, she stood every chance of becoming high priestess somewhere, and never needing to sweep a floor again. She had her place of safety, which had been her only motive in tagging along.

Had she and Matt ever truly been on the same side over anything? Why should she return the Shewstone to Insightful Sister Oracle? What was the point? Especially if Fortaine was about to be swallowed up by a new Rihtcynn empire. Was it not her birthright to be here in Cyningesburg at the dawn of a new age?

Eawynn was surprised at her instant gut rejection. She took a deep breath. There was no need to make her mind up instantly. She had nineteen days to think it through. There were all sorts of options. She could see to it that Matt was put on a caravan back to Sideamuda. Matt was quite resourceful enough to escape from there and make her own way back to Fortaine. They need never set eyes on each other again. Surely that would be best all round. The important thing was to take her time and make the right decisions.

Meanwhile, she had to think about the ceremonies. Eawynn turned to face the statue of the goddess. What would Anbeorht want? Traditionally, in Cyningesburg, she was the aspect of the changing moon which controlled the heavenly sign ruling over one's birth. Hundreds of miles from the ocean, Anbeorht never had been a sea goddess. So no getting up in the middle of the night for the Laudation of the Irresistible High Tide. And no dead animals.

Definitely no dead animals.

Matt could barely restrain her laughter. "So that's the scam, is it? They have the priestesses at Fortaine beat every way when it comes to the Shewstone."

"What do you mean?"

"It's a con trick. They're playing us for stooges." Eawynn looked even more confused. "You don't believe in demons and sylphs and magic, do you?"

"I didn't before."

"So what's changed?"

"Oswald told me—"

"A story. My ma used to tell me stories about the pixies, and I trusted her way more than I'd ever trust that shitbag. Doesn't make any of it true."

Eawynn continued looking baffled. Matt went to the window. Night had fallen, and candlelight flickered in rooms around the courtyard. She closed the wooden shutters and flexed the muscles in her shoulders, trying to shift the aches. While Eawynn had been listening to tales about sylphs, Matt had been ferrying reclaimed building blocks up from the lower town. Her back, arms, and legs were stiff, and likely to feel even worse tomorrow.

Matt returned to the bench, sitting close, so they could talk with no risk of being overheard, even if a spy outside stood with his ear pressed to the door. This also meant they were close enough for Matt to feel Eawynn's breath on her cheek when she spoke. Matt kept her hands safely clasping her own knees. But if she just let her head fall forward, she could nestle her face in the hollow of Eawynn's neck. She tried to push the temptation out of her mind. It would get her nothing but a slap, at the very least.

"You saw through Unsightly Sister Orifice and her fortune telling tricks. I don't understand why you've fallen for this."

"Because I don't see how the trick works. What will happen when the demon doesn't appear?"

"Depends on who's behind it and what their game is. Ceolwulf or Oswald. Oswald is the easy one to work out. He's letting his rival make a fool of himself. Ceolwulf says he's talked to Ipi-whatsit. I'd put my money on it being one of Oswald's followers in fancy dress. He's tricked Ceolwulf into believing in magical stones, and the dupe has taken the bait, hook, line, and sinker. He's even trying to impress on everyone that it's all his doing. They'll have a big ceremony with everyone watching, and when it goes tits up, Oswald becomes steward and Ceolwulf ends up a head shorter than he was before."

"And if it's Steward Ceolwulf behind it?"

"Then he's going to have to do a bit more work and put on a show. It doesn't need to be permanent. He just has to get the timing right. A bit of smoke, something to go flash-bang, a trickle of water. Nine out of ten watching will swear they heard the demon, smelt the sulphur, and saw the mighty river flow again. Some will even say they washed their underwear in it. By the time the story spreads, it won't matter what happened. And if thinking you've got a mighty demon on your side doesn't inspire your troops to a victory or two, then nothing will. From what you heard between them, Steward Ceolwulf is hoping to use the boost from this to get rid of Oswald."

Eawynn frowned. "I'm not sure."

"Or it could be somebody completely different, and this is a trick to get everyone in the same place, when the light is poor, and they're too excited to be alert. The perfect time to stage a backstab and coup."

"So if you're right, at least one person knows the Shewstone is a fake. Why did everyone go along with my story about it talking to me?"

"Steward Ceolwulf thinks you and Oswald have something going on and that Oswald told you to come here. That's obvious. But he doesn't have any proof to start throwing accusations around. If the scammer is Oswald..." Matt paused, thinking. "He said he hadn't realised you spoke Cynnreord. Back in Fortaine, he and his servant probably got into the bad habit of talking as if nobody around could understand them. It was two and a half months ago. By now he won't be able to remember whether they mentioned Cyningesburg when he went for the divination."

"I didn't overhear anything."

"But he won't know that. Perhaps he thinks you overheard and followed him because you've fallen hopelessly in love with his Rihtcynn charm and good looks."

"Don't be silly."

"I'm not. Has he been smiling at you? Standing close? Offering you his help and assistance?"

"Yes, but..."

"But nothing. Men can be very easy to flatter like that. Anyway, no matter who the scammer is, he could hardly say, *Oh no. The Shewstone can't have spoken to you because it's just an old ball of rock.*"

Eawynn still did not look completely won over.

"What else can it be?"

"I don't know. Oswald was so convincing."

"Yeah. He fooled my pa as well, and Edmund didn't fool easily. But he won't get the chance to fool many more." Matt felt the cold anger biting in her gut. Her grip on her knees tightened, this time a reflex that had nothing to do with the woman sitting so close.

Abruptly, Eawynn was no longer there. Matt watched her slip off the bench and start pacing the room. Neither said anything. What was there to say?

They came from different worlds. The priestesses lived in their safe cocoon, shielded behind every protection the state could erect. If someone wronged them, they could leave it to the city watch and the judges to sort it out with their hangman's noose, whipping post, and labour mines. The priestesses never had to dirty their hands. Eawynn could not understand the sort of man Edmund had been, nor the debt Matt owed him.

Eawynn returned to the bench, still refusing to meet Matt's eyes. Her face held the familiar disapproving pout, lips pressed hard together in a line. She drew in a sharp breath and released it slowly, as if trying to let go of her irritation. "Anyway. It doesn't matter whether it's a trick or not. The Shewstone is going to be destroyed. If we're going to get it back, we've got just nineteen days to do it in."

"I like a challenge."

"Do you think you can do it?"

"Just watch me."

❖

The library was the true glory of Cyningesburg. Only the temple had not been abandoned over the two centuries following the fall of the empire. The priests had preserved the books, and Eawynn could happily have spent the rest of her life immersed in them. Back in Fortaine, the priestesses had boasted of the hundred and forty-five books they owned. The shelves around Eawynn held thousands— histories, fables, works of religious and natural philosophy, and poetry:

Birds are happy in the trees,
Fish swim content in water,
Yet I am going mad,
I walk the earth, bound in sorrow,
For sake of the best of mortal blood,

Eawynn closed the book and returned it to the shelf. She had allowed herself half a month, fourteen days, to decide what she was going to do. Her time was up. What she decided might not be so important, if Matt did not manage to save the Shewstone in the next few days, but Eawynn did not want things to slip by default. She had to work out where she stood.

In her priestly robes, Eawynn was free to wander as she wished. Nobody would question or hinder her. She ended up on a terrace, overlooking the river valley below. Three thousand years before, her ancestors, the Rihtcynn horse tribes of the plains, had learned to exploit the bounty brought by the annual floods. On the banks of the Sidea, villages had sprung up and then towns, culminating in Cyningesburg, the first, the mightiest, and the most beautiful city the world had seen.

Much of what was written in the history books was slanted to tell the story the author wanted to be true. Digging through the bias to the truth could require cross-checking and a healthy dollop of scepticism. Yet, no matter how much of the self-glorification one dismissed, there was still no denying that civilisation had started here. Farming, irrigation, wheels, money, writing, and metal craft were all Rihtcynn inventions, along with swords and armies. Small wonder when the Rihtcynn rulers turned their attention to the outside world they met so little resistance. Stone knives were no match for Rihtcynn iron and steel.

Yet the conquered nations had benefited. The primitive peoples had been living hand to mouth, knowing nothing other than grinding poverty. Some dwelt in caves. Famine had been routine. Not one child in four lived to see its tenth birthday, and an old man or woman was a rare sight. Before it was conquered, the entire population of Pinettale numbered about a hundred and fifty thousand. As part of the empire, it grew into millions.

In some places, the Rihtcynn armies had even been welcomed, as defence against the marauders who plundered what little there was to take. Eawynn doubted the yellow haired people of the far north had ever eaten babies, as was claimed, but they had practised human sacrifice on a large scale until it was banned by the empire.

Impartial Rihtcynn law struck down the cruel restrictions found in many cultures, where taking a lover of the same sex was treated as a crime punishable by death—as had been the case on Pinettale before it became part of the empire. For the Rihtcynn, the choice of lover concerned no one but the parties involved.

Women had benefited beyond reckoning. The majority of the Rihtcynn army was male, but not all, certainly in the higher ranks, where a noble name guaranteed a command position. Most money and power might end up in men's hands, but sons and daughters inherited equally under Rihtcynn law. A woman could be a clan elder, own her own property, run her own life. In most cultures the Rihtcynn overturned, women had been possessions, controlled by their male relatives. In fact, depending on how you defined it, the proportion of slaves had gone down not up under Rihtcynn rule.

Maybe the ordinary people had not chosen the Rihtcynn overlords, but neither had they been given a say about the petty chieftains who preceded them—warrior elites who did nothing apart from fight among themselves and raid each other's land. Under the Rihtcynn, farmers could plant their fields with the certainty of a harvest. They would not see their homes and crops burned when a war band swept by. Eawynn was sure folk cared more about peace and prosperity than the colour of their rulers' hair. Of course they complained; people always complain about those in charge. You could give every single man and woman a vote in who was to be ruler, and they would still complain.

Even the fall of the empire was not as clear-cut as painted. In Pinettale, the Rihtcynn commander had led the break away from the empire. In Ferridia to the west, it was the Rihtcynn legions who had started the revolt, angry when their wages were cut. The people of Nabithe even sent an envoy to Cyningesburg, asking for more soldiers to be sent when raiders took advantage of the empire's retreat.

But that was not the full story.

Eawynn left the citadel, ambling down the wide avenue running from the central Plaza of the Emperors and out though the Lion Gates. The road carried on, gently sloping down. From where she stood, Eawynn had a clear view across the remains of the lower town. The sinking sun painted the sandstone with fire. Wind from the plains carried dust and grass seeds and snapped at the robe around her legs.

Hundreds, maybe thousands, of slaves were at work, manhandling the ancient stone, under the eyes and whips of overseers. Shouts rang out from all directions. The half dressed bodies were covered in dirt and sweat. Hair varied from blond to brown to black, but not a single redhead. Cyningesburg was being rebuilt as it had been built before, by unfree hands.

The scream made Eawynn jump. She followed the general drift toward the source. A naked slave was bound to a tall wooden post. Eawynn joined the crowd as the whip landed for the second time and the slave screamed again. Eawynn's stomach contracted painfully, her guts hardened like ice. She would have turned away, but she forced herself to stay and watch as a man's back was turned to bloody pulp. The whip bit so deep it cut to the bone. *This is also the heritage of the empire.* At last the screams became weaker and then stopped. The slave hung unconscious from the post. The audience wandered away. *That could have been Matt.* Eawynn was shaking.

Even in Fortaine, that could have been Matt. The priestesses did not go to witness the twice monthly entertainment, held outside the Courts of Justice. It would not have been seemly, joining in with the riotous mob who turned up every time to watch the flogging, branding, and hanging of criminals. By all accounts, the scene was every bit as barbaric as the one Eawynn had just witnessed. Yet, as she was sure Matt herself would agree, it was one thing to flog thieves for their crimes, and quite another to flog a man for the colour of his hair. What else had the slave truly been guilty of?

Eawynn retraced her steps back to the Plaza of the Emperors. The Rihtcynn had given so much to the world. What did they have left to give? Once, they had been the most advanced race in the world. Now everyone else had caught up. Did it matter if this was mainly due to the lessons they had learned from the empire? The Rihtcynn army was no longer the only one with steel swords. The new wars would not be the one-sided affairs of centuries past. They would be long, drawn-out, and bloody, and despite what everyone in Cyningesburg assumed, victory was not assured for either side.

Suppose the Rihtcynn won, and the empire was reborn? The Rihtcynn of old had looked down on the conquered nations. They had scorned the Thraelas, but had not hated them. They held no score to settle; they nursed no grudge. This time would be different. The Rihtcynn of Cyningesburg had rewritten the story of the empire's collapse as one of barbarity and treason. It had become a tale of savages, wantonly destroying a wonder, beyond their bestial ability to understand. The new empire would have nothing to teach, nothing to add, nothing to admire. It would be cruel and regressive, and she wanted no part in it.

Eawynn gave a sad half smile. What chance her decision would have gone any other way? But she would so miss the library.

The light was fading. Matt would soon be released from her work in the lower town. Eawynn returned to the apartment. On the way, she stopped by the kitchens and asked for food to be sent to her rooms. No need for Matt to do all the fetching and carrying.

Bread and stew arrived shortly, brought by kitchen slaves. Eawynn waited for Matt to return, but when time passed with no sign, she ate alone, before the food cooled. As the room darkened, she lit a candle. Now Eawynn was starting to worry. The image of the slave's bloody back kept picking at her thoughts, but at last the door opened. No need to wonder who. She had not heard footsteps on the stair.

"Sorry I'm late."

"Where've you been?"

"I had to pick something up and wanted a cover of darkness." Matt swung a pack off her shoulder and dumped it on the table. It landed with a solid thud.

"What is it?"

Matt pealed back the cloth to reveal a stone sphere. For the barest astonished instant, Eawynn thought Matt had already stolen the Shewstone. Then she looked again. The size was close enough, but the colour was off, and it did not glimmer in the candlelight.

"What? Why have you..."

Matt grinned. "It's a ball of marble. It's taken a lot of finding. There's been no end of sandstone ones, but they aren't smooth enough. I finally found this in the lower town this morning. I carted it up in a barrow of bricks and hid it so I could collect it on the way home."

"Why?"

"It's going to be a fake Shewstone, with a dab of paint and some sparkly bits. I'll need your help to get the colour right, and things. You've spent more time looking at the real one. I only had a quick peek."

"You won't fool anyone."

"I think I will, for just long enough. We need to swap it the evening before the ceremony. The less time we give people to study it, the better."

"You might get away with it in the crypt, but in daylight, it's going to be obvious."

"For one, how many people have ever seen the Shewstone in daylight to make the comparison? For two, the ceremony is at dawn, so it won't be much brighter than the crypt. And for three, even if they spot the swap they aren't going to say anything. Smashing a fake Shewstone will be just as good as smashing the real one. With everyone in Cyningesburg assembled, it'll be too embarrassing to stop the show and admit someone's stolen it."

Eawynn frowned, trying to find fault with the logic.

"The tricky bit comes afterward. We have to assume the fake gets spotted when they tidy up. They won't be able to launch a major hunt, because then they'd have to admit it wasn't the real stone used in the ceremony, but we still need a hiding place, where we can leave the Shewstone for as long as we need, until Ceolwulf, Oswald, and their henchmen have stopped looking."

"How do we make the swap?"

"That'll be easy."

"And you're going to need good paints."

"Believe it or not, I know the very person to ask."

CHAPTER TEN

Who takes a second look at a slave carrying a bucket of water and a scrubbing brush? Matt might have been invisible for all the notice she got from the two soldiers guarding the Shewstone. No one even asked to see the written note Eawynn had given her, although it was possible neither soldier could read. Matt put down her bucket to the right of the entrance. The crypt was exactly as Eawynn described. Matt knelt, dunked the brush in the water, and started scrubbing.

Eawynn had pulled her personal slave off stone hauling duties an hour earlier than normal. The overseer had not been happy, but was not about to argue with a priestess. Tomorrow, when the Shewstone ritual was over, Matt would try to avoid running into the same overseer again, just in case he wanted to take revenge for being out-bossed. She had already acquired a selection of cuts and bruises that could be put down to nothing more than petty malice.

Matt was tired from working in the lower city, but scrubbing the floor was oddly relaxing. Each tile was six inches square, decorated with a blue and white glazed design. Matt started counting them off as she worked her way along, mentally dividing the floor into rectangles.

She had turned the first corner when Eawynn arrived, dressed in priestly robes. This time the soldiers reacted. They stood up straighter and trained their eyes rigidly on the far wall. Matt kept her head down and carried on scrubbing.

Eawynn stopped in the centre of the four pillars and knelt. She launched into a droning chant. The words rose and fell like waves. Without understanding what was said, Matt could tell it was repetitious and very boring. The names of Anbeorht and Liffrea came up frequently. After a quarter hour, the soldiers' pose had reverted to the previous half slouch, and Matt had reached the rear wall. She was now behind the soldiers.

Matt worked her way over the tiles, row by row. She was within two feet of the altar when Eawynn stood. Still chanting, she took a half step to the left while bending her body to the right. Then she gave a quick double kick, a wave of the arms, and a swirl. Eawynn's whole body swayed in a slow, ungainly, and utterly ludicrous dance, in time with her chant. Her arms were held out horizontally. Her fingers and face pointed to the ceiling.

One soldier cleared his throat in a partly successful attempt to smother his laughter. Matt was hard put not to do likewise. For a moment, it seemed as if both soldiers might break down in a giggling fit, but their training held firm. Eawynn did not miss a beat. Her face showed no emotion except for religious rapture. She had been wasted in the temple. She was a natural and she had the soldiers' total attention. Standing sentry was notoriously boring. Eawynn's dance must have been easily the most entertaining thing they had witnessed in hours.

"Geblotsest us, Anbeorht. Geblotsest us." Eawynn trotted in a circle, hopping and kicking her feet left and right on each alternate step. She had lifted her robes, so the ankle twist was on full view. The soldiers were mesmerised.

Matt reached the base of the altar. Eawynn's dance became more vigorous. She spun in her most flamboyant twirl so far and her foot caught a candelabra, sending it bouncing off the pillar behind. Eawynn landed on the floor with a squeak. The clattering of the candelabra reverberated around the crypt. Loose candles rolled across the floor, still burning.

For an instant, everyone froze. Then one soldier sprang forward to help, while the other was again locked in a battle with stifled giggles.

Matt seized the moment. She scooped the fake Shewstone from the bucket, and dried it on the rag she had stuffed inside her shirt. The surface was still damp but no longer dripping. Another second and she had swapped it with the orb on the altar and hidden the real Shewstone beneath the grey, scummy water in the bucket.

Possibly the soldier heard a faint splash. He glanced back and caught Matt kneeling upright and looking at Eawynn, which was quite all right. It would have been suspicious if a slave had not stopped to watch.

"Aetfeolan thin weorc, wealh."

Which Matt was fairly sure meant, *Carry on with your work*, with an insult tacked on. She obeyed.

"Hwa alimpende?" A shout echoed down the stairs. The sound of the falling candelabra had obviously been heard by the sentries outside.

"Na uneadnessa," Eawynn shouted back. Her words were repeated by both soldiers.

Eawynn was now back on her feet, looking convincingly shamefaced. The smell of singed cloth and candle wax drifted around the crypt. Between Eawynn and the soldier, they got the fallen candelabra back in place and relit. The soldier then returned to his spot, Eawynn continued her chanting from a safe kneeling position, and Matt was past the altar with the Shewstone in her bucket.

Matt was lost in admiration. *Create a distraction*, had been her request. The show exceeded anything she had expected.

Eawynn continued chanting until Matt was halfway up the side of the crypt, then she rose, bowed to the altar, and went. The soldiers remained static until all sounds of her footsteps faded. First one and then the other started shaking with laughter. The nearer one lifted his foot to the side and wiggled it, in a tame imitation of Eawynn's dance. Maybe that night, with their comrades around the campfire, they might be less inhibited and would stage a re-enactment with the vigour it deserved.

After another quarter hour, the floor was finished. Scraping up spilt wax added a little to the job, but was more than worth it. The soldiers even stepped aside so Matt could scrub the bits under their feet. She picked up her bucket and left the crypt, attracting no more notice than on her arrival.

Soldiers could be every bit as easy as locks.

Dusk had fallen over Cyningesburg. A slave wandering around after nightfall was liable to attract attention. Matt wanted to be quick. She had the note from Eawynn, but would rather not rely on it. An overzealous soldier might decide to search her regardless. In fact, as Matt had discovered, some would do it for fun, the chance to humiliate a person of a lesser race. She grimaced at the memory. Lesser, but not so far beneath him a Rihtcynn could not enjoy a good grope. Although if that was his motive, a soldier would not be fishing about in dirty water.

Matt had picked a hiding spot for the Shewstone in a patch of garden a couple of courtyards away from Eawynn's rooms. An ancient, knotted tree was surrounded by waist high shrubs. The twisted branches were nearly devoid of leaves, as it went through its drawn-out, decades-long death. The tree was old enough to have borne witness to the height of the empire. It might even have stood when the horse tribes founded their first village in the valley below.

The roots clawed into the ground, digging deep for the last remnants of rain that had fallen the previous winter. The soil had blown away around the base of the tree, leaving deep clefts. Matt pushed partway into the shrubs and upended her bucket, like a slave watering the tree. The thud of the Shewstone on dry soil was covered by the splashing. Matt nudged the stone ball with her foot, rolling it into a hole under a curling root, and then scuffed dirt and dead leaves to cover it.

No footsteps or voices could be heard. Matt did not think anyone was around, but did not look to check. There was no point in knowing whether or not she was observed. She could not make a witness vanish. The trick was to act in such an unremarkable way nobody would bother investigating. Swinging the empty bucket, Matt continued on through the interlinked courtyards.

Eawynn was waiting, an unspoken query on her face.

"Job done." Matt grinned as she slipped onto the bench, close enough to whisper. "And you were amazing. You didn't hurt yourself, did you?"

"The pole cracked me on the leg. It'll leave a bruise, but that's all."

"Do you always dance like that?"

"The last time I danced was on my sixth birthday. We didn't do it in the temple. Dancing is not seemly for a priestess."

"I'd like to…" *dance with you,* Matt swallowed the words, "… congratulate you on your distraction. It was inspired."

"Thank you."

Eawynn blushed faintly, but even faint was noticeable on her white skin. Matt gripped her own knees firmly. Had she ever wanted so badly to hold a woman in her arms? "If ever you'd like to take up a life of crime, you've got a job waiting."

Eawynn shook her head, but she was smiling.

❖

Dawn was still an hour off. The Plaza of the Emperors was in darkness, broken only by the river of flaming torches. The procession of priests and priestesses flowed from the temple complex and onto the palace steps. Already, small clumps of civilians were scattered about the plaza, ready to watch the spectacle.

Eawynn ended up toward the back, at the top of the stairs. She stood, half hidden behind a column. It was not such a bad spot. She had a good view and was sheltered from the chill wind. If everything went wrong and the painted orb was denounced as a fake, her chances of getting away were slight, but at least her state of nerves was not so conspicuous. She did not want to draw attention to herself. Fortunately, nobody she knew was nearby.

Matt had been confident they were in no immediate danger. The ritual would go ahead, regardless of whether the fake was spotted. The light was on their side, and Eawynn had to concede Matt's artwork had been better than she expected. It might pass with somebody who had only glimpsed the Shewstone before. However, anyone familiar with the genuine artefact would not be fooled.

The Shewstone had been in Oswald's possession throughout the journey from Fortaine. Surely he would not be taken in for a second. Nor would he be the only one. The Shewstone had been in Cyningesburg for a month. How many others had taken the time to gloat over their prize?

The crack of marching feet ricocheted around the plaza. The army was coming from the encampment on the flood plain. Standard bearers led the way up the imperial avenue. When they reached the plaza, the column broke into cohorts and fanned out. The massed ranks came to a halt in ruler straight lines, twenty deep and spanning the width of the open space. History books claimed the fighting troops of six whole legions, fifteen thousand armed soldiers, could line up in the Plaza of the Emperors. This muster did not number a fifth of that, yet was still impressive.

Apart from the temple and court, a few Rihtcynn civilians lived in Cyningesburg, mainly merchants, overseers, craftsmen, and their families. Everyone had turned up. In contrast to the army's geometrically precise array, wads of civilians milled around on either side. In the darkness at the far end of the plaza, Eawynn sensed rather than saw the others, a mass huddling in the shadows. Even the slaves had come to witness the ritual.

To the east, a hint of dawn touched the sky. Sunrise was a half hour away. The doors of the palace swung open to the sound of grinding hinges. All heads turned to see the imperial retinue emerge. Empress Aedilhild Wisa Mearcweada Bregu Rihtcynn was a step in the lead, dressed in her most regal clothes. Steward Ceolwulf was at her shoulder, while Oswald and an elderly woman walked immediately behind. The entourage of courtiers and officers followed, in order of rank, escorted by a phalanx of ornate imperial guardsmen.

From the midpoint down, the flight of stairs was split in two by a stone buttress. The flat top had been made ready as a rostrum for the imperial party. Empress Aedilhild stopped in front of her throne, while Ceolwulf, Oswald, and the unknown woman carried on down the steps. A low, slab-like altar had been positioned in the plaza, some twenty yards from the bottom. The three went around the altar and faced the empress, forming a line with two torch-bearing guardsmen. Eawynn wondered if the woman was the envoy first sent to consult the Shewstone, now honoured with Oswald as its finder.

Steward Ceolwulf's voice rang out, loud enough to echo from the buildings opposite. "Your Imperial Majesty. Today will go down in the annals of the mighty Rihtcynn nation. Today, the Sidea will flow again. Cyningesburg will return to its true glory. Nothing will stand in our way. Let the Thraelas tremble and lament. The price of their treachery will be reclaimed in blood, sorrow, and servitude. Your name will shine as brightly as the greatest of your forebears. A new sword has been forged. Today, it will be raised. Tomorrow, it strikes."

A roar rose from the Rihtcynn, but not everyone cheered. As light seeped into the world, the mass of silent slaves acquired weight and form. Eawynn had not realised how many there were. Had anyone done the sums? They outnumbered the soldiers three to one. The slaves were unarmed and leaderless, but there were so many. A chill ran through Eawynn.

The empress replied. "Steward Ceolwulf Husa Elbacnola, we commend you for your tireless work in our service. Rest assured, all will receive what is due, both reward and penance. A new day dawns. We praise the gods that we have been blessed to witness it. Continue. Summon forth Iparikani. Reverse the ancient cataclysm." She sat down.

A new procession appeared on the western side of the plaza, leaving the temple gates. At its centre were four robed priests, bearing a litter. It was too far to see, but Eawynn knew the Shewstone was on it—the fake Shewstone. The moment they appeared, the assembled throng of clerics began the song of "Liffrea Light-bringer, Lord of the Skies," the oldest and most sacred of religious poems.

Normally, Eawynn would have been euphoric, to hear the beautiful words of Cynnreord, sung as they should be, by so many voices on such a stage, but dread blotted out all else. Why had they gone through with the swap? Matt had not questioned its wisdom. But why had she said nothing? Eawynn no longer wanted or needed the Shewstone.

The litter reached the waiting steward. Ceolwulf lifted the orb and held it high, so all might see, then placed it on the stone slab in front of him. The light was strengthening by the minute. Now Eawynn could see the altar was a rough block of granite, looking as if it was unworked since the day it had been lifted from the ground. What was its significance? Eawynn did not know.

A male goat was dragged, fighting and kicking to the altar, and a priest placed a knife in the steward's hand. Blood spurted as he cut the animal's throat. Ceolwulf, Oswald, and the elderly woman retreated a short way, while those who had carried the litter used the lifeless goat's body to draw a pentagram in blood around the granite slab. The four priests then bowed low to the empress before leaving, taking the dead goat with them.

The chanting ended. In the following silence, Ceolwulf shouted, "Behold the Orb of Celestial Captivity. May our gift be acceptable to Iparikani."

All eyes were on the altar. This was it. If the fraud was going to be challenged, it was now. Eawynn's mouth was dry. Who was close enough to see properly? The litter bearers had said nothing, but possibly they were not familiar with the genuine Shewstone. Ceolwulf had held the fake, but it was common knowledge his eyesight was failing with age.

Oswald was the greatest threat. He would be more familiar with the real Shewstone than anyone, and he was standing no more than five paces from the altar. Eawynn stared at him, while Oswald in turn stared at the counterfeit orb. His brows drew together in a frown. The beginnings of doubt were manifest on his face. He glanced to the east, as if trying to judge the speed of sunrise, as if hoping for better light.

Eawynn felt her stomach cramp. Why had she insisted Matt steal the Shewstone? Suddenly, looking at Oswald, part of an answer dropped into her head. As long as she was on a mission to reclaim the stone, she had a sop for her conscience.

Oswald Husa Eastandune was the man who had killed Edmund Flyming. He was the man on whom Matt had sworn revenge. Even though Eawynn now understood her suggestion that Matt report him to the legal authorities had been ridiculously naïve, she could not accept cold-blooded murder. So why had she not simply abandoned Matt and her quest?

Eawynn was not going back to the temple in Fortaine, and she was not going to become part of the new Rihtcynn Empire, but this did not mean her only other option was to stay with Matt. Yet, for all her deliberations, the one path she had not considered was simply abandoning Matt to complete her quest for revenge alone. Why? Instead Eawynn had stuck blindly to her own initial plans. Was it just because she did not want to search too deeply into her own heart to uncover her real motives?

"I call on the Captain of the Imperial Guard to stand forth." Ceolwulf's voice rang out one more time.

The captain was an impressively tall man. His uniform was the most elaborate Eawynn had seen. His embossed breastplate was gold, as was his helmet, with its stiff plume of dyed feathers. In his hands he carried a huge golden hammer.

Ceolwulf moved aside, well clear of the altar, followed by the elderly woman. Before joining them, Oswald hesitated a moment longer, giving the fake orb one last, hard look. His frown deepened, then he shook his head, and squared his shoulders. His expression cleared and he walked to where Ceolwulf was waiting.

A junior priest arrived with a leather bound volume. Oswald and the elderly woman held it open between them, acting as a human book rest. The ritual was about to begin in earnest, and nobody was going to challenge Matt's counterfeit. The surge of relief was so great, Eawynn had to put her hand on the column beside her for support.

However, it was not a complete end to her worries. She did not want Matt to kill Oswald in cold blood. She would do anything to stop her. So was that it? Had stealing the stone been a pointless, stupid delaying tactic? Eawynn understood how upset Matt was at the death of her adopted father. But when Matt killed Oswald, it would affect the way she saw Matt. And despite everything that had gone before, Eawynn was getting to like the way she saw Matt.

The view from the far side of the plaza was not good, even though Matt was better off than most. She had joined a group of more adventurous slaves and climbed onto the plinth of a statue. Normally, it was the sort of thing that would risk unpleasant consequences, but for once, the Rihtcynn seemed willing to ignore what the slaves were doing.

From her position, clinging to the tail of an iron griffin, Matt could see over the soldiers' heads. She had tried, without success, to pick Eawynn from the ranks of clerics on the palace steps. In fact, the only person she could identify with certainty was the empress, and that was purely because nobody else would be sitting on the throne.

After all her assurances, if Matt was honest, she would admit to a degree of relief once the ritual was definitely underway. The fake Shewstone must have been on the litter carried from the temple. She had seen the old man who did all the shouting pick it up and wave it in the air, before putting it down again. Standing on tiptoe, Matt was just able to catch the corner of a stone slab they were using as an altar, but she did not have the angle to see more, and now the flash officer with the pretty helmet was standing in the way.

The old man moved aside. He began talking again, although not as loudly as before. From the back of the plaza, his voice was a soft drone. Not that it made any difference, as far as Matt was concerned. Even when he was shouting, she had not understood a word of the Cynnreord. The old man appeared to be singing rather than speaking. Three times, the massed clerics joined in. Somebody somewhere was banging a gong. On a cue, all the torches were simultaneously put out. It was suitably dramatic, although to Matt's mind, could have been improved by another dance from Eawynn.

She tried to assess the mood around her. The slaves were not the target of the charade. The ones the grifters needed to con were the empress's followers. However, intimidating slaves would be a side benefit. How many were swallowing the farce?

Only a handful of stars remained in the pale blue above Matt's head, and off to the east, orange and pink filled the sky behind the roofs of Cyningesburg. Sunrise was scant minutes away. Suddenly, the old man's voice stopped. The big soldier with the helmet adopted a theatrical pose, holding over his head what looked like a golden sledgehammer.

Gold! Matt had to restrain her laughter. Who makes a hammer out of gold? Not just because of the cost or weight. If it were real, the shaft would bend double on the first strike. The hammer had to be painted iron, but it meant they were going for broke in the effort to impress.

On the opposite side of the plaza, the first ray of sunlight hit the tallest spire on the palace. The old man shouted one more time. This would be it. Matt shifted her grip on the griffin's tail and swung forward, not that it improved her view at all. What was it going to be, smoke and mirrors or an embarrassing anti-climax?

At first, the disturbance seemed like a dark speck, floating in Matt's vision. She blinked, trying to clear the blurred shadow, but instead it grew and deepened. Shouts began to ring out. It was not just her eyes. Others were seeing something as well, between the stone slab and the palace steps. The effect was as if dark water was flowing from nowhere into mid-air. Matt was impressed. It was far better than anything she expected. How were they doing it?

The rippling waves faded as the edge of the darkness solidified into a fixed oval, a dozen feet wide and twice as high, a hole in the air. Through it, Matt could see nothing. The empress and all her retinue were hidden from view. Then, deep inside the darkness, something moved—something swimming up from the depths of the void, something coming toward them, something seeking entrance to their world.

Close by, slaves yelled and a few even fled. On the palace steps, several of the assembled clerics also edged back. The first quiver of doubt quickened the beating in Matt's chest. It had to be a trick. It had to be, though she had no idea how it was being done. The effect was very convincing, but it had to be a trick. And yet, Matt could almost believe there was something in the darkness, waiting to emerge.

Suddenly, the darkness flexed, folded back on itself, and vanished, giving birth to a shape, five times the height of a man. The figure's skin was red and glistening. His head was an unholy mixture of pig and cat, with foot-long tusks and horns. Four hugely muscled arms reached upward, claws outstretched, as if wanting to rend the sky. A barbed tail flicked into view. From the waist down, matted, blood-red fur covered his body and legs, partially cloaking the bulging genitals. His feet ended in goat's hooves. Even without seeing, Matt just knew he had hooves. And it was no trick.

More slaves were now screaming and running away. A man almost knocked Matt from her vantage point in his scramble to get down, but she stayed, staring at the impossible figure. The demon threw back his head and roared. Over the shouts and shrieks, the old man was heard again. There was no hint of fear in his voice. Matt would give him that. The old man had guts. The soldier with the golden sledgehammer swung it over his head and down in an arc. The clink of metal on rock was just audible over the rising uproar. Matt guessed the blow smashed her fake Shewstone.

The demon took a step forward and roared again, and then a third time, but his tone was changing. Matt did not know if there were words in the roar, but she had no trouble understanding the fury and malice. It was the roar of a demon who thought he was being cheated, the roar of a very, very angry demon.

One massive hand reached down, picked up the stone altar, and hurled it across the plaza. It smashed into the temple façade. A barrage of ear-piercing screams erupted, some from those injured by falling debris. Yet, the main players by the palace had not moved. What sort of behaviour were they expecting from a demon? Did they know how badly awry their plans were going? Matt could see the idea dawning on some. The lower palace steps were emptying. Still, the soldier with the hammer held his ground, either frozen in fear or assuming all would work out well. The demon picked him up and slammed him headfirst into the ground.

Chaos and panic let rip. Clumps of Rihtcynn civilians broke and fled, following the slaves in a headlong rush from the plaza. At the front, the demon leapt onto the palace steps, his arms flying in a blur. Bodies were sent spinning skyward. Amid them, the broken throne tumbled through the air and crashed to the ground. The empress's chances were poor if she was still sitting on it. Bodies were lifted up in clawed hands and ripped apart.

"Eawynn." Matt's wild cry was pointless.

The demon turned from the palace and roared again. He swung two arms in a throwing action, like a child having a tantrum, hurling a toy. A ball of crackling blue flame shot from his hands. Those in its path had no hope. Men and women were scattered like straw on the wind. More fireballs followed, smashing into buildings and carving lines of death through the ranks of soldiers. The demon resumed his attack on the palace steps. Surging waves of bodies showed where clerics were trying to retreat, but they were too densely packed.

Eawynn would be among them. Desperately, Matt looked down from her perch. A torrent of people were gushing by below. If she left the plinth she would be swept away, or trampled. On the other side of the plaza, the flagstones were now deserted, apart from bodies and the demon. The remaining clerics were scrambling up the steps, a heaving mass, all trying to get through the palace doors at once. The demon hurled another fireball, the biggest so far. The front of the palace caved in. Another blast and the entire portico gave way, burying those trying to escape.

The demon's attack continued until the domed roofs had fallen. Black smoke billowed up. Where doors had once been was now the open entrance to a ruin. But not all were running away. To shouts from officers, the remaining cohorts had taken up battle formations. The soldiers advanced on the demon, weapons drawn. The outcome was short, bloody, and predictable. By the time the last black-cloaked figure had fallen or fled, the outpouring from the plaza had slowed.

Matt jumped from the plinth. Maybe the demon had grown tired of fireballs. He was now hurling anything within reach—bodies, broken columns, and ripped up flagstones. Matt took shelter behind the statue that had been her platform, but it would be no protection if the demon thought to use it as a missile.

While the demon tore man-size chunks of masonry from the ruins of the palace, Matt scurried around the edge of the plaza. There would be no safe hiding place if the demon spotted her, but she could not leave Eawynn. A loud crash announced that the demon had turned his attention from the palace to the temple. The Sanctuary of Liffrea was now minus an outer wall. Another crash, and the statue had also gone. Its head bounced across the plaza and cannoned into the front of another building.

Matt reached the corner of the palace. Screams and groans came from the rubble. Some clerics were still alive. What chance that Eawynn was one?

Another roar, but this time it signalled satisfaction. Matt ducked from sight, hiding behind a fallen column. The demon made a last circuit of the plaza, smashing or throwing anything that caught his eye. He passed close enough for Matt to feel the ground shake. A whiff of sulphur was carried on the air.

A last crash as a statue pounded the front of a building. A last scream cut short as a woman was ground beneath cloven hooves. As Matt had known he would, the demon had the feet of a goat. The stories had come from somewhere, after all.

The demon returned to the spot where he had first appeared. He slapped his chest in a final combative display and bellowed his challenge to the mortal world. And then, as implausibly as on his arrival, the demon folded in on himself and vanished.

Matt rose from behind the broken column. For a moment, the plaza was still deserted, then a few others emerged from hiding. The scattered figures stood in stunned, bewildered, horrified silence. The demon had gone, after destroying the dream of a new empire. It had not been a hoax.

"Well, bugger me."

Matt shook her head in the hope it would clear her thoughts. It did not help. The sun had risen high enough so the light of a new day flowed over the carnage in the Plaza of the Emperors. The attempt to rebuild Cyningesburg was broken and undone. Hundreds littered the plaza—dead, dying, or wounded.

The golden hammer lay where it had fallen, close by Matt. The paint had scraped away down one side, revealing the common iron beneath. Matt crouched and scratched off a few more flecks with her nail. There had been some trickery. She had not been completely wrong. Matt knew she could not have been completely wrong. Yet still, she was lost in disbelief over what she had just witnessed.

An agonised sob roused Matt from her daze. She had to find Eawynn.

❖

The roar faded away, leaving only agonised screams from the injured and the incessant muttering of the elderly priestess. "Blessed Bauthor save us. Hear our prayers. Mighty Liffrea aid us. Hear our prayers." The gods were not listening, but at least she had lowered her voice. Iparikani had ears.

The first surge for the palace doors had barged Eawynn and six others off the side of the steps. The drop had been about fifteen feet, and Eawynn had fared better than those she landed on. She had twisted her knee and would have a black eye from somebody's elbow. However, the priest at the bottom of the pile lay dead where he had fallen, and an elderly priestess had broken her leg. Eawynn and a junior priest had dragged her into the shelter of an alcove. The injured woman had screamed when moved, but then settled for her repetitive and unanswered appeals to the gods.

The others had staggered away. Two had escaped, including a woman with blood streaming down her face, but another had been caught by falling masonry.

Eawynn strained her ears. Was it safe to emerge? Had Iparikani gone? She stepped from the alcove.

"No. Stay here. It'll get you. Don't leave us." The young priest was panic-struck.

"I have to find someone. Look after her."

He made as if to pull her back, but Eawynn evaded his grasp and crept along the side of the palace. The priest took a half step after her, then stopped and retreated to the safety of the alcove.

His voice joined with that of the priestess. "Mighty Liffrea aid us. Hear our prayers."

Eawynn reached a corner where she had a clear view across the devastated plaza. There was no sign of Iparikani. A sudden crash made her jump, but it was just a damaged wall, collapsing under its own weight. Around a dozen people were wandering aimlessly across the broken flagstones or standing in shocked stupor.

The nearest figure was one Eawynn recognised, even from the back. Her heart leapt. "Matt."

Eawynn had no awareness of closing the distance between them. Suddenly, Matt's arms were around her, holding her tight. One hand was a solid reassurance, firm on her back. The other hand cradled Eawynn's head, fingers slipping through her hair. Matt's breath was loud in her ear. Their bodies were pressed so hard together she could feel Matt's heart beating.

Being held felt so good. Eawynn could almost block out the world—almost, but not quite. The edge of the iron collar dug into her neck, warm from Matt's body, but still an awkward intrusion. Then a drawn-out scream made her flinch. Shouts on the other side of the plaza turned to yells. Eawynn wriggled free from Matt's arms.

The ground around her was littered with smashed buildings and broken bodies. Blood smeared and splattered the stone. Lifeless faces stared, unseeing at the dawn sky, including one Eawynn knew, a library assistant who had recommended the poetry to her, just a few days ago.

"The demon was real." Eawynn bit her lip. Why state the obvious?

"Yes. I was wrong."

So many dead people, both men and women. Hardest of all, a few bodies were clearly children, the sons and daughters of the civilians. "We shouldn't have—"

"What?"

Guilt clawed at Eawynn. "We did this. We killed these people."

"No."

"If we hadn't swapped the stone, they'd still be alive."

"If we hadn't swapped the stone, they'd be on their way to crush the rest of the world. I—" Matt broke off, then started again. "I've spent the last month wishing something like this on the Rihtcynn."

"Now you've got it, how does it feel?"

Matt gazed around at the death and devastation. "Different."

"Better than you imagined? Worse?"

"Just different." Matt's tone was flat and cold.

Who am I to judge? Eawynn hung her head. *I'm not the one who's spent a month with an iron collar around my neck.*

"We need to go. It isn't safe here," Matt said.

"The demon's gone."

"It's not him." Matt pointed to a group of slaves who were scrabbling in a far corner.

"What's happening?"

"Looting. There's no shortage of stuff to take, but we don't want to become a target. Your hair isn't going to make you popular. We need to leave, now." Matt started walking.

"Wait."

"What?"

"There's someone hurt. We can't leave her."

"Rihtcynn?"

"An old woman with a broken leg."

For the space of four breaths, Matt stood still while a succession of emotions chased across her face. She shrugged, took one further step, then stopped and turned back. "All right."

She followed Eawynn around the ruins of the palace to the alcove. The young man was gone, but the old priestess still huddled in a corner, although her prayers had stopped. As Eawynn reached the alcove, she saw why. Blood was spreading down the front of the elderly woman's robe. Matt crouched and lifted her chin. More blood dripped from a raw gash across her throat. No living soul was in sight. Whoever slaughtered the old woman had fled.

Matt stood, staring at the blood on her fingertips. "Worse." She whispered the word.

Without more said, they returned to the plaza. Matt stopped by the bodies of two soldiers and pulled their swords free. She passed one to Eawynn.

"I don't know how to use it."

"You poke people with the pointy end."

"I've never stabbed anyone before."

"You won't do it now. We just make ourselves look like more trouble to rob than it's worth."

Again, Matt set off in the direction of their rooms, but something caught her attention and she turned aside. The charred remains of Steward Ceolwulf Husa Elbacnola lay, still clasping his book. His clothes and skin were blackened, but recognisable. A couple of yards away, Oswald's body was in a similar condition. Smoke wafted from his ceremonial robes.

Matt stood over Oswald's body, her face unreadable. "If you want someone to take responsibility, blame him. If he hadn't murdered Edmund, we'd still be in Fortaine, the river would be flowing, and the world would be in for a shitload of grief."

"You've had your revenge."

"Sort of." Matt pressed the point of the sword to his chest.

"He's dead."

"I know. But I promised to put a blade in his heart." Matt raised her eyes. "Edmund always kept his word. Every threat made good. Every promise honoured. That's what he taught me. He said I should always be very careful about giving my word on anything." Matt's expression started to break up. Her mouth worked, like somebody trying not to be sick. With a convulsive twist, she drove the sword into Oswald's body. Tears glinted in her eyes. "Come on. Let's go."

Eawynn hesitated, then pulled the book from Ceolwulf's hands. The cover was charred by the blue fire, but the pages remained intact. The library of Cyningesburg had been a wonder. She would keep one reminder of its glory.

They passed several looters on the way to the apartment, but nobody tried to intercept them. A man threw a stone that hit the wall above Eawynn's head, missing her by inches. In response, Matt scooped up a similar sized rock and her aim was on target. The stone thrower yelped, scrambling away, and no further missiles followed.

Columns of smoke rose above the ruins, either from Iparikani's fireballs, or from looters wanting to complete the demon's work. So far though, their rooms were untouched.

"What do we do now?" Eawynn asked.

"Grab our stuff and get the hell out."

"Can't we barricade ourselves in?" The mood in the city reminded Eawynn of her first days after being expelled from the temple.

"And get roasted when they set fire to downstairs?"

"Some of the army's left. Won't an officer pull the troops together?"

"Probably. Doesn't mean he'll try to retake the city today, or tomorrow, or even this month. The soldiers are outnumbered. With their training and weapons, I'd still give them the edge, but it doesn't matter who wins. If it's the army it won't be good for me, and if it's slaves it'll be worse for you." Matt was stuffing clothes and food into backpacks.

Eawynn plucked at her robes. "What about this?"

"Keep it on. You'll get more respect from soldiers and less trouble from slaves if they don't think you're an overseer."

They were soon ready to leave. Matt led the way. A few courtyards over, she stopped and passed her pack to Eawynn. "Here. Hold this a moment."

Matt burrowed into the bushes surrounding an ancient tree, then after a bit of scrabbling, backed out, holding the Shewstone. She offered it to Eawynn. "As promised." Her expression was a strange mixture of resolve and something much harder to categorise.

Matt had indeed promised the Shewstone. How many times had Eawynn doubted that promise? Matt might be a thief, but she still had her own code of ethics. Could you respect a moral standpoint you did not share? For what it was worth, Eawynn was not sure if she still respected her own. *I'm sorry I challenged you about the destruction in the plaza.* Now was not the time, but Eawynn would say it sometime and try to explain the confusion she was feeling about so many things.

Most activity in the citadel was centred around the Plaza of the Emperors. As they got farther away, they saw fewer slaves in smaller groups. The Lion Gates were unmanned when they passed. Outside the citadel, the streets were more exposed. They moved cautiously from cover to cover, alert for trouble ahead. Something alarming was going on a quarter mile downhill to the north. A clamour of shouts and screams resounded over the ruins.

"What's down there?" Eawynn asked.

"The pens where slaves got to live if they weren't lucky enough to be owned by someone with a nice house. Sounds like payback time. We probably don't want to go that way."

"So where do we go?"

"We need horses and an escort. Slaves who're looking for trouble will stick near the city. Those who aren't will run away. But just because they're running doesn't mean they'll turn down the chance for revenge on anyone with red hair. If we run into a group, I'd like some muscle in support."

"How do we get an escort?"

"We need to find a confused bunch of soldiers with horses—low rank legionnaires, who've got no idea what to do next, other than they'd like an excuse to get away."

"Is that likely?"

"I'm betting there's dozens who fit the bill. We just need to get to them before a senior officer does."

They crept through the lower town ruins avoiding gangs of slaves and one disciplined column of soldiers, a hundred strong, marching down to the valley encampment. Before long they were in a quieter region. No rebuilding work had taken place here. The ancient walls were crumbling. Grass and shrubs grew unchecked between the brickwork.

Matt pointed. "There."

One building was still intact and clearly occupied. The roof and door had been replaced and plants cleared from the front. Three soldiers stood, arguing among themselves. A string of horses were tethered nearby.

"Is it a sentry post?"

"Either that or a messenger relay station. Either way, it's our best bet. Leave the swords here." She smiled at Eawynn. "Just be bold. You've got the acting skills. I'll be right behind you."

Despite the reassurance, Eawynn's heart was pounding as she strode toward the building. The soldiers were locked in argument. "Well, I say we don't."

"You don't have a fucking—"

"You," Eawynn called when still some way off.

The three turned around sharply.

"Ma'am?" the oldest, a woman with a scarred face, answered uncertainly.

"I'll need a guard. I have to get to Sideamuda as quickly as possible. They must be told what's happened. We need reinforcements here."

"Uh." She looked left and right at her comrades for support. "Has the heretoga given permission?"

"No. Empress Aedilhild herself has. So don't waste time." Name-dropping could not hurt. They would be long gone before it was known for certain whether she had survived.

"The empress is alive?"

Eawynn glared at the speaker, putting as much condescension into her expression as she could. "Do I need to answer that?"

"No, ma'am." The decision was made. Eawynn could see it in the woman's eyes. "How many do you need?"

"You three will suffice. I'll need horses for myself and my handmaiden, but I see you have plenty."

For the first time, the soldiers looked at Matt. "You want her to come as well?"

"Unless one of you wants to do the cooking."

There were no volunteers. The rising sun cast long shadows as Eawynn, Matt, and their acquired bodyguard rode away from Cyningesburg.

CHAPTER ELEVEN

Matt needed two attempts before she managed to sit upright. Her back and legs did not want to move and let her know by launching stabs of pain when she forced them.

The kick from the soldier did not make her feel any better. "Hrere, wealh."

Matt rolled onto her knees. Dawn was an hour off. Even in summer, the night wind was freezing over the scrubland. Dry thornbushes rattled in the darkness. The campfire was cold, but all she needed was to hand. Thankfully, she had thought to gather brush the night before. The idea of scouring for firewood in her current state was not pleasant. How was she going to take another day on horseback?

There was little call for riding in Fortaine. Even visits to surrounding villages would take no more than a few hours at a relaxed pace. She had never covered anything close to the distance of the previous day, and her whole body was objecting.

"Cleace." *Hurry.* That was one word she knew.

By the time flames were snapping in the campfire, Matt's muscles were moving more freely, but she still did not think she would be able to ride. Eawynn was also moving slowly, and clearly in discomfort. Matt positioned a pot of spiced wine over the fire.

"Idelgeorne bicce." Which was something unflattering and accompanied by a cuff. The soldiers had not got over their terror from the day before, and were trying to cover it by being even more surly than normal.

Once the wine was steaming, Matt carried a mug to Eawynn. "How are you feeling?"

"Like I was dragged all the way here from Cyningesburg."

"Will you be able to ride today?"

Eawynn's expression was the answer.

"You should tell the soldiers to go on without us."

"Will it be safe?"

"Given a choice between having my throat slit and getting on a horse, I'll pick the cut throat."

"Yes. Me too." Eawynn gave a weak grin.

"Anyhow, we're far enough from Cyningesburg. There won't be any gangs of runaway ex-slaves."

"I'll be sure to tell our brave escort that."

"You think you can send them off without making them suspicious?"

"I'll say I'm too unwell to travel. They have to get to Sideamuda quickly, and I don't want to slow them down. The message is more important than my safety. That sort of stuff. From the way they've been muttering, I think they'll be glad to be rid of us."

Eawynn's prediction was right. The soldiers were in the saddle and away as soon as the sun rose. The sound of hooves faded, leaving only twists of dust carried on the wind.

Matt stood by the fire, watching the three dots disappear. "They didn't need much persuading."

"I'd thought as much. You probably didn't follow what they were saying yesterday. We were going too slow for their liking. They were also starting to wonder why a priestess was being used as a messenger. In another day or two they might have wanted answers."

"So they weren't as stupid as they looked. I wonder if they'll go to Sideamuda."

"You think they won't?"

"I wouldn't if I was them. Things are going to get nasty."

"True. How do you think it'll work out?"

"The Rihtcynn will keep control of the plains. Nobody's going to challenge them out here, but it'll go differently on the coast. Red hair won't be welcome."

"That could be a problem for me."

"We'll deal with it when we need to."

Matt lowered herself carefully to the ground and poured a mug of wine, something forbidden to a slave. She took a sip. The spices went only so far in covering the tartness, but the warmth was welcome.

Eawynn positioned herself on the other side of the fire. "Is there any left over?"

"Half a mug. We can brew more. There's plenty, and I don't think we'll be going far today." The soldiers had left not only a horse each, but also a pack mule and supplies.

"I won't argue with that."

"We'll need to go carefully. The news will be ahead of us, and we don't want to stumble into anything."

"Slow sounds good to me"

Matt grinned. It was nice when she and Eawynn were in agreement. "Have you ridden much before?"

"Last time was on my pony, Smudge, and I was six years old."

"You must be feeling worse than me."

"I don't know. I was able to collapse last night when we camped. You had to keep going."

Thankfully, that game was over. Matt took hold of the collar and pulled it around so a join was at the front. The false rivet heads were flat and did not give much to hold, but by placing a thumb on each side, she was able to twist them. Slowly, the halves unscrewed and came free. Matt tugged the slave collar from her neck. On the inside of one section was a hollowed recess, with Edmund's ring safely hidden. Now she had the right to wear it, if she wished.

She rubbed her fingers along spots on her throat where the iron had rubbed, still sore, although not as bad as on the first days. The breeze was cool on her newly exposed skin, but felt good.

Eawynn smiled. "It didn't suit you."

❖

The soldiers had picked a path west of the wagon trail. On the assumption it was the fastest way for anyone on horseback, Matt and

Eawynn stayed with it. It would go over a higher mountain pass than the one the caravan had crawled along, but the route was well enough marked there was little risk of getting lost.

On the seventh day after the soldiers left, the trail reached the foothills of the Stanscylfa Mountains, climbing though an open woodland of oak, birch, and rowan. Ferns and tall grasses covered the ground. The warbling of birdsong rippled between the branches, a joyful counterpart to the afternoon sunlight. Eawynn smiled as she rode.

Her body was getting used to the exercise and was no longer so tired and stiff at the end of each day. Eawynn had even gone so far as to name her horse Smudge II. Swapping the priestly robes for everyday clothing, better suited to riding, also helped. The new ease allowed her to take pleasure from her surroundings and pick up the pace. Even so, they would get to Sideamuda days after the soldiers. What would they find there? From her memories of the town, Eawynn was sure Matt's concern was well founded.

Matt had also swapped her slave garb for better clothes, including the boots she had worn in Fortaine. She rode in the lead, with the pack mule on a tether. The arrangement allowed Eawynn to study her at length. So far, they had restricted their conversation to mundane matters of food, weather, and the scenery, but at least they had not argued too often.

Eawynn returned her attention to the trees. What did she want to say? And if she managed to work out a satisfactory answer to that question, should she say it? The old litany: *She cheated me. She used me. She tricked and trapped me.* Could she fall for it again? Would she be making a fool of herself over someone who no longer even wanted to play the game? Of course, there were worse sorts of fool to be.

The ground was becoming broken. Fists of rock punched through the earth. Matt reined in her horse at the brow of another hill. When Eawynn stopped beside her, Smudge II immediately took advantage of this to chew on wayside flowers, much as his namesake would have done.

The valley ahead was cut by a winding river which the road crossed at a ford. The passage of hooves had worn down the banks on either side. Another narrower track came in from the south. It joined the one they were on just before the ford. Trees and wildflowers grew close to the water's edge. The scene looked pretty enough, but Matt was frowning.

"What's wrong?"

"I think there's something hidden in the trees."

"What?"

"Not sure."

"Do you think it might be dangerous?"

"Anything can be dangerous. But we don't have much option. If we leave the road, there's no saying where we'll be able to cross the river." Matt urged her horse forward. "We just stay alert."

Eawynn followed, casting around anxiously. Threats were not confined to humans. The howling of wolves had woken her the night before. The woodland seemed peaceful, but when they got close, she saw Matt had been right. Something was in the trees by the ford. Two naked bodies hung from a branch. Thick rope made nooses around their necks.

The casual display of cruelty was easily the aspect of Rihtcynn culture that Eawynn found hardest to deal with. Had the old empire been any different? Small wonder the subject races had rebelled. Yet almost immediately she realised her first assumption was wrong. The dead were not an example of harsh Rihtcynn justice. Both bodies had red hair. They twisted slowly in the breeze and, as they swung around, Eawynn saw one was an elderly man and the other a pregnant woman.

Matt reined her horse back. "Payback's a bitch."

"Who did this?"

"How would I know? I'd say they've been here a few days." Matt stood in the stirrups and looked around. "No sign of anyone now. Maybe our escort scared them away when they came through."

"The soldiers would have cut these people down and buried them properly."

"You're right. The Rihtcynn would take care of their own." Matt flicked the reins. "Let's hope whoever it was got bored of waiting for new victims and moved on, or that they only pick on people who can't fight back."

Before now, the dry ground held little in the way of prints, but thick mud beside the river was pockmarked by the passage of hooves and feet.

"Can you tell how old these are?"

Matt laughed. "I'm a townie. Your guess is as good as mine."

Eawynn peered nervously into the tangled wood. There was no trace of activity amidst the trees. She guided Smudge II down the river bank.

Smooth stones studded the bed. Water lapped around the horses' hooves as they entered the ford. By the time they reached the midway point it was up to their hocks. Eddies swirled around the animals' legs. The splashing drowned out the sound of birdsong, but then a piercing whistle cut above it all.

Three figures appeared from behind a rock stack up ahead, two men and a woman, dressed in a haphazard mixture of sacking, buckskin, and gentrified castoffs. All were carrying weapons. They charged down the hill to cut off the road. Eawynn glanced back. Two more had emerged from the woods by the hanging bodies.

"Come on." Already, Matt had spurred her horse forward, churning through the knee-high river.

Eawynn urged Smudge II to keep up. Passage through the water was agonisingly slow, and all the time the ambushers were getting closer. Matt reached dry land in the lead. Eawynn saw her release the mule's tether and set her horse off at a gallop. Smudge II gained the bank a length and a half behind.

The attackers had stopped in a knot, brandishing clubs and an old cutlass, trying to block the road by intimidation. Matt showed no sign of being deterred. If anything, she spurred her mount to greater speed. At the last moment, the ambushers' nerve broke, and they dived aside. Smudge II pounded through the gap, close behind. Shouts and curses followed Eawynn up the road.

Matt had not slowed. She was galloping, full pelt, climbing the hillside, but they had lost their pack mule. Eawynn made the mistake of looking back at the wrong moment. Smudge II swerved abruptly to the right. Eawynn grabbed for her saddle horn and missed. For the barest instant, she thought she could regain her balance, but then the saddle was no longer where it should be and her weight was working against her.

Eawynn had an eternity to worry about her foot getting caught in a stirrup, and how much the fall would hurt. The jolt came out of nowhere and rattled every bone in her body. Eawynn looked up at treetops and blue sky. She tried to remember hitting the ground, until the sound of running footsteps claimed her attention.

"Rihtcynn scum."

The larger of the two men had reached her. He hefted up a three-foot club hacked from a branch. The club joined the treetops in silhouette against the sky.

"No." Panic put an edge on Eawynn's scattered wits.

Then she heard hoofbeats. The club started to descend. The hoofbeats turned to thunder, a dark mass swept by, and suddenly, man and club were gone.

Eawynn levered herself up to sit. Matt was a dozen yards down the road, bringing her horse around while swinging a bag as if it were a flail. The man with the club was lying on the ground nearby, groaning. His two companions had stopped some way back.

Matt jumped from the horse. "Get on."

Eawynn tried to stand, but her legs were jelly.

Meanwhile, the fallen attacker was doing better. He heaved himself to his knees, and then his feet. Blood trickled down the side of his face, and his eyes were glazed. He had not picked up his club, but the sight emboldened the other two who joined him. Even with Matt's help, Eawynn could do no more than scrabble backward, putting another pointless yard between her and the gang.

"Why are you helping her?" the man with the sword shouted to Matt. His clothes were the least mismatched. Added to the assertive pose, it marked him as the leader.

"She's my friend."

"She's a Rihtcynn."

"She's my friend, from my hometown, on Pinettale."

"You're lying. I can see the rub line from here. Until a few days ago, you had a collar around your neck. So why are you on her side?"

"Do I have to repeat myself? She's my friend, and if you've got any sense, you'll back off."

More footsteps sounded. The leader glanced back. The other two had crossed the river and were running up the road. He faced Matt again. "You're the one lacking sense. You're outnumbered. Now, I've got no quarrel with you, but you're in my way. Leave the bitch to us." He took a step forward.

"I'm warning you."

The man smirked and took another step. He was less than a dozen feet away.

Their situation was hopeless. Eawynn was about to speak, to tell Matt to save herself. Before she could say a word, Matt dropped to one knee and her fingers slipped inside the loose roll top of her right boot.

"Last chance," Matt said.

The leader lifted his foot. Matt's arm moved, flicking forward. A blurred glint of metal flew from her fingertips, and the man stopped short, with an exhaled gasp. His hands clutched at his chest and came away bloody. The confusion on his face faded to nothing. He slumped to the ground and lay motionless, a dagger hilt marking the position of his heart. His followers froze.

"Who's next?" Matt's voice was as cold and as hard as iron. A second knife was in her hand.

The four surviving ambushers fled.

"Like I thought. Won't tackle anyone who can fight back." Matt walked over, tugged her knife free, then stood, staring down at the body.

Eawynn was now steady enough to get to her feet. The pack mule ambled past, swiping a mouthful of grass as it went to join Smudge II at a particularly juicy patch, farther up the road. Matt did not move.

"Are you all right?" Eawynn went to her side.

"Yeah. Sure."

"We should go."

"Yes." Matt's eyes remained locked on the dead man.

"Matt?"

"Yes. You're right. I'll get the horses." Matt lifted her head but still seemed unfocused. "You. How are you feeling? You fell."

"A bit shook up. I'll survive."

Matt nodded, then tottered up the road. Confused, Eawynn watched Matt's steps become more purposeful. *She just saved my life.* Eawynn thought. *And took another.*

The man's blood was forming a rivulet down the hill. His cutlass lay where it had dropped. The edge was nicked and pocked with rust, but it might deter another attack. Eawynn picked it up and saw the coin purse tied to the man's belt. Something else that might be useful. She slipped it free then hurried to catch up with Matt and their horses.

They did not stop until they were many miles farther on and dusk was falling. Their campsite was in the shelter of a birch grove. Matt had been silent the whole time. After dinner, she sat staring into the fire. Eawynn was also less outgoing than normal. She had a grazed cheek, wrenched knee, and collection of bruises, but made an effort to talk.

"You saved my life today."

Matt gave a one-shoulder shrug.

"Thank you."

Matt did not answer.

"Do you think we'll meet any more gangs?"

"Don't know."

An idea struck Eawynn. "Was that the first time you've killed anyone?"

Matt looked up sharply. "Yes."

"I'm grateful. Thank you."

Matt nodded and focused back on the flames.

What else could Eawynn say? *You gave him fair warning.* Matt knew that. *He murdered a pregnant woman.* But it was about what Matt had done, not her victim. *It wasn't in cold blood.* Was Matt also thinking that? How would she be feeling if she had stabbed Oswald Husa Eastandune in the back? Was she now relieved it had not come to that?

Eawynn pulled out her bedroll. "I'm going to sleep." She hesitated before shuffling around the campfire. Words were no use. She put her arm around Matt's shoulders and hugged her. For a moment, Matt relaxed into her embrace, but then pulled away.

Eawynn returned to her bedroll. Her bruises complained as she crawled in. Next time, she would pay more attention to where she was going. It was good advice, in all sorts of situations. Before trying to sleep, she looked across at where Matt sat motionless. The firelight picked out the planes and hollows of Matt's face in hot orange and warm shadows. There were many ways to fall, and you could do it more than once.

❖

With a wide-brimmed hat and a coating of dirt, Eawynn could scrape by, from a distance. Up close, she just looked like a dirty Rihtcynn. They had avoided any more trouble on the open trail, but the disguise would not get her through a busy port like Sideamuda.

Matt stood in the doorway of the abandoned barn and viewed the town walls, two miles distant, then turned to Eawynn, who sat inside, leaning against a wall. "I'll be back as soon as possible. Make sure the horses stay out of sight."

"We'll be fine." Eawynn pulled Ceolwulf's book from her pack.

The barn was clearly a casualty of war. The roof had gone, and the walls were blackened by fire. Two years' worth of dead leaves were piled in a corner. If the owners survived, Matt could only hope they would not choose today to check up on their property. The morning had dawned dry and calm, so no one was likely to be seeking shelter.

The road into Sideamuda ran along the bottom of the hillside, far enough away that passers-by would not be attracted by the sound of the horses. Matt would have taken them with her, except their rumps were marked with the army brand. Until she knew how things stood, being caught in possession of the animals was not a good idea.

When Matt reached the town gates, she found them manned, although not by Rihtcynn soldiers. The ragtag militia gave the impression of loitering, as much as standing guard. The only one wearing a helmet was presumably in command. He treated Matt to a quick once-over. "Where are you going?"

Matt pulled down the collar of her shirt to show the marks, just visible around her neck. "Home."

He smiled and waved her through.

The changes were equally obvious inside the town. Some of the government buildings had been burned out, while others showed signs of vandalism. The mood was volatile and dangerous. Matt could almost taste it. Violence could erupt without warning. No redheads were on the streets and slave collars were also missing. If the Rihtcynn nobles and soldiers were still alive, they were not advertising the fact. Where had they gone?

The answer, in at least some cases, greeted Matt in the main town square. A crudely constructed gallows stood in the centre, complete with a row of ten red-haired corpses, hanging from the crossbeam. Matt stood and looked up. Mostly they were older folk, dressed like wealthy merchants, but not all. One young woman and a couple of uniformed soldiers had also been hanged.

"We sorted them out." A man spoke at Matt's shoulder.

"What's happened? I've only just got to town."

"Word came, four days back. An army of slaves attacked Cyningesburg and killed the empress. First off, the fuckers here got nervous and tried to clamp down. They had a curfew, but fighting broke out by the docks. Next thing, they're packing up and heading out. We gave them a warm send off, and not all made it." He nodded at the gallows and smiled.

"Who's in charge now?"

"The harbour master and the merchant's guild are running the docks. It's not so clear cut in the rest of town."

Matt would have guessed as much. "Any idea what's going to happen next?"

"Some are talking about sending reinforcements to Cyningesburg. But I don't think it'll happen. Most want things to go back to normal and hang any red-haired bastard who comes within fifty miles."

Which was not good news for red-haired bastards. The town was definitely unsafe for Eawynn. The only good thing was that selling the horses would not be an issue. The money would come in useful—money always did—although they were well enough off for the moment. The gold coins in the purse Eawynn had taken from the dead gang leader would cover passage to Fortaine and more. Matt smiled at the thought. It had needed an ex-priestess to think of searching the body. *I must have been right off my game.*

The docks were less edgy than the main town. The business of trade was going on, unhampered. Possibly the number of ships in harbour was fewer than before, but not by much. Armed guards were highly visible, all wearing the badge of the merchants' guild, and looking far more alert than the militia on the gates. The harbour master's pennant hung outside what had been the portgerefan office.

Matt strolled along the quay. She could sense the tension, running below the surface, but already it felt more like home. Matt found the dock handler leaning against a wall with a clear view of the harbour master's door.

She took a spot beside him. "Hello again."

Fish Eye Ellis smiled in reply.

"How's business?"

"Getting better. You?"

"Sorted. Now, I need to go home."

"That would be Fortaine."

"Yes. Do you know who's bound there?"

"There's a few." Ellis waited until two stout merchants and their bodyguard had waddled by before continuing. "What's your main concern, speed, cost, or silence?"

"Silence."

"Try the *Song of Kalika*. She's berthed on the east quay. Due to sail early evening. Captain's called Leandros. He's a good man at minding his own business and he runs a quiet ship."

"Thanks." Matt had a coin ready. She then held up another. "There's something else I'd like."

"Anything along the lines of your last purchase?"

"No. Hair dye."

Ellis's face remained deadpan. "Dark enough to turn red hair black?"

"That'd be perfect."

"There's been a lot of demand for it recently."

"Really?"

"That's fashion for you. One day everyone wants red hair. The next day it's black." His tone was dryly ironic.

"Any shortage of supply?"

"Not if you know who to ask."

Matt grinned. Fish Eye Ellis would know who to ask, if anyone did. "It wouldn't hurt if it could do something about pale skin as well."

❖

From out at sea, the port of Sideamuda looked unchanged since the first time Eawynn had seen it, but although the view was the same, the sight provoked very different emotions. Back then she had been eager to visit her ancestral homeland. *It was good in parts.* Eawynn wrinkled her nose. *A shame those parts were so rare.* Her Rihtcynn blood might not be anything to brag about, but she still preferred it inside her rather than outside.

Eawynn wrinkled her nose again experimentally. The dye made her skin feel odd. She must ask Matt how long it would take to wear off. She stayed on the foredeck, watching and thinking, while Sideamuda shrunk to an indistinct jumble on the coast

Matt joined her. "I've been sorting out beds and stuff. Do you want to come and look?"

"I take it we don't have a cabin?"

"Nope. Leandros seems a decent captain, but he doesn't owe any favours." She directed Eawynn to a hatch in the deck. A ladder led down into the gloom. "We're in the forward hold. Afraid it isn't as fancy as the *Blue Puffin.*"

The words sounded ominous. Unduly so, to Eawynn's mind, once she reached the bottom of the steps. The hold was easily five times the size of their previous accommodation and less than half full, allowing them more space.

"Why's it so empty? Will they be taking on more cargo later?"

"As I understand it, the main hold is carrying iron ingots for tax purposes. The ship's got all the weight it can handle."

"Why would you carry ingots for tax purposes?"

"Tax purposes as in, some of the ingots look a lot like swords."

"They're smugglers."

"Who are they hurting?"

"The honest traders who have to pay extra taxes to make up the difference."

"Leandros isn't forcing anyone else to be honest."

"If nobody pays taxes, there'll be no money to maintain the harbours. Then what would he do?"

Matt grinned. "I still think you're being harsh. So he's smuggling out a hold full of swords and a Rihtcynn fugitive with her hair dyed black. If he was going to own up about one, you can't expect him to keep quiet about the other. You can't have it both ways."

She has a point. Eawynn sighed and let the matter drop. She looked around the hold. A row of barrels were braced along the one flat wall, while sacks where stacked against the curved sides of the ship and held in place by netting. A sweet, spicy scent came from the barrels, cloves and ginger at a guess. Their bags were piled in the middle of the floor, and on either side was a low bed, covered in blankets. Eawynn pressed down on one. Her hand disappeared up to her wrist. It was extremely soft.

Matt pointed to the sacks. "They're bales of wool. I've been arranging them. As beds go, they might be a bit on the bouncy side, but better than the floor."

"We've got the hold to ourselves?"

"Yes. The crew have hammocks in the stern. We don't have a porthole, but we can open the hatch in good weather, and there's a hook for a lantern."

"It'll do."

Eawynn climbed back on deck. A stiff breeze filled the sails, and seagulls swooped and wheeled over the ship's wake. They stood together at the stern and watched the land slip over the horizon.

"Are you sorry to see it go?" Matt asked.

"In some ways."

"Looking forward to getting home?"

Where is my home? "In some ways."

"You'll be taking the Shewstone to the temple."

"No."

"What?"

"I don't want to go back to being a priestess."

"When did you decide that?"

"Some time ago."

"You didn't…" Matt shrugged. "Guess I don't blame you. What are you going to do?"

"I don't know."

"You could sell the Shewstone. It's yours, you know. I want no part of it."

"I don't either."

"You're not going to toss it overboard?"

"No. I might see if I can free the sylph. I assume Oswald was right about one being imprisoned inside."

Matt looked surprised. "Haven't you had enough of supernatural beings?"

"Sylphs are safe. They're spirits of the ether who don't normally pay any attention to humans. But as Oswald said, they're notoriously helpful when they do."

"If you believe the stories."

"The stories were right about demons."

"Oh well, the *Song of Kalika* is making a straight run for Fortaine, but we still won't make landfall for over half a month, depending on the wind. You've got time to think it through."

"Maybe there'll be something in Ceolwulf's book. I started on it when I was waiting in the barn, but I haven't had another chance to read."

"You got your chance now. There won't be much—" Matt looked annoyed.

"What is it?"

"I'm starting to feel sick."

❖

Matt woke up from her first decent sleep since boarding the ship and felt all right. It was like a magic trick. Two and a half days of hell, and then overnight, her stomach gave up the attempt to swim back to shore without her. She lay on her improvised bed a while longer, looking at the roof and enjoying the sensation of not being ill. Her stomach then began a different complaint. It was empty. She rolled out of bed and pulled on her shirt and pants but left her boots behind. Barefoot would be fine on the sun-warmed deck.

The morning was well advanced when Matt clambered from the hatch. Captain Leandros hailed her from the tiller. "Got your sea legs now?"

"I hope so."

Leandros chuckled. He had found Matt's seasickness highly amusing, and it would seem the joke was not yet over. The *Song of Kalika* was smaller than the *Blue Puffin*, with a four-man crew. Only one other sailor was visible, up in the rigging. Eawynn sat on the foredeck, her book open on her lap. If she noticed Matt, she gave no sign.

The ship's galley was empty, breakfast long past. Matt helped herself to leftover porridge. She washed, using buckets of sea water, then went back to the hold and put on fresh clothes. Her hair was thick with salt, but she no longer smelt like a woman who has spent days hurling her guts up. By the time Matt returned to the deck, she felt almost human again.

What should she do now? On the previous voyage, she and Eawynn had kept as far apart as possible, but at that time, they could not spend two minutes together without arguing. They were getting along much better now. Did Matt want to push her luck? She could go and sit on the foredeck with Eawynn. They did not have to talk. Then a yawn caught Matt by surprise. Alternately, she could find somewhere sheltered and sunny for a nap and move to the foredeck later. Maybe by then Eawynn would like a break from her book.

Matt dozed on and off for the next few hours, until a thin cloud cover blew over and the sun went in. Hot food was only prepared at dawn and dusk. So Matt grabbed bread and salt pork for lunch and went to join Eawynn. She promised herself she would leave as soon as the conversation started to go sour. However, Eawynn and her book were no longer on the foredeck

"She went below, a while back," a sailor volunteered.

"Did she seem all right?"

"A bit unhappy, but that was all."

Matt leaned on the railing and chewed the last of the pork while wondering whether she ought to go find Eawynn. Could they become friends? Or would Eawynn work with her only when their lives were at stake? What was the worst possible outcome if she went down to the hold? Even without working out a full answer to that question, Matt felt her lungs grow tight. *What have you got to be frightened of?* Matt slapped her hand on the railing, hard enough to hurt. She was seriously losing patience with herself.

Matt crouched by the hatch and peered in, but it was too dark to see. "Eawynn?"

The lack of reply tipped her hand. Maybe Eawynn was unwell, or worse. Matt hopped down the ladder. Once her eyes adjusted to the gloom, she saw Eawynn sitting on a bed. The closed book lay on the floor by her feet.

"Eawynn, are you all right?"

"Not really."

Matt knelt beside her. "What is it?"

"The sylph."

By now, Matt's vision was strong enough to see tears forming in Eawynn's eyes. "What about it?"

"In the book. It's awful. I didn't know. I don't think any of us did."

"Know what? You're not making sense."

Eawynn rubbed her eyes. "Sylphs are simple spirits of the air. They just play and enjoy life. They're harmless. Like children."

"If children didn't do things like pulling legs off spiders?"

"Yes. No. I mean, yes." Eawynn shook her head. "They aren't malicious. They'd never hurt anyone."

Matt said nothing. Her previous remark had only caused confusion, and Eawynn clearly did not need any more of that.

"They're innocent spirits."

"You're saying it's safe to free it. What's the problem?"

"Lots. It has to be done carefully, with the right words, and in the right place."

Matt frowned. "Ceolwulf and Oswald were just going to smash the Shewstone open for the demon."

"That would have harmed the sylph. Which was why Iparikani would be able to consume it so easily. Normally, sylphs are nimble enough to escape. To be certain it's not injured, the Shewstone has to be opened in the exact same spot as where the sylph was first captured."

"In Cyningesburg?"

"No. Fortaine, at the Temple of Anberith. It happened during the last years of the empire. The Sister Oracle of the day tricked the sylph and sealed it in the orb. She was part of an underground Rihtcynn cult. They were evil." Eawynn buried her face in her hands.

Rihtcynn being evil. Now there's a surprise. "That was in the past."

"You don't understand."

I won't unless you tell me. "What?"

"The sylph is a prisoner inside the Shewstone. I don't think it can really foretell the future, but the old cult thought it could. When it wouldn't tell them anything, they used to torture it to make it speak. That became part of the ritual, and I used to do it. I lit a flame under the Shewstone and it made a noise. That was the sylph screaming."

Matt put a hand on Eawynn's leg. "You didn't know what you were doing, else you wouldn't have done it. It's the people who told you who are to blame."

"I don't think Insightful Sister Oracle understood. She was just copying what the priestess before her did."

I wouldn't rule it out. "It doesn't matter. You're innocent."

"No, I'm not."

Matt shifted around to sit on the bed beside Eawynn. "Then make what amends you can. Free the sylph."

"But how? They won't let me set foot in the temple."

"We'll find a way."

"We? You'd help me?"

"Of course.

"Why?"

Because I'm dangerously close to falling in love with you, and I like beating myself up. "I feel I owe you."

"You saved my life."

"If I hadn't stolen the Shewstone, you'd have been safely in Fortaine all along."

"Then I'm indebted to you, twice over. I was miserable in the temple. Once I got over my panic at the big wide world, there was no way I wanted to go back. And I'd still be taking part in torturing the sylph."

"So why did you stick with me? Carry on after the Shewstone?"

"I couldn't desert you."

"Why not? You've every reason to hate me."

"True. I got over it."

How much over? "I saw the marks on your back. You were flogged because of me."

"They wanted me gone. They'd have found another excuse. If not the key, then because someone said I dropped litter. That wasn't why I hated you."

Matt swallowed and dropped her gaze. They were both suffering with regrets for things done in ignorance, but her mistakes were far less forgivable. Nobody had told her to do it. Matt could not claim she had not known exactly what she was about. Yet she had not understood the consequences. She had thought flirting with Eawynn was a game, but it was actually one of the most serious things she had done in her life.

"I never meant to hurt you."

"But you did. Mostly my pride. You made a fool of me. Or you tricked me into making a juvenile fool of myself. I thought you were genuinely interested in me, when you were only after the Shewstone."

"No. I mean, I was only in the temple for the stone, but there were all sorts of ways I could have gone about stealing it. Flirting with you was the most fun option." Matt stopped. Probably she could have phrased that better.

"It was a game to you."

"Flirting always was. It didn't mean I wasn't gambling with my heart."

"You were betting your heart on me?" Eawynn sounded sceptical.

"More than I knew."

"You're serious?"

"Yes."

Eawynn turned her head. Matt found herself staring back. Her heart started to thump in her chest. The words could not be held back. "The day I met you, I thought you were one of the most attractive women I'd seen. Flirting with you was a game. I admit it. And I thought I was winning. Only since we've been travelling together I find that I've lost. With each day, I've become a little more lost. If we hadn't been bogged down with mundane things, like hiding from demons and running for our lives, I'd have gone crazy. And now I'm looking at days, stuck on this small boat with you, and I don't know how I'm going to cope."

Eawynn was silent for such a long time, Matt was giving up on a reply, but at least Eawynn was not running away. Eventually, she said, "If I kiss you again, and you steal something off my belt, I'm going to pitch you overboard."

"Do you think you might kiss me again?"

Instead of answering, Eawynn leaned closer and pressed her mouth against Matt's.

Eawynn's lips were soft and warm. Her body filled Matt's arms, firm and so very solid. A surge of desire ripped through Matt, from her toes to the tips of her hair, only to be washed away in something richer, deeper, and far more soul-searing. She slid down onto the blanket, pulling Eawynn with her.

They lay together on the wool sack bed, still fully dressed, exploring the texture of hands and faces, the soft and hard, the muscle and bone felt through cloth. After months of waiting, Matt could take her time and let Eawynn set the pace.

"I want more. I want to feel your skin against mine," Eawynn mumbled between kisses.

Matt sat and pulled her shirt over her head. Item by item, they shed their clothes. Eawynn's breasts were fuller than Matt had expected. She cupped one in her hand, entranced by the strips of pale white skin showing between her fingers. Eawynn's areolas were dark, the same colour as her lips. Matt sucked on both nipples in turn, feeling them harden under her tongue. Eawynn moaned, then reached under Matt's arms and pulled her up into another hard embrace.

A roll, and Eawynn lay on top, pressing Matt into the bedding. From neck to ankle, they touched, skin on skin. Matt's hands slid from the flat plains of Eawynn's shoulder blades, down the sharply defined column of her spine, and over the soft, smooth rounds below. She returned to Eawynn's head, sliding her fingers through hair, applying gentle pressure to guide the small movements as they kissed.

The need for release was building in Matt, but she would force herself to wait, just a little longer. She shifted free from the weight on top of her and pressed Eawynn back onto the bed. With the lightest finger pressure, she traced patterns over Eawynn's breasts and stomach, and then farther down. Starting at Eawynn's hip, she followed the line between body and thigh.

"Open your legs."

Eawynn's knees parted, and Matt's hand completed its journey. Eawynn was wet, and warm, and ready. Matt entered her with two fingers, while her thumb rubbed gently where it was needed, taking her timing from the gasped breaths. Eawynn was very close to the edge.

All the while, Matt stared at her face. Later, there would be time for tongues, and the more inventive games lovers could play, but this first time, she wanted to watch Eawynn's face as she came.

The stars were out. Eawynn sat on the foredeck with Matt's arms around her. As further protection against the night wind, they were wrapped in a blanket. She leaned her head into the hollow of Matt's neck. Had she ever felt so totally happy? Matt caught hold of her hand, interlacing their fingers.

Eawynn snuggled deeper into Matt's arms. "Of course, I reserve the right to hate you again, if you do something to upset me."

"If I do anything to upset you, I'll be hating myself."

"You can be irritating."

"Pot, meet kettle."

Eawynn gave a dig with her elbow.

"Ouch." Matt brushed a kiss across her cheek.

"Is it silly to worry about the future?"

"Yes. But if you can stop yourself doing it you'll be in a group of one."

"So what do you think?"

"We'll have a lot of fun on the boat, until we get to Fortaine. Once there, we'll work out how to get into the temple and free the sylph. Then, when that's over, we'll see how long we can go before one of us wants to kill the other."

"You think we'll last all the way to Fortaine?"

"I'm an optimist." Matt was laughing as she spoke.

The moon would not rise until dawn. Nothing challenged the array of stars carpeting the black velvet sky. The world was beautiful. She would free the sylph to enjoy its glory again.

"I need to read more of the book. I have to find the words to open the Shewstone safely."

"I promise to let you have some time to read." Matt nibbled gently on her neck, making it clear what she proposed doing the rest of the time.

Eawynn felt her insides flip and moved her neck away. "That tickles."

Matt left off nibbling. For a while they watched the stars in silence, and then Matt asked, "If the sylph was captured in Fortaine, how come the information ended up in a book in Cyningesburg?"

"From what I've read so far, Rihtcynn mystics discovered how to contact the otherworld centuries ago, but decided it was too dangerous. The temples banned its study. There's even talk of a prophesy that if they stirred things up, it would lead to the end of the empire."

"An easy bit of fortune telling, when you've got hindsight."

"Anyway, a cult started, with cells across the empire, mainly in cities. They thought the rule was just cowardice. They tried to capture a sylph in Cyningesburg, but failed. Obviously, the cultists in Fortaine were more successful. But then the river changed course, and it all fell apart."

Matt rested her chin on Eawynn's shoulder. "A month ago, I'd have said it was coincidence, but having seen a demon, could someone have done something stupid?"

"You mean, the prophesy wasn't just hindsight?"

"Maybe."

In which case, although the cultists might not have intended it, they had done the subject races a huge favour. Whatever benefits the Rihtcynn Empire had brought in the past, the world was better off now without it. She and Matt had just performed a similar role and saved countless thousands of people from decades of misery. But it was not going to put any beans on their table.

"After we've freed the sylph, do you think I'll be able to get work as a scribe in Fortaine?"

"Probably, if you want to."

"I need something to live on."

"Money won't be a problem."

"Maybe not for you. I won't be happy about it."

"Because it's stolen?" Matt squeezed her again. "When we get back, I'll have some family issues to sort out. After that's done, how about if I promise to only steal from bad people in future? It won't be hard. There's plenty of them about."

Chapter Twelve

Redoubtable Sister Door-warden was still guarding the atrium door. She jumped up when Matt approached. "Madam Hilda. We hadn't expected to see you again so soon."

Matt affected a confused frown. "Didn't you get my letter?"

"Letter? No, I don't think so."

"Oh dear." Matt gestured to the young man who was carrying her bags. "It's all right, you can put them down." She turned back. "I need to finish off the last of the paperwork for my uncle's affairs. I'd sent a letter ahead. I know it was short notice, but..." She bit her lip. "Do you know if there's room in the hostel? I'd be most unhappy about taking lodgings at a tavern. Although I suppose..." She let her voice trail off.

"I'll see what can be done. Please, take my seat. I'll send for Welcoming Sister Hosteller."

"Thank you."

Much bustling back and forth followed. Eventually, Welcoming Sister Hosteller appeared, with a junior priestess in tow. "A pleasure to see you again, Madam Hilda. I trust you've been keeping well."

"Yes, thank you."

"I believe you wish to stay with us."

"Just for a few nights."

Welcoming Sister Hosteller looked unhappy "We're rather busy, what with the royal wedding."

"I understand." Matt kept her fixed smile. Probably best not to admit she had no idea which royal was marrying who. Eawynn had said the hostel was never full. Typical bloody aristocrats to get in the way.

"Um...we have a free room until the tournament starts. Would that suffice?"

When was that? Matt hoped for the best. "Oh, that would be wonderful. I only expect to be here for two days."

Welcoming Sister Hosteller beamed. She had not been forced to say no to a guest. After Matt paid the porter, the priestess picked up the smaller of the bags, leaving the considerably larger one for her assistant. "Please, follow me."

Elbows by sides, small steps, squashed neck, and smile like an idiot. Matt had hoped she was done with the charade, but this time would not be for long. "Is all well at the temple? I recall a theft when I was here before. I pray there's been no repeat."

"No. The temple has been quite secure, and we were fortunate to recover the stolen items."

"You were? Praise the goddess."

"Indeed, our lady Anberith did have a hand in it."

"How so?"

Welcoming Sister Hosteller lowered her voice. "We didn't say at the time, but the most valuable thing lost was the Shewstone. But Most Reverend Insightful Sister Oracle led prayers for its recovery and told us to have faith. And truly, Anberith came to our aid. On the full moon after you left, the Shewstone reappeared overnight, at the feet of the statue in the sanctuary."

"A miracle." If anyone gave awards for acting, Matt reckoned she deserved one.

"Exactly. The hand of our goddess at work." They reached the hostel. "The room you stayed in before is in use, but you may have the one at the end."

"A change of view is always nice."

Welcoming Sister Hosteller opened the door and handed over the bag she had been carrying. "You know the rules and running of the hostel. I hope you have a pleasant time here."

"I did last time, very much so." Matt entered the room and then turned back. "Oh. One other thing. I'm expecting a clerk, a man, to visit tomorrow with confidential papers to sign. Will it be possible to make arrangements for me to see him in private?"

"I'll let Redoubtable Sister Door-warden know. I'm sure, depending on the time of day, either the schoolroom or the audience chamber can be made available."

"Thank you so much."

Matt closed the door after the priestesses left and smiled at the large bag the junior had dumped on the bed. Getting the Shewstone back into the temple had been even easier than taking it out.

Her view from the window was at a different angle than before, but still showed nothing except the neat rows of vegetables in the kitchen garden. Matt stood a while, watching the shadows cast by the beanpoles lengthen.

She had timed her arrival to miss the evening meal. Not only was food at The Jolly Wagoner better, but Matt would rather avoid the ordeal of keeping a simpering smile in place, while sitting within arm's reach of Most Repulsive Unsightly Sister Orifice. Matt had disliked the woman enough on her own account. Now she had the anger over the stripes on Eawynn's back to stoke the heat.

Just before sunset, the temple bell rang for yet another ceremony. The timing was perfect, late enough for poor light, but not so late as to be suspicious. Partly out of habit, Matt wanted to move the Shewstone. She transferred it to the smaller bag, the one that nestled in the small of her back, and pulled a cloak around her shoulders. Matt could think of no reason why anyone might search her room, but life in the sisterhood was dull. Who knew what the junior priestess who cleaned the room might do for entertainment? Safer if there was nothing out of the ordinary to find.

According to Eawynn, the Whatsit of Thingumy Day's End was one of the less well attended ceremonies, depending on how it conflicted with the tides. There was a chance of meeting a roving priestess. Matt covered the short distance at her best stately pace, keeping her head down and her hands clasped in front of her stomach. It looked reflective, and meant her elbows held the cloak open so it billowed behind her, just in case anyone was watching.

The platform under the statue had worked well as a hiding place before, and she intended to use it again. However, as Matt approached the shrine door, a priestess appeared from the other direction.

Unsightly Sister Orifice gave a manifestly insincere smile which got nowhere close to her eyes. "Madam Hilda. I heard you were with us again. I hope concluding your late uncle's affairs has proved beneficial." She still had not given up dreams of a donation to temple funds.

"We've managed to compensate most of his creditors. I'm sure his soul will sleep more easily."

"So we must pray." The smile became icy. Even the most determined beggar has to accept a no sometimes. "You didn't wish to join in the worship?"

"I'm tired from my journey. But I look forward to it tomorrow."

A frown appeared on the priestess's face. *So what are you doing, wandering around?* She was clearly trying to think of a subtler way to phrase it.

Matt saved her the bother. "I was hoping to borrow a book from the library to help me relax."

"Studious Sister Librarian will be in the sanctuary, but once she returns, I'm sure she'll be able to pick something suitable for you." She was as patronising as ever.

Matt forced herself to smile, remembering a book Eawynn had spoken about. "I understand you have a copy of Wilfrid's *Rise and Fall of the Rihtcynn Empire.* I'm hoping to see it."

"But that's written in…"

Something even an arrogant arsehole like you can't read. Of course, neither could Matt, but that did not stop her enjoying the flabbergasted expression. Matt followed up by reciting one of the more elaborate Cynnreord phrases she had picked up in the slave camp.

Unsightly Sister Orifice's smile was decidedly sickly. She clearly had no idea what Matt had just said.

"Beo gesund." She slurred the good-bye and retreated through the shrine door.

Matt sighed. An unnecessary risk, but she had been unable to resist, reckoning there was little chance the priestess would know Cynnreord for, *Go fuck yourself with a battering ram, shit-face.*

Matt continued around the atrium. The shrine was no longer available as a hiding place. Luckily, the library really was her second choice, and as expected, this room was empty. A priestess should not be doing anything as trivial as reading when prayers were in progress.

A row of bookshelves with scrollwork façades lined one wall. Matt pulled a chair over and climbed up. The ornate carving at the front rose considerably higher than the flat top of the case it was attached to. Easily high enough to hide a six-inch orb from anyone at ground level, and the thick dust showed it had not been cleaned for decades. Matt placed the Shewstone behind the highest section on the central cabinet. Eawynn had said they would need to visit the library tomorrow, so picking up the Shewstone would not require a detour.

There was just one more thing Matt wanted to do while the temple grounds were relatively priestess-free. The laundry was conveniently located alongside the hostel. This was another place where no priestess should be during a ceremony.

The room was cold and damp, with whitewashed stone walls and floor, and a water trough taking up all of one wall. Three huge wicker baskets for soiled clothes stood close by the entrance. Matt shut the door behind her and lifted the first lid. This was almost too easy. She grabbed what she needed, stuffed it in her bag, and left.

❖

Eawynn resisted the urge to check whether her beard was still in place. Even if it was askew, the last thing she wanted was to draw attention to it.

"I'm here to see Madam Hilda of Gimount." Eawynn tried to make her voice as deep as possible, but feared it only made her sound as if she was suffering from a cold.

"Oh yes, she's expecting you."

Redoubtable Sister Door-warden clearly saw nothing wrong. Her face held not the slightest hint of recognition. As Matt had assured Eawynn the day before, most people were very unobservant. Few would look beyond a beard and a change of clothing. A hat and a fresh application of the dye to skin and hair completed Eawynn's disguise.

The priestess slipped off her stone bench. "Follow me."

"Thank you."

"It's nice to see a new face in the temple. Do you attend the ceremonies often?"

"When I can."

"I'm always there, you know. I'm a member of the choir."

Something was wrong with Redoubtable Sister Door-warden. Her voice was a full octave higher than normal, and her shoulders wobbled back and forth as she strutted around the atrium. It was only after she threw a third bright smile over her shoulder that the stunning realisation hit. *She's trying to flirt with me.* Eawynn nearly choked.

"Are you all right?" Redoubtable Sister Door-warden put her hand on Eawynn's arm.

"I'll be fine." *If I don't pee myself.*

They stopped outside the audience chamber, and the priestess pushed open the door. "If you go in and wait, I'll make sure Madam Hilda knows you're here."

"Thank you."

Redoubtable Sister Door-warden replied with a girlish giggle. *I really didn't need to hear that.* Eawynn had a moment of dread when she thought she was about to be followed into the room and accosted. However, the simpering priestess only gave one last coy twitch of her shoulders and closed the door.

Eawynn collapsed on a chair—the same chair her father had sat on years before, when he gave her to the temple. Who would have guessed how life would turn out, for either of them? What would she say to her father, if they could meet? Or Hattie? Was the old cook still alive? Once the undertaking with the Shewstone was finished, Eawynn could go wherever she wanted. What was the likelihood she would be able to track down Hattie, or even her mother?

The door opened. "I'll be waiting out here." Redoubtable Sister Door-warden's voice had returned to its normal pitch.

Eawynn stood as Matt minced into the room. There was no other way to describe the way she was walking. *Did it look as ridiculous as that before, when she was playing the part?* Eawynn struggled with her memories. Was it just because she had got to know Matt so much better? Once the door closed, the grin was pure Matt. She wrapped her arms around Eawynn and kissed her soundly.

"Yep. I definitely prefer you without a beard." Matt spoke softly enough not to be overheard from outside the room. Redoubtable Sister Door-warden would be on guard.

"I'm not wild about it either."

"Everything went all right?"

"Fine."

Already, Matt was stripping off her clothes. Eawynn unlaced her boots, then dropped her leggings and tugged the shirt and jerkin over her head. Matt stared at her with clear intent in her eyes.

"Stop that. We don't have time."

"I know." Matt gave a dramatic sigh and handed over the dress.

Within minutes, they had swapped clothes, including changing the clerk's hat for Hilda's wig. Eawynn helped smooth down the edges of the false beard. She suspected Matt made a better boy than she did. Would Redoubtable Sister Door-warden notice the difference?

"How do I look?"

"Strangely appealing."

Matt pouted and then pulled her in for another searching kiss.

"Fair enough. You're right. It's better without the beard."

"Told you so." Matt released her and went to the door. "I was given the room at the far end of the corridor."

"Right. Oh, and before you go, I should warn you."

"What?"

"Don't let Redoubtable Sister Door-warden get you alone."

Matt frowned. "Eh?"

"You'll see what I mean."

Still looking bemused, Matt knocked and mouthed. "See you later."

The door swung open. "I'll escort you out." Redoubtable Sister Door-warden was back in flirtatious mode, and clearly oblivious to the fact the person under the beard had changed. A look of understanding flitted across Matt's face and then she was gone.

Eawynn waited until the sound of footsteps faded, then opened the door an inch and peered out. The atrium was silent and deserted. This would be one of the riskier bits. If she ran into anyone, her disguise amounted to no more than clothes, brown skin and a wavy wig. Even if this was enough to stop them recognising her as the former Dutiful Sister Custodian, it did not mean they would mistake her for Hilda of Gimount.

Still, there was no point hanging around. Her heart pounding, Eawynn slipped though the doorway. The temptation to run was overwhelming, but she remembered the way Matt had walked, the small mouse-like footsteps, the tight, bound in posture. Eawynn did her best to copy, but her shoes still clicked on the stone paving. How did Matt manage it? However, concentrating on the details of posture and movement helped. It stopped her thinking about anything else.

Eawynn left the atrium and crossed the open yard. She passed the elder tree with the bench around the trunk, the dried up fountain which had not worked for years, the spot where she had been caught throwing snowballs, aged seven. Step by step, she got closer to the relative safety of the hostel. The door came into view, and then she was inside, only to see Welcoming Sister Hosteller in her cubbyhole, just off the entrance.

The priestess glanced up. "Good afternoon, Madam Hilda. I trust your business went well."

"Yes. Thank you." Eawynn kept walking, and amazingly, that was it. No second look. No challenge or queries. No footsteps chasing after her.

She climbed the stairs and entered the room. Only once the door was closed did her pulse rate start to slow. That was the next stage over with. Now all she had to do was wait.

❖

"Do you think it's what Edmund would have wanted?" Benny clearly did not.

"He might have."

"He named you as his daughter."

"Didn't mean he thought I should become boss of the gang. I've never been into the management side of things."

"You're going to let Tobias's boy take over?"

Matt gave the question more thought, then shrugged. "Why not? I think he'll be good at it. Better then me." She went to the window and peered out. It was time for her to leave.

Benny had been waiting when she returned to The Jolly Wagoner, and the conversation had been going in circles ever since. "Something's changed with you."

"True. Some things have."

Benny ran his hand through his hair. "I'll tell the boys, but I don't think they're gonna like it. But it's good to see you back in town."

"Thanks."

He looked at the fake beard lying on the table. "You got a game on the go?"

"Sort of."

"There's no need to worry about Gilbert. You heard the handymen nailed him?"

"Yes, I heard, and that's not it. I've got unfinished business at the temple."

"The temple?"

"Yes." Matt smiled. "And I think Edmund would have approved, wholeheartedly."

Once Benny had gone, Matt completed her next transformation. A second set of clothes suitable for Hilda were hanging in the wardrobe. The style was loose enough to slip her set of lock picks inside the surcoat, as well as a pouch containing various items Eawynn had left ready.

The disagreement about succession in the Flyming gang had taken more time than Matt had allowed. However, with a bit of indecorous jogging, she was not far off schedule when she stopped in Silver Lady Square to buy flowers.

"I'd like a really large bunch."

"Carnations or roses, love?" the old woman asked.

"It's for an offering in the temple."

"Ah. Then you want lilies."

One previous lover had been annoyed when Matt gave her lilies. Supposedly, it symbolised something the lover did not appreciate. Obviously, Anberith was no ordinary girl.

Matt slowed her footsteps to Hilda's toddling pace as she crossed the sanctuary. Heavy clouds had arrived late afternoon, and the threat of a downpour was keeping the public areas emptier than normal. Was it right for worshippers of the sea goddess to worry at getting wet? Much about religion was a mystery to Matt. Not that she was complaining. The lack of observers made it easier to transfer Eawynn's bag to the middle of the bunch.

With the lilies in her arms, Matt reached the atrium gate, exactly when she had intended, just before the start of the evening meal. It was the one time each day when you could guarantee Redoubtable Sister Door-warden would not be on duty. Her deputy, who had recently taken over, was not to know Madam Hilda of Gimount had not left the temple earlier that afternoon.

The young priestess smiled at the lilies. "They look nice."

"I want to put them in the Shrine to the Oracle. Business has gone well, and I'd like to offer these for future good fortune."

"I'm sure Anberith will heed your prayers."

Matt nodded and continued on.

In the shrine, she placed the flowers at the foot of a statue, then on impulse, checked the door to the Shewstone room. It was locked, more the pity. She would have liked to see the new stone. How did Unsightly Sister Orifice's artwork compare with her own? Who held the key to the shrine now? Not that Matt had the slightest intention of kissing whichever priestess it was. A better bet was the lock picks, but the risk of using them was too much for the sake of idle curiosity.

The bell for dinner was ringing as Matt passed the refectory door. To keep in character she ought to join with the communal meal, but given the choice between Unsightly Sister Orifice's company and Eawynn's there was absolutely no competition. She stopped by the kitchen.

"Excuse me, I don't want to be a nuisance."

Yet she was being one. Matt could tell from the cook's expression. "Yes?"

"My stomach's unsettled. I don't think I could face food right now. Could I have a little bread and cold meat to take to my room, in case I feel better later?"

The cook was clearly rushing through last-minute preparations and scowled, pointing to a shelf. "Over there. Help yourself." Which was exactly what Matt was hoping to hear.

The hostel room was empty when Matt arrived, which was not to plan. She put the tray on the lid of the chest, fighting a sudden knot of tension in her gut. What had happened to Eawynn?

Then the door to the wardrobe opened and Eawynn stepped out. "It's you."

"Aren't you a little old for hide-and-seek?"

"I thought it safer."

"How long have you been in there?"

"Since I heard the door close downstairs."

Matt gave her a hug. "I've brought dinner."

"I don't think I can eat."

"Are you feeling ill?"

Eawynn sighed. "This really doesn't bother you, does it?"

"What?"

"Knowing at any minute someone could walk in and we'd be dead, maybe literally."

"Nerves? I've the perfect thing for that." Matt brandished the bottle of wine.

"You're hopeless."

After much effort, Matt was able to coax Eawynn into eating and drinking. They still had over three hours to kill, and Matt knew the perfect way to spend the time, but for once Eawynn was not interested, even when Matt stuck a chair under the door handle. It would not keep anyone out, but would allow enough time for Eawynn to get back in the wardrobe.

Instead, they simply lay side-by-side, with Matt's arm around Eawynn. The conversation with Benny kept drifting around in Matt's head. She really did not care about becoming head of the gang, but could not imagine leaving it. Yet Eawynn would never accept a life of crime. Realistically, what were their chances in the long term? Matt clenched her jaw. The thought of not being with Eawynn was unbearable.

In the end, all relationships floundered and broke up, unless you were lucky enough to find a person you were totally suited to. Matt wanted to think that person was Eawynn, but they were so different. Yet, despite it all, she could not stop herself thinking they were meant to be together. Matt knew she was deluding herself in this, but it felt like the same sort of delusion as telling herself she needed air to breathe. Lying fully clothed with Eawynn, she was happier than she had ever been before. The most energetic and imaginative sex was nothing compared to the satisfying weight of Eawynn's head on her shoulder. If Eawynn wanted, she could even call her Mattie.

Was this what love felt like?

❖

Eawynn wiggled from side to side, trying to adjust the weight of the robe. After three months out of them, they felt heavy, dragging on her shoulders.

"Any idea whose these were?"

"I grabbed the first two from the basket that looked the right size." Matt grinned. "Probably best if you don't think about it too much."

Eawynn gave up with the robe and pulled a cape over her head. Luckily, the weather was wet enough to justify it. "You don't think we need to shave our hair?"

"Nope. If anyone gets close enough to have a good look under the cape, the game will be up anyway."

Eawynn was not about to argue. It had taken her hair long enough to grow to its current two inches. She opened the shutter a fraction and peered out, not that she could see anything. The moon would be full and high overhead, but heavy cloud blocked all light. A distant roll of thunder rumbled over the vegetable garden.

"When does it start?" Matt asked.

"A half hour before midnight."

"It should be soon then."

Before Eawynn could reply, the chime of the temple bells sounded, dull and muffled by the hammering of rain. Even though nobody could see it, the Extolment of the Full Moon's Splendour would go ahead on schedule.

Matt joined her at the window. "We're lucky with the weather."

She was right. They would get wet, but not as badly as those in the sanctuary. Eawynn remembered nights, frozen stiff and soaked to the skin, as she suffered through the required ritual. Any priestess who could wrangle her way out of attending would do so and stay warm in her bed. The risk of running into anyone in the atrium was slim. Of course, the rain meant their own presence was more likely to raise questions if someone spotted them, but who would be nosey enough to step out into this sort of weather in search of answers?

"Everyone who's going should be in the sanctuary by now," Eawynn said.

"Yup. I agree." Matt lifted the lantern off its hook and beckoned Eawynn to follow, slipping silently down the stairs and out the hostel door.

Rain splattered off their capes. The hem of Eawynn's robe hung a little low and was sodden by the time they reached the shelter of the atrium. It slapped cold around her ankles and clung to her legs. Eawynn grimaced. Just one more reason to be glad about leaving the temple.

The rain had begun to ease, but still water gushed from the gargoyles and cascaded into the atrium garden. The flower beds must be awash by now. The small circle of lamp light was a beacon in the darkness of the covered walkway. They would be horribly conspicuous, if anyone was watching.

Matt stopped at the library door and pulled the roll of lock picks from her sleeve. "Here, hold the lantern for me."

"How long will it take?"

"I'll go as quick as I can." Matt flashed another grin.

This also was a game to her, Eawynn realised. Gambling with danger and breaking rules was part of Matt's world, and not a part Eawynn could ever be comfortable in. Quite aside from her nerves shredding, there would always be, at best, moral ambiguity. The line would not be an easy one to walk. Matt's skills might be used for good, honourable purposes, if not completely honest ones. What chance she could make Matt stick to this path?

Suddenly, an old memory surfaced, Hattie talking about Eawynn's mother, and about how women started out thinking their lovers were somebody other than who they really are. Then, when the illusion was broken, falling into the trap of assuming they could change their lovers to match their initial, mistaken ideal. *She never gave up thinking she could turn your pa into a noble hero who loved her.* Eawynn did not want Hilda of Gimount, so maybe she was starting out one step ahead. The real Matt was adorably incorrigible, and Eawynn could not imagine her any other way.

The beating rain softened enough for Eawynn to catch chanting from the sanctuary. Closer at hand, the lock picks produced a succession of clicks and dry metallic scratching. Then, with a last click and a whisper, the library door swung open. She followed Matt inside and shut the door.

"Where's the book you need?" Matt asked.

Eawynn pointed to the proscribed section. "I'm hoping it's in there."

Matt rattled the protective metal grill. "Locked."

"You can pick it, right?"

"I could, but..." Matt reached under a nearby shelf and pulled out a key. "...this is quicker."

"When did you put that key there?"

"I didn't. I spotted it the first day, when I was being shown around."

Eawynn was dumbfounded. "You mean it's been here all along?"

"Maybe."

"Do you know how much effort novices have put into trying to get a look at those books?"

"Then they ought to learn how to observe more carefully." Matt turned the key. "Which book do you want?"

A good question.

The general theory of celestial prisons had been known at Cyningesburg, but as their failure proved, they had not got it right. The priestess at Fortaine was the one who had made it work, and Eawynn was betting the difference was in the exact form of words. The bygone cultist would have recorded her discovery. Surely this must be where she would put her notes.

Eawynn examined the books, seven in total, bound in ancient black leather. Then she spotted one more, a thin volume at the end, pushed back and virtually hidden behind the others. She slipped it out and opened the cover. In dense clerical hieroglyphs was written *Diverse Explorations into the Mystery and Mastery of the Otherworld.* Had anybody read it since the fall of the empire? Most Reverend Insightful Sister Oracle certainly could not, even if she wanted to.

"This is it."

At the other side of the room, Matt was standing on a chair, doing something with the top of a bookcase. She hopped down and held up the Shewstone. "Here it is. Anything else you need?"

"Did you remember to bring the bag I left on the table in the Jolly Wagoner?" Eawynn was hit by a sudden doubt. She had not seen it yet, but Matt grinned.

"It's waiting for us in the shrine."

"Great."

"How much longer do we have before the sisters finish their singsong?"

Eawynn went to the library door and edged it open. The rain had stopped, and the distant sounds of the ceremony were clear. She listened for a moment. "They're on the sixth verse of 'Silver Lady of the Skies.'"

"Which means?"

"A quarter hour."

The lock on the second door gave Matt no more trouble than the first.

"Your bag is in the flowers." She pointed out a bouquet of lilies, lying before a statue of Anberith. "Now. Where's this crypt?"

In the corner of the Shrine to the Oracle was a trapdoor. Probably the only people to have lifted it in decades were curious novices. When Eawynn was ten, Beatrice had dared her to brave the spiral staircase below. They had crept down with a candle. At the bottom of the steps they found a long room, bedecked in cobwebs. Columns were carved from the bedrock on either side, and a plain granite altar stood at the end.

Eawynn had only the briefest glimpse before a draft puffed out the candle. They had screamed and fled. Five days later, they dared Agnes to go down. However, as a joke, they closed the trapdoor after her and then stood on it. They had not let her out until she was sobbing. Maybe childlike was not the best description for the innocent sylph.

Despite memories of Agnes's hysterical pleading, Eawynn felt happier once Matt had closed the trapdoor. For the time being, there was no risk of anyone disturbing them, and fortunately, the lantern was not as susceptible to drafts as the candle. The crypt was just as Eawynn remembered. It had to be the right place. Nowhere else in the temple was there an altar carved from granite. She walked the length of the underground room, opened the book on the altar, and placed the lantern in a convenient niche in a nearby pillar.

Matt handed over the Shewstone. "Now what?"

"I read the book until I find the bit I need."

"How long will that take?"

Eawynn planted a kiss on Matt's lips. "I'll go as quick as I can."

❖

Books were a lot slower than locks. Matt sat on the third step up and watched Eawynn at the other end of the crypt. Two hours gone, and she was still reading. At least, it felt like two hours, and Matt was normally a good judge of time. Up in the world above, the night would be well advanced, heading toward dawn. What would they do if Eawynn could not find the part she needed by then? It was too soon to start worrying or changing plans, but Matt felt the need to do something, other than sit and stare.

She levered herself up. The muscles in her thighs and shoulders cracked. "I'm going up to the shrine. I want to check out their new Shewstone."

"What? Which new Shewstone?"

"I forgot to tell you. Unsightly Sister Orifice did the same as us and made a fake. The hosteller was ever so thrilled about the hand of Anberith at work. I'm afraid even if you'd offered her the real one, she doesn't need it anymore." Matt turned to the stairs. "I'll pick the lock and be right back."

"No. Be sensible. Stay here."

"Why not?"

"You don't need to see it. It'll look like the one you made."

Matt shrugged. "Won't do any harm."

"It will if someone comes into the shrine and catches you."

The risk was slight, but Matt decided not to argue. "If it'll make you happy."

"You make me happy, but not when you do daft things."

You may be doomed to a fair bit of unhappiness ahead.

Eawynn returned to her book, and then glanced back. "She's made a fake Shewstone?"

"It's certainly not a real one up there."

"She's a bigger crook than you."

Matt was unsure whether to take that as a compliment.

Previous lovers had tried to stop her running unnecessary risks. Without exception, they had gone down the route of acting scared and tearful. It had always irritated Matt, to the point where she would deliberately provoke them. Eawynn, on the other hand, had acted like a schoolteacher with a harebrained pupil, and the result left Matt feeling absurdly protective. Edmund would have been highly amused.

Matt sat down again and tried to get comfy on the cold stone. The heavy robe was not as warm as might be supposed. She closed her eyes.

"Got it."

Matt jerked awake, slipping down a step. Why was it always the same way? She had just dozed off. She stood and brush cobwebs from her robe. "You're ready to go?"

"Yes."

"Do you need me to do anything?"

"I will in a moment."

Eawynn opened her bag and pulled out a tiny silver incense burner. Soon, the sweet scent of spice and jasmine filled the crypt.

"Did they use incense in Cyningesburg? I was too far back to tell," Matt said.

"No. To be honest, it's not totally necessary, but I think it might help."

"Definitely beats the smell of unwashed slaves."

The bag also contained red chalk, five squares of parchment, covered in squiggly lettering, and a small jeweller's hammer. The smooth wooden handle was also covered in symbols.

Eawynn passed the hammer to Matt. "Wait until I say to strike the Shewstone."

"I didn't think you'd get a gold sledgehammer in that bag. I take it size doesn't matter."

"Not if I get the words right."

With the chalk, Eawynn drew a five-pointed star on the altar around the Shewstone. "I guess you didn't see this either, but they killed a goat and used its blood for the pentagram in Cyningesburg. It was complete overkill."

"Especially from the goat's point of view."

Eawynn arranged the parchment squares, one at each point of the star and picked up the book. "Now we begin." She drew a deep breath and squared her shoulders. "Ic abiede tha heafonas hieren min gebeod."

Eawynn's words continued, flowing in a rhythm. Without understanding anything, Matt could sense a watchful force, seeping through the crypt, gathering around them. The air felt thick as she sucked it into her lungs. Hair on her arms and the back of her neck stood on end; even her scalp prickled. A haze crept over Matt, her thoughts slowed, her eyes grew heavy. Deep inside the Shewstone, the colours deepened. Wild patterns swirled in the depths. It shifted out of focus, became bigger. Lights from the stone raced across the roof of the crypt.

Suddenly, Matt was fully awake. Eawynn had stopped her chant. The Shewstone was at peace on the altar, radiating softly. Its outline was firm, although five times the size as before. A humanoid figure was inside the Shewstone, or the Shewstone was inside the figure, or the figure was inside Matt's head. Her eyes did not seem to be playing any role in identifying what she was seeing.

You are my friends. You will let me fly away home.

The words formed directly in Matt's head, neither a question nor a plea, but a statement of fact.

"Yes," Eawynn replied.

Knew you would. Always knew you were my friends. Always loved you.

"I'm sorry about what was done to you. If I'd known I wouldn't have—"

No. Don't talk about the sad time. The sad time is over. Now the dancing starts. It was not my friend's fault.

"Thank you."

No need to thank. I love my friends who will set me free.

"Yes. We'll release you right now." Eawynn gestured to Matt "Strike it with the hammer."

Wait, my friends.

Matt stopped.

When the stone breaks, I will go home. I would leave my friends with a present, because I love them.

"A present?"

What gift would my friends want?

A dozen ideas shot through Matt's head. What sort of presents could a sylph give? If only she had been forewarned a reward might be in the offing.

"We want no gifts." Eawynn got in first.

Matt sighed. But it was not really her show.

No present? Then I wish both my friends the best of luck. Now, let me fly home.

How hard did she need to strike? Presumably, if a jeweller's hammer was adequate, a mighty blow was not required. Matt tapped the top of the Shewstone.

Raw, undiluted joy flooded through Matt, so intense tears burst from her eyes. The ecstasy stopped the heart beating in her chest. Her whole body was filled to bursting, even her skin might rip and whirl away from the frenzy it was trying to contain. Then it was gone. Her heart faltered then picked up again, beating out the rhythm of life. Matt gasped. Mortal bodies were not built to withstand the experience. Beside her, Eawynn had dropped to her knees.

On the altar, the Shewstone was expanding again, now to the size of a man. Matt stumbled back, pulling Eawynn with her. How big was it going to get? Suddenly, the Shewstone rocketed upward, smashing a hole through the ceiling of the crypt and the ground above. The following crash would be the Shewstone bursting through the shrine. The thud of falling masonry shook dust and cobwebs from the roof of the crypt. A dazzling flash of blue light from the hole temporarily blinded Matt, accompanied by one final explosion, louder than any thunder.

Then silence.

In the light of the lantern, dust eddies danced in a breeze caused by the new ceiling breach. Still dazed, Matt tottered to the altar. A round hole tunnelled up through a dozen feet of earth and stone. Sounds floated down from the outside world, alarm bells, screams, shouts, and the distant barking of dogs.

There went her plans for a quiet getaway. "Oh, shit."

"I guess that would have been noticed." Eawynn joined her, looking up.

"If you weren't going to ask for a reward, you could have asked if the sylph would go quietly."

"There was nothing about it in the book. What do we do now?"

"I'm thinking an escape would be a good idea."

What were their chances? On the assumption there would be nobody around, Matt had intended to pick the lock on the gateway to the sanctuary and rely on the priestly robe to get Eawynn past the guards on the main gate. Matt would then return to the hostel and make her scheduled departure as Hilda of Gimount the next day. After the sylph's ear-splitting exit, they would be lucky even to get to their room without being caught.

Matt climbed the spiral staircase and blew out the lantern, then cautiously lifted the trapdoor an inch. At her shoulder, Eawynn muttered under her breath, "At least no one's standing on it."

Half the roof had gone. The full moon peeked in though a rip in the clouds. Already, several priestesses had arrived in what was left of the Shrine to the Oracle. They stood in a knot in the middle of the floor, pointing at the gaping ruins. The final explosion had ripped off the rear third of the room, leaving only a few unbalanced bits of wall sticking up through the rubble. Unsightly Sister Orifice would not only have to paint herself yet another Shewstone, she would need to find somewhere to keep it.

Fortunately, the location of the trapdoor meant everyone had their back to it. The chances of sneaking out unnoticed were not good, but would not get any better with waiting. Matt scrambled up the last few steps and lent a hand to Eawynn. Nobody looked around, but Matt could hear more people on the way. She and Eawynn made it to an alcove just in time. Three more priestesses trotted into the shrine. With squeaks of distress, they joined the horrified huddle.

Matt edged her way to the open doorway, listening intently. No new footsteps echoed around the atrium. She took Eawynn's hand

and slipped out. By the time the next agitated gaggle of priestesses appeared through the western archway, she and Eawynn were well clear of the shrine door and hidden in the darkest corner of the atrium.

"We go to the hostel?" Eawynn whispered.

"Yes. Pick up our stuff and make new plans."

So far things had gone their way, but how much longer could it last? At night, fewer priestesses would be in the eastern side of the grounds, but this would only make them more conspicuous in their borrowed robe if they were spotted.

With Matt in the lead, they crept from shadow to shadow. They saw no one until the hostel door came in sight. All the other guests were clustered outside, talking excitedly among themselves. Getting past them unseen would be impossible, but at that moment, Welcoming Sister Hosteller appeared.

"Please, go to your rooms. I'll find out what's happening." She spoke loudly enough for Matt to overhear.

The guests obediently trooped inside, and Welcoming Sister Hosteller waddled off in the direction of the shrine. As soon as the way was clear, Matt and Eawynn hurried to their room.

"You can still leave as Hilda tomorrow, but I don't know how I'm getting away," Eawynn said.

"A broken plan is a plan you drop. We pack up and get out now."

"Are you sure that's best?"

"At the moment, everybody is confused. It makes them unpredictable, but there'll be holes. Once things calm down, the guards' patrols will be tighter than a cat's bum. If they search the temple, we can't risk them finding you. I know where they look. They'll check under the bed and in the wardrobe, and there isn't space to hide you anywhere else. Our best chance is to go quickly."

But how? What were their options? The atrium would be the scene of much coming and going from now until daybreak and beyond. This ruled out any attempt to leave via the sanctuary and main gate. The garden wall would be a possibility if they had a ladder. Dropping from the hay door in the stable was doable, but would risk a broken ankle, and the armed guards would be on high alert. Did they have another way out?

"We need rope. Do you think we'll find some in the workshops or the stable?" Matt asked.

"We could try."

Somebody sneezed in the corridor outside. Immediately, Matt yanked the robe over her head, shoved it into Eawynn's arms, then pushed Eawynn into the wardrobe. A knock came at the door.

"Yes?"

The room door opened as the wardrobe door closed. Welcoming Sister Hosteller looked suitably abashed to see Matt standing in her underclothes.

"Ah...you must have heard the commotion."

"Yes, I did. And I'm sorry. I'm getting dressed right now and leaving. I just don't feel the temple is safe, first thefts and now this." Matt worked on sounding tearfully unhappy.

"I'm sure you don't need to worry."

"What was that loud bang?"

"We don't quite know, but Most Reverend Insightful Sister Oracle will be leading prayers shortly. Would you like to join us?" Welcoming Sister Hosteller's face showed she recognised the shortcomings in her answer.

"No."

"If you wait until morning, we'll be happy to assist you."

"I'll think about it, but if I don't see you tomorrow, thank you for everything."

Welcoming Sister Hosteller gave another regretful smile and left.

"Do you think a hostel guest could leave without being noticed?" Eawynn asked, once she emerged.

"Unlikely, but it'll be chaotic enough she won't be able to completely rule it out. Hopefully, nobody will be surprised if they never set eyes on Hilda of Gimount again."

Packing the few items they had and changing into everyday clothes did not take long. They had just finished when they heard the other guests leave to join in with whatever prayers were thought appropriate for things that go bang in the night.

Matt kissed Eawynn quickly and opened the door, then turned back and kissed her again, more soundly. If things went wrong, they might never get to kiss again.

❖

The clouds had blown away. The moonlight might make it easier to see where they were going, but it also made it easier for someone else to see them. Fortunately, it appeared everyone had gone to the sanctuary. Eawynn would have to admit, she was also a little curious about the prayers Insightful Sister Oracle would choose. There were none that completely fitted the form of, *Please, Anberith, don't let Enlightening Sister Astrologer become high priestess.*

"We might be able to get out the loading hatch in the hay loft over the stable," Matt whispered. "The biggest problem is that guards are posted nearby, and it's a long drop so we'll need a rope. If we're in luck, we'll find rope in the stable. But it's too much to hope the guards will have been pulled for hole watching duties. More likely they'll be patrolling the length of the wall. We'll have to try to dodge between them."

Matt slipped silently from the shadow around the hostel to that of the refectory, and then on to the kitchen. Eawynn followed, trying to match Matt's stealthy footsteps and failing. She could hear the crunch of gravel under her boots. From the kitchen, they moved to the wall separating the vegetable garden from the rest of the temple site. They passed the small doorway used by the cook and her helpers. Matt placed her hands flat on the wood, clearly thinking about its exit potential.

"The door is always locked at night," Eawynn whispered.

"I could pick it."

"We'd still have the outer wall to get over."

Matt nodded her agreement but turned the handle anyway.

To Eawynn's surprise, the door opened. "Somebody must have forgotten to lock it."

Matt poked her head around the edge and then stepped through, beckoning, "Come on."

The kitchen garden was an uneven shape, more bent triangle than anything else. From the door where they stood, the outer wall was fifty yards away at the nearest point. It was, if anything, even taller than the inner wall, a good fourteen feet high.

Matt pointed to a wagon parked in the far corner. "That'll do us."

After the rain, the gaps between the rows of plants were long troughs of water. Eawynn picked up several pounds of mud on her boots as they skirted the edge, but felt relatively safe. Apart from the hostel, no windows overlooked the garden.

When they reached it, they found the back of the wagon was piled high with bales of straw, wet and slimy after the rain, but easy to climb on. From the top, the outer wall was a small hop up. Even more fortunately, the wagon was parked by one of the spots where the broken glass coping was completely missing.

Eawynn peered over. Directly opposite, a narrow alleyway broke the row of houses, but as Matt had feared, the temple guards had changed their normal pattern. An armed man was stationed no more than thirty yards down the road, and they would be in plain sight when they jumped. They had little hope of reaching the alleyway without the alarm being raised. They both ducked back behind the wall.

"We'll have to risk it," Matt said.

"There's just one. Could we overpower him?"

Matt gave a tight smile. "I'll make a criminal of you yet. But more will turn up when he starts shouting, trust me. Speed is our best bet. When I give the word, jump down and run like hell."

Without warning, a fury of barking broke out. Eawynn looked back over the wall. A stray dog had taken a dislike to the guard, who was trying to chase it away. For the moment, his attention was fully occupied.

"Now! Go!" Matt whispered urgently. She tossed their bags over the wall then scrambled after.

Eawynn copied her actions, hanging by her hands for the barest instant before dropping to the ground. She grabbed her pack and scurried across the road, into the cover of the alleyway. The barking continued, and the guard's shouted obscenities were clearly directed solely at the dog. Eawynn set off at full pelt through the streets. If she had not needed her breath for running she would have laughed aloud. Maybe she could come to enjoy the adventure of breaking the rules, just now and then, when they were bad rules and in serious need of review.

Matt eventually caught up with her in a small square. The old oak in the middle held the sinking moon in its branches, but dawn was approaching, the sky paling to the east.

"It's all right. You didn't need to run since we weren't seen."

Eawynn leaned against the trunk, gasping. "It seemed like the thing to do."

"No. You don't run if you don't have to, because it attracts attention." Matt was laughing in between catching her breath. She rested a shoulder on the tree, took hold of Eawynn's hand, and raised their interlocked knuckles to her lips.

"We got away." Eawynn was not sure if she fully believed it.

"Yes, we did. And a lot easier than I expected."

"We were lucky. What with the door being unlocked, the wagon, and the dog." Even as she spoke, a silly idea slipped into Eawynn's head. She frowned, wondering if she should speak.

"Yes. And Sister Whatsit sneezing before she knocked on the door."

Was it silly? "The sylph wished us the best of luck."

"That's just a saying."

"It was a celestial spirit that said it."

"I don't believe in good luck."

"You didn't believe in demons either," Eawynn pointed out.

"Come on. You're teasing. You're just as sceptical as me."

"Maybe. Maybe not."

"Thieves who rely on luck don't last long."

Eawynn laughed and looked down. She did not believe in luck either, but it was always fun teasing Matt. The last beams of moonlight struck something in the dead leaves by her feet, something that glittered yellow. She scuffed the loose covering aside. Lying on the ground were three gold coins. Neither of them spoke for a long while.

After three false starts, Eawynn finally said. "Do you think this counts as implausibly good luck?"

"I don't know."

"I mean, I'm not saying we should do anything rash or stupid." Eawynn wondered whether she was being rash and stupid merely by considering the idea, but was it any more fanciful than the story of the Shewstone?

"No. We need to take it one day at a time."

"Agreed."

"We don't start visiting gambling dens."

"Oh no."

"We don't take risks."

"No." Eawynn picked up the coins and looped her arm through Matt's. "We'll just see how it goes."

"Right." Matt pulled her around for a long, slow kiss, then looked deep into her eyes. "Let's go see how this luck thing works."

Together, they walked away through the streets of Fortaine, while dawn proclaimed the start of a new day.

About the Author

Jane Fletcher is a GCLS award-winning writer and has also been short-listed for the Gaylactic Spectrum and Lambda Literary awards. She is author of two ongoing sets of fantasy/romance novels: the Celaeno series—*The Walls of Westernfort, Rangers at Roadsend, The Temple at Landfall, Dynasty of Rogues,* and *Shadow of the Knife*; and the Lyremouth Chronicles—*The Exile and The Sorcerer, The Traitor and The Chalice, The Empress and The Acolyte,* and *The High Priest and the Idol.*

Her love of fantasy began at the age of seven when she encountered Greek Mythology. This was compounded by a childhood spent clambering over every example of ancient masonry she could find (medieval castles, megalithic monuments, Roman villas). Her resolute ambition was to become an archaeologist when she grew up, so it was something of a surprise when she became a software engineer instead.

Born in Greenwich, London, in 1956, she now lives in southwest England where she keeps herself busy writing both computer software and fiction, although generally not at the same time.

Website: http://www.janefletcher.co.uk/

Books Available from Bold Strokes Books

A Reluctant Enterprise by Gun Brooke. When two women grow up learning nothing but distrust, unworthiness, and abandonment, it's no wonder they are apprehensive and fearful when an overwhelming love just won't be denied. (978-1-62639-500-8)

Above the Law by Carsen Taite. Love is the last thing on Agent Dale Nelson's mind, but reporter Lindsey Ryan's investigation could change the way she sees everything—her career, her past, and her future. (978-1-62639-558-9)

Actual Stop by Kara A. McLeod. When Special Agent Ryan O'Connor's present collides abruptly with her past, shots are fired, and the course of her life is irrevocably altered. (978-1-62639-675-3)

Embracing the Dawn by Jeannie Levig. When ex-con Jinx Tanner and business executive E. J. Bastien awaken after a one-night stand to find their lives inextricably entangled, love has its work cut out for it. (978-1-62639-576-3)

Jane's World: The Case of the Mail Order Bride by Paige Braddock. Jane's PayBuddy account gets hacked and she inadvertently purchases a mail order bride from the Eastern Block. (978-1-62639-494-0)

Love's Redemption by Donna K. Ford. For ex-convict Rhea Daniels and ex-priest Morgan Scott, redemption lies in the thin line between right and wrong. (978-1-62639-673-9)

The Shewstone by Jane Fletcher. The prophetic Shewstone is in Eawynn's care, but unfortunately for her, Matt is coming to steal it. (978-1-62639-554-1)

A Touch of Temptation by Julie Blair. Recent law school graduate Kate Dawson's ordained path to the perfect life gets thrown off course when handsome butch top Chris Brent initiates her to sexual pleasure. (978-1-62639-488-9)

Beneath the Waves by Ali Vali. Kai Merlin and Vivien Palmer love the water and the secrets trapped in the depths, but if Kai gives in to her feelings, it might come at a cost to her entire realm. (978-1-62639-609-8)

Girls on Campus edited by Sandy Lowe and Stacia Seaman. College: four years when rules are made to be broken. This collection is required reading for anyone looking to earn an A in sex ed. (978-1-62639-733-0)

Heart of the Pack by Jenny Frame. Human Selena Miller falls for the domineering Caden Wolfgang, but will their love survive Selena learning the Wolfgangs are werewolves? (978-1-62639-566-4)

Miss Match by Fiona Riley. Matchmaker Samantha Monteiro makes the impossible possible for everyone but herself. Is mysterious dancer Lucinda Moss her own perfect match? (978-1-62639-574-9)

Paladins of the Storm Lord by Barbara Ann Wright. Lieutenant Cordelia Ross must choose between duty and honor when a man with godlike powers forces her soldiers to provoke an alien threat. (978-1-62639-604-3)

Taking a Gamble by P.J. Trebelhorn. Storage auction buyer Cassidy Holmes and postal worker Erica Jacobs want different things out of life, but taking a gamble on love might prove lucky for them both. (978-1-62639-542-8)

The Copper Egg by Catherine Friend. Archeologist Claire Adams wants to find the buried treasure in Peru. Her ex, Sochi Castillo, wants to steal it. The last thing either of them wants is to still be in love. (978-1-62639-613-5)

The Iron Phoenix by Rebecca Harwell. Seventeen-year-old Nadya must master her unusual powers to stop a killer, prevent civil war, and rescue the girl she loves, while storms ravage her island city. (978-1-62639-744-6)

A Reunion to Remember by TJ Thomas. Reunited after a decade, Jo Adams and Rhonda Black must navigate a significant age difference, family dynamics, and their own desires and fears to explore an opportunity for love. (978-1-62639-534-3)

Built to Last by Aurora Rey. When Professor Olivia Bennett hires contractor Joss Bauer to restore her dilapidated farmhouse, she learns her heart, as much as her house, is in need of a renovation. (978-1-62639-552-7)

Capsized by Julie Cannon.What happens when a woman turns your life completely upside down? (978-1-62639-479-7)

Girls With Guns by Ali Vali, Carsen Taite, and Michelle Grubb. Three stories by three talented crime writers—Carsen Taite, Ali Vali, and Michelle Grubb—each packing her own special brand of heat. (978-1-62639-585-5)

Heartscapes by MJ Williamz. Will Odette ever recover her memory or is Jesse condemned to remember their love alone? (978-1-62639-532-9)

Murder on the Rocks by Clara Nipper. Detective Jill Rogers lives with two things on her mind: sex and murder. While an ice storm cripples Tulsa, two things stand in Jill's way: her lover and the DA. (978-1-62639-600-5)

Necromantia by Sheri Lewis Wohl. When seeing dead people is more than a movie tagline. (978-1-62639-611-1)

Salvation by I. Beacham. Claire's long-term partner now hates her, for all the wrong reasons, and she sees no future until she meets Regan, who challenges her to face the truth and find love. (978-1-62639-548-0)

Trigger by Jessica Webb. Dr. Kate Morrison races to discover how to defuse human bombs while learning to trust her increasingly strong feelings for the lead investigator, Sergeant Andy Wyles. (978-1-62639-669-2)

24/7 by Yolanda Wallace. When the trip of a lifetime becomes a pitched battle between life and death, will anyone survive? (978-1-62639-619-7)

A Return to Arms by Sheree Greer. When a police shooting makes national headlines, activists Folami and Toya struggle to balance their relationship and political allegiances, a struggle intensified after a fiery young artist enters their lives. (978-1-62639-681-4)

After the Fire by Emily Smith. Paramedic Connor Haus is convinced her time for love has come and gone, but when firefighter Logan Curtis comes into town, she learns it may not be too late after all. (978-1-62639-652-4)

Dian's Ghost by Justine Saracen. The road to genocide is paved with good intentions. (978-1-62639-594-7)

Fortunate Sum by M. Ullrich. Financial advisor Catherine Carter lives a calculated life, but after a collision with spunky Imogene Harris (her latest client) and unsolicited predictions, Catherine finds herself facing an unexpected variable: Love. (978-1-62639-530-5)

Soul to Keep by Rebekah Weatherspoon. What *won't* a vampire do for love… (978-1-62639-616-6)

boldstrokesbooks.com

Bold Strokes Books

Quality and Diversity in LGBTQ Literature

victory EDITIONS

Drama

MATINEE BOOKS

SCI-FI

E-BOOKS

MYSTERY

erotica

YOUNG
ADULT

EROTICA

LIBERTY

BOLD
STROKES
BOOKS

Romance

W·E·B·S·T·O·R·E

PRINT AND EBOOKS

31901059749475